THE OTHER WOMAN

THE OTHER WOMAN

Abigail Van Alyn

ISBN: 0692734791
ISBN-13 9780692734797
Library of Congress Control Number: 2016909598
ShadowWorks Press, Yreka, California

Acknowledgements

Thanks to all who read this book and encouraged me through its development, especially Leslie Keenan and her Book Passage writing group, Carole Deutch and our extraordinary salonistas, and my current writing companions Flannery Clouse and Jacalyn McNamara; to my long-time creative partners Saun Ellis and Pancho Drohojowski, Gina Hyams, Anita Barrows and Tony Taccone; to Sindri, Rik, Dorothy, Anna and Ellen, for their love and support; to J. H., for her great-hearted generosity; and finally to Leigh and Odette, brave adventurers in the arts.

Poetry in Anna's sculpture:

Bert Meyers' *One Morning*, from *The Dark Birds*, by permission, estate of Bert Meyers;
Rumi, and William Shakespeare

Whatever in the inner life is not made conscious returns from outside as fate.

C.G. Jung

1

Robert Buchanan, MD, PhD, leaned against Peet's counter waiting to be served. A storm was brewing outside and Berkeley's signature coffee house was packed with customers usually found lounging on the café's sidewalk benches—students with massive backpacks, professors engrossed in their laptops, retired radicals sipping by day and haunting political meetings by night. But the Doctor didn't mind the wait. His time was his own, he'd damn well earned it, and his lively mind never lacked for occupation. In his fist he clutched a *New York Times* and a buttery white sack holding two croissants from the bakery next door. He was torn between the *Times* headlines—more idiocy in Syria—and a large picture window. He could see himself in it, head to toe, looking in from the foggy street. Not to be caught looking, he invented a clever device. Like the old days on the MTA, with his briefcase on his lap and his *Globe* quarter-folded and balanced beside his coffee cup, he rested the *Times* on the counter and seemed to be reading while he studied himself in the glass.

What he saw made him smile with secret satisfaction. To anyone looking on, here was a handsome graying professor, lean and fit, a bit shaggy and conservatively stylish in cords and tweed complete with elbow patches. Even the shank of a thoughtfully chewed pipe stuck out of his breast pocket. As usual, several women in the little café were looking on as he pretended to engage the events of the world. And, as usual, he rejected them with a slight curl of his lip. He didn't dress for them. No, his pleasure came from the trickery of it, from his disguise, as complete as any Hollywood vampire's. Vampire?—he had the professional habit of challenging himself—why that? Well, it was everywhere, wasn't it, the culture's response to its own helplessness. The lust of the prey for the predator. But more aptly, he imagined, he was like a satyr, by Picasso, a satirical genius who understood as only Picasso and a few others had—Reich, for instance—the primal truth about sex, the drives, the instincts and their absolute hold on human beings. He understood it and he'd lived it and he'd helped others to live it. It was the source of his success and all his trouble. Oh yes, he understood it very well, sometimes even found a language for it. Words were essential to the inevitable mind games. But only instinct and sensation could be trusted. The sensation now for instance of stirring and rising as he looked at himself in the glass—*Gentleman Reading the Times*. Or, he revised, sobering up, *Gentleman with Buttery Sack*. The croissants were spoiling the effect, so he slid them under the counter top.

"Dr. Buchanan?" Two bright green eyes, then a little heart-shaped face with freckled nose and dimpled chin popped up beside the *Times*. "Same old?"

The counter girl, whatever her name was. Betty Boop.

"You always remember," he purred, tucking the paper away under his arm. "Aleppo. Terrible situation."

"Way scary." She sighed sympathetically. "Double Cap!!" She shouted his order down the line and took his money. "Sorry to interrupt."

"No, no. I'd rather be here with you anytime," he said, offering a satyr's smile. "If you can't make a difference don't worry about it."

She leaned over the counter, presenting herself to him in her deliciously unconscious way. Pert, that was the word. And every morning with every move she told him, I have gorgeous breasts under this little T-shirt.

"Think globally, act locally," she purred.

"So right," he murmured back. He leaned in, not quite touching her. She pressed his change into his hand and turned away laughing.

"One of these days I'll take you up on that," he called. She laughed again, dismissing him as she did every morning.

All right then, another day. He went out into the fog full of hunger and desire, those powers so keenly crafted, his gifts to those who were cut off from their own. He crossed the avenue, dodging traffic with athletic quickness, walked up a block and turned into a quiet street lined with old gnarled sycamores and oaks. As he walked he forced himself to focus on the patients ahead.

Wednesday. That meant starting with Anna Sheffield. Anna the Artistocrat. So deeply, passively, defiantly resistant. Anna the Mouse. For two years she's been saying she wanted to break through but refused to do it. Last week he'd told Craig Helsen, the colleague with whom he exchanged a monthly peer review, that she was the challenge every psychiatrist hopes for, the one for whom all the study was done, all the risks taken, all the sacrifices made. Because her life mattered. She had something to offer the world, and, unlike some he'd treated, she hadn't asked for or deserved what had happened to her.

He reached the two-story Colonial house where he practiced in partnership with Craig and two other therapists. His silver Mercedes, parked earlier in the driveway, lent an air of prestige to the otherwise unremarkable neighborhood. It had all been carefully planned. The home's plain white front, with its covered porch and columns and its tasteful dark green shutters and stairs, reminded him of Cambridge, of Princeton, the places of his early triumphs, and he'd wanted their comfort. And their cover. Only last year he'd finally felt safe enough to add the handsome car. It gave him comfort now to see it resting there.

He gathered his mail and went in. Each floor was divided into two spacious offices with a shared kitchen. The hallways served as waiting areas. On the first floor, a woman of forty or so was waiting with her small son, holding him on her lap and reading to him from *I Have Two Mommies*. Must be for Janice. Beside her, for their hypnotist colleague Kara, a tousled academic type hunched over a battered copy of *Time*, closing himself off from mother and child. Probably trying to quit, thought Robert, or hopelessly smitten by the leggy, doe-eyed Kara.

He climbed the thickly carpeted stairs. No one was waiting on his floor. On Wednesdays Craig had his first appointment at 11:00. Robert checked his watch: ten to 10:00. As part of her strategy of resistance Anna was always late, so he knew he had at least twenty minutes to relax, eat his croissants and listen to his messages. He unlocked his office door and went in. The windows had been closed overnight, and the comforting scents of pine, lavender and tobacco hung in the air. He crossed his treasured Persian carpet and opened the window behind his expansive walnut desk. Sipping his cappuccino, he looked out into the back garden with its lily borders, oaks and Chinese elms. The winter planting of chrysanthemums was in bloom—white, yellow and burgundy blossoms against the winter green. All peace, order and calm.

He'd insisted on the back corner office as acknowledgement of his status, the only MD in the group. In return he provided his colleagues with occasional prescriptions for Valium, Prozac, Zoloft and the like. He might even donate the odd sample of morphine. Without patient review he was taking a risk, but the privacy was worth it. And there was no trouble getting the stuff. He had drawers full of it, although he rarely prescribed anything himself. The mind, he believed, is like a great river whose wonders are dark pools and shadowy, often dangerous eddies. Mood elevators and painkillers are monstrous dams, drowning the river's mysteries, harnessing its powers to dull usefulness. Intervention went against his fundamental philosophy, that the vital energies are the key to everything—to growth, learning, meaning itself. And love? Of course there are those emergencies when you just can't help yourself.

Fog still hung in the trees, and a cold wind blew through the open window. Robert closed it again. Anticipating Anna's usual chill, he went to the fireplace, turned on the gas and lighted the metal logs. He'd rather have real ones, but with the weight of his debts the remodeling cost was prohibitive. Alimony, support of the kids, their schools, their cars, and then the loans he'd taken to pay the endless stream of lawyers. He sighed and stood warming himself, then lit a pipe and waited for his difficult patient to arrive.

Every morning for several days it had been the same. Anna would wake up and find herself huddled in the corner between her dresser and the closet door. Sometimes sunlight, paler as the season waned, lay across the floor in golden bars. Sometimes, like now, a pale suffocating fog seemed to seep in through the cracks. She'd force a breath. That would start the trembling, then the dry tearless sobbing. She'd hold her knees and keen into her sweaty gown, wondering how she'd gotten to the floor, what could have happened? Then it would start.

First the squealing of the iron gate. She held her breath, listening to the footsteps outside the window. But the steps weren't outside, they were in her, along with the images projected against the backs of her eyes, cinéma verité, the same show day after day. Angels, Holy Virgins, the small stone church with its high wall. Then the shuffling steps of three men, the slash of cold air on her breasts, their stinking mouths. And the sound track: TexMex blaring from the street, men grunting, swearing, a thin muffled scream, car radio, Latin beats, traffic, laughter. A woman's voice in an urgent whisper saying, "Please, please, you don't want to do this."

Here she would begin to flail and grunt like an animal dragged to the slaughter and rip her nightgown off and run naked into the shower. It was always the same. She'd wash and wash, the water beating on her face until it shut the movie down. She'd stay until the water ran cold. Then she'd climb out, look for herself in the mirror and quickly turn away from the sleep-tortured sad face. Finally she'd wrap herself in a towel and sit absently on the covered toilet, thinking it all over again.

Two and a half years earlier, not long after her forty-second birthday, she'd been raped. It was early evening, just after dark on a lovely April night in San Francisco. She'd been walking down Capp toward 18th Street, looking for a friend's new studio. They were talking about going in on it together, and this was a part of the Mission she used to know well. Now it had changed. She'd heard there were gangs but thought, what would a gang want with me? She'd always dressed inconspicuously, with a subtle sense of color and style but tending toward neglect in her appearance. "Cultivating the mad artist thing," her sister Claire had said long ago. She wasn't. She just didn't want to take the time. She would meet the friend, then go over to the Castro to join Colin for dinner. There was a new place he'd found with real couscous, Lebanese or something. So she was walking along the badly lit street, thinking about Beirut and wishing she could have seen it before the devastation. She was passing the church with its shadowy graveyard when she heard the squeal of the iron gate. They were hiding there, apparently, and the whole thing started.

Some time later she'd gone on walking and found the studio. No one was there. Her friend had left a note, angry that she'd forgotten. A lot of time must have passed. She'd looked at her watch. It was just after 9:00, but she couldn't remember when she was supposed to meet her friend or, in fact, the friend's name. So she sat on the stairs and waited for something to happen. Finally a woman who looked like an Olmec goddess passed, then came back and spoke to her gently in Spanish, pointing out that she was bleeding, from her elbows, the side of her face, and down the insides of her legs into her shoes. Later they'd find a knife wound on her inner thigh, that she couldn't let anyone touch even now. In spite of all that, she hadn't been able to cry, and she'd never felt even a trace of anger. That was the problem, Robert said. Between the gate and the friend's studio was nothing, a black hole. First the feelings, then the memories will come. Stick with it. We'll get there.

The towel was cooling and clinging to her skin. It brought back the other part of the story: damp clinging clothes, the rough voices and hard faces of the police, who couldn't help being tough though they were trying to be kind. And the hospital, sitting on a table waiting to be seen, on a crinkly paper so as to not mess things up. Then the matter-of-fact hands stitching and probing. And much later, to the rescue, Robert.

Robert! His name brought a rush of panic. She threw off the towel, ran into her closet and shuffled through the clothes, looking for something he might not have seen. Not that she cared what he thought, but he always commented on her appearance. Part of the job, probably, to make sure she was noticing, something like that. She threw something on and checked herself in the mirror. There was a tallish person pushing middle age, in a loose-fitting dress and a muffling baggy sweater, lace-up boots, her long brown hair in a thick braid, a plain face made interesting by intelligent sad brown eyes, and with strong rough long-fingered hands holding a silver barrette. She twisted her braid and pinned it to the crown of her head. Fine. Now she could pass unnoticed anywhere.

"All right, eat," she directed herself. "Cat."

Suki was sitting on the kitchen counter washing a gold and black paw. The cat cocked her head and made a tiny imploring sound. Anna picked her up. "Baby, baby." She took comfort in the soft fur. She put down milk and kibble. She glanced at the clock: 9:15. Good, she thought, I won't be late. For once I won't have to run the gantlet. She made tea and toast, then stood absently eating and gazing out of the kitchen window at the soft pearly mist outside. A slight breeze was blowing the curtain into the room in a riffling dance, and through it, across the garden, the blue door of her studio glowed like a patch of clear sky. Anna hadn't been near it in months. She drifted out across the patio and stood leaning against the studio wall. There was a small grubby window next to her, laced with spider webs. Which is more painful, she wondered—to look or not look? Why was the simplest question impossible to answer? A tiny sprout of anger uncurled itself somewhere near her heart. It pricked her. Make a damned decision. She brushed the webs aside and pressed her face to the glass.

Because of the fog, the skylights let in a dull blue glow. Everything was there, neat and orderly as she'd left it two years before. But after all this time it had the feeling of a capsized ship found at the bottom of the sea, everything cold, dead and perfectly preserved. The large piece of granite she'd been working on stood in the center of the room, draped with a sheet. But, she realized, a splash of rusty red had appeared, staining the sheet like a gash, a wound. She started to tremble. Was it blood? She pulled back from the window. She closed her eyes and tried to calm her breathing. She heard Robert say in his practiced tone, "You do this to yourself, Anna. You make the world you're in. Is it blood? Look!" She stared into the black hole. Yes, blood. My summer dress soaked with it, more blood than you'd think possible from sex, even forced dry sex. An incomprehensible amount of blood.

Robert said, "This blood is your path. It marks the trail back."

Another voice, rough and somehow familiar, said: "Cut the bitch!" A man laughed, a squealing howl. Blood gushed from her thigh.

"Robert! I'm seeing. I'm seeing!"

Before the fear could stop her, she took the key from above the door, ran in and pulled the drape away. There were the two forms, just as she'd left them, half human and hungrily entwined. But now that dark stain discolored the stone where a shoulder might take shape. She looked up, searching. There it was, a leak in the skylight. Only a leak in the skylight, she told herself, bringing down rust or something, that's all. She touched the damaged stone. In the time it might take to snap a photograph, she was pulling the blood into the granite, following it down to a new meaning, plowing it under, not wounding but opening, revealing—

Panic snapped her thoughts closed like a shutter. She ran out of the studio and through the house, dragging the drape behind her. She fell on her bed shaking and sobbing. After a minute, she took a picture from a drawer beside the bed, herself as she'd once been, with Colin on a street in Prague, heads together, arms wound around.

"You want tears?" she said to him. "Here! Here they are."

And wouldn't Robert be glad? She looked at the clock. Christ, 9:48! She dropped everything and ran for her coat. She'd be late again, but for the first time she had something momentous to report. On the offensive at last. As she drove down her quiet street she considered that this was a strange way to think about your therapist. And it was the first moment of clarity she'd had in two years with Robert Buchanan.

The morning rush was clearing up South of Market. Michele Palmer stood on the corner of Folsom and Dore, holding the baby and smoking. She looked down into the blaring onslaught of traffic, waiting for Joe. The smoke from her cigarette engulfed the baby's head. It blinked its eyes and twisted in her arms, trying to get away. She didn't notice, but if she had she wouldn't give a shit.

She wasn't so old, twenty-five, but she knew she'd been born at the wrong time. She wasn't some Millennial, Gen X or Y or whatever crap they came up with next. Her generation hadn't been invented yet. To show allegiance to her real tribe, she was subtly pierced with nose and ear studs—seven of them, a lucky number— and eyebrow rings and a big surprise underneath her layered clothes. These were black, and her hair was black, but that was it. She was too old and burdened by responsibility for black eyes and fingernails, looking like some drugged out pacifier-sucking E-freak. Or the Goth she saw inside. She had Robin, this real live baby clinging to her hair, leaving slobber marks on her sweater. That girl in Jerry McGuire had said it all: "I'm the oldest twenty-six-year-old alive." Michele could relate.

She was waiting for Joe, the father of record, to show up. He was supposed to give them a ride to BART, the train to Berkeley, and he was late as usual. Not that he was a bad guy, a deadbeat or anything. Really, he had no idea what a good friend he'd been to her. It was his car, an ancient VW Bug he liked to think was a Classic. Something was always falling apart on the twisted car and making him late. Still he was a good guy, better than he even knew, better she hoped than he would ever find out.

As she thought about his goodness, what popped up was his look when she'd told him, righteously pissed, that she was pregnant. A kind of searching—when? where?—and then pained strange joy, his little doggy face twisting into a smile he couldn't stuff for all his doubts. This was on her mind when he turned into the alley, the Bug rattling and smoking, his hands on the cracked wheel black with grease. It was a mystery, but no matter what good thoughts she was having before, the minute she set eyes on Joe she'd start hating him again. She stormed up to the driver's door and pulled it open before he'd even all the way stopped.

"You motherfucker!"

The baby bounced along on her hip saying, "Adadadada."

Joe looked tired and ashamed. "I couldn't help it, Shell, the wheel bearing started …"

"Do you think I give a shit?" With his little black paws waving around, he looked ridiculous. Eyeball to eyeball she gave him the cobra stare. "Do you seriously suppose I'm sympathetic?"

For effect she leaned in closer, accidentally bumping the baby's head on the side of the car. The little thing let out a squeak, then held her breath while her face turned white, then scarlet.

"Oh, Jesus, Jesus," said Joe, scrambling out. "Back off, Shelley, look what you did now."

He pushed Michele away and took the baby as she let out a huge painful scream. "Ooooh, baby, baby, let Daddy see." He rubbed her head where a red welt was starting to show. He kissed it, cooing to her as she bellowed. "Don't cry, sweetheart, Daddy's here, Daddy's here."

Michele tore into her bag for another cigarette. "Yeah, Daddy's here almost forty-five *fucking* minutes late, which means Mommy is going to be *late* to her extremely important meeting."

"Don't say fuck in front of Robin," Joe said solemnly. "She understands everything we say."

"I wish you understood everything I say. I told you, you j-e-r-k, that I had to be in f-u-c-k-i-n *Berkeley* at 10 o'clock, and it's almost 10 o'clock now, and I still have to get the goddamn BART!" They faced off among the dumpsters. "And shit! You're getting grease all over her jumper!"

She took the baby back and rocked her gently, her throat tightening with confusion and remorse. She turned her back on Joe so he wouldn't see.

"I love you, baby, I really do," she whispered. "Robin love Mama? You love Mama?"

"Mama," Robin said softly.

"Show Mama how much you love her. Give Mama kiss."

Mother and baby stood stroking and kissing, while Joe kicked at a tuft of grass sprouting through the cracked pavement.

"So what's this about? What's in Berkeley, Shell?"

"I don't have to tell you what I do."

"I might could take you."

"I wouldn't ride across the bridge in that piece of refuse."

Joe stood in front of her with his mouth drawn down like he might cry or scream. "I want to know where you're taking my daughter."

Although she generally thought of Joe with pity or contempt, sometimes he did scare her. She switched to a soothing contralto. "Don't get upset, Joe. I thought I told you. I'm going to see my shrink."

"Buchanan? Fuck, I thought you were done with that. How much is this going to cost me?"

"Nothing, it's just a meeting. I got something I need to talk over with him."

"And he does that for nothing? Gimme a break." Joe started to pace up and down the dirty alley. "You're starting back up, aren't you? You're back on disability. He's giving you Valium."

"No, Joe, it's nothing like that," she purred.

"Jesus, Michele, you're such a fucking liar! You've got some scam running here, and we have this kid to think about."

Spit was flying through his protruding teeth. Michele had never seen a rabid animal, but she thought this is what one must look like.

"Why do you want to go back to that asshole? What the hell good has he done in four years of this s-h-i-t? What's the fucking point, Michele? And anyway, I don't want you taking the baby."

Robin started to whimper, and Michele shifted her to her hip. She felt cold, had started to shiver. She never asked what brought on this chill, in fact she liked it. It helped her feel more deadly. "You never tried to do anything with yourself, Joe, so you could not possibly understand."

He shook his head, but didn't say a word.

"Gimme a twenty, I'm taking a cab." When he just kept glaring she tore like a cat at his pockets. The baby started to cry.

"Jesus!" Joe backed away, fishing for his money. "Okay, okay, chill will you?" He handed her a wadded up bill. "Now gimme the baby."

"Fuck off, Joe, I need her with me." Michele spun around and ran to the corner where a cab stopped right away. As they pulled into traffic, she caught a last glimpse of Joe pounding on the car with his fists.

"Berkeley, number 53 Santa Cruz," she said and pulled the crying baby tight against her breasts.

2

By 10:10 Robert had moved from the fireplace to the ample leather chair behind his desk. He'd swiveled toward the window and, with his feet resting comfortably on the sill, was listening to his messages and thumbing through the book of notes he kept on all his patients. He was thinking about rituals: how arriving late, apologetic, harried, was part of Anna's ritual and part of her process of will. So for him it was a matter of managing the anger he sometimes felt, as anyone would, at being kept waiting. And of working with her failure to take responsibility for it. She didn't accept her tardiness as a symptom of her buried rage, would not see it as something willed and deliberate, as he knew it to be. But it was all part of the job. The money was the same, and the one rule he always kept was that she leave on time.

He turned his attention to his book, always a source of pride and pleasure. Every therapist kept a notebook, but his was unique as far as he knew. Data had little value—that was something he'd come to believe in graduate school, studying Reich. You needed a lot more than that to guide a patient toward breakthrough. "Everything useful, all the conscious material, you know about in the first session, maybe two," he often said in his peer reviews with Craig Helsen. "Don't lose sleep over the context, what happened and all that. Who cares? What matters is your energies meeting theirs. That's the only thing that can help them, and you find the thread through instinct, imagination."

Craig would say, "Instinct?! Energies! What does that *mean*?"

And they'd go around and around, both sure they were right. But Robert knew more than that he was right. He knew how far he'd gone to test his theory, what courage that had taken. He had a wealth of secret knowledge that he gave free rein in this book of his.

It was a large clothbound artist's sketchbook with a tab for each patient. The tabs had the patient's first name, a slash, then her pet name, which might change once or twice over a long relationship. During a session, Robert noted the deeper meanings of things in inspired cartoons, at which he was rather talented. Taken out of context, he knew some might find these pornographic. But his field was sexual trauma, and you could not succeed without direct contact with your own fantasies and drives. Since you couldn't really know the other person's world and suffering, you could only be guided by your own responses. At the level of the primal energies these are the same in all people. In fact, this *is* the collective unconscious. What else could it possibly be? He thumbed on as he listened.

The disembodied voices purred from the speakerphone: Sally/(no pet name yet); Margot/ Cruella; Sylvia/Daisy Mae; Jane/ Bride of F; and Barbara/Blondie. Sally was new and wanted to be sure she understood, for the fourth time, when her appointment was. She had come to their first meeting clutching a tatty pink teddy bear, grubby from use. She'd told him, only when he asked, that she'd never been separated from it since her stepfather raped her at fourteen. As he listened to her thin little voice, he smiled at his drawing of the bear holding tiny Sally on its great male lap. Maybe "Piglet" would be good for her.

Margot asked in her seductive contralto whether she could switch to Wednesdays after the first of the year. In her substantial section of his book were many of his favorite pieces: for her lyrical moments, leafy forest scenes full of nymphs and satyrs in every kind of coupling; for the troubled times, surreal borrowings from Dali of melting beds, rivers of mud invading suburban family rooms, kewpie dolls' heads used as bowling balls against phallic pins. Sylvia's pinched falsetto followed, hemming and hawing about something or other; any excuse to call someone when no one wanted to hear from her. Sometimes his job seemed a great burden. Jane wanted to clarify the last moment of their meeting on Tuesday, and, as was his policy with all such messages, he deleted without listening. You had to manage the mental clutter. Finally Barbara was just saying hello. As much as he'd explained that they were not friends, had a professional relationship, and that he would never return such calls, she persisted.

He skipped on to find the all-too-familiar voice of his former wife, Frances. Thanksgiving, the children, only a few days left; Ben coming in from college in Connecticut, Camilla from her new job in L.A. Planes to meet, parties to be held. Did he want to come to any of them? Could they manage to be civil? She became more frustrated and dry as she demanded to know whether he'd put Ben's child support and tuition checks in the mail, and absolutely parched as she asked whether he remembered that Camilla's birthday came right after Thanksgiving.

He made a few notes, at the same time picking up his other line and dialing Margot. He let Fran scratch on through the dust as Margot's phone rang, and he left her a sultry-voiced message as a way of mirroring for her how she seemed to others. He said they would talk about Wednesdays when he saw her on Friday. In his view no change was insignificant, especially not within Margot's cunning system of manipulation. She wouldn't get by him so easily. As for the kids, or used-to-be kids—Robert sighed deeply and turned again to look out at the gray morning.

It had all been a terrible accident, really. There was Fran, standing at the door of his apartment on Beacon Hill with a look of sly mischief, as if she might produce a birthday present from behind her back. "I'm pregnant!!" She'd actually jumped up and down and squealed with joy. Seeing his face, she'd stopped cold, like a toy whose battery has suddenly failed. "Why are you looking like that? Of course I'm going to have it! We love each other."

How had she come to *that* conclusion?

The problem was that, having met Fran on a years-long rebound, he'd still been in love with another woman. An Argentinean stunner of mixed Spanish and ex-pat German descent. Laura Blaufeld, pronounced in the Spanish way. He conjured her from the past, whispering to himself, Laoora. He shifted uneasily in his chair. She was not someone he often let himself think about. But now and then when he was forced to idleness, memories broke through.

There she was, standing at the back of the lecture hall, her eyes boring through him, a sparkling Mediterranean blue. It was the fall of 1976. He'd fulfilled the athletic scholarship to Princeton, done the PhD, discovered Wilhelm Reich and decided to replace forever football with fornication. Now he was teaching a psych tutorial at Harvard, Reich and the Theory of Drives, as part of his residency at Mass General. And there he'd found Laura, his most willing research subject. His mind skipped nimbly over their year together, which he pictured as a mass of tangled sheets steaming with body fluids, and landed on the fatal turning point: the dreadful meeting with her parents. No, that wouldn't gain admission, not now. But the image of her luscious red mouth, open and laughing, broke through his defenses. And later, their last night together, his desperate weeping and pounding on the door when she'd shut him out, the landlord called, one humiliation after another. Robert pulled his chair close to the window, craning around to see the street. Where was that damned woman? The problem with this office, tucked in the back, you couldn't tell when someone was coming.

He jumped up and began to pace. The room seemed stifling. Why this sudden eruption of memory? The coming of the holidays, the latest terror attacks, the general climate of fear—it must be that. He turned down the logs. Anyway he'd loved her, had been devastated, too, after all. Had suffered those dreadful years of impotence and black depression from which Frances had saved him. And then, too soon after,

Camilla had been born. Babies. The bitterest fruit of human craving ....

Whatever else he might have thought was cut off by the sound, very faint, of a car door slamming. Gratefully, he scurried back to the leather chair and posed himself with his book in his lap. He opened it to Anna/Artistocrat. Clever as that was, some months ago he'd put a line through it and replaced it with /The Mouse. He turned to a fresh sheet. He uncapped his tortoiseshell pen, dated the page, and, by an act of will, pushed his miserable thoughts back into their caves. But it seemed an age from the slamming of the door to Anna's knock. He was left sitting there like a prop in a play. So when she entered, her face flushed and puffy, he said caustically, "You missed your cue." He looked down at his book and began idly doodling on the page.

Anna stopped on the threshold, suddenly wary and unsure of herself. All the way down the hill she'd imagined running to him with the gift of the morning's breakthrough. But once in front of the white façade she'd found herself reluctant to go in. She'd taken her time coming up, and even so here she was again, bewildered. She closed the door carefully behind her, like someone entering a sickroom. Robert was looking down at his book, drawing and refusing to look at her.

She took a stab at speaking. "My cue? I had ... had a ..."

"Rough morning?" he supplied. "You, too?" He looked up and said, suddenly avuncular, "Oh, yes, I can see that."

"Seeing ... I was ..." She put her hands up to her hair, smoothing down the stray ends. She wondered if she'd forgotten to brush it.

He said mildly, "Okay, come in and sit down. You now have …" he looked at his watch, "… about forty minutes, so let's make the most of them."

Dutifully, Anna made for her accustomed place in the far corner of the big leather couch. If things got testy she could sit there by the window and escape into the branches of the oak outside. She looked at it now as she took off her coat, its branches black on pearl, charcoal graffiti on the sky's gray wall. Then she sat in the silence, pulling her long sweater protectively around her. "You seem angry," she ventured.

Robert looked up. "Good for you. You hit the nail right on the head. I am angry. No, not really angry. I'm …" he searched theatrically for words, "… pissed off. That's all, just pissed off."

He leaned back in his chair, idly picking up a small pair of scissors from the desk and twirling them on his forefinger. They'd belonged to his grandmother, Anna remembered him saying. A familiar sensation stirred in her chest, like ants running around in her heart. Maybe the morning had been rougher than she thought. Something was scratching at the base of her throat, and Robert loomed toward her saying, "Take a breath, Anna. Take a breath." It was her own hand scratching for air. Robert sat beside her on the couch, guiding her breathing until things came back to normal.

"All right," she said. The ants retreated down their tunnels to wherever it was they went.

Robert took a pitcher of water from the desk and poured a glass for her. While she drank he said earnestly, "Listen, Anna, this is a moment when you could really get this. So stay with me here. I promised you I would always tell you the truth about my feelings. I don't believe in the silent therapist, the Great White Father lurking behind the couch, as you know. I am adamantly opposed to it. I will always tell you what I'm feeling, and it does not have to rock you like that. You can hear that I'm pissed off because you kept me waiting. You can handle it, Anna. Your choice."

She nodded, but he didn't go on. Now it seemed they were stuck in an awkward social moment, and she waited for her upbringing to save her. Should she thank him? Apologize? She summoned Gramma Price, who'd guided them all through the social catastrophe of the '70s: "Where manners fail, Breeding will never let you down." In that light she couldn't jump in with, "'Cut the bitch!" Besides, she wasn't sure that Robert would understand what it was like to hear the man's voice. She imagined him saying, "Okay, great, now what are you going to *do about it*?"

Robert was still leaning forward looking down at his clasped hands. Watching him, she suddenly understood a remark he'd made some months ago. She'd been rambling on about her family, and he'd interrupted, saying, "They obviously never read Nietzsche." What had seemed cutting at the time now struck her as quite clever. Maybe after all that is the therapy: to will him into his place, deny entry. If that's what he'd meant. Muster my Will, marshal my Powers, his favorite prescriptions. Mark my boundaries as he's always doing.

"Is something funny?" he asked. She realized she was smiling.

"This whole thing, in a way."

"Can you speak up? I can't hear you."

"Oh, sorry." She cleared her throat and raised her voice. "I was thinking about my grandmother."

"The matriarch. Interesting timing." Robert could feel how tight his jaw was. She looked at him warily, seeming to calculate whether it was safe enough to speak. God, the woman was a lot of work. He tried to soften, to soothe.

"Want to talk about her? You don't have to. Only if you think it will help."

While he waited for her to answer he revisited his last peer review with Craig. He'd been talking about Anna's resistance, how she thwarted all his efforts to put her in direct contact with her feelings.

"Sounds frustrating," Craig had said.

"You know what? I'm actually starting to get angry."

Craig had laughed. "Why? To just sit through a session taking notes while they stare out the window? Not to be raged at? Sounds incredibly restful to me. But don't let me project. Seriously, why?"

"She's touching the narcissistic wound. She won't respond to me! I want her to fight back, I want to grapple with it. She drains me. I hate that feeling."

And Craig had said, "You'll have to be careful not to project that onto her. She's not doing it on purpose, is she?"

He looked at her now, staring out the damned window, oblivious to him. Why can't she need me, he wondered? Is she doing it on purpose?

She heard him say stiffly, "So. Your grandmother. Anything there?"

Anna glanced secretly at her watch: half an hour to go. How could this happen? The man's voice, the bloody drape, the tears, all fading to black. Maybe, she thought, she'd dreamed that other Robert, the one who guided her. But no time for that. This one was shifting impatiently in his chair. Searching for material, she called up a memory. Her grandmother was standing on the porch of their sprawling house on Cape Cod, beautiful and commanding. She was wearing a blue summer dress, a red ribbon holding back her long gray hair, the wind blowing wisps of it into her face. She was looking out across the beach to the ocean, looking for the sailboat and "the boys": Anna's grandfather, her father and his friend Putnam Graves, whom at thirty-five everyone still called Pinky. It was the Fourth of July. The traditional meal of salmon and peas and boiled potatoes was on the table, covered with cheesecloth to keep off the flies. She described the scene for Robert.

"I was six that summer. Mother was upstairs feeding Claire, who was five months, and I was so hungry. I was sneaking chunks of salmon, stuffing them in my mouth and watching Gramma Price like a hawk. I turned away for one second to grab a potato, and when I turned back she was at the window looking in at me. She said, 'You are not yet a person who knows what to do!'"

"What did she mean by that? You were six."

"Yes, but I had BREEDING, in caps. I should Pull Myself Together. She often said things in caps, you see: 'A Person Who Knows What to Do, People Who Climb Out of Their Class. People Who Haven't Read Nietzsche.'" Anna felt like winking but restrained herself.

Robert looked startled. "You remember that."

"Oh, yes." She went on lightly. "She'd married wealth but then had to make her own way after my grandfather died. The Depression, his drinking, his 'straying.' She was well enough off when he died, but she used his money to go into real estate in the '70's and made a fortune. I have a lot to thank her for. And so do you."

"Why's that?"

"How could I afford you? How could I afford this much time off?"

That wasn't at all how she felt about it, but what mattered now was keeping the upper hand. Robert looked at her with hard eyes, and she wondered for the first time about *his* background, whether he'd Climbed Out of His Class, whether he envied her.

"And what would she advise you to do now, do you think?" he asked coldly.

She froze, sensing a trap. "Now that …?"

"Now that you're incapacitated."

So there it was, the gantlet. She felt a small crumbling inside. "You think I'm incapacitated?"

"Well, you're living on Gramma's largesse, coming late to your appointments, sitting around here whistling while Rome burns …"

"Fiddling," Anna whispered.

"Whistling, fiddling. It's been more than two years, and still you come late, repeat yourself, over and over the same ground. You look awful. Something happened today. Why aren't you talking about it?"

"I don't know. Just more of the same. Anyway, it's over now."

They glared at one another, then Robert sighed. He spoke softly, reasonably. "You know, I don't usually go this route, but I just want to say, I think you're simply unusually anxious. The bombings down south, terror attacks on the home turf, you're not immune. We've talked about this. We could loosen things up if you'd be willing to try ..."

"Valium? Paxil? Absolutely not."

Anna moved back into the corner of the couch and curled into a tight ball. There was such a tension in her throat she thought she'd choke. He was right, of course, she was making an awful mess. She longed for the hour to be over.

3

The news from Syria was blaring in the cab as it crept through crazy traffic over the Bay Bridge. Robin had fallen asleep on the seat, lying heavily against her mother's arm. Michele pulled at the arm and thrashed around trying to get comfortable. It was amazing how babies slept, that dead weight. She thought, I could just open the door and she'd fall out into the traffic, and she'd never feel … But the wave of nauseating guilt that hit her made her take the sleeping child onto her lap and hold her in a suffocating embrace.

"I love you, baby. I love you love you love you," she whispered into the sleeping ear.

The driver looked back in the rear view mirror. "How you doin' back there?"

"Great." He had a jolly fat face and seemed sympathetic. The meter was clicking away, and she only had the twenty and an extra ten and a BART ticket. Maybe he wouldn't charge her for the time in traffic. She'd work it somehow.

He was saying, "… never ends, those poor people aren't going to have a country left. That Aleppo already looks like a fuckin' nuke … oh, sorry! Anyhow, New York next, you watch. Anyway, they won't do Frisco, who wants to nuke a million LBG whatevers. Don't get me wrong. I hate terrorists as much as the next guy …"

This guy really needed to shut up, but she wanted him on her sweet side. She managed, "Yeah, it sucks." And then, very nice, "Could you turn the radio down? I need to think."

He looked disappointed, but he did, as the newscaster announced, "10:28, traffic and weather together."

It wasn't just his fucked-up opinions, she did need to think. She pulled an envelope out of her purse. It was fresh and white compared to the little bundle of yellowish newspaper articles inside. She looked in at them again, like she had several times that morning. She wanted to think about how she was going to do this. But instead she kept thinking about the first time she and Robert met.

She was sitting in the hall, a funky excuse for a waiting room. On the wall was a poster of a whale swimming up toward the sun, in a sort of halo effect. It said, Deep Light. She started to read *People* magazine. She'd been worried about how the doctor would treat her, since this was being paid for by Medi-Cal. She imagined an older guy with, like, a little gray ponytail; an old hippie with granny glasses and sandals, maybe a leather vest and a guitar leaning against the wall. A guy like that might have once had food stamps, he might be nice to her about the disability money. Then she looked up, and he was standing in the doorway to his office taking her in. He was older but strong looking, a great looking sexy guy with a cool sizing-up look. It flashed her on clubs, those guys who stand around the walls and drive BMWs and pick up E-babies and drop rufies in their drinks. She remembered feeling her scared little girl face dissolve into her nightcrawling face as she looked him over. And he actually blushed.

Looking back at herself from the back seat of the cab, she rose to meet him like a snake uncoiling from a basket.

She put on her Madonna voice. "You're Doctor Buchanan?"

He seemed flustered. "Yeah, yes. Michele?"

She laughed at his awkwardness and said, "With one 'l.' It's French. Just gotta be me." Her hair brushed his jacket as she moved past him into his office. She looked back at him standing in the doorway with his arms crossed and his "I see your bones" look. She laughed, and he shut the door behind them.

That first time was like an interview, so many questions, and only one thing stuck with her still. He'd asked what her home life was like.

"I live in the Garden," she'd said. He hadn't yet seen the tattoo that covered most of her body, the Garden and the Serpent, but he got that she was testing him.

"The garden." He'd written something in his notebook. "What garden is that?"

"Eden."

This seemed to touch him somehow. He'd looked kind of soft and said, "So you're Eve."

And she'd said, "Guess again."

The look in his eyes had gone dark and distant, and they'd locked onto each other, she thought now, like a pair of scorpions in a cage.

She couldn't really remember how it had gone for the weeks after that, just a feeling of being high on seeing him every time and dancing around the things he wanted to know, to see how he would handle it. And the energy she got from him, the animal thing. And then about three months into it, the day she'd finally told him her story. She was standing in front of the fireplace with the stupid gas logs she always teased him about. Her back was to him while she played with some of the stuff on the mantle. She especially liked looking at a postcard he had framed there, a hilly little town in Mexico of blue and pink and yellow houses that seemed to be growing out of the jungle. *Papantla*, the card said. Robert was sitting behind the desk, not out in front in the big leather chair like he did when he wanted to get heavy. He was leaning back in his chair, twirling a pair of little scissors on his finger, letting her know they were just fooling around. That had gone on for two minutes or so, and then he asked her where she'd been the night before. She said, "What'll you give me to tell you?"

He was silent for so long that she finally turned around. He was nailing her with cold, dead eyes. It scared her, and she said, "What's the matter?"

He just looked at his watch. Then he rubbed his hands together, staring at her, and the idea flashed on her that he was thinking of strangling her. She sat on the couch with her hands clenched between her knees like she was eight and being scolded at school.

Finally he said, "Okay, Michele. You have thirty-five minutes left today. And this will be your last session, so maybe you'd like to use the time to get some closure."

"But I'm not any better! You can't just do that."

He just kept staring. "Do you remember on the first day I told you I'd always be straight with you? I'd always tell you what I was feeling? Okay, I'm angry. You're wasting my time. You're not better because you're bullshitting me. You have to be straight with someone for once in your life, and here I am. You've got half an hour to tell me why you're here, or we will say goodbye."

So of course she told him. All about the complicated arrangements in her family, her father dying and her mother having an affair with her aunt's husband Andy, mostly during the afternoons when she was in third grade and trying to do her homework. The grunting and shouting. And Andy always coming into her room right after smelling of sweat and salt and dead fish and sitting on her bed in his shorts, asking her did she know where babies come from, while her mother was taking a shower. And then finally making his move, once when her mother went out to get beer, rubbing his thing all over her face and finally coming in her hair. And then shoving her in her clothes into the shower, saying he'd drown her if she told. And then when her mother came back, him saying, "Michele got in the shower in her clothes! What's going on with this kid?" And years of weirdness after that, until she was fifteen and finally busted him to her aunt, and him beating her up, and then her mother beating her up, and no one believing her, and the foster homes and finally the day she'd gone at Andy with the broken bottle and all that. The time she'd finally decided to protect herself.

She remembered crying and writhing on the couch, thinking how strange it was that Robert just sat there behind the desk watching her. Her saying something like, "So that's why it's so hard for me, and I need, I need ..."

And him asking gently, "What do you need, Michele?"

And her saying, "I need you. I need you to come here. Please come here."

But he didn't. He just said, "You don't need me, Michele. You need a part of yourself to come back to you. And that will take some doing. That's why you're here. You've finally figured it out. And it will take some time."

That had seemed so true. So they started the therapy for real. She hoped that now her life would get easier, but it wasn't like that. It was hard to understand what he wanted her to do. He had an idea of how she could make things better, but it wasn't easy. She didn't really know what it was, even.

Thinking about this, she remembered another session, an important one in hindsight. She'd taken to crying about everything. She'd tell him about her stupid life the way it was then, dancing in clubs and doing a bunch of drugs and shit like that, some porn on the side, and he'd ask her if the things that were happening reminded her of her past, and she'd cry and cry, sometimes scream. He didn't seem to mind, up to a certain volume, when he'd remind her of the neighbors. And this would keep things going, but wasn't making her feel any better, or her life improve. And then came the one-eighty.

He was sitting behind his desk. She'd been crying about the owner of the club where she was tending bar and how he looked at her, scaring her by reminding her of her uncle.

He wasn't like Andy at all, but he was a creep and it was the easiest explanation. She was hoping Robert would offer her a Kleenex from the box on the corner of his desk, but he didn't. He sat staring out from under his eyebrows with a look that seemed to say, "Every word you say is bullshit." The Kleenex box was on her side of the big desk, so she got up and took a few, and then she walked up right beside him, she wasn't sure why. He seemed to force himself not to flinch. She stood over him blowing her nose and waiting for—okay, provoking—a response.

Finally he said, "How does that work with a nose stud? I've always wanted to ask someone."

She was amazed at her own reaction. She was suddenly in a rage and spit at him, "You're a superior motherfucking punkass cocksucker!!"

Robert laughed. "Okay! And you're a poor sad little girl without a clue, just so powerless and helpless and sad, and life has been so, sooo hard on you. So what do you want to *do about it?*"

Michele felt her face redden and her whole body start to shake. "I don't know!! That's why I'm here, you fucked up dickhead!!"

"Okay, that's a start. Stop trying to please me, Michele. You have no idea what I think or what I want, so sit down and we'll talk about it."

His voice was even, steady, low. This made him even more scary. In fact, she thought, he was trying to scare her. She felt miserable and confused, with no idea what to do but to stand over him and appear to have the upper hand.

But it didn't work. He stood up suddenly, right in front of her. He said, "Siddown!!" He was taller and much stronger than she was. He commanded her like a dog, "Sit Down Now!!"

And just like a dog, she dropped to the floor. She hid her face and for the first time in his presence really cried. Robert knelt beside her. He stroked her hair. He took her hands away from her face and wiped her tears with his palms. He murmured close to her ear, "Finally, finally, finally. Can you feel it? Now you're crying from the real source of your pain. And these tears will heal you, Michele. So let's figure out what your life holds right now. Because now is the only time we live. Right now."

She remembered sobbing, "I want to kill myself."

And him laughing, like he was sharing a joke. "Be careful how you throw ideas like that around. I have to report that to the police if I think you're serious. So don't say that unless you mean it."

"I do mean it," she said, not sure what she really meant.

He moved in closer and sat down with her on the thick soft rug. "No, I think you mean something else." He took her face in his hands.

She remembered looking into his dark confusing eyes. "What? What do I mean?" She really wanted to know.

"I think you mean you want to be free of the pain you feel, and you want something rich and vital to happen to you. You're a beautiful, deeply intelligent woman, Michele. You know it. You want that to mean something, and it does mean something. To me. It means something to me."

He was holding her face firmly in his warm hands. That was the first time she felt it: wet and swollen and wanting his hands all over her.

"What it means to you, you have to choose," he'd said. "That's the part only you can do. However much I may love you …."

He'd said that, he *had* said that, and he'd wanted that, and her, no matter how much he lied about it later.

"Which way do I turn on Santa Cruz?" The driver startled her. Robin woke up and started to whimper.

"Left," she said. "Then it's on the right. Fifty-three. A white building. Like a regular house."

4

Inside the house, up in the warm scented office, Robert sat drawing in his book and waiting for Anna to speak. She had an uncanny ability to hold a silence, to disappear, and she could always outlast him. He had better things to do, and she was driving him to the hottest edge of boredom. He looked down at his drawing, of two trees standing in a clearing, and reflected on the odd asexuality of all his Mouse material. For the hell of it he asked, "What are you doing?"

She turned to look at him, her eyes childlike. "I'm sorry, what?"

"We'd come right up to the edge there. It's important to talk about it."

"What time is it?"

"You're wearing a watch."

She blushed and checked it. Technically, she had five minutes left of the fifty-minute hour. "I'd like to go," she said politely and began to gather her things.

"Mmmm, well." Robert leaned back, stretching like a lazy cat. "We agreed, no matter what, we stick out the hour. That's the deal."

"I'd like to go."

Their eyes met, neither looked away, and both heard a car door slam outside.

"Of course," he broke the silence, "you can go if you like, but that's the end of the relationship. It's entirely up to you." He gestured expansively toward the door. "Feel free."

Much as she wanted to laugh at his posturing, Anna felt bound in her place, miserably wrestling. And then with marvelous *éclat*, like a doorbell ringing in a French farce, there was a loud knock on the office door. Robert seemed genuinely startled.

"Who the hell?" he asked Anna, making her really laugh and answer without thinking, "How would I know?"

Looking furiously annoyed, he went to the door and tore it open. A young woman, strikingly thin and pale, was standing there draped in layers of black. The red-haired, pink-clad baby she was holding seemed to have dropped into her arms from some other world. Her eyes, two beams of electric blue, shot their light straight into Robert's face. She knew him, that was obvious, and he knew her. He stepped quickly out and pulled the door behind him, forcing the girl back into the waiting room. Through the cleft, Anna could see the length of his tweedy arm, his hand with white knuckles on the knob.

"What are you doing here?" he asked, as if talking to an errant teenager.

There was trouble. Maybe his daughter?

"You didn't call me back." The girl was teasing, provoking.

"I told you never to come here without an appointment. That means never."

The girl's voice was low and mocking. "How can I make an appointment, Doctor, if you don't call me back? I didn't have a *choice*."

No, not the daughter. Their voices tumbled over each other.

"You can email, or write to me …."

"Just get your little black book, Robert, and let's pick a time to …"

"That's the only way that I will …"

"Oh, yeah? Well get this …"

"… permit you to communicate …"

The girl raised her voice. "*Permit*? Hey listen, you don't permit or not permit me. I am not letting you …"

Anna was ashamed to be eavesdropping. She tiptoed across the room and peeked through the crack. Robert opened the door, looking at her with a face she didn't recognize, hardened and compressed as it was with anger. Or was it fear?

"Sorry," she said lamely. "It's really okay, Robert, if you want to, go ahead with …." She waved a hand toward the young woman. "If you need to stop now I'm ready to go."

Before Robert could respond, the girl broke in. "I'm so sorry. I didn't realize someone was here." The teen rebel was gone, replaced by a soap opera socialite in silks and pearls. "If you'd just take a second, Doctor Buchanan, to make an appointment. I've come all the way from the city with the baby. I did try to call."

With effort, Robert was pulling himself together. "I'm sorry about this, Anna."

But the girl went on undeterred. "You didn't say someone was here." She looked over the tweed shoulder, the blue eyes now limpid with sympathy. "I would never have …."

"Okay, Michele," Robert cut her off sharply. "Just wait. I'll get my book. Anna, come inside for a second."

He took Anna's arm, escorted her back into the office and closed the door sharply.

"Wait for one minute. I want to end this session. I'm sorry. I want to get closure with you. Can you wait?"

Anna hesitated. What she really wanted was to watch this strange scene play out, but of course she couldn't say that. "Who is that?" she asked instead.

Robert seemed abject. "Okay, Anna," he said, leading her toward the desk. "Again, I apologize. This never happens. I'm appalled."

"No," said Anna, "it never has. What's going on?"

As Robert reached for his appointment book, Anna caught a glimpse of his open notebook, a drawing of tree limbs intertwined—or were they arms? Seeing her looking, Robert flipped it shut.

"My stuff entirely. You don't have to take it on." He tucked the appointment book under his arm.

Anna said, "No, but I'm here."

Robert nodded mechanically, his mind clearly on the girl and her pink baby. "We'll have to talk about it next time. I just wanted to be sure you were okay."

"A gift from the gods."

Robert smiled stiffly. "Good choice, Anna." He patted her shoulder. "See you in a week."

Anna scooped up her coat and purse from the couch, hurried past the girl and down the stairs. As she went she heard their voices start again.

"I'm completely booked through the New Year."

"Okay then, I'll just sit here every day until 2016."

Anna paused on the stairs and heard Robert say coldly, "I see. Okay, I have 9:00 next Wednesday, or, no—9:30. That's it."

"That or nothing?" Michele had gone back to her Lolita voice.

"I'm afraid so. Very, very busy."

"I'll bet," Michele answered with cunning suggestion. "And what if I need more than half an hour?"

"You'll just have to be concise."

Now was the time for Anna to go, or admit that she was staying on purpose. She stayed.

"Do you want this appointment?"

"I certainly do."

The baby let out a frustrated squeak. Michele said with dripping sarcasm, "Thank you so much, Doctor." The baby made a louder protest. "Say goodbye to her, Robert. You never even said hello."

But he didn't. "I will see you at 9:30 next Wednesday." He was guiding or possibly pushing her toward the stairwell. "Do *not* be late."

Anna heard Robert's door slam shut, a rustling at the top of the stairs, and the baby's small sounds growing louder. She imagined being caught there, the blue lasers turning on her. As Michele's footsteps came closer, she slipped quietly down, then back along the front hall. She ducked into a little alcove under the stairs and crouched there trembling in the dusty corner. The girl paused for a second beside the front door, adjusting the baby and her bags.

She said, "Step one, baby girl, step one, step one. Can you say, step one?"

The baby said, "Bawa jooz!"

Michele laughed and went out, closing the door solidly behind her.

Anna sat on the floor, breathing in the way she'd learned at Rape Crisis. Three counts in. Step One sounded ominous. Toward what? Five counts out. Whatever it was, it had nothing to do with her. Three in, five out. Still there'd be lots to talk about next time. Thinking the girl must be gone by now, she got up, dusted herself off and bundled into her coat for the dash to her car.

Outside a stormy wind was blowing. At the foot of the stairs Michele sat smoking a cigarette. What, waiting? The baby's pallid face peered back over her mother's black shoulder with puffy half-open eyes. There was a large red welt on her forehead. A trail of grayish smoke swirled up and was carried away by the wind. Michele turned at the sound of the door, and Anna felt a shameful need to explain.

"I stopped off in the ladies' room."

Michele took another drag from her cigarette. "Whatever." She watched with quiet Siamese eyes as Anna came down the stairs. "I was just wondering," she said, "whether you're going across the bridge."

Yes, waiting. For me, Anna thought. "I live on this side," she said. "Sorry."

"No problem." Michele blew smoke at the dark sky. "Going anywhere near a BART station?"

Looking down at the two bundles at her feet, Anna felt like a fool. It was Robert's ambiguity, his strange behavior that had frightened her, not these sad little girls. It was her own isolation. She'd become wary with people, even with this child who was young enough to be her student. Once, anyway. Her daughter.

"Sure. It's not far. Right on my way," she lied.

Michele jumped up, gathering her purse and the baby's blanket. "Cool. Oh yeah, I'm Michele and this is Robin. Say hi, Robin. Say hi." She waved the baby's knotted fist.

Robin said, "Wa jooz, jooz." She reached out toward Anna. Her face was dirty and her brow was wrinkled with worry. The welt on her forehead was darkening into a bruise. Anna took the grubby hand and stroked it.

"Hi, Robin. I'm Anna." To Michele she said again, "Anna."

Robin shouted, "Nana! Wa jooz!"

"Juice. Her basic word." Michele ground her cigarette out on Robert's step. "But you know what?" Michele cocked her head to one side, sweet and appealing. "I gotta change her before we go. And I'm dying for some caffeine. Would it be okaaay ... if we went ...?" She gestured toward the line of shops along the avenue.

Anna took a deep breath. "Sure. Why not." They pushed against the wind toward the bright steamy windows of the Matrix Café.

Inside the trendy eatery, its walls lined with posters of Neo, Morpheus, Trinity, and Smith, the lunchtime crowd was already gathering. Michele shoved her way to a table by the window—"Excuse me, I *have* a *baby*?"—threw off her sweater, ordered an orange juice and double cap as if Anna were the waiter, then took Robin off to the ladies' room. Left on her own, Anna felt suddenly claustrophobic and afraid she might panic. Why had she agreed to this? She wanted to be alone, thinking about the morning, the black hole opening and closing, all that dark matter, even her strange session with Robert. Could she cut it short, say she had an appointment she'd forgotten, order to go? On the other hand, here was someone who came from another part of Robert's life, who stood up to him, who frightened him. Who might give her a new perspective. She ordered the cappuccino and two juices.

Soon Michele came back, flung herself down and plopped the baby into a chair beside her. Robin let out a wail. "Shit, girl," said Michele, snatching her up again. She turned to Anna. "You order?"

"Yes," Anna said. To the baby she added, "You'll have your juice."

"The bomb." Michele looked sourly around the little café. "What's going on, a sweatpants convention?"

"Berkeley isn't about appearances," Anna murmured.

"Radical grunge," Michele said to herself. She turned away to the window, winding her legs around the legs of the chair and rocking mechanically back and forth, whether to comfort herself or the baby wasn't clear.

The callous attitude was nothing new to Anna. She'd seen plenty at the Art Institute: black clad students with fuchsia hair, pierced and tattooed and tough as nails, hanging in the fierce space and wanting you to know it. Then producing visual screams. Pretending to study the menu, Anna studied the girl. Her first impression had been that Michele was anorexic. But the arms holding the baby, bared now that she'd shed the sweater, were strong and supple. At close range the girl was exotically beautiful. Her flat broad forehead and high cheekbones, strong straight nose and wide full-lipped mouth gave her a gypsy look. Turkish, Finnish? She might be Cajun, Anna thought, except for the eyes. Tropical sea eyes, feverish and magnetic. Had they magnetized Robert? Surely not. Judging by the diplomas and awards all over his walls, he was one of the elite. Doctor, author, celebrated specialist—not one to fall for beauty without class. So what kind of relationship could they possibly have?

The eyes turned on her, making her start. "What?" Michele demanded. Now that she had what she wanted, why bother to be nice?

"I was just wondering if Robin might be hungry," Anna said.

"She's always hungry," Michele said defensively. "She's a baby." She poured orange juice more or less into Robin's mouth.

"I'd like to get her something to eat," Anna said. "And you, if you like."

Michele softened a little. "Okay, that's cool."

They ordered soup, salad and bread. Then Anna took the plunge. "So, how is it you know Robert?"

Michele didn't look at her. "Same as you, I guess."

Anna tried to hide her surprise. "You're a patient?" Robert's services didn't come cheap. But it helped to explain the anger. Something terrible had been done to her, too.

Michele's mouth twisted into an unpleasant smile. "Patient? You could say that. I *was*, anyway."

"I've been seeing him for two years," Anna offered.

"Me, too. Before ..." Michele nodded at the baby on her lap. "I stopped in 2013."

"I started then. October."

"Huh. You sort of took my spot, I guess. Wednesdays at 10:00."

Anna tried to imagine Michele in her place on the couch, a coiled dark form confronting the powerful doctor. "Is it the terrorism?" she asked.

"Is what?"

"That brought you back to Robert. The terrorist attacks, the wars."

Michele seemed to find this funny. "Terrorism! Yeah, that's it."

Robin started to fuss. Michele held her out to Anna, kicking and squirming. "You want her?"

"Sure, I'll hold her. You could probably use a break."

"No shit."

The baby was passed over and sat quietly on Anna's lap playing with a spoon. For something more to say, Anna offered, "I have a niece. She's four, my sister's daughter. How old is Robin?"

"Eighteen months. You don't have kids?" Michele wiped some juice from Robin's chin with the sleeve of her sweater.

"No, but I used to spend a lot of time with my niece. I'm her godmother. But then they moved, to Oregon."

Michele looked bored. Still, Anna pressed on. "They're both lawyers. They got terrific jobs, so they couldn't say no. My niece's name is Jessica. She has red hair, too."

The blue lights shot up at her. "It won't last," Michele said. "Both me and her dad are dark."

"Well, if you're both dark, there must be at least one red-haired grandparent." How pedantic, Anna thought. But Michele perked up.

"Not my parents. Except my mom out of a bottle. My dad had lighter hair, I think. I don't really remember."

"Probably through your husband, then."

"I don't have a husband," said Michele, in that sly, provocative way Anna was coming to know and dislike.

"I'm sorry. I shouldn't assume ..."

"Whatever. Anyway, I don't really know about her dad's parents. But I should find out." She looked over at Robin. "Mama should find out about Daddy's parents." She shook the baby's hand hard enough to make her head wobble. "Yes she should. Yes she should." Then she went back into her private world, jiggling her feet and looking out toward Robert's office.

Mercifully the food came. Michele ate hungrily, now and then tossing bits of bread onto Anna's placemat for the baby to snatch up and stuff into her mouth. Like feeding a bird, Anna thought. She fished some vegetables and chicken out of her soup, mashed them and helped Robin feed herself.

Michele took no notice. Then out of nowhere, she laughed. "How about those drives?"

"Sorry?"

"Did you ever get a look in Robert's notebook?" She leaned back in her chair, pretending to have the book in front of her, flipping through its pages. "Okay, Anna, I see we're going to have a day ..." she glared under her eyebrows, "... of denial. Now there's a winning strategy." The delivery was languid, seductive, Robert at his most confusing. In the imaginary book, Michele made an air sketch with her fork. It seemed to be the curves of a woman's naked body. "No matter. One day you'll rejoin the living. You can't escape the fundamental drives."

Anna allowed herself a guilty laugh. She didn't understand the drawing, but she knew the line. He'd said that to her only two weeks before.

Michele leaned over the table and said in her Robert voice, "Good, Anna, that's it. Laugh! Can you feel those primal energies moving through you?"

Anna hunched in embarrassment over her food, but that just egged the girl on. "Mooooving right through all the hurt and the pain!" she cried. "Come to Jesus! Come on to Jesus, baby girl!"

Robin flapped her arms and chirped, "Ma! Ma! Ma!"

"I know what you mean," Anna whispered. "But I do think he knows what he's doing. I think he's very skilled."

"Oh, yeah," Michele said bitterly. She put out her arms for the baby. "He's skilled. I'm down with that."

This was the door Anna had been looking for, but she found she couldn't go in. It was too dark in there. And now people were looking. She called the waiter while Michele put on the baby's coat. When the check came Michele slapped her hand over her heart and said pathetically, "Oh, shit. I don't have any money. Just enough for the BART ticket."

"No, no," said Anna, "I'll get it. I wanted to ..."

Before she could finish, Michele had recovered. "Fantastic." She looked at the clock on the café wall. "Can we hurry? Maybe we can make the one o'clock from North Berkeley."

At last a fine rain was falling. Anna put the tail of her coat over the baby's head as they ran for the car.

5

They drove through the empty neighborhoods, rain coming steadily down. As soon as the car was moving Robin fell into a deep sleep, heavy in her mother's lap. Looking down at the baby's soft head, her red hair wisping off in all directions, Michele realized how exhausted she was, how she'd love to put her head back and go out—far, far out. The energy of the morning had drained away, and she just wanted to sleep the sleep of the dead, then wake up to find the baby gone, all grown up, the whole thing over or never having been. Nothing and no one. The meeting with Robert hadn't worked out. Maybe it never would. She sighed and sank back.

"It must be hard without a car," Anna said without looking at her.

Michele felt slighted. "I have a car. Joe … the father does. He just had to use it today."

"Okay. I see."

"Robert has a Mercedes."

For some reason Anna smiled, making Michele think she'd better shut up. But she kept an eye on the woman, on the sly. This was not the kind of person she usually spent time with. She wasn't used to politeness and consideration. She wasn't used to driving this slow, creeping along like old ladies through the rain. Still, there was something about

Anna. She didn't bother with any of the things that mattered to Michele: hair, makeup, jewelry, the stuff that makes men look and want. But she had some kind of quiet about her. She looked right into you. Michele wasn't used to being looked at like that. It made her edgy. But on the plus side, that all added up to money. Even though Anna dressed like a bag lady, her stuff was good. Expensive shoes, a sweater that might even be cashmere, her dress that thick, velvety silk. Her hands on the wheel were long-fingered and white, but not weak or soft. And she had that gentle, strong voice, like the house mistress in a TV show about old furniture, who wears brown wool skirts and has a cocker spaniel. She leads you around a museum, or a huge house in the English countryside, using words like handsome, elegant, regal. Michele sometimes watched stuff like that, her face twisted in a smirk while she fought back a painful longing. But how had Anna wound up with Robert?

She risked it. "So you and Robert. What's up with that?"

She guessed Anna might be too shy to talk about it, but she was wrong. "I'm glad you asked," Anna said, then just went on driving. Michele could barely hear her when she finally said, "Well, okay. I was raped, about two years ago."

"That's funky." But not a big deal in Michele's world. "Date thing?"

"Oh no, no." Anna sounded like the question hurt her feelings. "No. It was a group, or gang. I think three. Men, boys—I don't know. They grabbed me off the street and dragged me into a cemetery."

"I hope you got a piece of 'em."

"A piece? Oh. No, but they got one of me. I was injured, well, wounded, and I couldn't help the police find them. I can't remember what they looked like. Even now. I went to Rape Crisis, and they recommended therapy. It took a couple of months to find Robert. He's the Top Man—I mean, sorry—one of the best in his field."

Michele didn't want to argue, but she stuck out her tongue and let her eyes roll back in her head. Top Man, fuck that. They happened to be at a stop sign, and Anna caught her doing it. What a surprise—she laughed.

"What does that mean?"

Michele played innocent. "What?"

"This," Anna said. She dropped her head and rolled her eyes. "This Saint-Joan-in-the-flames-I-don't-really-think-Robert-is-the-best-in-his-field look."

Someone behind them honked, making Anna jump and laugh harder as she jerked forward. She pulled to the curb and put her head down on the steering wheel. Michele wasn't sure what had just happened.

"Who's Saint Joan?" She couldn't tell if Anna was laughing or crying. Whatever it was, Anna started talking fast, like she was running out of time.

"I don't know, I guess I just don't know whether Robert is really helping me. No. I take it back. I'm better. I am, I think. But I've lost so much in the two years I've been with him. I've lost my partner, I mean, my … lover. My husband, really. My sister moved away, and Jessica, who I miss so much. I've lost my job. Although they'd have me back of course if I felt I could do it."

"Why can't you do it? Why can't you be with ...? What's his name, anyway?"

"Colin. Colin. We separated ..." Anna turned to Michele. She was crying. "I'm so sorry. I never do this. Joan-of-Arc. They burned her for witchcraft, after all she'd done for them." She wiped her eyes with her palms and looked back out at the rain. "I'm not with Colin because we, I mean I ... I can't. Be intimate. We tried, for months afterward. It was especially bad because we'd been trying for a baby. But I just couldn't do it. I have flashbacks. If anything happens that brings up the, the—incident, I panic. Is it like that for you?" She didn't wait for the answer. "I never know when it's going to happen, so I stay away from people. I mean, I have friends—my friends have been loyal, my family's been terrific, but everything is so ... pale. I'm like a ghost visiting my life from another world."

Michele made little sympathy noises, with no idea what to say. She didn't get it. Worse things had happened to her, but she didn't feel like a ghost. More like a fireball raging through an oil refinery. She couldn't be alone. She needed people. Men, sex, action. But right now, she thought, it was Anna she needed. She liked sitting in the Volvo with its heated leather seats. She liked the easy way Anna had with money. She liked having someone to help with the baby. And most of all, it was dawning on her that Anna might also help with the Robert problem. She put a hand on Anna's arm, like a friend. Anna reached in her pocket for a tissue, breaking away. But Michele didn't let go.

"So what world are you visiting from?"

"My past, I guess. Manchester-by-the-Sea. A town north of Boston. Little seaside village, all blue and white. A safe place." Anna turned off the engine.

Things seemed to be going in the right direction. "That's where you grew up?" Michele asked.

"There, and Cope Cod and a winter place we had in New Hampshire, a cabin for skiing."

"So you were rich." Michele hoped that wasn't going too far. But Anna didn't seem to mind. She went on in a dreamy voice.

"Not really rich, but well off. Our neighbors were a lot richer. My father was a painter. Well, a lawyer, but really a painter. He practiced law because he wanted his freedom. The family money came from my mother's side and he didn't want to be dependent on my grandmother. What a waste. He was a good painter, but he only did it on the weekends. We were very close. The Inward People, my mother used to call us, huddled together over our books. She was an activist, you see, every cause and committee you ever heard of. The Three Managers, my Dad used to call them—my mother, my sister, my grandmother—desperate to keep us on the straight and narrow. But by the time I was in my teens she'd given up on organizing Dad. Anyway, he died in his early sixties of a heart attack, I'm sure from doing work he didn't really like. But my mother's still working on me." She put a period on it. "She's going strong at seventy. In fact she's probably wondering where in the world I am."

"Your *mother*?" Michele couldn't believe a middle-aged woman would have a mother worrying about her.

"She calls every Wednesday, after Robert, to see if I'm cured."

This Michele got, and they laughed together. Anna turned the rearview mirror and looked at herself. She smoothed her hair with a disappointed sigh.

"I'm sorry. I'm sorry to blurt all that out."

"Want some lipstick?" Michele thought that would help more than anything.

"Sure, why not." Like she'd been offered some new kind of drug.

Michele fished in her bag. She had Black Plum, too dark, Urban Decay, an olive green that looked great under black light, and a howling red that might work okay. She handed it over.

Anna looked at the bottom. "*Cherry Bomb*," she read, and laughed. While she dabbed it on, Michele kept at it.

"So, what do you do? What's the job you lost?"

"I don't do much anymore," Anna said, working at the lipstick. "I used to teach. And, well … I'm an artist, I guess. A sculptor. I used to work in stone. And clay, both stone and clay."

"You make, like, statues and stuff?"

"Used to. And pottery, ceramic objects, that kind of thing. I haven't done anything for a while." Anna fished a Kleenex out of her pocket. "What about you?" She blotted the lipstick almost to nothing.

Michele knew Anna was just being polite, but she wanted her to know. "A bunch of stuff. Waitressing, tending bar, retail … in really nice places." That was stretching it. Anna wouldn't be caught dead in the Blue Rose or the Ashbury Boutique, but that didn't mean they weren't cool. "Then I was an exotic dancer for a while. That's what I like the most."

She hoped that would get her attention, but Anna just nodded, looked at her watch, and pulled out into traffic.

"My professional name's Jolie, like French, or Angelina. Jo-*lee*. You make a lot of money, depending on the club. You know, tips? I'm very, very good at it."

Michele leaned forward, making Robin's head fall awkwardly sideways. She wanted Anna to look at her, to see how powerful she was in the black leather thong and stilettos. "Do you know what I'm talking about?" The baby was hanging over her arm like a rag doll. "It's not stripping, you know. Do you know what exotic dancing is?"

Instead of answering, Anna said, "Sorry, I'm worried about the baby. Could you protect her head? We really should have her in a car seat. It's dangerous."

Anna was looking intently at the road, so Michele did the St. Joan, thinking, "Like you're a mother, like you would know." But she pulled the sleeping baby to her. "Like we're going to have an accident," she muttered. "It'd be faster to walk."

Anna only smiled. Moments later they came to the North Berkeley BART station. As Michele gathered her things, the sky opened and rain thundered down on the roof of the car. She wanted to ask for Anna's number, but couldn't think how to do it. "Shit," she whispered. When she opened the door, the baby startled awake, screaming.

"Oh fuck, here we go."

Within seconds Robin was writhing and pitching like a wild colt. Michele tried to get out, but the baby was thrashing and kicking, wriggling out of her clothes and down onto the floor. Michele was stuck in the open with the rain dripping onto her lap and running down into her boots. She yanked the baby up and held her by the arms, screaming, "You stop it, Robin. I hate this shit! Stop It!" Then she gave her a shake. Robin stopped kicking but kept on screaming.

"Here," said Anna, "let me see if I can help. Close the door, you're getting soaked." She took the baby. "Do you have a bottle for her?"

Michele slammed the door, dug in her purse and handed over a grubby bottle half full of juice. Then she started hitting her legs with her fists, breathing in short, hard bursts. She wanted to scream like she did at home when it all got too much, but she held back. Anna chimed in with Robert's breath coaching.

"Breathe out, breathe out. Now, take a slow breath in."

Michele didn't need it, but she went along. Soon she was sitting silent and coiled, while Anna comforted the baby.

"I know I'm not supposed to shake her," she said finally. "I did take the parenting class. She just drives me fucking nuts!"

She looked at the baby's blotchy red face, streaked with dirt and old food, and felt her blood start to boil. But before she could do anything about it, Anna said, "You've missed your train. I can't send you out in this. I'll take you home."

"You're kidding."

"No. But listen, we can't drive on the freeway without a baby seat. I was just wondering if you have one? I mean, obviously not with you, but if you could use another one? I have one at home, for Jessica. You can have it, if you want."

"To keep? Oh, wow, that's so great! Robin, Anna's going to take us home!" She reached for the ragged baby, stood her up on her lap and bounced her up and down. It had been a long time since anyone gave her anything. "And a new car seat! Can you say thank you to Anna? Wow, that's so great." She hugged the pink bundle until it squeaked.

Minutes later they turned off Grizzly Peak onto Cypress Street, winding around the hillside through tall pines and huddled acacias. A few houses down, they turned into Anna's drive. Although hers was a comfortable two-bedroom bungalow at the back of the property, everyone called it "The Cottage." The imposing Tudor facing the street made The Cottage look like a doll's house. Anna and Colin called that one "The Manor." When they had kids, they'd planned to move into it themselves. Jane and Howard Barton, both Classics professors at Cal, lived there now on a long-term lease. The Barton's Lexus was gone, so Anna and her guest seemed to have the place to themselves.

Anna parked while Michele gaped at the The Manor. "Wow," she whispered. She was trying not to wake Robin, half-asleep again in her arms.

"Mine's the cottage," Anna whispered back.

She could feel Michele's disappointment. But when they went inside, the little house gave a different impression. Its broad entryway swept through a wide arch and hallway that led to the dining room whose French doors overlooked the garden. Outside a Japanese maple was glowing like a desert sunrise against the silver rain. Anna turned on the lights, filling the house with color: pumpkin, rose, sea green. The paintings and sculpture, the comfortable furniture and subtly patterned rugs all invited ease, comfort, safety. Seeing it fresh through Michele's eyes, Anna was embarrassed to have all this and be so idle. But Michele stood marveling like a kid at a carnival.

"Wow, great stuff!" she said.

"I'm glad you like it."

"Awesome."

Michele approached one of Anna's pieces, standing just inside the living room—an enormous basket woven from strips of clay—snakes whose tails, writhing above the rim, turned into metallic fire.

"Way cool. You made this?"

"Yes. Thank you," said Anna. It crossed her mind to say that the piece had once shown at the Whitney Museum in New York. But that had stopped mattering a long time ago, and anyway it wouldn't mean anything to Michele. "I'll get the car seat, then we'll go."

"But could I change her?" The ingratiating whine Michele had used on Robert. "It's going to be super funky if I don't."

Anna didn't want Michele exploring the house, but how could she refuse? She led the way into her bedroom. The bed was unmade, the stained drape still tangled on the floor along with Colin's picture. She'd almost forgotten the revelations of the morning, it seemed so long ago. She threw things together and spread a towel on the bed for a makeshift changing table. While Michele changed the baby, Anna went to the guest room, where a large armoire held toys and books and clothes standing by for Jess. The car seat should be there somewhere. Before she could look for it Michele called out, "Where's the bathroom?" Good, the baby would finally get a wash.

Anna led the way through her dressing room into the sky-lighted bath. Closing the door to give her guests some privacy, she was going back for the car seat when she noticed Michele's purse upended on the floor, her things spilling out onto the bedside rug. Makeup, tattered wallet, diapers, teething rings lay in a heap. At the bottom, face down, was a fresh white business-size envelope. Several pieces of yellowed newsprint stuck out. The header, "*Boston* ...", caught Anna's eye. She couldn't help seeing below it a partial headline: "Boy Won ..."

She knew that typeface very well. Of all things, it was a clipping from *The Boston Globe*, the paper that had sat beside her father's plate every morning of her childhood. The headline suggested a contest. Behind it were several other clippings, one in the familiar font of *The New York Times*. She glanced guiltily toward the bathroom, listening. Over the sound of running water, Michele kept up a steady monologue of complaint. Anna turned the envelope over. "Robert" was scrawled across the front.

A boy had won something. What did that have to do with Robert? Michele didn't read the *Times*, Anna would have thought, and certainly not *The Boston Globe*. But she was collecting clippings? Old ones, by the look of them. She'd come that morning without an appointment. Were they meant to be a surprise? A revelation? In the bathroom the water stopped, and Anna could faintly hear the rustle of clothes. She pulled the envelope open just enough to see that "Boy Won ..." was in fact "Boy Wonder ..." and to catch, on another page, the odd phrase "... Priced Shrink ...". If the price were high, both could describe Robert himself. To read more, she'd have to rearrange the papers. She picked up the envelope just as Michele turned off the bathroom light. In a panic, she slid it back under the pile, ran back to the armoire and began rummaging.

"Don't know why you wanted kids," Michele said, as Anna met her carrying the car seat.

"It was Jessica's. My niece, I told you." Anna hoped she didn't sound breathless.

"The redhead, the lawyers. I remember." Michele put Robin on the bed and crammed everything back into her purse. The envelope went last, tucked in and patted into place. As Anna started out Michele said, "You go ahead. I'll be there in a sec." She jerked a thumb back toward the bathroom.

"I'll put the seat in. Just—turn off the lights, okay?" Anna didn't like leaving Michele in the house, but there was no way around it.

Hearing the front door close, Michele left Robin lying on the bed and went out into the hall. She slipped along it to the dining room. She looked out the French doors, across a stone patio where a garden sloped down the hill. Beyond it you could see houses and trees going down toward the Bay, half hidden in mist. When it was clear you could probably see the city, the Golden Gate, like from Robert's house. She turned back to the softly lit rooms: the dining table the color of honey, where eight people could sit and have their lamb chops and wine, by candlelight; the apricot kitchen with brushed steel appliances and marble counter tops; the kitchen opening out onto the huge sunken living room, a couch you could sink down in forever in front of a big open fire, looking up at the beamed ceiling. *In Style* good, *Lifestyles* fabulous.

Back in the bedroom Robin started to wail, and a bomb went off in Michele's chest. She wanted to run through the place breaking it all to pieces. She wanted to pick up this honey-colored chair, smash it through the pretty door and let the rain wash it all away. But she wouldn't do it. Anna was out there, prissing around in her late model Volvo, so fucking nice about everything, waiting to take the orphans home. She ran back to the bedroom and caught Robin crawling head first off the bed. She threw the baby under her arm and grabbed her purse. Turning to go, she saw a small green statue on Anna's bedside table, a little Buddha sitting inside some kind of flower. She picked it up and shoved it in her pocket. Then she smacked Robin's bottom hard and put a hand over her mouth.

"You shut up. You cry, I'm gonna fuck you up. So don't."

6

They drove silently down toward the Bay. Robin, who'd seemed happy enough before, was hysterical while her mother strapped her roughly into the seat. Michele, too, had dropped into a dark mood. She sat tightly bundled, shivering and turning something over and over in her pocket. Anna began to think she'd been found out, that Michele knew she'd been looking at that envelope. Or she'd said too much, shown too much. Still not speaking, they drove across the bridge until the buildings along the Embarcadero were below them, framed in their holiday lights, twinkling as they rose up out of the fog. They got off at Fifth and drove down Harrison. As they crossed Tenth Street, Anna felt her throat tighten, the ants begin to crawl.

"Do you live in the Mission?"

"South of Market," said Michele.

"It's just that, it all happened there. On Capp."

Michele was dismissive. "We're nowhere near Capp. Don't worry about it."

Minutes later they turned into an alley called Dore. The rain had stopped, but the sky to the west was darkening again, and the streetlights had come on, splashing their garish yellow over jagged puddles and potholes, trashcans and broken sidewalks. Someone had hung a sad strand of early Christmas lights on a building farther down. The alley was deserted, except for a dark figure trotting toward them, a young Asian man in ragged happi coat and flip-flops, balancing a huge plastic bag on his head. The bag rattled and tinkled with old cans and bottles. Traffic roared, sirens wailed.

"Downright nasty," Michele said in a Texas twang. "Stop at 56."

They stopped, and Michele gathered her things, the white envelope just visible inside her purse. The wisest course, Anna thought, would be to let it go. The envelope, the girl, her moods, her secrets. Instead she said, "Before you go …." The blue beams turned coldly toward her. "I was wondering … I hope this won't seem too intrusive. I, I wanted to tell you that I saw …"

She stopped in mid-stammer. Over Michele's shoulder, a sinewy, angry-looking man threw open the door of Number 56. Before she could warn Michele, he flung himself against her window, pounding on the glass.

"Hey, Shelley! Where the fuck you been?"

Michele jumped as if she'd been shocked. When she saw who it was, she threw the door open, leapt out and started hitting the man. "Joe, you fucking asshole! You scared the living shit out of me!"

Now Robin woke up with a start and cried out in a thin wail. Anna crawled into the back seat as Joe protested, "Where you been? I called home and you weren't …. Hey cut it out, cut it out *now*!"

He grabbed Michele's wrists and pulled her to him. "I was worried about you, Shelley. I was worried about Robin. And who the hell is this?"

Michele tore herself away from him. "Not that it's any of your fucking business, this is Anna. She's been helping me, now *there's* a concept."

They both turned to the strange woman, rocking the baby in the back seat of the Volvo.

"Oh, yeah, like I don't help you." Joe went to Anna. His thin face was sweaty, his dark blonde hair stuck to his forehead. "Thanks for your help. Can I have my daughter please?"

Robin said, "Dada," and started to cry again.

Michele ran around the car and pushed Joe aside. "Give her to me," she ordered Anna. When she held out her arms, Anna could see red welts where Joe had hurt her.

"Michele," Anna whispered, "who is this? Is this okay?"

"It's Joe," Michele answered impatiently. "My ... the father. Just give her to me."

Behind her, Joe was pacing and muttering to himself.

Anna hugged the crying baby closer. "Listen, let's calm down a minute. This isn't good. Robin's frightened."

Michele looked at her with real menace. Anna relaxed her hold on the baby and Michele snatched Robin away, snarling, "You shut up. Shut up or I'm going to smack you so hard! We just got you a car seat, what the fuck more do you want?!"

Sitting desolately in the back seat, Anna could still feel the small body lying against her. She looked out at Robin, red-faced and haggard, sobbing with her hands curled against her forehead, and clambered out onto the street.

Joe and Michele were faced off and Joe was saying, "You took a car seat? What's she gonna want for that? You're fuckin' unbelievable."

Anna went to them and put her hand lightly on Michele's arm. "She's only a baby, she doesn't understand. Let me take her while you two calm down."

Michele turned on her. "Oh, so now you're going to tell me how to raise my kid? What the fuck do you know about it?"

She paused, inviting a reaction, but Anna was too stunned to speak.

"Joe's right," Michele taunted. "People always want something."

The familiar fogginess came over Anna. The iron gate, the struggling and begging would be along any minute. She heard her mother say, you've had enough for one day. Blank faced and empty, she walked back to the car and started to open the door.

Michele handed the baby to Joe and ran after her. "I'm sorry, I'm sorry." She leaned against the car door so Anna couldn't open it. "I didn't mean that. I'm just so stressed out. This has been a hard day, I mean it's been a great day thanks to you, but hard. Really hard. I'm sorry."

From inside the sheltering fog, Anna saw a very young girl begging not to be left, not to be hit again on an old wound. Like her, Michele had had two years with Robert. Had he helped her at all? Was there any hope for either of them? She heard herself say, "I'd like to talk to you for a minute in private."

Michele squirmed, turning away so Joe couldn't hear. "Why? I said I was sorry."

"I just want to ask you a couple of things. In the car, if you want."

"Hey, Joe," Michele called. "You guys go on inside. I'll be up in a minute."

Joe hesitated, looking suspicious. She went to him cooing. "God, Joe, take her inside, give her some food. Does this woman look like she's going to hurt me? She's trying to help us. What's the matter with you?" She kissed him lightly on the cheek. "I'll be right there. Oh, wait!" She took Robin's arm and shook it, making the dirty little hand flap up and down. "Say bye to Anna," she said in a baby voice. "She was so nice to us, wasn't she? Say bye-bye."

"Ba Nana."

"Bye, Robin," Anna called. "Goodbye."

She got into the car. As father and baby went up the stairs, Michele got in beside her muttering, "He is so dumb." She sat staring out of the window. "Listen, you don't have to tell me, I know I was wrong."

"It's not that." Anna, too, spoke to the slate gray sky, the empty street. "I just want to know, why were you seeing Robert? I told you why I am, and I'd like to know."

Michele sighed. "Damn. Okay. Just … stuff, you know. Shit that happened when I was a kid."

"What happened when you were a kid?" Anna asked gently.

Michele took cover in the tough girl act. "Stuff in my, sort of, family. Incest, okay? But not my dad, my dad was gone. My stepfather, my mother's boyfriend, who was actually my aunt's husband, my mother's own sister. Getting the picture? So it wasn't, like, hard core. If I'd got pregnant I wouldn't have had a retard or anything." She laughed a hard little laugh. "But anyway you don't get pregnant with the stuff we did."

"But the pain's the same, isn't it? How old were you?"

"Nine to about fifteen." Michele began to rifle through her purse and the white envelope rose again to the surface. She pushed it back down. "Where are my fucking cigarettes?" She gave up the search and settled for gnawing on her nails as she went on.

"I was put in some foster homes, in and out. Him and my mom had got married. Can you believe it? Which blew the family thing totally apart. They even got born again, but it didn't take on him. So then," she turned to Anna, holding a dramatic pause, "I tried to kill him. Whoa. And went to juvie for a while, but my lawyer got me off. 'Impairment,' some shit. I didn't seriously try to kill him, I was protecting myself with a broken beer bottle. They said it was a deadly weapon. I mean, fuck that, Andy was five times as big as me. But I did kind of mess him up. He's got some scars. So. How's that? That do it for ya?"

Anna tried to be gentle. "You're lucky to have Joe. And Robin."

"Oh, yeah," Michele said sarcastically. But she turned away and seemed about to cry. "Joe's been good to me," she said softly. "We're a lot alike. We were raised the same kind of way. He did his time in juvie—stealing cars, little stuff. But then he went to Iraq, and it straightened him out. He works hard. We're together four years, sort of. It was Joe wanted me to go to Robert, or get therapy anyway. But then he said I changed." She wiped her nose with the back of her hand, and let out a bitter laugh. "He doesn't know the half of it."

Changed how? The half of what? But it seemed cruel to press her. Anna said simply, "I'm sorry. I'm so sorry." Before she could think better of it she took paper and pen from the glove compartment, wrote her name and phone number and gave them to Michele. "Here. Call me. I'd like to talk some more. If you want to."

As she took the number, Michele's face opened. Sweet, Anna thought, when you caught her off guard. Breakable.

"Wow," Michele said softly. She held the paper for a moment, then looked up at Anna with childlike eyes. "Does this mean I can keep the car seat?"

As Anna drove away Michele carried her present up the dimly lit stairs and into the little studio she sometimes shared with Joe. As usual, the place was trashed—the bed unmade, unfolded laundry spilling out of the battered armchair, Robin's stuff all over the place, dirty dishes piled on the counter in the makeshift kitchen. It was a little place Joe's uncle had found for them when Joe told him they were having a baby. His Uncle Frank owned a dump called Sweetcakes, a strip club in North Beach where Michele used to dance, and this building, which had offices and live/work spaces packed together like sardines. Theirs was one large room with a bathroom down the hall, shared with some artist's studio. Joe had made a partition that stuck out a few feet from where she stood, so Robin had a sort of room. Now it was a jumble of clothes and toys and junk.

With Anna's paradise burning in her brain, Michele was disgusted with the whole scene. And with Joe, who was sitting at the table—the "kitchen" table, the only table—with the baby in his lap, helping her spoon rice and pea glop out of a baby food bottle. She felt painfully soft, like she wanted to cry. She closed the door quietly behind her and leaned against the wall. Joe looked up, sheepish and suspicious at the same time. Their eyes met, a rare and uncomfortable thing.

Michele held the car seat out in front of her. "Sweet?" She carried it to the table and sat beside them.

Joe held her eyes. "What happened with Buchanan?"

"Nothing. He wasn't there."

"What? He's a fucking therapist, for God's sake. He has to be …"

"The holidays, whatever."

"Why didn't you call me?"

"With what? You took my phone, Joe. You didn't pay the bill!" Seeing his face darken, she quickly said, "Let's drop it." She lifted the car seat and did her Vanna White thing. "Behind door Number One! Look at it, Joe. It's a really good one. She was just being nice."

Joe sighed, sensing some kind of truce. "Where'd you meet her?"

"At a café." She didn't want to reopen the Robert can of worms. "I'd gone in to change Robin, and she let us sit at her table. We started talking … you know. She really liked Robin." She stroked the baby's head. "Didn't she, baby girl?"

Robin turned to her mother, smiling a gooey greenish smile. "Wyepee!" She waved her little fist. Joe and Michele laughed.

"Why peas?" said Joe. "I ask myself that all the time." Then he got serious. "So how did that turn into a hundred dollar present?"

"You are so fucking suspicious of everybody," Michele said mildly. "It was pouring rain, she felt sorry for us, whatever. Anyway, she's loaded."

She put the car seat carefully against the wall and began searching through the flimsy metal cabinet over the kitchen counter. "What do you think, she's going to exploit us?"

"Exploit? Shelley, you don't know what the fuck you're talking about. What are you looking for?"

"Weed," she said. "I do, too." She watched the news all the time. No one was going to call her stupid. "'Take advantage of.' 'Use.' Exploit." She pulled a little glass bottle out from behind the cans of soup and cracker boxes. A few shreds of green lay at the bottom. "Shit. You got any?"

"Well, yes." Joe put the baby in her high chair and patted the pockets of his jacket. He pulled out a slightly bent joint and a pack of matches.

"Here you are, my lady," he said, holding them out to her. She reached for them, but he pulled them back. "What do I get?"

Michele sat down beside the baby. The tearful feeling was stronger than ever and she just wanted it to stop. She didn't want to have to get angry, either. She was sick of it. "I don't feel like playing, Joe. Just give it to me."

He pretended to mull it over, leaning on the table looking down at her. With his tight jeans showing off his stuff, his work shirt streaked with grease, the sleeves rolled up baring his sinewy forearms and their pale blonde hair, he didn't look half bad. If it wasn't for those teeth he'd be a real winner. Even those, in profile, gave him a pouty look that sometimes, like now, she found sexy. She got hold of his belt and pulled him toward her.

He lit the joint, took a hit and passed it to her. She took two, then turned to the baby who was starting to fret.

"Go take a shower. I'll put her to bed."

"Let's do it later. I gotta help Frank move a refrigerator. Fuck, Shelley, it's Wednesday! It's a work day, girl!"

Michele stood up and started to undo his belt. "I might not want to later." She pulled the belt off and hid it behind her back. "Fuck the refrigerator."

"Now there's a picture," Joe said.

"You might not get a second chance, funny boy."

Joe knew it was true. He grabbed his cell phone. Texting as he went, he ran down the hall to the bathroom. When he came back five minutes later, Michele had hastily straightened out the bed and was lying there naked, pale, her black hair curling over her shoulders and out across the sheet. The anaconda tat wound around her waist, its head twisting on her belly so its scarlet red eye stared out from her navel. Its flaming tongue licked down between her legs, and its scaly tail wrapped around one perfect breast. It lived in the Garden of Eden, painted in flowery detail all over her body. In the background, Robin was making singing noises in her crib, while her music-box pony played *All the Pretty Little Horses*. Joe threw off the towel around his waist, straddled Michele and looked into her very stoned, crazy blue eyes.

"Where's the joint?"

"All gone," she said.

"Shit, Shelley," he began, but she pulled him to her.

"Com 'ere," she murmured. "Come into the Garden." She closed her eyes and held Robert Buchanan in her arms.

Twenty minutes later Joe was scrambling into his clothes, real quiet so he wouldn't wake the baby. Michele sat up in bed, smoking and watching him with a faraway look. He stopped at the end of the bed and kissed her foot.

She said vaguely, "Go on, Frank's waiting," and he went.

Michele wasn't really there. She was deep in her Mrs. Robert Buchanan dream, living in his house in the Berkeley Hills. In real life she knew the place, she'd gone up there once while she was pregnant, to get him to give her money. She'd found the address in his desk, the same place she'd found the clippings, in the locked drawer. The house was gorgeous, some kind of red clay, with trees and flowers everywhere. On an old show, *Lifestyles of the Rich and Famous*, she'd seen something like it, a villa in France where the ancient singer Tina Turner lived. "I'm a STAAAAR!" Only theirs would be in Mexico, Papantla, rising out of the jungle. By the pool in a thick, luscious bathrobe, reading *Vogue* and *Elle*, she'd pick out her summer wardrobe, sipping rum and Coke. Robin would be with her nanny, looking so cute in her pink flowered bathing suit.

Michele put out her cigarette and looked around the shabby room. Anger rose like nausea. She threw on her sweater, grabbed her purse and turned it upside down over the bed. A pile of junk fell out with the "Robert" envelope on top. Taking great care, she arranged the clippings on the table. There were three of them altogether, the parts from the back pages stuck on with see-through Scotch tape.

Monday, June 12,1988
T h e B o s t o n G l o b e

Ivy League Boy Wonder Faces Licensing Board

Wednesday, June 28, 1988
East Village Jive

High-Priced Shrink Does Double Duty

Tuesday, May 19, 1989
The New York Times

Respected Psychiatrist Exonerated In Paternity Case

Looking at this treasure she felt tremendous pride. It hadn't been easy to come by. It was back in the spring of 2013, when she'd known for sure she was pregnant. She'd been, whatever— involved—with Robert for a year or so.

Well, there'd been that break, after they'd kissed and pawed each other, and he'd made her leave early. He'd called later to say he was taking a month off, he needed a break from his practice. Yeah, right. When he came back, there were some weeks of nothing, just those horrible sessions with him behind the desk never letting her come near him, so cold and clinical. Of course she was sleeping with Joe all this time, and Robert was with someone probably, so it wasn't like she needed it. She just wanted him, it was all she could think about. She wanted the deep expert kisses and the hard hands so slow and enslaving. She used Joe to make love to him all the time, but she wanted to know for real what he would do, what it would be like.

Finally one day she'd come in, walked into the middle of the room and taken her clothes off, like she did at the club. She told him she thought it was time he knew what her life was all about. This was before the baby and getting so wasted looking. She'd had the most fabulous body, everybody said so. He probably thought he could resist, but he couldn't. When he saw the Garden and the Serpent he completely fell apart. They did it on the floor, with their hands over each other's mouths so people in the building wouldn't hear them moaning. There'd been a few other times, with weeks in between when he seemed to be trying to stop, or was making her work all the harder to get him.

Then somewhere in there she got pregnant. She waited until she knew for sure, then she went to a session and tearfully told him. She was sure he'd say, "This isn't how I wanted it, but I'll take care of you. You can't raise this child on your own. Besides, Michele, I love you." Or some other lines from *Days of Our Lives*. But instead he started flipping through his Rolodex. He handed her a card and said, "This is the best place in the Bay Area. They take Medi-Cal. It should be fully covered. Anything that isn't, I'm sure you and Joe can pay for over time."

"It's got nothing to do with Joe."

"How do you know?" he said.

"A woman always knows."

He said, "Bullshit."

So then the war between them really started. She kept coming to her weekly appointments, and he let her. She guessed he hadn't wanted to just kick her out. It would look strange if anyone was watching, like this Craig guy he talked so much about. She figured he wanted to keep control of her, to have time to talk her into an abortion. And she wanted something on him. But she knew the time was short and she'd better make the most of it. So she started faking morning sickness, groaning on the couch until he went to get her tea. Then she'd go through his things. She knew where he kept his keys and after several tries found the one to that locked drawer in his desk. There she discovered the folder full of clippings and blindly took three out of the middle. There were letters, too, and other old stuff, and a stack of notebooks like the one on his desk. In her boldest move, she ripped a bunch of pages out of one and stuffed them in her purse just as she heard his footstep outside the door. That time, when he came back in she was sweating for real.

She picked up the *Boston Globe* article and read:

> Prominent Cambridge psychiatrist Dr. Robert Buchanan may lose his license to practice medicine in Massachusetts, according to sources close to the state's Board of Registration in Licensing. A hearing has been scheduled, following a complaint filed with the Board last week by former patient Maura Quinlan of Boston. Ms. Quinlan has alleged that the doctor, a leading authority on sexual trauma and recovery, involved her in a sexual affair ...

Attached to that was a letter from Dr. Jules Traneau, some big deal at Harvard:

> ... it is easy to envision a scenario in which a young woman, having relations outside the therapy, could imagine that a pregnancy created with her real partner was a result of her fantasies about the therapist. It has been known to happen, many times.

Blah blah. The punk was actually defending him. That infuriated her. But it made you think. It had stopped her cold the first time she'd read it. This was how these guys put their world together. Once she'd read them all, she knew it took money to go up against Robert, just like he'd warned her. It took lawyers and DNA, all kinds of shit. And you had to have a trial, and testify, and he would do everything to make her seem sick and crazy like he did to that other woman. And then there was the problem of Joe, who was so excited about being a dad, in spite of having no money and nothing in his future but crawling around under broken down wrecks. And so she'd hesitated, until today.

She got up, lit a cigarette, went to their one grubby window at the foot of Robin's crib and looked out at the rain. Why had she picked today? It was one week until Thanksgiving, heading toward Robin's second Christmas. Robert would be going on his vacation, probably down in Mexico with some bimbo. Even if her plan got nowhere, she'd wanted to spoil that for him. And it was her old time, Wednesdays at 10:00. But out of the blue, there was Anna. That was the real reason. She'd gone today because this was the day to meet Anna. Hallelujah, her mother would say. Hallelujah!

Michele turned to look at the baby, sprawled out in the crib, her face and hair all gummy with dinner. A terrible feeling of tenderness came over her. She went to the edge of the crib. "It is not going to turn out that you ruined my life, baby girl." She ran a finger along the tender cheek. "But now there's Anna. She likes you. How do I get her to feel that way about me? What do you think she wants, baby girl? Everybody wants something. What does she need?"

Michele went back to the bed. She rifled through the stuff from her purse until she found the paper: *Anna Sheffield* in strong handwriting, and the number. She spent a minute memorizing the number, just in case, then took the little green Buddha out of her coat pocket and put it on the table beside the bed. "Anna," she said. That strange shivering cold came over her, so she lit another cigarette and went back to pacing up and down.

7

At four o'clock the door mercifully closed on the last patient. All day Robert had bravely maintained his usual routine, doing his best to put Michele out of his mind. But finally, when he leaned back in his big leather chair, he found that instead of a deep sigh of satisfaction and transition, he emitted a loud, painful groan. He covered his eyes with his hands and bent forward over the desk like someone about to be sick. Unwanted images flooded in—judges taking the bench, hard-eyed lawyers leaning across tables to depose him, reporters like packs of jackals. It had all happened once and could easily happen again if he somehow lost control. He saw the mystically Celtic Maura Quinlan weeping at the plaintiff's table as he testified to her borderline personality, her fits of jealous rage and the likely benefits of institutionalization. He'd paid a bloody fortune to get away with that.

And then there were the other deals, the other costs he'd kept in the dark—from his partners, his lawyers, from that conniving bitch he'd been married to for too many years. How could anyone understand the unimaginable losses? He fought an impulse to open his meds drawer and take a little something, as again a memory erupted of Laura, her long bare legs twisted around the sheets, the frantic calls for help, the inquiries. Yes, he had these samples, he was a doctor, but the drawer was always locked. She must have found the key somehow. Yes, she could be devious, but who knew she was so lost? Or was it just a wild experiment, Ativan and gin? She was wild, that's all, and more desperate than anyone knew. He'd collapsed there in the stark interrogation room, overcome that Laura had abandoned him with these hard men. But mercifully they'd decided: death by suicide. They'd left him alone until Maura betrayed him. And yet again he'd carried the day. He was still paying, but he'd prevailed. Yes, he told himself, he had prevailed.

He went to the window and slammed it shut, then sat again at his desk with three dreadful letters repeating themselves like some witch's curse: D-N-A. Since Maura, DNA testing had come into its own, and he knew all too well that a sample wasn't hard to come by. But luckily this patient was malleable. She came from his own class and he understood her better than she knew. For all her fire and rage, Michele wouldn't know how to bring an action against him. The word "lawyer," he was sure, brought chilling associations of juvenile detention and family court justice. When he told her DNA tests were prohibitively expensive and easily contested in court, she'd believed him. And, he'd added for good measure, her criminal record was bound to come into it. Better she be satisfied with what she had: a healthy child and a faithful mate, Joe, who adored her no matter what she did. And sure enough, after a sad attempt to shame him into giving her money, nothing more had happened. Until now. The holidays, he told himself. They do strange things to people. Anna was off balance, perhaps he was a little, too. Let it go.

Feeling reassured, he began to put the office to bed for the night. Right now he needed to turn his attention to the evening. He'd made a date with Fran to drop by for a drink, then take Camilla out to dinner. Turning off lamps, he paused beside a table in his reading alcove, where his daughter's college graduation picture was on display. A strong, handsome face reflecting her defiant way with the world. She'd been a baby when the trouble with Maura began, almost three when they'd fled to California, just thirteen when he and Fran divorced. She had been so angry then that she'd hit him once, pounding her fist into his shoulder over and over. He remembered the scene painfully as he tidied the office. How she'd cried while he explained that she couldn't really understand this complex situation, and she'd said that was a bunch of parental bullshit. So he'd opened up to her, told her about his early life, how gray and full of drudgery his days had been. He'd spent too much of his youth in school, he theorized, trying to escape the poverty and degradation of his dreary family, trying to emulate those pompous Yalies he'd hated so much in his youth. And in the prison of his ambition and fear, women had been his only refuge. He loved women, he'd confessed to his teenage daughter, who sat glaring at him from behind a curtain of flaming cellophaned hair. Glorious creatures, far superior to men. Terrible things were done to them, as she must be aware, and he would do anything, had dedicated his life, to help and heal them. He'd paused then, considering how to open a more frank conversation with her about sex, the drives and her own experiences, when Fran had come in raging and dragged Camilla out, hissing back at him, "You are utterly shameless." Fran hated the truth above all things.

He tucked his notebook into the top desk drawer and shut the blinds. Putting on his coat, he realized he'd left the logs going. As he crossed the room to turn them off, an unwelcome memory returned, Michele's spectacular rainbow body in the firelight, the first time she'd taken off her clothes down to the thong. The artful undulations, the Eden she became, what strokes of genius she could perform, the anaconda's tongue inviting him down to taste forbidden fruit, her black hair giving off purple sparks in the firelight. And now here she was standing at his door with this dreadful red-haired baby. Did it look like him? Just stick to your guns—it isn't yours.

On the way out he heard voices in the little kitchen down the hall. He looked in and found Craig and Janice leaning on opposite counters waiting for the kettle to boil.

"Staying late?" he asked.

"Yeah," said Craig, "we've both got six o'clocks. Where're you off to?"

"Camilla's up for Thanksgiving. Taking her to dinner, drinks first with Medusa." Janice shot him a look over the tops of her glasses. "Sorry, Janny," he added insincerely. She was a Jungian and didn't like it when he belittled her icons.

"I know, you can't help it," Janice said lightly. "It's a form of Tourette's with you. Maybe you should see someone."

"Oh, geez, let's not start this," said Craig, ever the peacemaker. "You have to be somewhere, and we have twenty minutes, then back to the trenches."

Robert left them murmuring to each other and ran out into the stormy twilight. On the way home he picked up some flowers and a bottle of Tanqueray for a decent martini. Since Fran had fallen in love with gin some years ago she'd been buying a cheaper product by the gallon and today he just couldn't face it. He popped in a CD and let Bill Evans carry him up into the hills. He was feeling decidedly better.

Once home he ran up to his big Arts and Crafts bedroom and searched his closet for something with the right touch for the evening ahead. The Euro film producer outfit should do it: black slacks with a great Italian cut, sueded silk shirt in a dusky blue, black jacket. It was sure to raise Fran's hackles. But he shouldn't play too hard with her, at least not in front of Camilla. Though he couldn't understand it, the girl went on loving her mother. He began to undress with the unpleasant sensation of being watched. Fran's watery blue stare followed him into the bath where, as he soaked, he found himself back in Boston, at the Newbury Street gallery where they'd met.

The eyes hadn't always been bleary and bloodshot. He saw her standing there, offering a tray of hors d'oeuvres, a small, perky person whose most striking feature was the color and clarity of her eyes—a vibrant cornflower blue. She was serving finger food when their paths crossed. She worked at the gallery part time, hoping to become a dealer. He'd come there because his practice was going well and he'd taken a small interest in collecting. Later she told him she'd spotted him coming in the door and made sure the encounter would take place. She wore her long hair pulled smartly back in a ponytail, leaving her pink ears and round, fresh face innocently exposed. Nice little lips, nice little nose, rosebud cheeks, like some cherub of the prairie.

"Are you enjoying the show?" she asked.

"It's all right." He took a shrimp roll and looked away at the canvasses covered with what seemed to be veins of coal and beds of lava. But she stayed.

"Are you really interested in painting, or just dropping in for cookies?"

"Ooo, are there cookies?" he said, in his drollest Harvard manner.

"Ha, ha." She turned away with a swish of the ponytail. "If you have any questions, I have answers."

He watched her for a while, swishing here and there with her shrimps. Her little black cocktail dress was matched by a velvet ribbon pinned just above the ponytail, to hide the rubber band. It was all too sweet. He got some wine, made a tour of the paintings and came back to dump his glass just as, fatefully, she was arriving at the bar with a tray full of empties. She pretended not to notice him and began chatting brightly with the bartender. She was making him feel small and she was doing it on purpose. He had a fleeting fantasy of tying her to a bed and using her for hours until she bled and cried for mercy. Watching her ponytail bob up and down as she rattled on, he felt a stirring. He said:

"I have a question."

Of course the question was what was she doing later, and the answer was, far from being tied to a bed, sitting on a bench in the Common and talking about her family life in Cincinnati, where her father was in business and her mother raised four kids. Just a cut above his own family. Charlie Potter did marketing for Hormel, Jimmy Buchanan sold aluminum siding. Robert found this comforting. After a few pro forma dates he'd gotten her to bed where he found her soothing, malleable, sweet. She loved to stroke his dark hair, which he kept at a Chopinesque, artful length; stroke and stroke as though he were a big black dog. She thought he was brilliant, brave, wonderful to look at, and told him so constantly. He thought this would soon become tedious. But the months went by, his work was demanding, and he found himself looking forward to those evenings of rest in her arms, if not in her company. When he talked about the cases of rape and assault he worked with at the hospital she'd listen briefly with large-eyed horror, then wave her hands as if fighting off bees. "Oh, no, no, honey! I don't want to hear any more. Oh, that's so awful." And so she was unaware of what he did when he was away from her, and that was fine with both of them. Then, after a couple of years, she got pregnant.

He wanted an abortion; she wouldn't even consider it. There were scenes and tears. But finally it had dawned on him that doing the right thing had ancillary benefits. A wall might be built between him and his past, for good. Stability, fatherhood, would enhance his reputation. Through Fran's trust and naiveté he'd put Laura behind him, finally, forever, and remake himself in his wife's innocent blue-eyed gaze. So, clenching his teeth all the way down the aisle, he'd participated in a big white and pink, Midwestern wedding, with ice blue accents, a mountain of tacky cut glass gifts and a five-story sugar and lard cake.

Yes, he thought as he shaved, that cake with its plastic bride and groom had said it all. She couldn't live up to his daring. She was too small to tolerate the vast spaces of his inner being. And he was glad when she'd betrayed him and the tie to her was finally broken. But he had to give her this: she'd never told the kids any of it—whether from fairness or fear didn't matter. She'd left him that small sanctuary, the unconditional admiration of his daughter. He stood in front of the mirror, trying on a wry, knowing smile.

Minutes later he pulled up in front of Fran's pleasant shingled house on the south side of campus. Camilla answered his knock and they stood appraising one another. Her sleek brown hair hung down to her shoulders and her strong athletic body was poured perfectly into a long liquid silver and black thing.

"Wow!" He whistled appreciatively.

"I'm fat," she said, giving him a quick kiss on the cheek. She twined her arm through his, steering him down the hall toward the kitchen. As they passed the living room, he caught a glimpse of a plump pink leg dangling from the wingback chair. Fran's foot, squeezed into its little black pump, was beating time to some CD of Camilla's, some Latin number. A fat hand shot up. She waved and sang merrily, "Hola, Roberto! Hel-lo!"

"Here, Dad," said Camilla, "give me your coat, you're drenched." As she was helping him out of it she saw the bottle of gin and added, "She's on her third. We're having so much fun!" Camilla could be quite a snake when she wanted to. She stepped back and looked her father over. "Ow, Daddy! You're just too hot for Berkeley." She put the flowers on the counter, took his arm and led him back to the living room. "You've really got to set up in L.A. It's perfect for you. Everybody's traumatized."

Fran peeped around the wing of the chair. "Oh God, there's that word again. It follows you around like The Furies." She waved her hand around her head, demonstrating how it pursued him. "*Les Mouches*. Whatever."

Robert thought she must have gained another five pounds since he'd seen her a month ago, and this perm made her look like a poodle. He stood in front of her chair looking down at her.

"Hello, Fran. You're looking terrific."

Their eyes met briefly, cold and hostile.

"Uk! Puh-lease," said Fran, "You're such a liar. And what's this?" She swept her hand through the air, indicting his clothes. "Isn't this the wrong time of year for Cannes?" She was cooking up something better when she caught sight of the green bottle. "But this is lovely of you. So thoughtful. Honey," she said sweetly to Camilla, "do the drinks. Show Daddy why he put you through grad school."

Camilla made a great show of mixing the martinis, making them both laugh. Then they sat on the edges of their chairs drinking them for twenty agonizing minutes, until Fran broke in abruptly with "Why don't you two run along and wallow at Chez P? Leave Mommy alone with *Monsieur* Tanqueray."

Sweet release. Soon they were sitting upstairs at Chez Panisse, in the back room, eating oysters and drinking champagne. Camilla was telling him all about the job, buying art for wealthy industry types. How much she was enjoying her research at MOCA and her decision to definitely settle in contemporary art. They had just ordered dinner when she suddenly said, "Oh, Daddy, I'm such an airhead, I almost forgot about this." She opened her purse and took out a neatly folded paper, apparently torn from a magazine. She held it against her chest and leaned conspiratorially across the table.

"Remember you told me one of your patients was an artist, a sculptor?" She carefully straightened out the folds and handed it to him, asking, "Her?"

Irrationally, the question frightened him. It must be Anna, nothing to worry about there. But why all the excitement? Daring to look, he met the penetrating gaze of his problem patient. In a small photo, part of an article on contemporary sculpture from some art magazine, Anna was radiant, holding her large, beautiful hands in front of her as if shaping something. She was dressed in an elegant Japanese costume, dark green and gold, a regal presence. A man stood beside her with an arm around her waist, a strong-looking guy with full, slightly lecherous lips, a craggy Slavic face and wild dark hair graying at the temples. While Anna seemed to be speaking with someone behind the camera, the man was posing for it like a model for an Art Edition of *GQ*. The caption read "Anna Sheffield and Marco Gravatsky".

So that's Gravatsky, Robert thought uncomfortably. From Anna's descriptions, he'd imagined a smaller, softer man, a sort of Bill Moyers type. He looked away quickly to a box framing a quotation:

> *What I've tried to do is to make visible the hand of the maker in the things I make. Ritual objects are our messages back. They say, we specks of consciousness belong here, too, though we suffer so much doubt about that. When we touch our world, we make each other. Rilke said it better: "Nothing was complete before I saw it. All becoming stood still."*
>
> ANNA SHEFFIELD

Below that was a tall, slender object, rounded at the base into a burl of rough burnished bronze and green. A crazy-looking fossilized tree, it seemed, or possibly a jar of some kind, a ritual vessel pouring spirits out into the air. Whatever it was, it seemed to have been buried for centuries, with the power of the long-forgotten. "Mana," Janice would say. The caption read "The Offering, Anna Sheffield, 1999, copper and clay." Up one side of the photo, in tiny print, it said "Courtesy of Whitney Museum, New York."

"Isn't that fantastic?" Camilla exclaimed. "Is she the one?"

Robert could not have been more disturbed if she'd handed him a summons. He'd just found his way into a cozy room with a warm fire and a wrecker's ball had smashed through the wall. He'd spent months hacking away at Anna's defenses, giving everything he had, and she'd never told him, never even hinted that she'd had *that* life, a celebrated artist, shows at the Whitney, someone written about in the national press!

"What is it, Daddy?" Camilla reached across the table. "I thought you'd love it. I mean, look, the Whitney, my client is dying to get hold ..." She trailed off. "What's wrong?"

He could hardly say what he was thinking. Look at her, damn it! With me she's withdrawn, hostile, a washed-up wreck. Now here she is, whole and happy, damn her. In two years I've done absolutely nothing to help her. This is who she's meant to be, and she won't let me help her! And darker, less altruistic thoughts were breaking through. This man she'd been with, half-Polish, half-Italian he seemed to remember, a well-known painter, an important influence on contemporary .... His thoughts kept falling apart. He'd had her for years, six or seven, all through her youth, and the guy looked like a real stud. Now his own fantasies with Anna would have something tougher to chew on.

But he didn't want that. He didn't want it. He looked up into his daughter's anxious face and tried to speak. He didn't believe in shame, he wasn't afraid of The Mouse, for God's sake. He felt his mouth hanging open like an idiot's and his skin was cold and clammy. Some unconscious material was bubbling up. Michele stood before him with the red-haired baby, eyes like laser weapons, as Anna said, "I'm here." While he faced off with Michele, she'd slipped away down the stairs. He couldn't be sure he'd heard the front door close behind her. Was it possible that the two of them had met?

"Sorry, so sorry," he managed. Still clutching the paper, he dashed for the men's room.

8

Anna crept back across the bridge in the rush hour traffic, feeling as turbulent as the world outside. Wind beat against the car, sea birds fell through the clouds, then tumbled away like scraps of paper across the Bay. Just past Treasure Island an accident brought the mass of cars to a dead stop, giving Anna her first chance to reflect. She found herself thinking in headlines: "Boy Wonder", "Priced Shrink"—almost certainly descriptions of Robert, old news from his time in Boston years ago. Harvard, Mass General, his diplomas said. She saw him standing at the door, pale and angry. He'd tried not to give Michele an appointment, but had relented. A girl who'd once tried to kill her abuser with a beer bottle—he'd know that, obviously. Could he be afraid of her? Or was he just embarrassed to have a lunatic like that camping on his doorstep. Another woman, like herself, on whom his therapies hadn't taken?

At last the traffic crawled off the bridge into the East Bay. Even though it would be longer, she took the scenic route, inching north through what was left of the Bay's wetlands. At University Avenue she should turn east toward home. Suki would be waiting by the door, the phone ringing and ringing with her mother's suffocating concern. But Robert broke in. "You don't have to. Home is a trap. You need the storm." She turned down toward the Bay and soon found herself at Chavez Park, almost alone in the parking circle that overlooked the Berkeley harbor. This had once been the city dump, transformed now to a landscaped promontory thrusting out into the Bay. The only other car was an ancient Chevrolet, painted all over with graffiti and plastered with bumper stickers. The driver, a man with a white beard, tidily dressed, sat behind the wheel absorbed in a book. Anna parked across from him and studied his slogans. *Hell No* and *Pueblo Unido* were half blotted out by *No Blood for Oil*, *Occupy!* and strangely, *Copulate Don't Populate*. The twin towers, smoke billowing, had *He Knew* stenciled across, and the names of all the attacks since were scattered here and there. Anna had been to many of those protests and wakes, the great gatherings in Central Park, the marches along Wall Street, but now both wars and protests seemed alien, the peculiar behaviors of another species. Still, she too had scraps for an assemblage: the voice of the man who had raped her, the strange session with Robert, the wild-eyed girl with the red-haired baby—an assemblage whose pieces refused to fall together. And look, she thought, I've already put that girl in a box. Even though she touched me. Even though she's the only one I've told about the rape, all the losses—Colin. Without editing. With tears. Why did I do that? Does it matter?

She turned away from the Protest Man and looked out at the storm, the heart of it still miles out to sea. The park, usually lively with bikers and skaters, kitefliers and dog walkers, was battered and desolate now, reminding her of Gloucester, Plum Island, the winter beaches of the North Atlantic. There were no beaches here, only the rocky breakfront and the boats tossing in the chop. Under the charcoal clouds now shedding a light rain you could see across the Bay, through the swag of the Golden Gate and out into the Pacific. Far away to the west the green water grew black, then liquid silver under some distant sun. A painter's dream. She saw her father standing on the rocks with his sketch book, trying to "get the clouds." He was always trying to get the clouds. Careless of the driving wind, she got out and walked along a gravel path toward the park's northern edge.

Artists should be a little crazy, her father had said once, shaking his head over some landscape of his. I'm just too sane to be any good. She'd been seven, looking up at him with a child's helpless love. Leaning into the wind, she felt herself tearing along their beach through the snow. She'd been tall for her age, with hair that hung down to the middle of her back. If she wet it thoroughly with hair spray, she'd imagined one stormy day, and ran the frozen beach as fast as she could, flinging it up behind her with both hands, it would freeze into the shape of a wing or a sail. Then, she'd later told her father from the safety of a hot bath, she'd fly away to the crazy place. And leave me? He'd pretended to be stricken. No, never, she'd said. I'd find out how to get crazy, and I'd bring you back some. You're lucky your nose isn't frostbitten, her mother had called from the hall. How did she always hear everything? I'd leave the Three Managers, Anna had whispered.

Later, about thirteen, all the girls were talking about astrology and signs. They were living in a special time, it turned out, the Age of Aquarius. One of them had gotten hold of her parents' album of *Hair* and spread the word. Anna had learned she was a Pisces: dreamy, artistic, prone to addiction and ruling the House of Birth and Death. That was great news. Those summer nights on the Cape, she'd sneak out after midnight, drop her nightgown on the rocks and lie naked in the waves, offering her changing body to the subtle influence of the stars. She'd wonder what the addiction would be, how she would handle it. It turned out to be an obsessive search for beauty that took her to the craziest places she could find: Indonesia, Afghanistan, Mongolia. If her mother said that a place was too dangerous, she'd have a ticket by the end of the day, and she'd go alone.

"How can I thrive as an artist if I don't study ancient cultures, Mother? These people *invented* The Pot," she'd argued, as her father stood protectively in the doorway.

After one of those fights—the one about Mongolia, the Junior Year Abroad fight—her mother had shouted, "Why not Italy? The Etruscans!! That's what you should be doing, Italy!"

"I'm inventing new forms. New forms, Mother! You wouldn't recognize a new form if it bit you!" She'd bolted away, rolling her eyes at her father. He'd come after her, taken her into his study and closed the door.

"I want to be clear about something. You're old enough"—she was nineteen—"to hear this now. I love your mother. I'm not trapped. I chose the life I have, and I keep on choosing it. But you should soar. You have it in you. You can't do it with me, and don't do it for me. Or against her. Do it for yourself.

Sail the Sea of Marmara, walk the Atlas Mountains, meet the dragons of Sumatra."

And she'd done it. Every one of those things.

She looked up and saw she'd covered the north leg of the trail. The path was turning east, back toward the hills. The light was failing, and they were hidden still in cloud, her home up there somewhere. Michele's dingy alley suddenly appeared, stopping her short with a nasty feeling of guilt. To have so much and do so little with it. I've become a coward, she thought. Maybe it's as simple as that, Daddy. Good girls don't soar. I'd rather live in a box, Robert. Let's start next time with that. She looked at her watch. Well after 5:00. Poor Mummy. The rain was starting again, as she crept through traffic back into her life of privilege and obligation.

When she pulled up to the cottage twenty minutes later, her neighbor Jane Barton threw open the back door and ran out with a newspaper over her head. She hunched down to look in the car window.

"My God, everyone's frantic. Are you all right?"

"I'm so sorry," Anna said. "Were you expecting me?" She hadn't laid eyes on Jane in days.

"It's Sarah—your mother. She called about 2:00. Apparently she'd been trying you all morning. Then she called again at 3:00, and Colin came by shortly after …"

Anna's heart skipped. "Colin?"

"He said he'd be back around 7:00." Jane shifted uncomfortably under her paper tent.

"You're getting soaked," Anna said. "Come inside."

"No, no. I just wanted to make sure you were okay. I'm in the middle ...." she trailed off.

Their friendship was another casualty of The Thing That Had Happened. "Sure. Thank you, Jane. I'm sorry you were put out. I'll call Mother right away."

As she stepped inside, Suki rushed her, frantic at being abandoned for so long. She tucked the cat under her arm and went around the house turning on lights and heat and putting the kettle on for tea. Finally she speed dialed the familiar number. It rang once.

"Yes?" The voice was both anxious and controlled.

"Hi, Mother."

"Anna! Where are you?"

"I'm at home. I just got in. I'm fine, Mummy. You didn't have to ..."

"All right, dear." The voice shed its anxiety, became firm, crisp and unavailable for criticism. "I'm glad you're safe. What happened?"

Anna hesitated, not sure how to make the day sit well with Mummy. "I ... I ran into a friend, and gave her a ride to the city."

"Aren't you having an awful storm out there?"

Her mother would imagine the nor'easters of the Cape, the battering rams of green waves smashing the gray barricades of the houses.

"Nothing much. Really," Anna lied.

"Well, you sound better. Whatever it was, I think it was good for you. How was your session?"

Anna knew her mother didn't want the gory details. And the session was hardly the point. "About the same. Listen, Mother, I can't talk long. I need some time for myself before … well, Jane told me you called Colin. I wish you hadn't done that."

"It'll do you good to see him." Her mother put her foot down. "He sounded very concerned. He loves you, Anna. He misses you."

"Mother, he's in a relationship."

"What a ridiculous phrase. I have no idea what that means."

Having settled the Colin issue, Mother went on decisively to the next. "I'm getting you a cell phone. I want you to promise to use it and call me if anything of this kind happens again."

"Oh, Mummy, a cell phone? Please, I hate all that …"

"Now, Anna, it's already been sent. Just keep it in the car. It's ridiculous that you don't have one. You're the last person on earth! It's got a Bluetooth so you can keep your hands on the wheel. Wonderful invention. Now—you said you needed to have some time to yourself, so why don't you run along. I think Colin's coming at 7:00."

Anna had to laugh, conceding everything. She'd never figure out how to use the thing anyway. She'd put it in a drawer and forget it. And Mummy was charging on.

"It's good to hear you laugh, darling. Sounds as if we're making progress." Which was how she always left it.

With Murray Perahia playing Schubert, Anna built a fire, then ran around the living room dusting with her hands and making sure there was nothing she didn't want Colin to see. Like this picture of them together on the boat in Portland. That was less than a year ago. Anna held Jessie and pretended to smile while Colin rested his hand on her shoulder. Tentative, she thought, unsure of himself with her. She took the photo out of its frame and stuck it on the far side of the fridge with a sushi magnet over their faces. Yellowtail, their favorite. Well, you can't erase everything. Finally she settled with tea and cat in front of the fire to plan what she would say.

Instead she found herself back at the beginning, in Kyoto, helping Sensei prepare for the next class—in the studio whitened with clay dust, putting a mound of hard paste porcelain at each student's place. Out of nowhere a tall man, a boy really, with a monstrous backpack burst in and came clanking toward them, down the row of empty benches. The kind of person who runs everywhere. He arrived panting and laughing, a hazel-eyed treasure with dark curls, a crooked grin and the long, sleek muscles of a swimmer or a dancer. A California mountaineer, as it turned out, a nature lover.

"Am I too early or too late?"

Sensei, having no idea who he was, said calmly, "Just on time."

Surely. She was twenty-five, he was twenty-two, both alone. He was on his way to Indonesia for a stint in the Peace Corps, taking a month to dabble in the arts of Japan. She would have dropped everything, but her apprenticeship lasted six more months. When he went away to Borneo they exchanged long, important letters about art and love and their short lives. On her way home they met in Bali for a month, on the north side where no one cared that they did nothing but make love all day. He'd joined a non-profit working to save the rainforests and had to go back to Jakarta. So she went on alone through Turkey, Greece, Morocco and back to New York.

Then she took the job at Cooper Union and waited for letters that came less and less often. Then mourning, then Marco. Marco Gravatsky, the king of postmodern surrealism. Unwillingly, she saw him leaning in the doorway of their loft with that Klaus Kinski look of spiteful, impotent injury. After five years together, the night of her first major show, when he'd felt her standing in his light, when things really began to unravel. The acid-tongued fights had started. She was losing herself, so she left. Slept on a cot in her studio, had serial affairs, a real Bohemian. Then 9/11 threw them all into chaos. And then the letter from California came, just on time again. Colin had settled out there, gotten a law degree, taken an important job in forest preservation. He'd seen a piece of hers in a show at MOMA, was overcome by a feeling of loss ....

Now it was half a year since their last meeting, when he'd told her about Elizabeth. She'd been distant and distracted, hadn't felt a thing. Dissociated, Robert had said. Sometimes he said things that were quite helpful.

"It isn't that you don't care, you just can't handle any more loss."

That was it. Claire and Jess had left just two months before. She'd met Colin at a restaurant because they'd agreed that meeting at the cottage would be too hard. As it turned out, everything was too hard.

He'd said, "You're not the same person," or something like that. "But if you find your way back …."

Back? Was there such a place? She couldn't remember all he'd said. Michele and Joe broke in, brawling in the rain, the way people managed on the far side of the moon. None of this politesse and delicate concern for others' feelings.

"Oh, to hell with it!" She threw Schubert aside and put on Annie Lennox. Exotic dancing—did she know what it was? She tried a move or two. Not grinding music, but so what? She ripped off her sweater. She sang *Here Comes The Rain Again*, rolling in the deep blue of Annie's longing …

The doorbell startled her. She ran for it, flushed and out of breath. Colin was there, cool and somehow paternal, wearing the black overcoat they'd bought on their last trip to Paris. His face was more lined, there was more gray in the dark hair.

"You're dancing. I guess you're all right." He must have seen her shadow against the blinds. He stood there looking wet and miserable.

"I'm so sorry, Colin. Mother was impossible."

"Reformer, reform thyself." He thrust his hands deep in his pockets. "So? Should I …?"

"Come in. I'm sorry she dragged you into it. Come in. It's cold out there."

Anna closed the door and leaned against it. Suki ran over and tried to climb up Colin's coat. He picked her up and nuzzled her.

"So you haven't forgotten me."

"Of course she hasn't." They stood close together, watching the cat writhing under Colin's hands. "You've still got the coat." She brushed her hand lightly along his sleeve. "You look thinner. Tired."

"Fighting the good fight. So? Is there anything I can do? Anything you want to talk about?" He put Suki down and looked at her, a hard look she didn't understand.

"No. What do you ...?"

He cut her off. "Something's up, Anna. I can't be ..."

"What, on call?"

"Sarah scared the hell out of me. I need to know what's going on."

"I'm ... You need to? I missed my call with Mother!"

"You never do that. Never."

"Colin. We haven't spoken in six months." For the first time she noticed how sad he seemed, and lonely. She softened. "Something came unstuck today, finally. I hope. It's exciting, it's frightening, I don't know what to say about it yet. Except that I'm not ready."

"Ready for what?"

"For this."

His voice hardened again. "Just tell me if there's something I should know."

"I need time to think." She took his hands. They were cold. He let her hold them. "Can I call you? Will it be all right with Elizabeth?"

"We don't see each other that often." He took a step back, then said, "Yes. Call me." He turned to go and said with his back to her, "Are you seeing someone? Is that where you were?" Right away he seemed to regret it. "I'm sorry. I have absolutely no right ..."

"Oh, for God's sake, what rights? The day just keeps coming apart. It's not your fault. I'm glad you came." Anna opened the door, letting in a cold wind. "I did meet someone, but it's not ..."

Colin cut her off. "Okay, then, I'm not ready for this either. Take time to think." He stood facing her in the doorway, then took her face in his hands. He brushed his thumb softly across her lips. "Lipstick," he said and kissed her, just long enough to let her know he meant it. "Yes. Call me."

"It's not a man!" she called after him, but with his long loping stride he was already down the driveway.

Anna watched until the lights of his car disappeared, then slammed the door and threw herself on the couch, her hands over her eyes. Mother, you fool, making him come here! It was terrible to see him like that, standing in the hall, a stranger in his own home. He was living now in a studio on the south side, in the student quarter, "in transition." She lay back, her hand moving along his sleeve as he leaned down to kiss her. A burst of heat in her belly made her groan and roll onto her side, clutching herself as if she were in pain. But it wasn't pain. This was what she wanted, wasn't it? Wanting him?

"Cut the bitch!" The voice came back clearer than before, high-pitched with a strong Spanish accent. Anna sat up, pulled up her dress and looked at the place where they'd cut her, a two inch line of thick scar tissue high up inside her right thigh. They'd meant to do something worse, the nurse had said. You're lucky. She cupped the place with her palm and closed her eyes. Lucky. The man's face hovered just out of sight. Why hadn't she told Robert she'd heard his voice? Maybe together they could make him show himself. Maybe she should call. He'd said he was available in emergencies, had given her a special number. Did this qualify as an emergency? A big enough job for Boy Wonder?

"Another day of denial, now there's a winning strategy," Michele mocked. She stood outside Robert's office, skewering him with those eyes: "You don't *permit* me!" Anna lay down again and curled around herself. What she'd give to be that angry, that guiltless, like the Bay roiling in the storm. A broken beer bottle, he has a few scars. And Robert? Had the girl gotten a piece of him? Until Anna knew more about that she'd never be able to sit with him again, much less dial the emergency number.

The phone rang, dragging her out of the brambles. Thinking it might be Colin, she stumbled up and ran for it.

"Anna?" It was the voice she'd just been hearing. "It's me. It's Michele."

9

Early Friday afternoon Anna sat waiting at the North Berkeley BART station. There was finally a break in the storm. A sharp cold wind was blowing, the trees were gleaming, the bright confetti of their leaves tumbled through the air glowing red and pink and yellow. Towering cumulus clouds streamed golden light from some mysterious source and every puddle was a well of cerulean blue. A Fauve masterpiece. Even the turbaned cabbies, who usually made Anna think of teeming cities and women bruised underneath their veils, seemed jovial and benign.

"I'm so, sooo sorry," Michele had said on Wednesday night. Her Lolita voice, seducing, sucking up. She'd thanked Anna over and over for taking them home; said that she was sometimes just so stressed she couldn't help getting angry, and that was too bad after Anna had been so nice and generous. Finally Anna had put a stop to it. She'd seen the envelope, she confessed, and wanted to know what had happened between Michele and Robert, if the anger had anything to do with him.

The girl had taken a long drag on her cigarette. In a low, suggestive croon she'd asked, "How much time have you got?"

Some game was being played. Anna realized she didn't care. "An endless supply," she'd said.

But Michele had held back. The stuff was dynamite, she'd said, and she'd rather "hook up." They'd have things to talk about, for sure. On Friday Joe's Aunt Ruthie could take the baby. They'd just have to wait until then.

So Anna had resigned herself and gone to bed without eating. She woke up late, hungry and exhausted. Rain tap danced on the roof and hissed among the trees and the day before might have been a dream. A damaged child with a sad pink baby and an envelope full of tattered newsprint—was it plausible that she had some power over Robert? Empty theatrics, more likely, some desperate way of lashing out. Anna lay listening to the faint humming of the house as it warmed itself against the storm. She wondered if she should call Michele and cancel, but realized she didn't have her number. And anyway the harm was done, her relationship with Robert had taken a turn. Without realizing it, she had given him her trust. She couldn't let him in, but that was something different: her new cowardice. Silently, she talked to him all the time. Her world had narrowed to him and Mother. Now another man had peeked out from behind the mask. She needed badly to see the face he was hiding.

Only two things had happened since then. Midafternoon, the FedEx man had delivered the cell phone. Jane's husband Howard helped her with the parts that belonged in the car: ear buds, charger, something that was called, but wasn't, a blue tooth. He said the phone was great, a top of the line smartphone, cutting edge. Later, after supper, she'd been straightening the bedroom and realized that the little Buddha on her bedside table was gone. It was there on Wednesday morning, she was sure, and it frightened her to find it missing. Sensei had given it to her when they'd said goodbye, wishing her happiness in life and love, knowing they wouldn't meet again. Its disappearance seemed a sort of omen. After searching for an hour, she'd collapsed into bed and cried herself to sleep. Still, that morning she'd woken in her bed and not in the corner cringing.

Now, with the bright world gleaming all around her, Anna felt sharp and clear. Whatever Michele had in mind it could only be for the good. Two days without flashbacks, with tears and a full night of sleep! She imagined herself next Wednesday sitting in her place across from Robert, the spotlight now turned on him. Michele's knock on the window caught Anna laughing. She hadn't seen her coming. She was wearing Wednesday's clothes, and an oversized leather jacket. There were headphones around her neck, their wires running down to some device inside her purse. She looked tired and peevish. Anna flipped the lock and Michele climbed in.

"How was the trip?" That was a stupid way to start, but now that the girl was actually there she couldn't think of anything else.

"The shit never ends," said Michele. She pulled the jacket around her and started bouncing her feet up and down. "I'm freezing."

"How's Robin?"

But Michele was already distracted. She pointed to a tight-faced woman standing on the curb. "See that hag? She was sitting right across from me. I thought she was going to call 911."

"Why?"

"My music, I guess. Fuck, I'm wearing the headphones." Under the dashboard, she gave the woman an emphatic finger. "Bitch," she muttered, then said mildly, "Wanna go?"

Anna started the car. "Where do you want to have lunch?"

Michele turned sharply toward her. "This has got to be totally private."

That hadn't occurred to her. Taking Michele home was the last thing she wanted. The first time had been bad enough. But then, it had brought her here. "Of course, I'm so sorry. I'm just not used to having people over. I guess I can throw something together."

"You're not exactly having me over. And I don't care about lunch." Michele leaned against the door, studying her. "Wanna hear something cool?"

"What is it?"

"Don't you like surprises?"

"Not recently, no."

Michele ignored that. "It's ancient but still cool. Linkin Park, out of L.A." She pulled a disc from her purse. "Old school," she said. "Joe confiscated my cell." She slid the disc into Anna's player. A blast of raw noise, maybe the meltdown of a nuclear power plant, was followed by the agonized screams of two young men. They jolted Michele into wild gyrations.

"What are they saying?" Anna asked.

Michele hit pause. "You try to get a fix on what's going on, but everybody's wearing a mask. *You're* wearing a mask, and it's like stuck to your face. But do you really want to see what's under there?"

"Just what I've been thinking," Anna said. "Please put on your seatbelt."

Michele gave Anna the Saint Joan, cranked up the sound, and the men went on screaming as they drove into the sun-drenched hills.

At the cottage Michele didn't wait for an invitation. She went to the dining room, threw her purse on a chair and dug a pack of Camels out of her pocket. While Anna put her own things away Michele wandered around the living room examining paintings, books, objects. Anna hovered near, afraid she might break something. Finally Michele stopped in front of Marco's drawings: Anna's long naked body, like a pale eel, she now thought, abandoned on a subway platform, then draped around the body of a burned and gutted car, then sleeping in the furrow of a field plowed by a robotic monster. These were studies for Marco's "Subterranean Series", that in the early '90s had taken New York by storm. Though they'd always hung there, Anna hadn't really noticed them in years. She and Michele stood side by side, looking.

"Me," Anna said, feeling awkward and shy.

"Yeah, I got that. That's cool."

"It's Marco Gravatsky." What a stupid thing to say. Michele wouldn't know who that was, Anna guessed, and would care even less. But she was wrong.

"Everything got covered in ash. I saw it on some show a few days after 9/11. Intense foreign guy in a big loft in Soho, with lots of windows. I guess that's near the Towers?"

"You were a child!"

"I was nine, practically an adult. Anyway, stuff like that sticks with you. I watched it for days. And this guy, he's like …" Michele struck a pose, both sullen and craving attention, a Marco clown. "'I am so deeply wounded by these events'." She made him sound vaguely Russian. "'I had many paintings in both Towers'—and he's making sure he's got some chest hair showing. 'Of course friends as well.' Side issue. Major bullshit artist. But sexy. I think he looks a lot like Johnny Cash. That's my Mom's favorite."

"Johnny Cash," was all Anna could manage. She'd been at a meeting in Chelsea, where they'd watched from the roof as the Towers came down. Over the next two weeks she'd tried to find friends and helped dig out studios in Soho. Along the way she'd heard that Marco was alive and she'd let it go at that. Looking at her long ago self, innocently provocative, recklessly open, she imagined their loft filled with ash and felt strangely relieved.

Michele broke away, tapped a cigarette out of the pack. "I don't guess I can smoke in here."

"If you don't mind." Anna followed the girl into the garden. "Is a toasted cheese sandwich all right? Some salad?"

"Whatever." Michele lit a cigarette, took a hard drag, and leaned against the house. Anna left her looking up at the sky and jiggling her foot. Putting their lunch together, she watched the girl wander toward the studio, wipe off the dirty window with her fingers, and press her face against the glass. Anna put the sandwiches aside and went out.

"My studio," she said. "My work space."

"I know what a studio is."

"Good. Want to look inside?"

"Is this where you made that snake thing?"

"Part of it." Anna took the key from the lintel above the blue door. "That's clay, so I had to fire it in a kiln—a furnace kind of thing. Then I painted it with metallic paint and fired it again."

She opened the door. A shaft of brilliant white from the skylight lit up the far side of the granite pillar, making her work on the piece disappear. She didn't turn on the lights. She didn't really want Michele to go in, or to have to ask her not to touch. But Michele seemed content to stand in the doorway and look.

"It's dusty," she finally said.

"I haven't worked in a while."

"The rape thing?" As if a little thing like that would never stop *her*.

"Since then, anyway. I'm afraid to be in here alone. And I can't … I can't decide …." Anna stopped, thinking Michele wouldn't understand. But the girl was good at proving her wrong.

"You can't decide what you want this to be."

"That stone was hard to find. And hard to get in here. We had to take the roof off. I don't want to ruin it."

They were standing close together in the sunlight streaming through the door. Michele stepped inside, then turned back, dramatically flipping her hair out of her face. Her eyes were gemlike in the glare.

"I'm an artist, too," she said. "Wanna see?"

"Sure. But please don't touch anything, if you don't mind."

Michele gave the hair another flip. She dropped the leather coat at her feet, then the little velvet jacket underneath. She slipped off her lace and rhinestone T-shirt and held it over her head with both hands. She was wearing a black lace bra that covered almost nothing. A silver mesh belt held her skirt just above the hip bones, baring her lean white torso, the canvas for a spectacular painting. The head of a serpent, red, turquoise and black, was tattooed on her belly, its body winding around her waist, its tail draped over her right shoulder, circling her breast. On her left breast, a single apple. All around the serpent were trees and flowers of every kind and color.

"Eden," Anna said. "It's beautiful. You do tattoos?"

Michele sighed petulantly. "It's not a picture of a snake," she said, still holding up the shirt. "It *is* a snake when I say so. You should know that. You do snakes."

Making percussive sounds under her breath, she began to undulate. On her quivering belly the serpent opened and closed its eye, winking and smirking. Michele writhed and turned, making the scaly flesh ripple across her body. As Anna watched, her attention drifted to the granite block with its rusty stain. The new forms Anna had seen there days ago sparked to life again, more intensely. Michele moved between her and the stone, looking at her through a curtain of purple black hair.

"Wanna see the rest?"

"I do."

Michele slid her skirt slowly down her muscular thighs and let it drop to the floor. She stepped out of the bundle of clothes at her feet, turning into the light as she unhooked the bra and tossed it aside. Now she was wearing only a thong and thick black boots with soles like gondolas. The snake's tongue, a jet of flame, curled along her left thigh, its tip turning up to point enticingly toward the strip of black leather hiding buried treasures. Like the snake, Michele put out her pink tongue and licked the air in time to a series of full body rolls. Anna wondered vaguely if the girl might be coming on to her, but her veiled, inward look said no. The pleasure she promised was only for herself. "False fire," Sensei would say. Skillful as it was, the whole performance left Anna cold. And Robert? Had he been invited to the dance, asked if he'd like to see the rest? Anna felt suddenly anxious and realized she was shivering.

"You must be freezing," she said.

Michele stopped abruptly and stared at her.

"Don't be offended. You're beautiful. It's just not the best time for this. Come on, let's get warm."

Michele threw on her clothes, petulant as a five-year-old, and stomped back toward the house, muttering, "Try a little of that on that man of yours, he'll know what I'm talking about."

Anna locked the door and replaced the key. With Michele outside smoking and pacing she served their food, then called Michele to the table. The girl threw herself into a chair, sulking.

"That tat took a year, y'know. I had to trade or the fucker would have charged me two grand."

"You traded …?"

"Blow jobs." Again, the taunting smile. "The way to a man's heart." Then she reached into her purse and pulled out the Robert envelope, now stained and dog-eared. "But it's paid for itself," she said. "Almost." She held the envelope against her heart and stared dramatically into Anna's eyes. Playing magician, she took out three newspaper articles and laid them face down on her place mat.

"Okay then," she said. "You ready?"

"Should I pick a card?" Anna joked.

Michele was stern, parental. "Just take a deep breath. In about one minute it's not going to seem that funny."

10

That was an understatement. Michele turned the first article over and spread it out in front of Anna. While she read, the girl watched with quiet, feral eyes.

Monday, June 12,1988
T h e B o s t o n G l o b e

Ivy League Boy Wonder Faces Licensing Board

"So," said Anna, "it wasn't a prize."
"What wasn't?"
"'Boy Wonder'. I thought he'd won a prize."
"He did, sort of. Keep going."
Anna read on.

Prominent Cambridge psychiatrist Dr. Robert Buchanan may lose his license to practice medicine in Massachusetts, according to sources close to the state's Board of Registration in Licensing. A hearing has been scheduled, following a complaint filed with the Board by Maura Quinlan, a former patient. She has alleged that the doctor, a leading authority on sexual trauma and recovery, involved her in a sexual affair …

"God!" Anna looked up. "He had an affair with a patient?"

"Yeah. God!" Michele mocked. "Go on, it gets better."

> ... culminating in the birth of a child last fall. Dr. Buchanan has denied any involvement with the patient, according to sources. But Ms. Quinlan intends to bring a civil suit, whatever the licensing board decides.

Anna stopped and caught her breath. Before saying anything, she read the passage again. "Okay, I see. It's a former patient. And—was he married or anything, at the time?"

"She wasn't former when she got pregnant. Keep reading."

> Buchanan, the son of blue-collar workers in New Haven, CT, obtained a public school education there, excelling as a scholar and an athlete. He went on to Princeton University on a football scholarship in 1967 and graduated Summa Cum Laude in 1971. From there he matriculated to Harvard, earning a PhD in Psychology and an MD with a specialization in psychiatry. He is currently in private practice in Cambridge.
>
> Dr. Buchanan is held to be "among the top ten men practicing in his field," according to JPP, the *Journal of Psychiatric Practice*, which reports on groundbreaking work in clinical psychology and psychiatry. He is thirty-eight years old, married to the former Frances

Potter of Cincinnati, Ohio, and the father of a one-year-old daughter.

It went on, but Anna stopped reading, attracted to a short clipping attached to the article, apparently a letter to the editor. Judging by the familiar typeface, it had been printed in *The New York Times*. She read aloud:

> Robert Buchanan is a pioneer in the treatment of posttraumatic stress disorders resulting from sexual trauma and abuse. His clinical work, his book, and his published papers are held in the highest degree of respect by his peers.
>
> In work like Dr. Buchanan's, it is very easy for patients to misunderstand some of the things that are said in therapeutic sessions. Also, patients tend to act out. They may test the doctor, who is of course restrained from responding both by social mores and the licensing board. Still, traumatic experiences leave very deep scars, and patients become confused at points in the work of healing. It is easy to envision a scenario in which a young woman, having relations outside the therapy, imagines that a pregnancy created with her real partner is a result of her fantasy relations with the therapist. It has been known to happen, many times.
>
> Therapeutic intervention in traumatic experience is a delicate matter. This is not the first difficulty for a

doctor working in this arena and we must not rush to judgment in this case.

Dr. Jules Traneau
Editor-in-Chief, Journal of Psychiatric Practice
Professor Emeritus, Harvard University

Michele grabbed Anna's wrist, hard. "Doesn't that just fry your brain? The fucker's blaming it on her!" She got up and started to pace. "He's blaming the whole thing on her."

But Anna was going in another direction, drawn by the sensible voice of the Harvard professor. She was thinking of many sessions where she herself had "become confused." But not like that. Robert was attractive but there were no sparks between them. Well, there were no sparks coming from her at all. He drove her crazy sometimes, but he was trying to help, she believed that. She felt small and foolish. She felt numb, as though she'd been walking for hours in the cold. Still, she said, "Show me the rest."

Michele set a single column in front of her. It was headlined My Patient, My Lover …, with the byline "Street Wise," from *The East Village Jive*.

"I don't know what this is, but it rocks," said Michele.

"It's from New York, a neighborhood on the Lower East Side. I used to live there," Anna said blankly. "Dated two weeks later."

Red Alert, all you Feminist readers. Here's one for the books. Remember Chinatown? My patient, my lover; my patient AND my lover! AND bonus! The mother of my child! This is the predicament of well-known Boston psychiatrist Robert Buchanan. Or is it? The Massachusetts Board of Registration in Licensing couldn't decide, so they settled for censure in a case that has rocked the psychiatric community and gained national attention. They could have taken the guy's license, but, citing lack of compelling evidence, hey, guess what? They slapped his wrist and sent him home to practice another day. And that's *before* the civil suit has come to court ...

"Okay," said Anna, "they censured him. They didn't take away his license. They must have interviewed the woman and they didn't believe her."

She looked up at Michele, whose face contorted in disgust. "I don't fucking believe it! You should have been one of the judges. You want to take his side, you'll love this one."

Without the theatrics she shoved the last article across the table. Anna scanned down and stopped at the third paragraph.

Tuesday, May 19, 1989
The New York Times

Respected Psychiatrist Exonerated in Paternity Case

In spite of repeated delays by Buchanan's counsel, noted defense attorney Harvey Schultz, a blood sample was finally obtained which excluded Dr.

> Buchanan as the child's father. The outcome visibly shocked both the plaintiff and her attorney, Patricia Stimson. Ms. Stimson had repeatedly accused Mr. Schultz of dragging his feet in producing a blood sample, demonstrating her certainty of the outcome. Ms. Quinlan held her counsel's hand and wept as the judge announced the test results.
>
> Ms. Stimson spoke with reporters after the case was dismissed.
>
> "I can only say I wish the science of DNA forensics was more advanced. But it'll be a decade before we have a foolproof system."
>
> Asked if her remark suggested the sample had been manipulated, she refused further comment.

Michele was right. What little fun there was had gone out of it. But could a blood sample be wrong? There'd been no other test at the time, no recourse, but now there would be. It hadn't taken a decade after all, the science of DNA forensics. Anna read quickly on, stopping at this paragraph:

> Maura Quinlan, 28, the plaintiff in the case, called a press conference shortly after the hearing concluded. She stood on the steps of the court house holding her two-year-old son.
>
> "This is a terrible injustice," she said. "Now I'll have to raise my child without a father, or financial support. It just shows the power of the male establishment that controls the whole medical field. I've been raped twice."

> Ms. Quinlan had sought therapy from Dr. Buchanan following a 1985 stranger rape in Cambridge. She said she intends to move out of the state, but did not further disclose her plans.

Anna's heart was pounding. "I've been raped twice." That's how it would feel, if she let go and saw what Michele wanted her to see. But why should it? It had happened years ago, to someone else. Even if it were true, things happen, people grow. And what was this girl after, anyway? The tattoo had paid for itself, "almost." Was she going to blackmail Robert? Anna pushed the articles away and put her head in her hands. She felt slightly dizzy. She heard Michele get up and start her cat-like pacing. It finally occurred to her to ask, "Where did you get these?"

"What difference does that make? So? What do you think now?"

"I don't know what to think. I mean, we know him."

"Oh yeah?"

"We've trusted him. I don't know about you, but I have trusted him with …"

"Oh yeah, I trusted him …"

"… some big secrets, confidences."

"I trusted him with more than that. I trusted him more than you!"

"Then don't you hope this isn't true?"

Michele moved close enough to bite her. "Hope? I know. I *know* it's true."

Anna stood up. She was surprised by the strength in her voice. "The man was cleared, don't you understand that?"

There was no sympathy, only anger, and she didn't know why. Michele held her jacket around her as if she were freezing. "And it makes a big difference where you got these. Where did you get them? What're you planning to do with them? Why are you showing them to me?"

Michele had obviously expected a different response. She backed away, against the French doors. Her mouth was drawn down, it seemed she might cry, but she screamed instead.

"You stupid bitch!" She broke down sobbing. "I'm sorry," she whispered, huddling against the wall. "I didn't mean that. But you've read all these books, and you still don't get it? Robin? That precious little girl you like so much? She's his, okay?"

All the strength seemed to drain from Anna's legs. She sat down again.

"Yeah, that's right. Are you getting it now? She's Robert's. His kid. He's the father. He raped me. He fucked me right on his pretty carpet, okay? And when I got pregnant he did exactly what he did to Maura, he kicked me out. So I stole these out of his desk. He has this locked drawer, maybe you noticed. And he has something else in there. The Book?"

She rummaged through her purse and pulled out a bundle of papers. With tears dripping onto the pages, she spread out three large sheets covered with doodles and notes and drawings. A large naked woman with a handsome horse's head, on hands and knees, looking back over her shoulder and laughing a toothsome horsy laugh. A tiny man dressed in a business suit and holding a whip shimmying up her leg. "Cruella de Ville" was scrawled across the top. A caption read: "He's so abusive!"

Anna stared at the pages. The black hole opened and the movie started, angels and Holy Virgins in graveyard ranks, men grunting and swearing. Latin beats, laughter, a woman's muffled screams. Four shadowy figures struggled across a stone courtyard. An urgent whisper, "Please, please, you don't want to do this."

"But that's why I came to you."

"What?"

Michele looked odd, as though she were made of wax, as though she were floating. "He won't help me. I thought you would." Her black mascara was running down her thin cheeks. One of those gravestones, a nihilist Madonna. But there was nothing Anna could do about it.

"Michele," she said, as though dictating, "I'm willing to help you, but right now I'm having—an episode. I mean, I don't know if it works this way for you, but I start remembering things, from the rape, involuntarily." That sounded absurd, but she couldn't help it. "So I need to be alone for a while. I'll get you a cab. Then call me later today and we'll talk about this."

"There's nothing to say if you're not going to help me."

"Just not now."

For once, Michele had no come back. Anna picked up an untouched sandwich from the table, took it to the kitchen and wrapped it carefully in cellophane.

"You'll be hungry," she said mechanically. "I'll pay for a cab. I'll give you some money." From some far away place she heard herself say, "I'll pay for everything."

Minutes later the girl was driven away, looking back through the cab's rear window, needy and helpless. Anna ran to her bed, put her face in a pillow and screamed over and over. Then she lay on her back and put all her effort into quieting her breath. If Robert went, there would be nothing. No one. Mother.

Questions buzzed around like hornets. The first moment she'd seen Michele, standing outside Robert's door—was that the look of someone who'd been raped, in the very room she wanted to enter? And Robert—was he furious, or terrified? She held Robin's sad little face against a picture she'd seen on Robert's desk, his kids when they were small. Yes. Especially the daughter. The daughter's graduation picture she'd once caught a glimpse of—Robin at twenty-one? Except there'd be no college, no privilege of any kind. There'd be drugs, jail, maybe insanity. Michele was self-involved, unpredictable, damaged, but she was trying to be a good mother. Without Robert, no one. Anna's thoughts spun around. A weight, like Goya's *Nightmare*, held her down. She called out to nobody, "I can't!"

From the phone beside the bed she dialed Colin's number. "Hi, I'm away from the phone…" Friday afternoon. Of course, he was out there saving the world. She did her best to sound cool and self-contained.

"It's Anna. I need your help. Could you come over later? I'll be here."

She hung up and glanced at the clock. It was only 2:30, a long way to go until Colin's day was over. She sat there in the fog. A woman's voice said, "I've been raped twice." Maura Quinlan. She jumped out of bed and ran to her computer.

Michele, flying away in the cab, couldn't shake the cold. She wished Robin was there to comfort her and hugged her purse against her chest instead. This hadn't gone the way she'd wanted, not at all. She'd played all her cards and come away with cab fare. The whole thing had been so spooky. She thought about Anna's face, how white she'd turned when she saw Robert's drawings. How she'd walked around and talked like a zombie. You had to be careful with people who'd been sheltered and spoiled all their lives. She knew the pictures were porn and none of Robert's patients would want to see themselves like that. She'd relied on their shock value. But they were funny, too. They were cool in lots of ways. You had to keep a sense of humor. Still, Anna had left the door open. She just needed to calm down, maybe. She'd said call her, she wanted to talk some more, and who knew what she might come up with. Most important, she'd said she'd pay for everything.

"You can't get anything straight, can you?" Robert said. He sat behind the desk, looking across at her with cold dark eyes. "You're so self-absorbed all you see is the inside of your own head."

"You think so?" She answered him out loud, making the cabbie shrink a little more into himself. She lowered her voice. "Well, I see *you*. I'm locked in on you."

The first job was to make Anna believe. And there was someone else who might help out. This Maura. To find her, she'd have to go back to the source, a much harder job than the first time. Tomorrow was Saturday. Robert didn't work on weekends, she knew, but some of the others might. If the building was open, she might figure a way into his office. It was worth a try.

"But don't you worry, baby girl," she whispered to a faraway Robin. "We'll get there. Yes we will. We'll get that motherfucker."

The cabbie threw her an anxious glance in the rear view mirror and she gave back a lethal dose of icy blue.

11

Yes, Anna whispered to herself, I do. I really want to see what's under the mask. The worst of the nightmare had passed and she felt quick and curious again. Bit by bit her search had yielded its fruits, and now she had the sketch of a life, at least the part since the birth of Maura's illegitimate child. After almost three hours, she sat back to reflect.

Maura was out there, living in Florida as Mrs. Gary Timms. And she wasn't crazy. No, it seemed she'd led an exemplary life. After Boston she'd moved to Atlanta, where she'd founded Women Take Charge, an organization for victims of rape and domestic violence. It offered self-defense classes, access to legal advice, support groups and counseling. Not therapy, Anna noticed. Five years later, Maura had moved to Florida, Fort Myers, where she married Gary Timms. This Anna learned through the website of the National Association of Kindergarten Teachers, who'd given Mrs. Timms an award last year for Promoting Creativity in the Classroom. She'd looked for Maura in the Fort Myers white pages but the Timms' phone was unlisted. Probably, like Robert, Maura dealt with a lot of troubled people. And there the trail ended.

Anna wanted to find the kindergarten where Maura taught, but that would have to wait. It was long after 5:00 on the east coast, and then the weekend. Still, there was one thing she could do. Using the address on their website, she composed an email to the current director of Women Take Charge.

> Dear Ms. Hernandez,
>
> My name is Anna Sheffield, and I'm hoping to start an organization like yours in the San Francisco Bay Area. I'm particularly interested in speaking with your founder, Maura Timms (nee Quinlan), who I understand now lives in Florida. I've tried reaching her there, but her number is unlisted....

An odd noise outside stopped her. Suki ran for the door, crying. It must be Colin's bicycle crunching down the drive. She wrote quickly:

> Could you contact Mrs. Timms and ask her to call the number below in Berkeley, at her earliest convenience? Your help is greatly appreciated.

She signed, sent, and ran for the door. This time Colin didn't wait but walked right in and put his arms around her. "What is it? What's happened?" He held her at arm's length, doing a quick evaluation. She imagined she looked even crazier than last time.

"I'm sorry, Colin. I'm behaving like a lunatic," Anna said. "Can you stay a minute? I have a lot to tell you."

He followed her in and sat at one end of the sofa. She sat at the other.

"Let me see if I can make sense of this," she said. "So much has happened. I'll try to make it quick."

"I have time." He was calm, soothing. He was good at quick shifts like that, and she began to relax a little.

"I'm sorry to drag you into this."

That hard look came back into his eyes. "Is this about him?"

"What 'him'?" She remembered their last moment, days ago. "No, no no no. I met someone, but it isn't what you think. But would it matter?"

He moved closer, put a hand on the cushion beside her. "How could it not matter?" Without thinking, she covered his hand with hers.

He pulled away. "So? Who is it?"

"It's a woman, a patient of Robert's. A lost child, really. She came to his office during my session last Wednesday, with her baby. A little girl." She told him about the confrontation with Robert, about meeting the waifs and their lunch together, leaving out the part about hiding under the stairs. "It's the first time I've talked with anyone who knows Robert, who's been through the same ..." Colin shifted uncomfortably beside her. "I know, you're thinking I should have gone to a group, a woman, whatever. But that's not the point. The girl had an envelope full of newspaper clippings, with Robert's name on it."

She told him about the headlines, "Boy Wonder". She sketched in the trip to the city, leaving out Joe and the angry scene in the street. But she had to tell him she'd given the girl her number. Colin looked alarmed.

"Does this person have a name?"

"Yes, of course. Michele." She was glad she didn't know the last name. She wasn't sure what Colin might do once he'd heard the rest.

"And what do you know about her?"

"She's intelligent, sweet in her way. Sometimes. And angry. She's been an exotic dancer, a stripper I guess, maybe a prostitute, I don't know. I'm sure she does drugs of some sort. She's nervous, unpredictable. And she's been hurt, worse than I have. So I gave her my number." Anna found herself slipping back into the defensive stance she always took when they talked about Robert. She got up and began to pace. "Anyway, she came over today, to show me the clippings, and it's worse than I thought. 'Boy Wonder' turns out to be—well, ironic."

Colin was watching her with worried, questioning eyes. He looked exhausted, probably hadn't eaten. She should just get on with it.

"Robert was involved in a paternity suit. He may have gotten one of his patients pregnant, a long time ago, in Boston. She took him to court, he won. He was exonerated."

Colin didn't flinch. He was good at waiting until all the facts were in. But it was a long minute before he said, "Okay. And why is Michele telling you all this?"

"It's complicated." Anna took a deep breath. "She believes Robert *is* the father, in spite of a blood test. And her child's father as well."

Colin stared at her for a moment, then said "What." It wasn't a question.

"I know, it looks terrible. But should I believe her? That's why I wanted you, I mean to talk to you, although I know you've never liked Robert, or the idea of Robert, or whatever it is."

Colin seemed ready to jump to his feet.

"Wait, let me finish." Anna sat down beside him, closer this time. "I want to talk to the woman from Boston. Her name's Maura Quinlan, or was. I spent the day trying to find her through the Web, and I got close. But you're so much better at these things. I need to find her, to hear her side. If I'm going to help them I need to know if this is true."

"What!" This wasn't a question either. "Anna." Colin took her hand and held it hard. "You know we've wondered over the years—okay, months that seemed like years—whether this guy was helping you."

Anna made a small attempt to pull away and Colin immediately let her go. But she stayed close, almost touching.

"He did. He did help me," she said. "I'm starting to remember things, I haven't had a chance to tell you."

"Okay, great. I want to hear. But focus on this now. It doesn't matter what the truth is about this Michele, or anything else. A paternity suit is enough in my book. You have to move on. No matter what the outcome was. Great, he helped you. Now let someone else work with you for a while. How about a woman? I mean, doesn't this just blow your trust wide open? If you ever had any. How can you feel safe with the guy after this?"

"Life's about living in danger and getting used to it. Getting stronger because of it. Isn't it? That's what Robert would say."

"Is that what he said about us, too? How about staying together? I never believed he gave a damn about that. And *are* you getting stronger? This is hard to say, but haven't you been hiding in your house for almost two years? Who left who?"

Once that would have made her crawl into her corner, but not now. "Okay, I have. I did. I left you. I disappeared. But something's been changing. For the better, I think. Robert can be complicated and imperfect and still be good at this." Imperfect? The horse-headed woman came to mind, her little man with his whip. She'd keep *that* to herself, along with all the other things. "I know it seems contradictory, and you're right, I can't exactly trust him after ..."

"Then what more do you need to know?" Colin shifted to face her. "Anna. Here's what you have to do. Walk away. Don't ever see either of them again. Not Robert, not this girl. Call him—now. Leave a message. Tell him you won't be seeing him again. And the same with her. Just stop it cold. We'll find someone else."

She noticed the "we," how it touched her. Even so, she said, "I can't. I have to find out what happened. I've spent two years of my life with him. And I can't just abandon them. Michele, I mean. And Robin." She felt tears coming.

"Robin?"

"The baby."

Or is Robin a stand-in for our baby? She knew he was thinking it, too. He wiped her tears with his palm.

"I wasn't thinking you should go to a group," Colin said. "I was thinking I should have been there. I was ten blocks away, waiting for you. Furious with you for being so preoccupied. Eating couscous, for God's sake. I could have run there in five minutes, I could have done something. Killed them."

"You've never said this."

"Because it wasn't about me. It couldn't have been, at the time. We didn't know yet it had happened to both of us."

There was nothing left to say. She reached for him, drew him to her. She hadn't meant to kiss him, but without any help from her, lips and hands found their familiar pathways. They lay back together, going deeper and deeper. There was a moment of panic when Anna felt his weight pressing her down, and all the times she'd panicked, panting, gasping for breath, came flooding back. How she'd beg him to wait, to stop. And then the storm of images would engulf her, and he'd withdraw, close off from her, slowly disappear. Then would come the hours of miserable, pointless talking. She closed her eyes, breathed in his scent of yeast and salt and wood smoke. A winking, smiling serpent uncoiled from the place where their bodies met.

"Let this be about you, then," Anna said. Her voice was husky, unfamiliar even to herself. She lifted his shirt and stroked his long smooth back, feeling it ripple like warm clay under her strong hands, making him groan. He pulled away just enough to look into her eyes.

"Be sure this time."

"I'm sure enough. But maybe you'd like to take off your coat?"

They made their way to the bedroom, leaving a trail of clothes behind. As they fell onto the bed—their bed—the phone rang. Colin sat up and looked at her.

"No," she said. The answering machine clicked on, recording a message. She pulled him down again. "And don't be careful." She slid his hand between her thighs, covering the scar. "I'm through with all that."

A couple of hours later they tumbled out, dressed in a pair of Anna's kimonos, giddy and ravenous. They threw together a meal, almost afraid to look at each other, standing side by side at the kitchen counter talking about his work, the war, the people they knew who'd been near the latest bombings or lost friends. Paris had happened only two weeks ago, and they hadn't talked about it. They ate in front of the fire, then lay watching it with Suki curled between them.

About midnight Colin said, "I have a conference this weekend, until Sunday night."

"You'd better go, then."

"I don't want to."

"We won't sleep if you stay. Let's leave it for now."

As he was dressing, Anna went to the answering machine, turned the volume low and listened to that last message.

"Hey, it's Michele." There was a pause, a sound of sharp inhaling. "Listen, I'm very creeped out about today. I hope you're thinking this over, 'cause I could really use your help. I hope you'll call me. Please call me." And she left her number.

Before Anna could write it down, Colin came in and stood at the living room door, buttoning his shirt.

"Everything okay?"

"Just one of those scams."

A few minutes later they stood by the door with their arms resting on each other's shoulders. "So." Colin tucked a strand of hair behind Anna's ear, one of those old habits. "Are you going to call him?"

"No."

He turned away, trying to contain his distress. She pulled him back to her.

"But I'll do this. I see him on Wednesday. I'll work on it until then, and if I haven't found anything, I'll just ask him. I'll tell him I know, see what he does, then decide what to do. That feels stronger to me."

"It's up to you. It has to be."

"Will I see you tomorrow?"

"The conference. I'm supposed to give an award."

Of course. Their lives wouldn't come back to them just like that. "Sunday, then. Come here when it's over. I hope you can rest. You look exhausted."

"It's you, really. I've been worried. I still am." He kissed the top of her head, started to go, then turned back. "The victim will have a strong bias," he said, the lawyer in him finally engaging. "That needs to be balanced by someone. Who would that be? And who would have the most comprehensive knowledge?"

Anna scanned quickly over the few things she knew about Robert: a life years ago in Boston, Harvard, colleagues in his practice, two children, a divorce. A name somewhere—*the former Frances Potter, of Cincinnati, Ohio.*

"He was married at the time. A woman named Frances."

"Google both their names. Obviously he'll turn up. But most people have some sort of trail. Or maybe they were still married when he came to California. Try the phone book." He kissed her. "Just stay anonymous. Trust me, you don't want him to know you're looking. I'll call tomorrow night."

She stood on the porch watching him wheel the battered old bike down the driveway. When he'd disappeared into the fog she went to the phone book. The search for Robert's ex-wife wasn't long. The former Ms. Potter was right there, in Berkeley, listed with a complete address on Piedmont Avenue. Or at least some Frances Buchanan. Too late now, the call would have to wait. She went to bed and lay for a while holding Colin's pillow, his lean sweetness lying beside her, opening to her as they took each other back. Soon, she imagined, there'd be a night without fear. She might even dare to think about a future.

12

For the first time in months Michele woke up on a Saturday with something big to do. The day was dark, but the rain was holding off for now. Joe had already gone, doing some emergency roof patch on one of Uncle Frank's apartments. Frank's boys, a bunch of illegals from Honduras, had picked him up at 7:00, and she'd heard him say he was leaving the keys to the Bug. With Robin at Aunt Ruthie's until late afternoon, there was nothing to stop her. After scraping together a joint from a bunch of old roaches she put on her straightest looking clothes—black skinny jeans, a plain T-shirt and a baggy purple sweater she'd picked up at a garage sale. With the long black sweater coat, and the Garden under cover, she might be presentable. Like a free-box version of Anna Sheffield. She took out all her rings and studs, put her hair in a long braid, grabbed a sweet roll to eat in the car and took off a little after noon.

Half an hour later she turned onto Santa Cruz. She parked a few doors down in case anyone was watching. There was no Mercedes at Number 53, in fact no sign of life except a dim glow through the glass panels of the front door and one lamp lighting up the blinds downstairs. She hoped that was the hypnotist lady. If it was, she had a plan. She'd wait for her in the hallway, then tell her she'd been in the day before to see Robert and had left something in his office. Something she had to have, something life or death important. But if no one was there, there was the big tree in back that practically leaned into Robert's window. Maybe she could climb it. Maybe, since his office was upstairs, he left his windows unlocked on the weekends. One way or another, she was getting into that office. Then she knew where he kept his extra set of keys, including the one to that locked drawer. There'd been other things in there she hadn't had time to get into. Bundles of letters, some old check books, that pile of fat notebooks. Maybe something would lead her to Maura Quinlan. That old shivery feeling grabbed hold of her, so she got out and walked decisively up to the front door. It was unlocked. Hallelujah. She went in and closed it softly behind her.

At first the building seemed absolutely still and only her shallow breath disturbed the silence. She tiptoed along the carpeted hallway. About halfway down was the hypnotist's door. She pressed her ear against it and listened. Nothing. Would a hypnotized person talk? Would the hypnotist? She had no idea. As she listened she began to hear a rhythmic shooshing filtering down from the floor above. She crept back to the stairway and looked up. An upright vacuum was standing at the top, with a feather duster hanging from its handle. She went quietly up and peered through the banisters, back toward the kitchen where Robert used to make their tea. A woman's denim-clad rump filled the doorway, wagging back and forth as she scrubbed the tiles, down on all fours.

Okay then, time for her Anna act. She glided regally down the hall. With a few feet to go she called softly, "Excuse me." The woman let out a shriek and pivoted around on her knees, lost her balance and fell backward onto the slippery floor. She was maybe forty, with olive brown skin and a puffy pockmarked face, wearing secondhand clothes a size too small. She lay there with her hand over her heart, calling out in Spanish to some saints or something. Michele wanted to laugh, but knowing Anna would never do that, she went to the kitchen door and offered a hand.

"I'm so sorry," she said sweetly, helping the woman sit up. "Are you okay?"

"*Quién es usted*?" The woman pulled her hand away and scrambled to her feet. "What you want?"

Michele wondered what the woman saw in her that made her act like that. Still, Anna would not get angry. Anna would have sympathy for the poor bitch. "I really am sorry I scared you," Michele purred. "I'm a patient of Dr. Buchanan's. I was here yesterday and left something very important in his office."

"I clean in there already. I don't find nothing." The woman was suspicious, but starting to calm down, smooth her clothes, pat her hair. So Michele went ahead without a plan.

"I suppose he might have picked them up and put them somewhere." She was imagining papers, but the woman said, "What? Glasses or something?"

That's a good idea. "Yes, glasses. I have another pair, but I left them in my husband's car."

The woman looked impatiently at her watch. "Ay yai," she said to herself. "Okay, I let you look quick, but I got to get this done, I got another job to go to."

"That's fine," Michele said soothingly, heading back toward Robert's door. "I'll just be a minute."

The woman followed, searching through a chain of keys hanging from her waistband. She opened the door. "I come back in five minutes and lock up," she said. "You let me know if you find them." And she bustled back down the hall, picking up the vacuum as she went.

Leaving the door ajar so the woman wouldn't wonder, Michele went straight to the desk, to the second small drawer on the left. Carefully and silently she slid it open. The spare set of keys was still hanging from a hook attached to the back panel. She put her hand around them to stop any jingling, lifted them out and put them in her lap. She recognized the big one to Robert's office door, slid it off, and dropped it in her purse. But several looked like the one she wanted. Finding that one would take trial and error.

With the keys silenced in her fist she crossed the room and looked along the hall. A door was standing open, down near the kitchen, apparently leading into a large utility closet. By the sounds coming out, the cleaning woman was inside putting her mops and brooms away. Michele's heart kicked up to a higher gear. She could take the keys and come back later, but the building might be locked. She couldn't stand outside in broad daylight going through them all. Or in the middle of the night either. As she watched the closet door, a brown arm shot out, thrusting itself into the sleeve of a raincoat. In seconds the woman would be coming to lock up.

Michele darted into the alcove where Robert kept his red leather reading chair, a little table for his tea and pipe and kid photos, and a standing lamp. The space was only a few feet deep, but one corner was completely hidden from anyone standing at the office door. She pressed herself into it and held her breath. Robert's daughter, in her graduation robes, was looking right at her, smiling in that sick way they both had: I'm smarter than you, I'm better than you, you can never get to me. We'll see about that, Michele thought, and held the girl's eyes as footsteps thumped closer, then stopped. Michele could hear the cleaning woman's heavy breathing.

"Lady?" she called, and took a step in. "Hey, *chica*!" She was silent for a moment, then muttered "*Qué grosería*!" and slammed the door and locked it.

Michele didn't move until she heard the front door close and its lock snap into place. Then she ran to the desk, sat in front of the big drawer on the lower right, and started through the keys. The sixth one did the trick. Everything inside was just like she remembered it: the pile of notebooks on the bottom, the folder with the newspaper articles, a stack of used up checkbooks, and then a manila envelope she hadn't noticed before. Hottest of all, a large stained envelope held a bundle of letters yellowing with age and held together with a thick rubber band—the first order of business. As she pulled it away, the rubber band disintegrated, leaving gummy marks on the letters. Good thing Robert never looked in there and wouldn't know the difference.

She started at the top of the stack and spread the first letter out on the carpet. It was on thick, creamy paper, almost like cloth, and the handwriting was loopy and foreign-looking.

Mi Corazon,

How I miss you, adore you, want you. Switzerland is glorious, you would love it here. The snow is perfect although it is spring. Don't forget me even for one minute. I kiss you everywhere, I tame you with kisses mi tigre—Laura.

Full dark pink lips had been pressed against the page. And there was a little faded snapshot of a dark haired girl on skis, like a model in super fancy ski clothes, designer shades, perfect white teeth. Maybe this was the girl who made Papantla worth a place on the mantle. Michele stuck the picture back in the envelope and moved on. There were three more letters from Laura, sent not from Mexico but Argentina. Fatter, but basically the same gushy crap: *mi amor, alma mía, mi tigre, mi sol.*

Michele felt like stuffing it all in a shredder, but stopped herself. You never know what might be useful later on. She set the Laura letters aside. There were only a few others, the first on nice stationary, too, though not as nice as the ones from Hot Lips. It was still in its envelope from a place called Peabody, Hawkins, Schultz & Graves, Attorneys at Law, 147 Providence St., Boston, Massachusetts.

July 18, 1988
Dear Dr. Buchanan,

We are in receipt of materials dated 7/12/1988, which will be handled appropriately. Otherwise there is nothing we can do in this regard but to advise you. As per our telephone conversation, it is imperative that you neither initiate nor allow further contact with Mr. Neal and his associates. If you do so, we will not be able to continue our representation of your interests. The Somerville location should also remain strictly off limits.

I hope you will regard this matter with the utmost seriousness.

Yours truly,
Charles W. Peabody III, Esq.

Michele read the letter over a couple of times, trying to understand. The date was the first important thing. It was about two months after the Maura Quinlan court case was settled, and Robert's lawyer was warning him off some guy named Neal "and his associates." Translated, the thing seemed to say, "See these guys again and I can't be your lawyer. I'm even putting that in writing. Don't see them, contact them, let them contact you." That could only mean some crime was going down. Some crime that would make their client look bad, which was all lawyers cared about—not was he bad, but how did he look. Like Andy's lawyer, who looked bad himself, like he got his stuff at Goodwill, even that rug he wore on his head for hair. He knew that Andy was a rapist but he tied himself in knots trying to make the judge see a hard working citizen, an upstanding member of his Pentecostal congregation hoping someday to be a deacon of the church. Up against that, Michele was advised to plead impairment and beg for leniency.

Same thing in this deal. It was important to Charles W. Peabody III—Esq, whatever that meant—that Robert stay clean. But clean from what? Drugs maybe, from the stress? What "materials" would Robert send about that? She couldn't figure it out, so she went on to the last four letters, all from his lawyers, short and boring. And that was that. Just a lot of questions with nothing to nail them down to.

Feeling burned, she shoved all the letters back inside the big envelope. But they didn't fit any more. Something was in the way. She fished around inside and pulled out a small crumpled paper. It must have been stuck somewhere in the bundle of letters, and when she took them out it had fallen to the bottom. It was a little piece of note paper, like people keep by the phone, and a logo on the top said it came from MedSource Labs. The note was handwritten in tight little scribble. She imagined the writer would have a high-pitched voice, like a cartoon rabbit.

Dr. B.!
How did you find me? You the man.
Couple of guys at

FSL might be interested. Re yr query,
nothing's changed
since MG. And looks like you've still got
<u>your</u>
monkey, so it's auld lang syne. We'll be
in Somerville,
same time same place. Or 374-8250.
L.

God damn. Same place, your monkey, auld lang syne? Some "we"? Were these the associates, possibly including Mr. No-Contact Neal? And the Somerville location—somebody's house, or just an alley? There was a phone number. Could be a cell, or maybe a restaurant, like in *The Sopranos*? L worked at MedSource Labs back then and he'd known Robert a while—since MG. A person? A place? Anyway, L was a lab guy, a guy who dealt with blood and stuff like that. Which made him the hands-on guy for a paternity test. But L didn't want to do the work himself, he wanted his buddies to do it at this FSL. Why was that? Whatever, this wasn't the first time L and Robert had crossed paths. Auld lang syne meant long time gone, back in the day. And then there were the monkeys. Your monkey, my monkey. That was a funny way for a lab tech to talk to a doctor.

Michele took her treasure over to the coffee table in front of that couch she knew so well. She sat staring at Robert's desk, all polished and gleaming, his fat leather chair, his diplomas in their gilt frames. Princeton BA, Harvard PhD, MD, Doctor of Psychiatry, Mass—. "MG." Massachusetts General

Hospital. Robert had known L since he was in school. Interns were famous for hitting up lab guys, to get through the long nights. But Michele had never known Robert to take an interest in substance abuse. She'd had to get hysterical for him to give her the Valium. Still, drugs were mixed up in it somehow, or some other addiction. What was Robert's monkey? Getting his clients pregnant? Not much of a monkey, twice in 25 years. And anyway what was the kick in that for him?

She thumbed through the stack of letters, found Peabody, Hawkins, and read it again. Now the picture was coming clearer. L had some connection with Robert from his student days. Could he be Mr. Neal? He'd done something for him before, something to do with his addiction. When Maura Quinlan got pregnant, Robert turned to L again for help, this time to switch the blood samples. Just like Maura's lawyer had thought. By '89, the whole thing was settled, but L wanted more. He had the drop on Robert and he went for it. The materials were extortion letters, payoffs, maybe death threats.

"So, Dr. PhD, you found yourself another badass motherfucker," said Michele in the general direction of the diplomas.

But then what? Here was Robert living high in California, doing his great work of healing. So what had happened to Mr. Neal? She took out the folder of newspaper clippings and looked through them to see if he would turn up anywhere. The ones on top were really old and mostly about Robert's scholarships and shit, then a whole bunch from the Maura Quinlan thing. Then at the back of the folder there was one from the Boston paper, headlined "Harvard Student's Death Ruled Suicide". There was the girl from the letters, posing in black dress and pearls. Gorgeous Laura Blaufeld, undergraduate, it said, in psychology; honors, wealth, Argentina, Germany, now dead at 23. What in holy hell did that have to do with anything?

Michele got up and started to pace. Here was the Big Question: why would Robert keep this stuff that made him look so bad? Answer: because he didn't see it that way. When it came to the newspaper clippings, everything he'd kept would make a sick guy like him feel good about himself. Like the train wreck you walk away from without a scratch. Judges, deans, lawyers, and licensing boards—everyone who mattered had found him squeaky clean. He'd beaten the rap, and just knowing what was in that locked drawer was enough to keep him on a high. Protected, above it all. But what was Laura's story doing in the pile? And how did she connect to Mass General, the monkey, and auld lang syne? Right now there was nothing in the world Michele wanted more than to talk to Mr. Whatshisface Neal.

She looked at the clock above the door: 1:08. Back east it was late afternoon. If the Somerville place was a house, people might be home. If it was a restaurant, it might be open by now. She had that number, so what the hell. Michele went to the door, unlocked the deadbolt and looked out into the hall. She stopped breathing so she could hear every sound. Faintly, far off, she could just hear cars shooshing by on the avenue, the roar of a bus, the blast of a horn. But inside there was only the gurgling of the old refrigerator down the hall. She closed and bolted the door, went back to Robert's desk and sat in his big leather chair. First she got the area code, that was easy. Now the number. Feeling high, she turned to look down at Robert's lovely garden, then put her feet on the window sill and waited for someone to pick up. On the sixth ring, someone did.

"Rinds!" It sounded like that anyway. The guy was shouting over the background noise. A bar, Michele guessed, in full Saturday afternoon swing.

"Who've I got?" she asked. But the guy was a wiseass.

"Well that depends on who's calling." He spoke with a lilt, and now Michele knew what he'd said: Ryan's. A bunch of Irish guys tossing back the boilermakers, watching college ball on satellite TV. She put on a crisp, deep voice, working to sound forty and official.

"I'm looking for a Mr. Neal? This is the number he gave."

"We got a gaggle o' Mr. Neals. And who might you be?" He wasn't hostile exactly, just protecting the customers.

"Mr. L. Neal. He's a lab technician."

"Larry Neal?" It wasn't like he didn't know the guy, more like he was making sure he'd heard right. Maybe L for Larry was now a dead Neal. "You're calling for Larry? Who the hell is this?"

Before she could think what to say, some guy in the background said, "For Larry? What's up?"

"Some female, says he left this number somewhere."

"Yeah, that's likely," said the second man. The two held a muffled conference, then the other guy took over, sounding grim. "Hi. This is Mike Neal, Larry's cousin. What's this about?"

There was obviously some big problem with calling there for Larry. But on the bright side, this was the place, they knew him and knew him well. She'd thought up a great story about a problem with his driver's license that would let her ask for his current address and phone number. But before she could get into it she was distracted by a noise downstairs, a clicking, snapping sound—keys turning in the front door locks. Michele said, "I'm from the DMV. There's a problem with Mr. Neal's license," as the downstairs door opened.

Down below, an unfamiliar man's voice said, "... catching up on (something), it's (something) the holidays."

And Robert responded, "Just picking up the mail, then I've got to run. Ben came in last night. We're going skating."

Michele bolted out of the chair and ran to the office door, taking the phone with her. The sound of Robert's voice started the old shaking, but she didn't have time for that. She guessed the other man was that Craig guy, Robert's partner. In Michele's ear, Mike said, "You fucking kidding me? Larry hasn't driven since 1992. He had a stroke. He's in a wheelchair."

She ran back to the desk, whispering urgently, "A stroke?" This completely changed her picture of the clever Mr. Neal. A drooler, going nowhere even faster than before.

"Yeah, ya morons. Update your records how about it?" And Mike hung up.

Downstairs, the two men went on talking, still standing by the door for some reason. There just might be time to call back, find out whether she even had the right guy. But then Craig said, "Okay, tea!" and the men started up the stairs. Crouching behind the desk, Michele dialed Anna's number so someone would know where she was in case something bad happened. Anna's message kicked in. Then Craig called out, "Rosario?" And Robert said, "I'll take mine to go." They were nearing the second floor.

Michele put down the phone, her body on fire with fear. She scooped up the letters, grabbed the big manila envelope, shoved everything in it and stuck it in her purse. She replaced the newspaper folder—minus the suicide article—closed the drawer and fumbled for the key. But she couldn't remember what it looked like. Fuck it, he never looked in there anyway. More important to put the ring back on its hook. She managed it, as the footsteps came closer. Then she ran to the window, thinking she'd jump if she had to. But that wouldn't be possible. Robert and his goddamn locks, she should have known he'd have the kind that fit into the frame and need a key. She froze, sweating and shaking, her mind scrambling for a way out.

"Darjeeling?" said Craig. They were right outside the door. "I've got some great new oolong, flinty, but smooth, really good stuff."

"I need a stiff martini." Their voices moved on down the hall.

"It's only a week. Okay, what'll it be?" Then the faint rattling of cups.

"The oolong."

Michele ran to the door and turned the lock. All she had to do was get outside the office, then she could tell them anything. No point in checking first—if they were looking her way she was fucked no matter what. Deftly she stepped into the hall and pulled the door closed behind her. In the kitchen

Craig had opened a cabinet on the far wall and was rummaging around for the tea. At a glance he reminded her of the counselors at juvie, slightly rumpled with a bad haircut. Robert, his old sleek self, was leaning in the doorway with his back to the hall. She slipped silently away, down the stairs and out into the cold. She sprinted down the street, laughing hysterically, heading with her treasure to the Matrix, the nearest source of caffeine. Then to Anna. To Anna.

13

It was just after 1:00 when Anna finally got her courage up. Sitting by the phone, she'd been trying to make herself dial, thinking it through from every angle. She'd slept long and deeply and woken free of the nightmares. Colin was right. Just walk away and put it all behind us. But as she'd dressed, the trap of her thoughts had closed her in again. Every day for the rest of her life she'd wonder what was happening to Michele, what had become of Robin. If the girl left her alone. There could be calls in the middle of the night, unwelcome visits. It could go on for years. And you started it after all, she told herself. You took them in, promised your help. And then there was Robert. If Michele was right, she couldn't turn her back on what he'd done to her. If not, it was her duty to protect him from the girl. Him, and the small progress they'd made, whatever it was he'd done for her.

She gazed out at her garden. The maple was subdued, its fire banked by fog, a silver cloud perfectly still among the branches. Time and weather had come to a stop, waiting for her as they had for so long now. She dialed. The answering voice was young, feminine.

"May I speak with Frances Buchanan?" Anna asked.

"Who is it?"

Anna felt the blood rush to her face. Stay anonymous! She couldn't call as herself. If Robert found out it would ruin everything.

"It's … Michele," she said. No! Not Michele! "Mimi, uh, Buchanan."

She waited for questions but none came. The girl simply shouted, "Mom, it's Mimi," into what sounded like a large house. After a long silence the girl said, "Sorry, she'll be right here," and Anna scrambled to invent a biography for Michele's alter ego.

Soon an impatient voice said, "Yes, what is it?"

"Hi, Frances," Anna tried to sound breezy. "My name is Mimi Buchanan. I'm looking for a distant cousin of mine named Robert, who used to live in New Haven. I'm wondering if you can help me."

She was ready with more, but the woman said abruptly, "He'll be here in ten minutes. But as far as I know he doesn't have a cousin named Mimi."

It was absurd to take offense, but she didn't like the woman's tone. "He may not know I'm his cousin," she said coolly.

"Well, whatever. Give me a number and I'll have him call."

Again Anna was caught off guard. "I'm, uh, calling from a pay phone. At the airport. Could I call back?"

"Oh, for God's sake, I really don't have time for this. This isn't Robert's home and hasn't been for a long time. Contact him at his office, he's in the book." And she hung up.

So that's the ex. Poor Robert. Or did they deserve each other? Anna looked again at Frances Buchanan's phone book entry. The address was right there. Without giving herself time to think she grabbed her coat and ran for the car.

Twenty minutes later she pulled to the curb, across the street from a shingled house on a quiet, tree-lined block of Piedmont Avenue. Robert's silver Mercedes was parked in front. Through the wide picture windows that opened onto the living and dining rooms, she could see the people of Robert's world moving from room to room, apparently getting ready to go out. There was an athletic young woman whom she recognized as Camilla, a gangly, stoop-shouldered boy of maybe twenty, and a petite plump blonde in a pink dressing gown, who seemed mostly to stand by a portable bar and call out to people. Finally, after a minute or two, Robert himself came into the living room and took up a position by the door, leaning against the wall and fiddling with a cell phone while talking first in the direction of the bustling kids, then toward Frances at her watery pursuits. Apparently only Robert and the kids were going somewhere. Frances would stay behind to drown her sorrows.

Anna had wondered on the way over what she would feel if she saw Robert there. Her revulsion at his casual arrogance was no surprise. But she had to admit there was a painful touch of tenderness. Looking through Michele's lens, the handsome tweedy clothes were now such an obvious disguise, the mask he wore for his family. A working class boy from a grubby industrial town made even more pathetic by the presence of the great Yale University. Maybe he'd married a princess, and that's why he had to posture for her even now. She wondered what it had been like for her, this Frances. She'd stuck it out for years after the Quinlan affair. What had finally done them in?

With a start, Anna realized she'd drifted off into her thoughts. While she was wandering Robert had crossed the room and was looking out. The street was narrow. He could easily see her if she somehow attracted his attention. She wasn't sure whether he had ever seen her car, and he seemed unaware of her now, tucked away in the shadows of a giant sycamore. Still, she held her breath. Then, horribly loud and rasping, the opening notes of Handel's Hallelujah Chorus sounded from somewhere under her dashboard. Her mother's idea, to have a unique ring for the stupid cell phone. She'd forgotten all about it, even where she'd put it. Must be the glove compartment. She scrambled for it.

"Anna!" Mother of course. No one else had this number. "Darling, why do you sound so far away? Is the phone not working properly?"

Robert moved off, apparently into a hallway between the living and dining rooms. Only Frances was visible now, facing away. Was he going to the door?

"No, Mother, it's fine," Anna said, keeping an eye on the house.

"Speak up, darling. I can hardly hear you."

Frances looked toward the hall. First one kid, then the other, came in and kissed her on the cheek. They were wearing coats and scarves and carrying ice skates over their shoulders.

"Mother, I can't talk now."

"Stop being so mysterious."

Robert came into the room and patted Frances awkwardly on the arm. She brushed his hand away, turning the gesture into a little shooing wave. "Bye-bye. Have a good time," she mouthed.

Anna whispered urgently, "Mother, I cannot talk. I'll call you in a minute. Oh, God."

Across the street the door opened and the little group spilled out onto the porch. Anna plunged head first across the passenger seat. The phone, crushed against her chest, made muffled Mother noises. She heard car doors slamming across the street and pulled the phone out just enough to find the red button. She lay there until the street grew quiet again, then sat up and looked back at the house. Frances had moved to a wing-back chair and sat holding a highball, gazing vacantly out of the window, her slippered foot bouncing up and down to distant music. Anna was about to get out of the car when she remembered and dialed her mother.

"Mummy, I can't talk right now. I'm at a … surprise party! For a friend."

"Oh! Well, that's wonderful, darling, you're starting to get out …"

"Here they come. I'll call you later."

Not waiting for her mother's response she ran across the street and rang the bell. When Frances Buchanan's peevish face appeared at the long window beside the walnut door she called out, "Hi! I'm Mimi Buchanan."

Frances opened the door and said caustically, "Well, the cousin Mimi, uninvited and equally unwelcome."

That was meant to intimidate, but the shot fell short of the mark. For one thing *A Chorus Line* was playing softly in the background. And the face, though even-featured and probably once pretty, was rumpled and puffy, the voice equally unkempt. The woman was falling apart. There was nothing to be afraid of.

"I'm sorry," Anna said and stood her ground.

Fran looked Anna up and down and, for some reason, softened. "I'm Fran, the former spouse. You just missed Robert, but—oh hell, why don't you come in?"

In contrast to her disheveled host, the house was light and airy, decorated to give the appearance of affluence if not of originality. Hardwoods, brocade, and chintz. It might have been put together by a stylist from Ethan Allen, except for four or five very good abstract paintings hanging in the spacious entrance hall. One, she knew, was the work of her old friend Jerry Kantor at The Art Institute. They must have been part of the divorce settlement. In their first session Robert had said he had an interest in abstract art.

Fran led the way into the living room, flipping off the stereo and retaking her post in the wing-back chair. "Do have a seat," she said, indicating a faux Empire loveseat. Anna couldn't tell if she was posturing or mocking.

"Thank you," she said. "I'm so sorry to barge in on you like this." She could do a fine Boston Brahmin herself, if called upon. "But you'd said Robert would be here, and I thought I might surprise him."

Fran was appraising her over her drink. "You sure would have. Sorry, but I didn't mention you. I'd forgotten all about it. Can I pour you a Bloody Mary?" Fran didn't sound at all as if she wanted to.

"No thanks. Water would be fine."

Sighing heavily, Fran hoisted herself from her chair and made the trip to the bar worthwhile by topping up her own drink. With the refreshment ceremonials out of the way, she settled in as if she intended to dig for gold.

"So, Mimi, what brings you to the Bay Area?"

"I'm on vacation."

"From ...?"

"New York. I work ... I work in one of the museums there."

Fran sat forward, for the first time genuinely interested. "Really! What do you do?"

"I'm assistant to the curator for modern sculpture."

"Oh!" Fran pressed her hand over her heart. "That's just amazing! I'm an art history major. Modern painting!" She sounded twenty years younger.

Anna's mind raced. So the paintings were Fran's. She'd have to be careful, they might even have friends in common.

"Which museum do you work with?" Fran was asking.

Anna quickly switched from the Whitney to an obscure museum in Brooklyn and was relieved to see Fran's bemusement.

"I know. We're not on the map yet. We're just building our collection. But tell me about you. You have some wonderful paintings here."

"Well, thank you. It's so rare to find someone who knows that."

Punctuated by trips to the jug of gin, Fran talked for twenty minutes about her youth: the bleakness of Ohio, the thrill of Cambridge, trips to New York, her hopes for a job there, maybe someday her own gallery. From there she drifted to meeting Robert, their courtship, the innocence of their wedding.

"It was all so absurd. The froth! But it's once in a lifetime," she rolled her eyes clownishly, "and I just had to have it all. Our cake was yea big!"

She gestured hugely, spilling her drink on the arm of the chair. "Oops." She patted at it with her cocktail napkin. "Bad Frances," she scolded.

Then something seemed to come unstuck. Fran seemed to forget who Mimi was, her blood ties to the awful ex. She reached over, took Anna's hand, and gave it a moist, sticky squeeze. She looked with desperate sadness into her guest's eyes, giving Anna the opening she'd hoped for.

"So you and Robert haven't been together for a while?"

"Eight years. Officially. Really more like eighteen." Now Fran became more sour, more angry. "Or, you could say we had five years together out of the eighteen we were married. Or maybe just one. He wasn't around much. Such a hard worker. Oh yes indeedy, Robert was a busy boy." She sipped her drink and stared sharply at Anna over the rim of the glass. "You know what happened to us?"

"No," said Anna. She tried to sound as innocent as she had been two days ago. "What happened?"

Fran didn't answer, but got up and took a step, then gripped the arm of the chair for support. "I need coffee. Want some?"

"Let me help."

Fran lead the way toward the kitchen. "So, *how* are you related to Robert?"

"Oh, not very closely at all," Anna said lightly. "My great grandparents are from Scotland, on my father's side, and my mother's interested in genealogy." All this happened to be true. She went on with the performance as they made coffee. "I grew up north of Boston, and some years ago my mother read something in the paper about a Dr. Robert Buchanan—an award he'd gotten, I think—and she thought we were related, quite far back I guess. The more obscure the connection the better she likes it." Anna silently asked her mother's forgiveness. "I was in my teens and didn't pay much attention. But I did remember she'd showed me his picture, and how handsome he was."

"Señor Fabulooh-so," Fran sang softly as Anna went on.

"Then Mother said something about it again last year. She was watching a program about—what was it?" Anna fished for inspiration. "Oh yes, medical ethics." That made Fran wince, but Anna ploughed ahead. "And she said, 'that's just the question they raised about our cousin Robert at his trial,' or something like that. I have no idea where she gets these things, but she's often right." Anna paused. Since she'd met Michele, she'd become quite the little gamer. But it seemed to have its rewards. She took the next step. "Was there a trial?"

"Not exactly." Fran handed her a steaming mug. She went on with false gaiety as they made their way back to the living room. "There was the licensing board, and then a big fat civil hearing, and then another one, with lots of lawyers in between. More than a year's worth. And there I was with an infant, for Christ's sake. Camilla, my oldest. What fun. A paternity suit, one of his patients." She sat heavily in her chair, again splashing herself but not bothering to dab. "Maura Quinlan!" She said the name as though she were reading a 24-point headline. "And I stuck by my man, oh my God! Not for one second did I believe he'd done the dreadful deed. I believed every word about little Maura: that she was borderline psychotic, a nymphomaniac, should be locked up."

She took a long drink of coffee and exclaimed as it burned her mouth. She fished a piece of ice from her abandoned drink and popped it in to dull the pain.

"What's blinder than a bat?" she asked, spluttering around the ice. "Maybe a mollusk. Whatever it is, that was me. Well, I was young, ten years younger than him. Him? He? Anyway, he kept us strictly away from it all, right up to the last moment. Our Protector!" She laughed harshly and spit the ice back into her glass. "But I went to the last hearing. I put my foot down. I had to fight with him about that. And I saw them for the first time, Maura and her child and her family. That Maura was gorgeous, just a knockout—black haired, blue-eyed Irish—and the boy was so like Camilla. He had this head of red hair like hers, and Robert's, too, when he was little. I sat there staring at them, and I was sticking by my man, and I was staring, and sticking ... And somewhere inside myself I'm saying, 'Frances, you mollusk! Wake up!' And he was sitting up there ..." She mimicked Robert perfectly, that way he had of withdrawing to the heights and looking down on the little people below. "… all shut up inside himself. It was entirely about Him, you see. *His* career, *his* reputation, *his* house with the wife and kiddies inside. My Fabulous World! Photo op! *Life*, please take a picture."

She lolled back in her chair, remembering. "And then they said the blood test had come back. Negative! He wasn't the father. I should have been relieved, but I was stunned. I didn't believe it—his own wife. Because he was so pleased with himself. And the way he looked at her, at Maura, when they said it. I mean, the moment wasn't dramatic, just their lawyers droning back and forth, and the judge dismissing the matter. But Robert was looking at Maura with this look of triumph and, I don't know, something darker. He was *gloating*. And this poor girl, who was supposed to be certifiable, gave him back the steadiest look of—what?—knowing. Deep knowing.

"That look stayed with me for ages. And then seven long years later, I decided I had to talk to this woman. Not that Robert was doing anything overt, but Camilla was growing up, and I didn't like the way he was with her. And Maura started haunting me. And then my boy Ben, when he came along, was a dead ringer for her kid. Dead ringer. So I got in touch with her lawyer back in Boston. I sent her a letter. She was living in Atlanta, running some battered women's shelter. God, of all things! I said I now believed that Robert was guilty as sin. I had no idea how he'd wriggled out of it, but if there was anything I could do to help her prove it, I would. Really, I would have thrown everything away—" she gestured to indicate the house, the art, "—to get to him. Well, not the kids. I'd come to see him as a deeply troubled, even dangerous person."

Fran was gazing up at the ceiling, talking to herself, in communion with Maura Quinlan. "And she actually wrote me back. She said she didn't want the trauma of another court battle and no longer needed the support. Still, she wanted to put the question to rest for her family. She was absolutely sure, herself. And she apologized, all that. She was very nice. Intelligent. I liked her. And by that time I could care less what her part in it had been. She asked me to send his toothbrush so she could get a DNA test. The cheek cells are almost as good as blood. If I couldn't get that, I could get hair, but it had to include the roots. What a pleasure *that* would have been."

She paused again to sip her coffee with exaggerated care. Anna held her breath.

"And I did!" Fran finally went on. "I sent her the toothbrush, a handful of hair from his brush, and some underwear. Just for fun. Silk boxers with chili peppers on them I got him once for Valentine's Day. I dug them out of the laundry. We were still living together at the time, you see, in deep misery. So a few weeks later she sent me a copy of the results, and his boxers—the things that happen in this crazy life!—both of which I left in front of his door at the office one day, in a plain brown envelope. Oh, that was delicious. He called and said, 'Is this your handiwork?' And I said, just very lighthearted, 'Robert, can't you ever focus on the *positive*?' He hung up on me. And that was the end of it. Neither of us has ever mentioned it again."

Fran seemed to have forgotten all about Anna. She looked longingly toward the bar.

"But was he ...?" Anna probed.

"Of course! 'Positive'—get it? Somehow he switched the blood."

"Is that possible?"

"For him, sure. He knew people in the labs. He'd worked in hospitals around the area. He has no conscience. Who cares how? He did it, and no doubt broke quite a few laws in the process. So I did very well in the divorce, let me tell you. Very nicely indeed. Turns out to be enough that he knows that I know. I get everything I ask for."

Fran looked triumphantly at Anna, then her eyes widened in realization. "Oh, my God!" She tottered over to sit beside her guest on the little sofa. "Mimi! Please forgive me, I'm so sorry. This is your cousin we're talking about."

"Very distant," said Anna. "Don't feel bad. I should be sorry. I've upset you."

"No, no, you were sweet to listen. And I thought you should know. You're such a nice person." Fran sighed deeply. "People should know what their relatives are capable of. God! And I thought *I* could learn something from *you*."

Releasing little sounds of disgust and self-loathing, Fran sat back and covered her face with her hands. Tears seeped out between her fingers. At this close range Anna could see that the blonde perm was gray at the roots, and unwashed. The former Mrs. Robert Buchanan smelled faintly of sweat and alcohol and day-old perfume.

"I'm sorry," Anna said again. "I shouldn't have come. I really should go, but I don't want to leave you like this."

Fran, however, snapped up out of her seat and walked away, pulling a wad of tissue from her dressing gown and copiously blowing her nose. "No, no. I'm fine. I have a great day planned," she said, plainly lying. "Going out for drinks with some girlfriends." She ran a hand through her hair, fluffing it. "Jesus, I must look like the wrath of God. Well!" She stuffed the tissue back in her pocket and extended a damp hand, then immediately withdrew it. "Sorry. Bet you're glad it's not me you're related to, however distantly."

Murmuring denials Anna made for the door, with Fran trailing behind. "Don't tell Robert I was here, will you?"

"Oh, God no," said Fran. "Why should he know?"

"Right. I mean, I don't think we'll pursue it, you know, the family connection."

"Don't worry about it. I'm a great secret keeper."

Yes, Anna had just gotten a taste of that. With Fran peering out the window behind her, she crossed to the Volvo. Her hands were shaking as she reached for her keys. She stumbled into the car and put her forehead on the steering wheel, feeling a little sick. The brave protector of the poor and abused. She who would save the world from the Monstrous Predator. What had she been thinking? All she wanted was home, and Colin. What was she after, really? To make it right for Michele, for Robin? Or to show Robert who was the stronger. A shameful way to go about it, dragging other people into it like this. Fran's manic babbling covered depths of loneliness and pain and there was nothing she could do about it. Robert was corrupt. Face it. Walk away. There was strength in that, too. Do it for yourself. It might be an expensive proposition, but there was only one thing to do now: call Michele, then Robert, and call it all off.

14

It was drizzling as Anna turned into the driveway, and she ducked under the porch just as the downpour began. Inside she went straight to the answering machine to retrieve Michele's number, but before she could do it the phone rang. Irrationally, Anna felt the girl reaching out to her from somewhere. She knew who she'd find on the other end.

"Michele. I was just going to call."

But a velvety voice responded, "I'm sorry, this isn't Michele. Is this Anna Sheffield?"

"Yes. Who's this?"

"Maura Quinlan. Maura Timms."

"Oh, my God." It was as if she and Fran had conjured the woman out of the past. "Thank you. I'm sorry. Thank you."

But Maura was all business. "A volunteer at WTC in Atlanta sent your email yesterday. I'm going to be very busy with the holiday next week, so I wanted to get back to you now." The voice was controlled but warm, like the voice of a doctor, someone who's chosen to live near a lot of suffering. "I want to applaud you for your courage in taking this step and see if there's anything I can do to help get this …"

What step? Anna's mind raced back to her email, the fictional women's shelter she was founding.

"Sorry," she said, "sorry to interrupt. But that's not really the reason I wanted to talk to you. It's something else, actually."

Maura hesitated. "Oh?"

"I'm a client, a patient, of Robert Buchanan's, here in Berkeley."

There was a little groaning sound, followed by silence. Anna rushed on. "I'm sorry I didn't say that in my email, but I was afraid you wouldn't respond. At the time I needed to know what had happened, what had really happened in the case you brought against him. But now I've …"

"How did you get my name?" The voice was now tight and defensive. "How did you know about the case?"

"I have a friend who follows this kind of thing. She's in … family law …" Okay, more deceit, but why make it harder for her? "… and she stumbled across it. So in any case, it made me doubtful of the treatment I'm getting …"

"Rightly so," said Maura emphatically.

"… and needing to know what really happened. Because you lost the case. I'm so sorry to bring all this up for you again. I know how hard this must be."

Maura sighed heavily. "No, actually I'm past it, thank God. And maybe it'll help you to know that that is possible, you can get past it, whatever may have happened to you. You're alive, that's what counts. As for Robert, I did finally get a DNA test, but I decided not to pursue it. I'm happily married, with two more children. And my husband adores Brian, that's my son with, well, *by* Robert. Gary's adopted him. It's behind us. I want to keep it that way."

"I'm so glad to hear that."

Warming to Anna's sincerity, Maura went on. "But just so you know, the test was positive. Odds in the hundreds of millions. So obviously Robert switched blood samples, I don't know how. He had the will and the money. Anyway …" She seemed to be thinking something through. "I wonder if you'd like to see my son? He's twenty-seven now and looks exactly like his father. But a totally different person I'm happy to say. Maybe that would make it real for you."

Anna hesitated.

"Not in person. We have a website, a family album. My husband and I both have huge families. It's the cheapest way to keep them up on what we're doing." She gave Anna the URL. "So I'm going to leave it there. But about working with Robert? He has his gifts, but he can't control himself. He lost himself somewhere. I hope this isn't too hard to hear. There are some fine therapists out there, so just cut the cord. Okay?"

"Thank you, Maura. Thank you, you've been a great help."

"Okay, Anna, you take care. Find a group, it really helps. Hang in there. You do get through it." And she hung up.

Anna sat for a minute, wrestling. An introduction to Maura, a parting gift that might appease Michele. Ammunition for her solo fight. With the end in sight, and a glimmer of curiosity, she went to her office and soon was welcomed to The Timms/Quinlan home page. "*Failte*!" it said. Gaelic, probably. And "Ya'll Come on Down!" Timmses and Quinlans by the score were gathered on a spacious sandy lawn dotted with palm trees. An attractive couple was centered in the front row, with a crowd of children at their feet. Maura was broad-hipped and large breasted, her long black hair dramatically streaked with white. A Gaston Lachaise goddess transported from the Pennsylvania coalfields to a Florida resort. Next to her Gary, a big, jovial, fair-haired man, held a fishing pole in one hand and a long silver fish in the other.

Along the margin of the page were links to Boston Celtics, Moonlight in the Pines, The Kids .... Without looking further, Anna clicked this one. There were formal portraits of Faith and Mary, blue-eyed, fair-haired girls of sixteen and twelve. Maura's kids with Gary Timms. And Brian, at twenty-one (the caption said), even more like Robert than Ben was: rugged featured, with a forced glittering smile and sad dark eyes full of questions. Maura had said Brian was a great, happy young man, but his picture said something else. How could Robert live with himself? What did he tell himself in order to face his kids, or Fran? She saw him lounging against the living room wall while Michele and Robin made their way up a dark stairwell.

Anna was dragging the cursor toward a button labeled Baby Pix when she heard a car tearing down the drive. She looked out. A rusty yellow VW Bug swung in beside the Volvo, kicking up gravel. Michele scrambled out. More synchronicity, Anna thought, of the unhappy kind. Now she'd have to deal with Michele in person. And she looked manic. Seeing Anna at the window she raised her purse over her head like a trophy and ran toward the house waving it in the air. Anna met her at the door.

"Fucking, fucking unbelievable!" Michele greeted her.

Before Anna could react she ran into the living room and turned the purse upside down over the coffee table. A fat manila envelope fell out, opened up, spilled across the floor along with wallet, lipsticks, and a Huggie. Seeing Anna standing speechless in the hall, she ran back, grabbed her arm and dragged her to the couch.

"You are not gonna believe this, it's way gnarlier than we thought."

Anna tried to protest but Michele wasn't listening. "Don't trip, just look at this!" She scooped a wad of papers from the floor and arranged them on the coffee table—letters, a small snapshot of a girl on skis, a rumpled note. She put the note down with care, and under it spread an official looking letter, apparently from a legal firm. Peabody, Hawkins, Schultz & Graves. Schultz, Anna remembered, was Robert's lawyer in Maura's case. And Graves—a common enough name, but uncanny to see it now, when she'd mentioned her father's old friend Putnam Graves to Robert only days ago. And this letter, too, was addressed to Robert. The ants started to crawl.

"Have you been back to Robert's office?"

"Whatever!" Michele picked up the note. "So this is Larry," she said. With the other hand, she held up a newspaper clipping, headlined:

Friday, July 8, 1978
T h e B o s t o n G l o b e
Harvard Student's Death Ruled Suicide

"And this is Laura." There was a small, grainy picture of a dark-haired girl, in black dress and pearls, the classic Harvard grad.

"Who is she?" Anna asked.

"Read it."

"I don't want to."

"Yeah you do. It's Laura. Blaufeld. *Was.*" Michele held up the snapshot of the same girl, on skis. "Robert's student, the suicide."

"Was she a patient? Don't tell me she was pregnant."

"I have no idea. But she suddenly OD'ed or something. Her letters were right there with all the other stuff."

That was it, the limit. Methodically Anna took the photo out of Michele's hands, put it back in the envelope, and put the envelope in Michele's purse. She swept the other things in after it. "I was going to call you today, Michele. I'm sorry, but I can't. I can't go on with this. Now you've stolen these! Do you understand what that means? This is all a delusion. You're making it all up, anything to have this your way. I'm glad you have the car. Please take these back if you can. If not, just take them away." She tried to put the purse in Michele's lap, but the girl threw it on the floor. She jumped to her feet.

"You need to hear this! They said she committed suicide, but why would she do that? She was rich, smart, she was gorgeous. Maybe she *was* pregnant, like, Catholic, a shame thing. She took some kind of drug, some lethal combination. That's Larry's thing, he knew Robert back then."

"What Larry?" Anna asked without wanting to.

"I just showed you! Larry Neal!"

Michele pawed through her purse and found the lawyer's letter. "After the Maura thing, Robert's lawyers wrote him this letter." She read, stumbling over the words, "'We are in receipt of materials,' blah, blah, 'imperative that you neither initiate nor allow further contact with Mr. Neal and his associates. The Somerville location should also remain strictly off limits!' That's Ryan's! Larry's a lab guy. His boys switched the blood in the Maura Quinlan thing. So then he was blackmailing Robert, I just know it."

Anna felt dizzy. "You can't possibly *just* know that," she managed. She picked up the purse and took it toward the door. Michele followed, waving the damning letter.

"He wrote Robert that note, I found it stuffed in with the letters. No way was it supposed to be there." Then something about a bar in Somerville, Larry's cousin. "He said the guy had a stroke—how about *that* coincidence? He's blackmailing Robert and suddenly has a stroke? Stroke? Overdose? Think about it!"

"I'm not going to think about it. I don't care." Anna stopped at the entrance to the hall. "I should tell you that I found Maura."

"No way! What'd she say?" Michele ran past her to block her way to the door. "Was it him?"

"Yes. There was a DNA test later. And you may be right about the blood. Maura thought so. And Fran."

"Fran? His *wife*? You are so totally fucking kidding me!"

"Or you may just be after money, I don't know." Anna pushed past her and opened the door. "I don't care. This has gone too far, way past me. Please go, Michele. Just go."

When the girl didn't move, Anna glanced up the drive to see if the Barton's Lexus was there. She was about to make a scene and she didn't want to drag them into it. The car was gone, so she threw the purse out into the rain. As Anna hoped, Michele ran out and snatched it up. Clutching it to her, she screamed back, "Yes, I want money! I want that motherfucker to pay!! And now there's all this other shit. You can't make it go away! You can't make *me*!"

Mechanically, Anna closed the door, chained it, turned the deadbolt and went back to her study. She heard Michele run onto the porch, shouting that Anna was a spoiled bitch, asking if she was fucking blind. She pounded and kicked the door while Anna stood looking at Brian Timms' picture. The cursor pointed to Baby Pix. She heard Michele ranting in the drive, then a car door slammed shut, then tires screeched out on the street. Imagining this to be her last gesture, Anna picked up the mouse and clicked. A baby boy was holding himself up on his stroller in an autumn wood, his red hair as flamboyant as the maple leaves behind him. It could be Ben, it could be Robin. Looking down at the boy Anna felt she was peeping in windows. Shame was followed quickly by fear. She closed the page, went to her day bed and lay down, a cold sweat oozing into her clothes.

She'd said she was through but she couldn't help herself. Thoughts churned on. Robert had made a youthful mistake, perhaps out of grief at the loss of his first love, this Laura. After all Maura, like Michele, had an exotic quality, the blue-eyed, black-haired gypsy type Robert seemed to prefer. Fran the dead opposite. Laura, Maura .... As Jules Traneau had said in his letter to the *Times*, Robert might have become confused, mistaking one woman for the other. And the blood sample? Sheer panic. He'd only just started a family of his own and he couldn't put them through it. The minute Maura gave birth Fran had gotten pregnant. God! But murder? This Larry hired to do it, then hired again for the Maura case? If that's what Michele was implying. Ridiculous. He couldn't have done that, much less gotten away with it. Anna didn't watch television, she didn't read salacious news, she didn't read crime fiction. Still she knew that murders took place in middle class homes, among people like those she'd grown up with. And like them she'd always believed it couldn't happen to her. Of course, that only meant, as Michele had said, that she was blind, that she was spoiled, that all sorts of horrors were going on around her that she still couldn't imagine, in spite of the terrible things she'd experienced.

The squeal of rusting iron cut through her thoughts. Here they come again. She closed her eyes, waiting for the men to take her. When nothing happened, she whispered, "Where are you?" She sat up and screamed into the empty house, "Come to me! Show me!!" She put her hands over her eyes, rocking back and forth and found herself not in the little churchyard, but on the beach at Cape Cod. In the distance a huge gray stone stood like a pillar at the edge of the water. She ran to it, reached out for it. She could feel the sun's heat trapped inside even before she touched the rough surface. Under her hands it moved like flesh.

She jumped up and ran into the garden, in the gathering dusk. By the light spilling out from the kitchen she found the key above the blue door. She went to her tools, laid out neatly in rows and covered with a thick layer of fine dust. The great stone stood there in an attitude of challenge, its new stain like a bloody wound. "All right, you won't? Then I'm coming for you." She fumbled among the tools for a chisel and a hammer and without a plan began to hack out a pathway for the blood-red mark.

When Robert returned with the kids in the late afternoon, the house was dark and silent. Fran might have gone out, he imagined. Drinks with her coven of divorcees, stirring their poisonous brew. It had just begun to rain and they all trooped in, shedding watery coats. Camilla and Ben rushed into the living room to lay claim to the stereo, jostling each other and arguing playfully about the relative demerits of hip hop and rap. Robert was just following them in to give his professional opinion when a husky voice drifted down from the landing above.

"What a festive little group." Fran had apparently been napping and now stood, disheveled and smirking, at the top of the stairs.

"Well hi, Fran." Robert rested one foot rakishly on the bottom step. "Have a nice nap?"

"Oh, yes, thanks so much for asking. I needed it. I've been such a busy girl."

Fran always taunted, but this was unusually sharp. Robert armed himself. "What have you been up to, you witch?" he asked, sotto voce.

"I had a visitor today, out of the blue."

"Uh-huh?" He feigned disinterest, but the fear that had haunted him all week crept up like a shadow moving in a dark room.

"She wanted to know all about *you*, of all things!"

He felt himself flush. "She? What do you mean? Who did?"

"I told her I wouldn't say. Someone you'd find very interesting, though. And now she knows a lot more about you than she did when she came."

A vision of Michele sitting on Fran's French settee, bouncing the red-haired baby, telling and hearing all, compelled him up the stairs. "What did she want? What did she look like?"

"Oh, calm down," cooed Fran. "She wasn't one of yours. Not your type at all. Much too sweet and thoughtful, not at all exotic, much too East Coast." She was backing away along the railing as Robert took step after step toward her. "I'll give you another hint: you've been keeping a little family secret. Oh yes, and she's artistic."

In his office, the wind rattled the branches of the oak, and Anna Sheffield sat gazing at him with deep, intelligent eyes. Then Ben bounded in from the living room. "Hey Dad, did you get the tickets to the Sharks for Tues …"

Seeing his parents faced off like that, he stopped short. Robert froze, too, in mid-flight up the stairs, his eyes still fixed on Medusa.

"What's going on?" Ben asked.

Before either parent could answer, Camilla stormed in and up the stairs, took Robert's hand and dragged him down behind her.

"Okay, parents, here's the 411," she said, holding Robert in place and facing off with her mother. "We are not having this kind of holiday. If you guys are going to do this, I'm getting right on a plane and going back to L.A., and I'm taking Ben with me. And you, Daddy, can pay for the whole thing." In the background Ben said coolly, "Why wait?" as Camilla went on. "So pull yourselves together and cut it out, right now. Mom, get dressed. Take a shower, for God's sake, you actually smell. Dad, get out of here. We'll see you tomorrow."

Robert started to turn back toward Fran, to see if he could wrest the vital information from her, but Camilla was having none of it. "Go!" She opened the door, handing him his coat. He fled down the front stairs, shrill voices rising behind the heavy door. As he made his escape, Camilla's "disgusting!" and Fran's "just like him, you little bitch!" trailed after him.

What the hell was happening? He ran to his car and sat there trying to put the pieces together, all the things that had happened since the Queen of Chaos had come to his door on Wednesday. Michele's gaunt face, that dreadful baby; Anna, like Ben, asking "What's going on?"; Camilla with her art magazine, Anna and Gravatsky, his own helpless retching while the maître d' tapped on the men's room door, hoping to God it wasn't the oysters. There weren't enough pieces to make a picture. And now, this visit from some woman whose description raised the specter yet again of Anna Sheffield.

Either it really was Anna, or he was becoming fixated on her, perhaps delusional.

With shaking hands Robert tapped out a text and was relieved when his old friend answered right away. The soonest Craig could see him was after dinner, about 8:00. "Kids on hands, got 45 max." They agreed to meet at the office. Robert's "Hurry!!" must have raised an alarm, because Craig's parting words were, "U ok til then?"

15

In the dark and the cold, Robert sat on the stairs in front of his building waiting for Craig to appear. By 7:00 the rain had lightened, and now, a little after 8:00, a fine mist swirled like snow under the street lamps. For some minutes he stared out empty-headed, breathing in the sharp November air and watching with envy as two young cats frisked merrily across the lawn next door. But then he began to form the coming conversation and he realized there was a substantial problem. While he was desperate to find relief, he absolutely could not tell Craig the truth or anything approaching it.

He revisited the awful thought that Michele and Anna might somehow have met. Anna's wealth and moral rectitude coupled with Michele's rage would make a deadly combination. Did Anna's visit to Fran, if that's who it was, have something to do with that crazy bitch? He needed an open exploration of the possibilities, but he couldn't share any of the week's events with Craig without sharing them all. He couldn't share his fears about Anna. He didn't dare tell Craig that Michele even existed. He'd succeeded so far in keeping her under wraps, and he must continue to do so. Could he expect Craig, for instance, to strategize with him on ways to keep Michele's dirty little claws off his few remaining assets? No. Craig would exhort him to "do the right thing," "get the test and settle it once and for all," and so on in that self-righteous vein. And if his relationship with Michele were known, what else might somehow leak out?

The loneliness of his struggle cut him as sharply as the night air. He thought of Joseph Campbell and The Hero's Journey, of the demons that had beset him all his life and the battles he'd fought against them. The time for action might soon come again, and Craig, with his innocent nature and his obsessive positive regard, would make the perfect Wolfram to his Parsifal. Or was that Tannhäuser? Tannhäuser, of course, the ultimate Tragic Romantic. Parsifal was obsessed with the Holy Grail, for which Robert could give a good goddamn.

"For Christ's sake, snap out of it," he said and forced himself to focus. He'd need all his energy and skill in the coming exchange, where, he began to imagine, seeds might be planted for a future harvest.

"Of what?" he asked himself and felt a terrible dread.

He jumped to his feet and began to pace up and down the damp walkway. He looked at his watch. Craig had said he'd "try" for somewhere close to 8:00. That could mean anything. He'd feel better in the safety of his office, he decided, and ran in and up, turning on lights as he went.

The cleaning lady had been in earlier and he noted with annoyance she'd left his door unlocked. When he flipped on the overhead light he saw that his phone was sitting in the middle of the desk. Rosario was getting sloppy again, or making multiple calls to Mexico City. Chastisement was a job for Janice, who was gifted at these trivial negotiations. He'd leave her a note. Glad for something else to occupy his mind, he circled the desk and opened the top drawer to get a pad. As he closed it again, a little white flag caught his eye, the corner of a piece of newsprint sticking out of the bottom drawer.

What the hell? He froze, staring at it. He hadn't been in that drawer in months, maybe longer. As if he were opening a tarantula's cage, he pulled the handle toward him. The drawer yielded just enough to show the clutter inside. He collapsed in his chair as though he'd been struck. This couldn't be Rosario. She'd have no use at all for what was hidden in there. Michele, on the other hand … He looked again into the drawer. The stack of old notebooks was there, the bankbooks and the envelope full of press clippings. But the letters … The drawer had been locked when he left on Friday, he was certain. How could she have done it? On Saturday morning the building would be open, though not his office. He could call Rosario and find out if anything unusual had happened, but he didn't have the number. If he asked Janice for it, he'd have to explain. And Michele? He'd erased her from his books two years ago.

A vise-grip threatened to crush his heart. He forced himself to bend forward, to catch a breath. Why in hell had he kept those letters? Because, he realized, his little bundles made him feel safe. And proud, yes, that too. He'd won out before, and he could do it again. Even now, surely. And face it—they were his darlings. He treasured them. He straightened and took a deeper breath. There was one thing he could do, he realized. The thief had apparently used the phone. He picked it up, dialed *69 and waited. It was a woman's voice, a voice he knew well—smooth, elegant and burdened. "You've reached Anna Sheffield. Sorry I can't take your call …"

So. Michele and Anna had met. Downstairs, the door opened.

"Robert?" Craig called up, then took the stairs two at a time. He looked in, smiling broadly. "My place or yours?" The man loved to put a happy spin on everything.

Robert quickly closed the bottom drawer. "Yours," he said, longing to get away. He started to cross the room, then stopped as a plan began to form. "No, wait. I only have one thing to say. We might as well stay."

Craig came in and Robert gestured him toward the couch. He sat on the edge of the desk. Neither moved to take off his coat.

"My God, you look really sick," Craig offered.

"It's like a letter dropped into a glacier," Robert muttered, feeling his way forward.

No stranger to the odd metaphor, Craig said only, "What is?"

"My mind. Completely frozen."

Some clever therapist, Robert for instance, might have asked, "What's in the letter?" Craig's pragmatism led him elsewhere. "Is this about your mind or has something happened? When you called earlier I got the idea that something had happened."

"Yeah," said Robert, "that's good. Let's take that tack." He paused, then took the leap. "I think I'm being stalked."

Craig had been waiting patiently, his angular Norman Rockwell face all benign curiosity. Now he pulled his mouth down into an expression of grave concern, and it seemed to Robert he was trying not to laugh.

"Stalked? Who by?"

"One of my patients. Anna Sheffield."

"The *Mouse*?" Craig remembered many of Robert's little nicknames. "The Artistocrat? What makes you think that?"

"She's become more and more hostile. I don't know which way to go with it. I think I'm losing her. In the last session she was completely withdrawn, refused to talk about medication. And then, this is the kicker, she showed up at Fran's house. And the kids are in town. She knew that, I'd told her."

"Whoa, wait a minute," said Craig. "Let me see if I'm following you ..."

But the way forward was opening now, and Robert plunged ahead.

"Fran wouldn't tell me what actually happened or what they said, only that this woman wanted information—about me. Personal stuff. Fran was loving every minute of it, the castrating bitch. Luckily, Anna had gone by the time the kids and I got back, or God knows what might have happened. And there's more. She sent me this."

He pulled from his coat pocket the article Camilla had brought him. Craig took it and studied it for a moment.

"Wow," he said. "The Whitney! Did you know she worked at that level?" He looked again, this time at Anna's picture. "She's really beautiful here, isn't she? God, when I see the damage, I'd like to get those monsters by the balls ..."

Robert found himself standing and raising his voice. “That’s not the point, goddamn it!” He snatched the article back and shoved it in his pocket.

“Okay, take it easy. Then what do you mean by ‘sent’? Did she bring it to session? Mail it? Maybe she’s just saying she feels you don’t see her as she is.”

Robert couldn’t restrain a derisive laugh. “I found it on my desk just now. She got in somehow.”

Craig narrowed his eyes and twisted his head around as if trying to swallow a tough piece of meat. “Now wait a minute,” he said. “This doesn’t fit the profile at all. From everything you’ve told me, it’s her strength that drives you crazy …”

“Strength? God, you never listen. Resistance! And anyway that conversation was before all these attacks. Bombings, hostages, no place is safe. This climate of terror is hitting her hard. She rarely leaves the house, never sees anyone. She’s clearly fixating on me, and now she’s jumped the wall …”

Craig put his hands up as if warding off a blow. He got up and began to pace. Robert knew he was thinking about the practice, their security, the devastation if one of them were really to be stalked. Craig went to the window and looked out into the branches of the oak while Robert held his breath.

“Okay, okay then,” he finally said. “What’s your plan?”

Robert talked quickly. “My fear is this is moving toward psychosis. First I’ll try again with medication. Then I may need to recommend an institution. Short term, of course. Fortunately she’s wealthy. I think very wealthy. She can afford the best.”

He imagined Anna safely tucked away at twelve grand a month, giving art lessons to the other inmates. Without her Michele could be easily dealt with. But Craig was thinking otherwise.

"You know that sort of rejection can lead to suicide." Sweat broke out on Robert's face and he had to turn away as Craig went on, "We should notify the police, then find her another therapist, get her out of here ..."

Robert broke in, trying to sound calm. "Rejection no matter what I do. But not police, not yet. I could be wrong. I see her on Wednesday. Let me see what I can do."

He went to the door and held it open, inviting Craig to go out. The poor man made for the stairs, looking pale and shaken.

"All the books say don't wait, it only escalates. Take action," Craig said, sounding anything but decisive.

"There's more than one kind of action," said Robert, locking the office door. But Craig didn't seem to hear.

Once outside, the two men stood for a moment on the porch, looking into a thick fog that had crept over their quiet little town. Now that the way was clear, Robert felt enormously relieved and grateful for his friend's simplicity. The primal energies were flowing once again.

"Who said, 'I am vast, I contain multitudes'?" he asked.

"I have no idea." Craig sounded weary, his mind now full of worries. "Shakespeare?"

"Never mind." Impulsively, Robert spread his arms out like the wings of a great bird. "Ahhhhhh!" he cried into the night. He put an arm around Craig's shoulders and held him for a moment in a comradely embrace. "Just a little genuine caring. Breakthrough, my friend. Good work." Leaving Craig amazed and full of fear, he ran off into the fog.

Anna wasn't sure she'd heard it. The whine of the polisher drowned out everything, even her thoughts. But a persistent overtone finally persuaded her to turn off the machine and listen. It was the doorbell. She looked at her watch and was startled to find it was already after 9:00. It must be Colin. Somehow he'd managed to get away. Without bothering to dust herself off, she ran through the house and flung open the door.

"Hello, Anna."

It was Robert Buchanan, still dressed for skating with the same jaunty scarf around his neck. As he stood appraising her, his look of aggrieved pity shifted to one of deprecating amusement. "Have you been cooking?"

Anna looked down at herself. She was covered in fine flour-like dust. "Working," she said. "Rock dust."

"Well, that's a shift. You've found a new energy source, it seems." Robert took a step toward her. Reflexively, Anna backed away. With easy grace he came into the hall.

"Thank you," he said, as if she'd invited him in.

Anna stood beside the open door, her mind racing. Had he seen her after all, spying on his family? Or had Fran told him something that had brought him here? She looked toward the Manor. The Bartons were throwing a party, the lights blazing, people coming and going from the kitchen with glasses of wine and plates of hors d'oeuvres. Feeling safer, she closed the door. Every move she'd made so far radiated guilt and she tried now to put on a show of outrage.

"What on earth are you doing here?"

Of course it was too late. Robert only smiled. "We're both making house calls," he said.

"I don't know what you mean." Anna couldn't keep her voice from shaking.

Robert sighed deeply. "May I take off my coat?"

"No, I don't think so." It came out in a whisper.

They stood for a moment staring into each other's eyes. Then Robert strolled into the living room.

"This is a very lovely house. Maybeck?" Anna nodded. He stopped to look at the fire serpents. "Ah! Magnificent." He moved on to Marco's studies. "Gravatsky," he read. "So that's Marco. Very interesting—terrific! You, I guess?" He turned to look at her appraisingly. "Mmmmm."

Anna found her voice. "Robert, it's extremely inappropriate for you to be here. Whatever it is, I'll see you Wednesday, and we can …"

But he moved smoothly to the couch and sat down. "Yes, but I want to clear up a couple of things before then. So I can have some kind of weekend. I know you saw Fran today, that you went to her for information about me. There's only one reason you'd do such a thing, as far as I can see. That would be a young woman named Michele Palmer. You know who I mean, I can see that. She broke in on our session on Wednesday. Why don't you come and sit down?"

Anna was still standing in the archway between the hall and living room. Only because her legs felt weak, she moved to a small chair and sat on the edge.

"Good," said Robert. "Now first you should know that Michele has a severe personality disorder. Another way of putting that is, she's not entirely sane. She's actually, well, quite dangerous. That's why I came here, really. To warn you." He was speaking in his good daddy voice, as though Anna were five years old. "I had to move her out of my practice because she became fixated on me. It used to be called hysteria and that's a pretty good name for it in her case. She has an idea that her child is mine. And to be honest with you, I was involved in a paternity suit back in Boston years ago. That's what put the idea into her head, to blackmail me. I was found not to be the father, by the way, whatever crazy notions my ex-wife may have. But I'm guessing you already know this."

Anna said nothing.

"Do you?" Robert sat forward on the couch, his voice dropping to a lower, hypnotic register, his dark eyes demanding an answer. "Did you meet Michele? Did Fran tell you about the Quinlan business?"

Having no idea what he might know, Anna thought she should give him a crumb. "I gave Michele a ride to BART. We chatted. As for this paternity case, I'm shocked that you would come to my home …"

"Yes, well, I feel the same. My family's home. My children have been dragged into it."

Fran, the great secret keeper. Anna felt herself blush. Robert obviously noticed. He stood up, took a step toward her.

"You're a very naïve person, Anna, as you've said yourself. Did you give Michele any personal information, invite her to contact you? For God's sake, don't be stupid. The girl's using you."

Anna stood, too. "I told her my name. I'm in the phone book. And it's really not your business. I want you to leave."

She moved toward the kitchen and the phone that sat on the counter separating it from the living room. Robert turned to watch her, but didn't follow.

"I'm deeply concerned for you, that's all," he said easily, as she dialed. "Who are you calling? There's really no need ..."

Colin's cell picked up and delivered his short greeting. Anna turned away, walking toward the dining room. "Sweetheart!" It was almost a shout, so Robert would know she, too, could make demands. He walked toward the fire and stood warming himself. Over her shoulder, she watched as he turned to look at her. He smiled when their eyes met.

"Colin," he mouthed and raised a thumb in approval.

"I'm fine," she said into the dead air. "You won't believe it, but Robert's here." She pretended to listen, then added, "Yes, Buchanan." She went on in a whisper, turning away and curling around the phone. "He won't leave. Call as soon as you get in." Then, not wanting Robert to think she was cringing, she circled back toward the kitchen. He was no longer looking at her but focused intently on something in front of the couch, apparently something lying on the floor.

In a show of bravado she walked toward him, saying, "The police?"

But Robert didn't react. He bent down and picked something up.

"All right, ten minutes," Anna said. The couch was blocking her view so she moved closer, trying to see what Robert had found. When he stood up again both hands were in his jacket pockets and his face was hard and chalky. Anna's heart started to race. "Thank you, darling," she said weakly. When she'd hung up she kept the phone in her hand, thinking she might need a weapon.

"Ten minutes," Robert said stiffly. "I understand. And I'm sorry if I frightened you. Just let me just say this: whatever Michele is up to can only bring you trouble. She's dangerous. Believe me, I know. I can't say more, for obvious reasons. But I'll see you on Wednesday and we'll sort all this out."

He moved toward the door, looking as if he'd aged ten years. Anna followed. She wanted to scream that she wouldn't see him on Wednesday, that she'd never see him again. But she didn't know what had just happened, what he'd found. She said instead, "Yes, all right, Wednesday."

He stopped in the hall and turned to face her, making an attempt to be suave. "I'm glad Colin is back in your life. Was that the big secret last session? How did you manage it?"

Anna opened the door. "That's just the kind of question I won't ever answer again."

Strangely, Robert laughed. "So this is who you are when you get hold of a little power," he said. "Good. I like it. All right, then. See you Wednesday."

The moment he heard Anna's door close behind him Robert sprinted down the driveway toward his car. Because of the party in the neighboring house he'd had to park quite far down the street. He couldn't wait, but stopped under the nearest streetlight to examine the thing in his pocket. Not that it wasn't already well-known to him, but he had to be sure it was real, that his fears weren't causing delusions. He pulled it out, a piece of wrinkled paper. It had been wedged under a leg of Anna's couch, and when he'd picked it up part of it had torn away. Now he saw:

Couple of guys at
query, nothing's changed
like you've still got your
auld lang syne. We'll be in Somerville
place Wednesday about 9. Or call
374-8250.

That note should have been in the packet he'd sent years ago to Harvey Schultz. Somehow he'd missed it, and Michele, in her rat-like sniffing and searching, had found it in his drawer. He tried to imagine how, and when, it had come to rest under Anna's couch. She was a neat, fastidious person. Her house was immaculate, so it must have happened within hours. Then Anna had lied. Michele had been there. She had broken into his office, stolen his secrets and was peddling them on the open market. But what would Anna want with them? There was just a chance she'd sent Michele away empty-handed. If not, it would be out of some moral impulse, he thought, some weak-kneed pity. Well, that could be used, that could be turned his way. But Michele?

The damp night air was chilling and he roused himself and walked back toward his car. With Michele he should be prepared for the worst. She had a substantial bundle of evidence and must be after money—more money probably than he had. She could ruin him if she came to understand what those papers and letters meant. As for Larry, Robert didn't know the law, statutes of limitations and all that. He didn't know what might happen if those matters were reopened. Laura's letters and pictures and press clippings were emblems of love, that's all, and Larry as far as he knew couldn't talk. But what about Larry's friends at Forensic Science Labs, whom he'd never met and never wanted to meet? Was there a trail from them to him? The Quinlan blood alone would finish his career.

His thoughts were broken apart by laughter. A small group of people, going to the party at the neighbors' house, approached him smiling through the fog. With breezy presumption someone called out, "Leaving already?" Their Burberrys and drooping velvets and soapy scent reeked of Academia. If they only knew, he thought, who they were crowding off into the street. They were the ones who would judge him most harshly, though he'd only done what they hungered for themselves—lived in the raw fury of reality. He said nothing, but stood in the gutter while they passed. He wouldn't be pilloried by them. And his children, Camilla .... He imagined her dark eyes veiled with hate. No, it couldn't come to that. He ran the last few yards to the Mercedes. Take precautions now, so there's minimum proximity to the moment. If the moment came. He locked himself in and speed dialed from his cell.

"Sherman's 24-Hour Pharmacy. Is this a physician?"

"Yes, it's Dr. Buchanan, Robert Buchanan in Berkeley." He tried but failed to keep his voice steady. "I need a prescription filled tonight."

"Patient's name?"

Robert hesitated. Michele was out of the books and off the record. Besides, he now had Craig's cover. He should keep it that way. "Sheffield," he said, though he hoped for her sake that fear would win out, that she'd see reason and disappear forever from his life. "Anna Sheffield."

16

Standing where Robert had stood in front of the fire, Anna searched the floor for some hint as to what he might have found there. Whatever it was it had frightened him badly. Finding nothing, she pushed the coffee table aside. Something rolled away under the couch. She dropped to her knees and chased it with her hand. A lipstick, labeled *Urban Decay*. Could it be that? As she turned to put it on the table a jagged edge of white caught her eye, a bit of paper trapped under a leg of the couch. Carefully she pulled it free and sat on the floor to examine it. It was the note Michele had shown her, now torn in half but leaving the crisp blue and white logo of something called MedSource Labs, "Your Source for Reliable Results." It said:

Dr. B.!
How did you find me? You the man
FSL might be interested. Re yr
since MG, and looks
monkey, so it's
same old
L.

Anna couldn't keep Michele's voice out of her head. "Laura. The suicide." And something about Somerville, a bar and Larry Neal. This "L," the blackmailer, a trace of whom Robert now had in his pocket? Would he guess Michele had been with Anna? Of course. He'd said she was dangerous so he must have guessed already. Robert was right, she was hopelessly naïve.

She tried to imagine what might happen if she did nothing. On Wednesday Michele would go to her appointment, unaware that Robert was many steps ahead of her. No matter what she'd confront him with, he'd already outwitted her. He had the note, or half anyway. She'd stolen from him and he knew it. Maybe the police would be waiting when she got there, she'd do something reckless, they'd take Robin away. But he wouldn't want the police, surely, if he'd really .... The paper in her hand was getting damp with sweat. It was soiled with all the hands it had passed through. She only wanted to be rid of it, to be rid of it all. She got up to throw it in the fire, and the phone rang.

"Sweetheart! It's Colin." In the background she heard loud conversation, music, the clattering of plates. "Can you hear me?"

"Yes, where are you?"

He was still at the hotel in San Francisco. "You scared the hell out of me. What's going on? Is Buchanan still there?" He sounded a little frantic and strangely unfamiliar.

"No, sweetheart, he's gone. He came to ..." What now, lie to him, too? But there she was again, in a world he wouldn't understand. "He only came to give me some advice."

"Advice!? What the hell does that mean?"

"About the holidays. He was at the Barton's for a drink, and he realized it was the same address ..."

Colin shouted over the hotel din: "Buchanan knows the Bartons?" He admired Jane and Howard and couldn't imagine them inviting a person like Robert even for a drink. From this side of the rift, those old values seemed so simple and loveable. So remote.

"No, he came with someone who does," she saved him. "I panicked, that's all. He apologized. He realized it was inappropriate. He was just curious. I mean—I don't know."

Colin got tough. "Anna, that's bizarre. Do you get that? Look, I can't deal with this now, I have to go. We'll sort it out tomorrow. You're safe, yes?" He sounded distant. "I'm one of the sponsors of this thing ..."

"I know. It's all right. I'm safe. And I'm getting out of it. Don't worry, you're more important to me than any of that."

But Colin had moved on. "See you tomorrow, about 6:00." He hung up. Dutiful, resigned. The way he'd sounded last spring, toward the end. Was he thinking now, as she was, this will never end?

Anna stood staring out of the kitchen window, perfectly hollowed out. Gradually she realized she was looking into her studio, where she'd left the door open and the lights blazing. It seemed she'd done some awful violence to her perfect granite pillar. It looked as if it had been ripped apart by lightning. She went out and stood shivering in the studio doorway, trying to remember what mad thought had driven her to open that wound from shoulder to navel. What came instead was the note. FSL, MG, monkey, same old. A monkey is an addiction or obsession, isn't it?

What she should do, she thought, was to call the police. And what would she tell them? Michele was the one with the evidence, but faced with police she'd just deny it all. What was it she was saying while Anna was throwing her out? Larry had a stroke. She wished she'd read that article on Laura Blaufeld's suicide. Michele thought they'd both overdosed, was that it? With drugs supplied by Robert? Assuming the worst, Michele would be the perfect target. She was under pressure, behaving erratically, had a brutal past. No one would question an overdose. Only Anna would know why it had happened, and without those papers she couldn't prove it. But if she called Michele to warn her, who knew what the crazy girl might do? And if the police got involved they'd have only conjecture and the word of two crazy girls.

A creeping cold spread out from Anna's heart. She saw Robert standing in front of Marco's pictures, turning to her and licking his lips. A burst of anger kicked her thoughts into high gear. In 1978, the year of Laura's suicide, Anna had been seven. If the news of Laura's death had rocked the North Shore it would be carefully kept from the children. But someone back home might remember. Peabody, Hawkins, Schultz & Graves. Could Graves really be her father's old friend Pinky who used to sail with them every Fourth on the Cape? There were many possibilities and they were all in Boston. She heard Colin's voice, frustrated and burdened already.

"You cannot have him," she said to the ravaged stone. She locked the studio door and ran for the house. First she called

Colin's landline. He was staying in the city, so he'd get it after she'd gone. She was bone-weary, she said. She loved him, was sorry she'd scared him. Maybe they were going too fast. She wanted to give them both time and she'd call him after Robert on Wednesday. She was ending it, they'd start again, put it all behind them.

Then she called her mother who, though she must have been sound asleep, answered promptly: "What on earth!"

"Mummy, it's me. Sorry to wake you, but I wanted to warn you. I'm coming home."

"Hey! Watch the fuckin' finish." Joe's uncle, Frank Pierello, snatched the scrubbie away from Michele and threw it the length of the bar into the sink. As usual for a 2:00 a.m., his heavy, hound dog face was bright red from a long night of boilermakers, and his breath reeked of booze and stale cigar. "Goddamnit, girl, can't you ever just act normal?" He ran a hand along his precious mahogany bar top, feeling for scratches.

"You want it clean or not?" Michele snapped. "This place is crusty, Frank."

"You're the expert on clean, God knows." The ash from his fat cigar fell on her just-washed space and she let it lie there. He went to the register, took out five twenties and shoved them into her hand. "Go home to your kid, you're driving me crazy." And he gave her the usual smack on the butt.

Out of habit, she stuck the bills in her bra. "Don't ever turn the lights up, that's my advice to you."

So another fucked up Saturday night at Sweetcakes was finally coming to an end. Frank's girls, waitresses and dancers both, were sitting together at a table in the back rubbing their feet, having a drink, and filling the place with smoke. San Francisco had non-smoking laws everywhere, but all the bars on Broadway thought that was a joke, especially after 1:00 a.m. Michele sat down at an empty table to change her shoes. A fucked up day dragging on into a fucked up night. Robin with her screaming and slobber and endless needs. Joe on her case about her mothering skills, or none. Those two gel-haired techies who'd kept diving across the bar and pulling down her skirt every time she served them, wanting to see where the snake went. Only her need for that hundred had kept her from grabbing them by the short spikes and smashing their heads together. And of course, top of list, Robert Buchanan. Right now she loathed everyone she knew and everyone she'd ever known. But the real seething hatred she reserved for Anna Sheffield. That bitch had thrown her out into the street. The evidence she'd worked so hard to find had rain spots on it. And if things stayed this way, she'd have to go it alone with Robert. That's where this black mood came from. The only relief would be finding some way to get Anna pointed back toward Robert again.

From the table in the back her old friend Sharee motioned her to come down and sit with her. As she approached the other girls turned away, letting her know what a bitch she'd been all night. Fuck them, she wasn't about to apologize. Sharee laced her long fingers between Michele's and gave her hand a warm squeeze. She had a round dolly face and short red dreads, the sweetest thing, and her dark silky hand made Michele's look chalky white. They'd had a little fun together from time to time.

"Hey, Jolie. Wussup, girlfriend? You lookin' beat up. Wanna come over for some pizza and watch a movie? I got Denzel, *Devil in a Blue Dress*." She pulled Michele closer so the others wouldn't hear. "I got some glad."

Sharee was a country girl from Indiana and had a funny way of putting things, but Michele knew what she meant. Perfect. Another couple hours away from that funky apartment, Joe's bitching, Robin's whining complaints. And the coke would clear her head. She needed to chill. She needed to think. She needed a plan.

Out in the Haight they settled on Sharee's bed in her overheated studio, surrounded by faux fur drapes and throws and pillows, and posters of Denzel as Malcolm X and a rebel slave in Amistad, and of the super sexy Idris Elba in *The Wire*. But they decided it was too late for a movie since Michele had to take care of the kid later that day. So Sharee sat on the end of the bed painting her toenails with Michele propped up behind her, eating pizza and flipping through the channels. They'd caught up on all the news from the club, ragged on their boyfriends, and shared fantasies of a three-way with Idris. But Michele couldn't even pretend she was really there. She kept getting up, pacing, looking out the window at the drunks and junkies who owned the Haight at night. The coke had only made things worse. She was jumping out of her skin. Finally Sharee just couldn't stand it.

"What's wrong with you, girl? Sit down, eat some pizza, you're making me mess up my toes."

"Okay, okay." Michele sat twitching on the edge of the bed.

"So what you doing for Thanksgiving?" Sharee was all set to get her mind off whatever was eating her.

She played along. "Frank and Ruthie, like always."

"What's that like? He grab your ass every five seconds?"

"Not with Joe around. But Ruthie's all, like, 'Blah blah, you're doing everything wrong, you're so fucked up.' And there's Frank and Joe getting wasted, watching football with all the freaky cousins. And I'm like, 'Excuse me, can I just go in the bathroom and slit my wrists?'"

"On Christmas too?" Like it broke Sharee's heart to think of anyone having a shitty Christmas.

"We used to go up to Frank's cabin, up near Placerville. It's on this mountain called Wildcat Ridge. When me and Joe got together Frank was always saying, 'I got the perfect place for you, girl. Wildcat Ridge, ha ha!' Asshole." She took a bite of pizza and pushed mute so she could hear herself think. "It's this place he uses for hunting and stuff. Him and Joe go out and shoot some deer, or try to. Joe's pretty good, from being in the army. They hang them up in the shed and cut their guts out. It's disgusting."

"You ski and everything?" Sharee asked, turning away from this dreadful picture.

"Right. You see Frank on skis?" Michele did an imitation with Frank's paunch sticking out and his cigar, carried away flailing down a scary slope. Sharee rolled around laughing.

"Anyway, it's pretty up there, the woods and all, hardly any people around. But we don't go anymore, with the baby and shit."

"Want another line?" Sharee asked sympathetically. Her toes held safely apart by cotton swabs, she cut a couple.

"I'll save it for later." She wrapped the white powder in a scrap of paper while Sharee settled on Judge Joe Brown. Judge Joe was tearing some poor guy a new one over child support. Suddenly Michele was sober and focused.

"All that bullshit for ninety bucks a week," Sharee was saying. "That is truly pathetic."

"It's the principle of the thing."

"What'd you say?"

But Michele didn't want to get into it. The way had opened up, just like that. Anna Sheffield had a lot in common with Judge Joe Brown. What that woman wanted more than anything was to be Good. Like Sharee, but with a difference: she also loved to Do Right. Righteousness was what made her tick. Not like she didn't feel things, but she wanted everything to stay in bounds. It was the idea of blackmail that had upset her so bad. And wrong done to a child, that was way outside the rules. It was Robin Anna cared about. And stuff Done Right, in a courtroom. She'd be willing to pay for that.

The papers with their rain spots were hidden away in Michele's underwear drawer, off limits to Joe, out of reach for Robin. Now all Michele had to do was get Anna's attention for five minutes and stay cool. That would be the hardest part, not to let on how she really felt. To show Anna they could take Robert in court, without fuss or muss. And to get it done before Wednesday morning. They'd go together, with the papers, maybe take a lawyer. That sister of hers, why not. Like she'd promised, Anna would pay for everything.

Sharee, pulled roughly to her feet and handed her coat, complained that her toes weren't ready.

"Fuck your toes," said Michele, back to her old self. "Come on, girl, get me home. I got things to do."

17

"Now. What's this all about?" Anna's mother eyed her sharply over the tops of her glasses. "Why the burning need to see Putnam Graves?"

They were at the old oak table in the Sheffield family kitchen, the remains of an egg and pancake breakfast before them. Since flying was the last thing on earth anyone wanted to do after the latest scare, Anna had easily gotten a business class seat on the redeye. She'd hoped to sleep but her dreams wouldn't let her. A dark forest in murky water where strange shapes slithered below the surface—swampy nightmares had left her wrung out. And the airport only made matters worse. Cheerless at the best of times, Logan seemed still haunted by 9/11 and the marathon bombings. With a handful of morning travelers she'd hurried out to the taxi ranks and, expensive as it was, taken a town car to Manchester. She'd brought the cell—Mummy had to be appeased—and called ahead to let her know.

When she'd arrived Sarah was waiting, looking tiny on their wide front porch. The day was overcast and in the dull light the house looked elderly, sagging a little on its frost-bitten lawn, its pale gray paint in need of a fresh coat. But the traditional wreath of red and gold bittersweet was on the door, and Sarah was calling, "My God, you look dreadful!" So Anna knew she was home.

She stretched and looked away, not meeting her mother's eyes. "Just the time of year, I guess. Thanksgiving, missing Daddy. You know." Luckily her mother had never understood her and wouldn't suspect that she was lying. "But what about Uncle Pinky? Did you reach him?"

"Putnam," her mother corrected. "We have to help him grow out of this Pinky business. Well! I hope you'll be happy. I started those calls at 8:00 on the dot"—it was now 11:00—"making myself very popular. Men don't have the stamina of women, you know. The man's only seventy-two, but he was still in bed, if you can believe it. You'd asked if he was a partner in Peabody, Hawkins and so forth, in the '80s. I don't know why I didn't know the answer. I suppose because I never liked him as much as your father did. But long story short, he was, had been for twenty years. Now one of his sons is filling the slot. And he'll be here for drinks at 4:00. He's coming on his own. Marianne has some sort of do to go to. He was actually pleased—to be seeing you, anyway. I haven't seen him much since Daddy died. I just couldn't."

"I know, Mummy. Thank you. You're a wonder."

"Years of practice, darling. But you look exhausted. Don't you want to get a little sleep?"

They went up together to her old room, still decorated with her father's watercolors and early work of her own. Flowers, stones, the sea. Sarah turned down the bed. When

Anna was tucked in, she lingered there. "If you're going to be that pale," she said, "you might as well winter over with me."

"I may not look it, Mummy, but I'm better than I've been for a long time."

"If you say so, dear." Sarah closed the door softly behind her.

Seconds later, it seemed, a light tapping woke her, and her mother's voice whispered through the door. "Anna. It's almost 4:00. Putnam's here. Try to hurry, darling."

She found them sitting in the parlor in two high-backed chairs with a tray of sherry and cookies on a small table between them. Though it was nearly twilight only two small lamps were lit, off in a corner. Sarah, it seemed, had no intention of letting Putnam get comfortable. With great relief he jumped up to greet Anna, arms outstretched.

"Lovely girl, so good to see you. It's been too long."

It was ten years since she'd last seen him, at her father's funeral. She'd forgotten how tall he was, and how like an enormous baby, with large innocent blue eyes and a perfectly round head covered in downy white curls. He'd put on twenty pounds or so, and the exertion of getting up brought out the famous Pinky flush on his freshly shaved cheeks. He was dressed in a green blazer and red plaid tie, tasseled loafers and dark red and green Tartan wool trousers.

"You're looking very festive," Anna said after shaking his big, soft hand. She couldn't help wondering if after all this was someone she could rely on.

"And you," he said, "very California."

She'd put on a long maroon silk dress, brown sweater to her knees, a dark gold scarf and sandals with thick black socks. Behind her Sarah made a small, exasperated sound. But for Anna the sting of the community's disapproval had worn off long ago.

"Not what they're wearing in Manchester-by-the-Sea?" she joked.

But after all Pinky was gallant. "They might start when they see you. Can I pour you a sherry?"

"I'll bet you'd like something stronger." She went to the hutch where her father had kept the whiskey and was touched to find that her mother had left it there. Off by the windows Sarah was pretending to be busy with the drapes, closing them for the night. When their eyes met she gave Anna a sharp Three Managers look: Get this over with!

"Mummy," Anna said lightly as she poured two whiskeys, "I wonder if I could have a minute with Putnam alone?"

Her mother responded almost too quickly, "Of course, darling, I have a million things to do," and all but ran out of the room. Once her light steps had faded away into the house Anna turned to Putnam. He looked thoroughly puzzled.

"Putnam …" she began, offering him a glass. But he interrupted.

"Indulge me, Anna. Call me Uncle Pinky, like the old days." He took his drink and settled into an overstuffed arm chair. "That used to tickle me no end. Those breezy days of youth. The Cape, the Sea!" He took a long draw on the whiskey. "Ahhh, that's more like it." He looked up at her with soft, boyish eyes. "Want to talk about Johnny—about your Dad, do you?"

"No. I need your help with something." Anna brought a small chair and sat nearby. "It's something of my own and I have to ask you not to tell Mother under any circumstances. She absolutely must not know about this."

"Good grief." He chuckled as if she were sharing some girlish prank. "All right, I suppose I can promise that. What is it?"

"In the late '80s your firm had a partner, Harvey Schultz, who represented a doctor in Cambridge. Robert Buchanan, a paternity suit."

"Did he?" Pinky took a sip of his drink, looking bemused. "Not my line, that kind of thing."

"Robert Buchanan is my therapist, in Berkeley."

"Therapist!?" Pinky put down his glass and peered at her across the darkening room. "Anna! I'm so awfully sorry." She knew it wasn't the paternity suit he was sorry for. In their part of the world seeking therapy was a sign of profound mental weakness.

"I was raped. I was assaulted and raped by a group of men in San Francisco, two years ago. You didn't hear about it?"

"Good God, no!" Pinky fell back into his chair, his face reddening as if he might cry. "That's ghastly, just awful! Little Anna," he said weakly. "Little Anna with the pigtails and the wonderful talent for art."

"Thank you. But what I really need now is your help."

The poor man's look changed to one of alarm. "Help?' he said and reached again for his drink. "I'm a Corporate Man,

Anna. I really don't know what I could do about a—God! About a rape."

He took a gulp of whiskey and seemed about to stand, maybe to go. Afraid she might lose him, Anna went to him and sat on the ottoman at his feet. She reached for his hand. "Uncle Pinky, please. If Daddy were here, I'd go to him, of course."

Pinky looked stricken. "My God, you had to go through all that without a father. But what can I possibly do?"

"My confidence was shaken when I found out about this paternity suit. Of course Dr. Buchanan was exonerated, he's fully licensed and so on. But when I looked into it there were other problems. The blood test may have been compromised. There was a man involved, a technician named Larry Neal. He may have been blackmailing ..."

"Wait, wait," said Pinky. "Are you asking me to represent you somehow? Because I'm semi-retired, you know, and criminal law is not my, well, Thing, as you kids say."

"No, no, I just need information. I want to talk to Larry Neal, to find out what really happened. There's a place in Somerville where people know him, a bar or something. I don't know the name, that's the problem."

"And you think that's in the record somewhere?"

"Yes. I'm sure it is. Harvey Schultz knows about it, and I think Charles Peabody as well."

"As far as that goes, Harvey's moved to New York and Charlie Peabody died three years ago. But in any case, that's privileged information. Even if I got hold of Harvey, or the files, there's nothing I could share with you. And if this Neal is some sort of extortionist, it could be dangerous. It's the police who should handle ..."

"No, I can't do that. I know what the police would do. And there are other people involved. Anyway, Larry Neal is an invalid now. He's harmless."

"And how do you know that if you don't know where he is?"

"I have a source." She saw Michele standing in the drive, locked out and abandoned, and a pang of guilt hit hard. Guilt and regret. She should have listened. She should have studied those papers.

Pinky got up and began to pace. He crossed the room, turned on another lamp and stood gazing at a picture. It was her father's painting of the Cape house with a storm coming up behind and a cat rigged ketch making for shore. When he turned back to her, there was the shrewd lawyer her father had always admired. "Pinky Graves may look like a blustering fool, but you should see him command a courtroom." He'd decided, it seemed. Johnny Sheffield would want him to help his favorite daughter and that was all that mattered.

"Any other way we can come at this? Where did this Neal character work, do you know?"

"At something called MedSource Labs, sometime in the '80s, and I think at Mass General earlier. Robert was an intern there, then taught at Harvard. That's another piece of the puzzle, a girl he was involved with—Robert, I mean—a student of his who died. Suicide, or possibly a drug overdose. And Larry Neal may have supplied ..."

"Anna!" Pinky interrupted. "This is quite a nasty tangle. If I had any sort of doctor where things like this came to light, well! I'd simply leave his practice. No, run for the exit. Why haven't you?"

"Fate," Anna said lightly. "I happened to meet a former patient of his, a damaged young woman. Robert may have fathered her child. I feel for her, or with her."

He stood for a long time looking down at her, the wheels turning. "Is there a particular story you'd rather find, once you start searching?"

"What do you mean?"

"Facts have a curious way of organizing themselves around our wishes."

She thought about Robert as she'd seen him yesterday, coming to her home "to warn her." He'd been cool, controlled, controlling, just as he was in their sessions. And everything he'd said about Michele might well be true. She might be the real danger, and now Anna was dragging Pinky into it. On the other hand, Robert had hidden something in his pocket, the other half of that note, she was sure. He'd gone ashen. But perhaps it meant nothing. He was a vain man, Anna could see that now. Michele's intrusion alone might make him feel small. And finally, did any of that matter?

"I've lived in a trap for two and a half years. It's a failure of memory. I have a marriage—not an official one, but still, it depends on the outcome. I'm not sure this is about Robert, or the girl. I've cowered in my corner long enough, that's all. I need to know."

"Not a formula for objectivity," Pinky said kindly. "If you're going to look into it I'd better come with you. Let me do a little work on this in the morning, then I'll fetch you around 10:00. I think I'll start at Harvard and work forward. I'm a Harvard Man. I Know People."

"We'll have to be quick. I have to be home by Wednesday morning."

Michele sat in Joe's car at the corner of Cypress and Grizzly Peak, sucking on the dregs of a mocha. She had to calm down before she saw Anna. The setup had been harder than she'd imagined, getting both herself and Robin in a pathetic state for real. That meant getting Joe worked up enough to fight her. She'd started by waking him up with a wet towel in his face. She'd said she was leaving, she couldn't take it anymore. She was leaving and taking the car. They'd struggled for the keys and he'd thrown her brand-new cell phone out the window. He wasn't paying for her shit ever again! She'd grabbed Joe's hair, then spit on him until finally he'd started choking her. Robin was hysterical. All the better. Anna had to get the whole picture.

It had worked. She had bruises on her arms and Joe's hand print on her neck, covered up by a long black scarf. With the crying baby in her arms and the Robert papers in her purse she figured she was on track to get Anna back. But when she looked at herself in the rearview mirror she saw a problem. She was shaking all over from exhaustion, from life in general, and looked like death warmed over. She wanted to go on foot, like she'd walked all the way there, but if somebody saw her like this they might call the cops. She checked around to see if anyone was watching. The street was like some sci-fi movie where all the people have been vaporized. No cover, fucking Berkeley. And she had to get by the Manor. She took the stud out of her nose and the ring out of her eyebrow. She fished in her purse and found a barrette, quickly braided her hair like Anna's and pinned it to the top of her head. With the hem of her skirt she rubbed off the Black Plum lipstick. Now she might pass for Anna's kid, home from college for Thanksgiving after a horrible week of midterms.

"Yes, I'm a graduate student," she purred. "In sexology, at Buchanan University."

She laughed so hard that Robin woke up with a loud cry. Perfect. Might as well go for it. She got out, took the blubbering baby and went along the empty street to Anna's house. Once in the driveway she noticed that both the cars—Anna's Volvo and the neighbor's Lexus—were gone. That got her head spinning. The woman was practically a shut-in. Where the hell could she be on a Sunday? Michele crunched along the gravel drive to the cottage and knocked softly on the door. Nothing. The shutters on all the windows were closed, so she couldn't see in. But there were no curtains on the dining room doors, she remembered that. The doors might even be unlocked. There was a path leading around by the studio and she had just started toward it when the back door of the Manor flew open.

"Excuse me!" A pretty little woman with hennaed hair came out with a spoon in her hand, dripping something dark onto the gravel. "May I help you?" Luckily Robin reached out for the spoon and softened the woman up. "Are you looking for Anna?"

"Yes, that's right." The grad student voice, weary from exams. "We had an appointment. Will she be back soon?"

"Not for a few days," the woman said. "She didn't mention an appointment, but I guess she was in a hurry. She left last night. Are you a student?"

Remembering that Anna no longer taught, Michele said, "I used to be." She wanted to ask, left for where, but didn't think a student would.

"Well, I'm sorry you missed her," the woman said. She looked back into the kitchen, obviously dying to get out of there. "Would you like to leave a note?"

"Yeah, I'll just sit here and do it. I'll leave it in her mailbox."

When the woman closed her door, Michele slumped down onto Anna's porch. So the bitch had really done it. She'd really left her, after all she'd said about wanting to help. Maybe she'd gone away for Thanksgiving. That meant she wouldn't be there on Wednesday and Michele would face Robert alone. It was one thing to confront him with the baby, but this blackmail shit, this Laura thing .... She'd only stolen that stuff to please Anna. And the fight with Joe, the bruises for nothing. She felt tears coming and put her hand around her throat, squeezing hard. Her mother used to do that, and it sobered you right up.

Okay. If Anna thought she could get away with this, she didn't know who she was dealing with. She was involved, and Michele intended to keep it that way. She tried to imagine what might happen if she went to Robert alone and he turned her down. She'd tell him the evidence of his crimes was ready for mailing to the police. He'd dive for his precious hiding place, see that she was way ahead, give her that deadly stare. "You're delusional, bringing in the police. You think they'll believe you?" "Not me, Anna. It's all her idea. She's got the papers. Ask her to show you around her studio." If she couldn't get some money, at least she'd have her revenge.

Hiking the baby onto her hip, she looked toward the Manor. There was no one in the kitchen so she took the path to the studio. The key was there on the ledge where Anna had left it. She slipped inside, closing the blue door behind her. The baby was heavy in her arms, so she put her down and let her crawl in the fine white dust that covered everything. In the half light the big stone seemed to be hunching toward her. It had a long gash down one side, like the earth after an earthquake. Inside it was colored a deep blackish red.

"Shit, she's losing it." Michele hurried on with her task. She took out Robert's papers and stuffed them into the manila envelope. All but the sexiest thing, the suicide article. That would stay with her, as bait. That and the Maura clippings. And yesterday she'd had a brainwave, to copy the lawyer letter. She'd leave the original hidden here. The articles didn't matter so much—if, say, Robert went crazy and destroyed them. They could be replaced, but not the letter. She looked around for a hiding place. A tall narrow cupboard stood off in a spidery corner. If Anna came in before Robert, Michele guessed she wouldn't go in there. Nobody had in ages. Michele opened it and found some big power tools and a shelf of rags and sand paper and steel wool. She shoved the papers behind all that and closed the door tight. Then she scooped Robin up from the floor. Without looking back she locked the studio door, replaced the key and, keeping this time to the silencing grass of the lawn, drifted out onto the deserted street.

18

Anna waited on the porch of a Wedgewood blue Victorian, lost in the forest of last night's dream. It was a redwood forest, but full of the copper beeches of her youth, and it ran toward the sea and into the sea, right out into the waves. She'd run through the trees, searching for Colin, over the sand and down to the water's edge. There she'd watched the trees go on and on, deeper and deeper, and finally drown far out in the Sound. The descent from the Atlas mountains, maybe, she in a chador, into the desert, the sea of sand. The first time she'd lost Colin.

How had she imagined that he wouldn't find her? Of course he'd called Sarah, Sarah had said too much, giving the lie to Anna's story that she'd come home for Thanksgiving with Mummy.

"This trip has something to do with Buchanan, doesn't it? Who exactly is Putnam Graves?"

"My Uncle Pinky. You remember."

"A lawyer, isn't he?"

"He loved my father."

The trip was for herself, she'd promised, a break before the meeting on Wednesday. Concern for her mother. She wasn't sure that he'd believed her.

A tap of Pinky's horn snapped her back to the porch on Hawthorne Street and the handsome house on this narrow lane between the Charles River and Harvard Yard. Parked at the curb he gestured that, having knocked, she should try ringing the bell. Pinky had proved himself again. In just a couple of hours that morning he'd bonded with the chairman of the Department of Psychology at Harvard, who had guided him to Rebecca Guthrie. She was to be Anna's first "interview," while Pinky went off to Mass General, on the trail of Larry Neal. Professor Guthrie, as she now was, had been a roommate of Laura Blaufeld's at Harvard, a student of psychology and of Robert Buchanan's as well.

Anna rang the bell and waved to Pinky. He'd said he'd wait, to be sure Professor Guthrie was at home, but also to establish provenance. In the fiction he'd devised, this imposing figure in the dark green Jaguar was Anna's employer, so you'd be wise to cooperate. Pinky was turning out to be a showman as well as a strategist.

Footsteps sounded in the hall. A woman's face, angular and alert, half hidden by a mass of dark curly hair, appeared in Cubist form behind the front door's cut glass panel. Pinky had worried about Anna's California gear, so she'd stolen a stylish Burberry from Claire's closet. With her lace-up boots and the maroon and white Harvard scarf Pinky had lent her, she might be a fellow professor coming in from the cold. Apparently that was reassuring. The door opened.

"Professor Guthrie?"

"Yes?"

"I'm Anna Sheffield. Putnam Graves called you earlier?" She gestured toward the curb.

Dr. Guthrie looked past her to the Jaguar. Pinky waved a jaunty sailor's salute, which the professor returned.

"Oh, sure, you're the investigator. About Laura Blaufeld. Gosh, that seems so long ago, but anyway, come in. It's freezing out here. There's a nor'easter due in tonight. Let's go back to the kitchen, it gets the best light." Talking all the way, the professor led Anna back to a cozy French country kitchen. "Excuse the mess. I like to work down here. Would you like some tea, Anna? And please call me Rebecca." She offered Anna a seat at the rustic dining table. Books and papers were scattered everywhere. Rebecca put a kettle on, while Anna waited for her to take a breath.

"I can't give you very much time," she said. "I have to finish these midterms by Thanksgiving or it's all over. But take your coat off. Wow, I've got to tell you, I was just amazed to get Mr. Graves' call this morning. I'd have thought all the statutes had run out on everything to do with Laura and all that. But I don't really know much about how those things work. Is this a civil suit? The Blaufelds? Aren't they all dead by now?"

"The next generation, I suppose," Anna invented. "Mr. Graves doesn't share all the details, just gives me the questions."

"Sure, sure. Laura's brother is behind it, I'll bet. *Les Enfants Terrible*. Anyway, sorry to be in such a rush, but I'm very pressed for time. Kids coming home from college, etcetera, etcetera." Rebecca filled a tea pot and put out two cups. "There was plenty to wonder about, that's for sure."

"I'll try to be quick. You were Laura's roommate, I understand. Can you tell me something about her?"

"Right! Senior year. Four of us moved off campus into an apartment. Laura and I had a class together as well, with a young associate named Robert Buchanan. Reich and the Theory of Drives. Pretty darn steamy for a sheltered Jewish girl from the Bronx."

Jewish? Guthrie? But there had been a mezuzah at the front door, and a menorah on the mantle as they passed the living room.

"But Laura couldn't get enough. Laoora. Took Robert on as a full-time tutor. I guess he's the one the brother's most interested in?"

"That's a name we're looking into," Anna said, feeling herself blush. Luckily Rebecca was preoccupied with pouring tea.

"Let me just say," the professor sped on, "I don't know how much time Robert Buchanan had spent in the Orgone box, but boy, he had it in spades. If you don't know, Orgone was Reich's term for life force. The sex drive, the will. He thought it was floating around all over the place and he'd trap it in this metal box, stick a patient in there and cure their neuroses in a flash. Don't get me started! Anyway, not only was Robert the poster boy for narcissism—that's the diagnosis I'd give him today—but he was the guy the term "charismatic" was made for. He just—what?—*exuded* that mysterious energy some people have. And Laura wasn't exactly a shrinking violet. Those two put on quite a show. Robert had this red Mustang convertible, some collector's item from the '60s, and they drove around that fall like the Duke and Duchess of Windsor." She demonstrated how Laura's hair flew in the wind. "But here, I'm going on and on, and you have questions!"

"No, no, this is all helpful." Anna couldn't help savoring the image of Robert in an Orgone box. In her mental picture it was very small. "But I wonder, looking back, do you think that Buchanan's energy may have come from drugs?"

"Well, sure, that's what you'd want to know. Given what happened." Rebecca dove back into the current of her thoughts. "Okay, so these two were together for less than a year, met fall semester and she died the next summer. At first Laura was laying a trap, teasing him, toying with him. She was wild, and I thought troubled. I was the fifth wheel, you see, in our foursome. She and I were never really friends but I saw what was going on from my quiet corner. Behind his back she'd sneer at Robert, his lack of sophistication, a proletarian from the wrong side of New Haven. And that was the thrill, the princess and the stable boy. None of us ever said anything. She had a problem with anger. Well, let's face it—we were scared of her! It all came from that father of hers, *Sturmhauptführer* Blaufeld. That's what we called him. First name was Reinhardt, really, I think. He visited a few times. I remember the first time, he shook my hand and just said, 'Corman'—that was my maiden name—'Corman,' in this deliberate way. He was wondering if I was Jewish. And I am. Secular, all about the rituals, the symbols and so on. But my family lost people. It chilled me to the bone."

"Because the family was German? Weren't you jumping to conclusions?"

"Of course you'd think that, but no. The Blaufelds lived in Argentina, and Laura admitted her father had been a Nazi. A member of the party, who knows at what level. So in my view, she was running as fast as she could from that horror, and at the same time she was scarred by it, or maybe enthralled. Somewhere she was hypereroticized."

Rebecca took a gulp of her tea and stared out at the yard, where fallen leaves were swirling in a rising wind. "Oh!" She brought herself back. "But you were asking about drugs. Herr Blaufeld had 'addict' written all over him, probably opioids. There was something wrong with him, thin as a rail. So for Laura drugs were familiar territory. And I know she and Robert played with psychedelics. For exams she could get uppers, some kind of speed, so sure. But it was everywhere anyway, you could get almost anything on the street."

Anna made herself press on. "What about whatever killed Laura?"

"They didn't disclose that. But it was some kind of sedative combined with alcohol. We all thought, potent sedatives you don't find in Harvard Square. Then, anyway. Maybe in Daddy's medicine chest."

"Knowing her as you did, do you, or did your roommates, believe she'd committed suicide?"

"That's a tough one. A more likely finding would have been accidental overdose. It would have been something Robert told them that got them thinking otherwise. He was the last to see her alive, except the landlord of the apartment building, who tried to revive her. So Robert was the main person of interest. They talked to all of us, but they really grilled him. In fact, now that I think of it, he came over right after the first interrogation and he especially wanted to talk to *me*, in private. I guess he picked me as the only psych major in the bunch, someone who thought deeply about people and their motivations, and he said, 'Becky, Laura committed suicide. Someday I'll tell you all about it, but she was far more unstable than anyone knew.' And he cried. Brokenheartedly. Sobbed. 'She did it to hurt me. To overpower me.' I held him, I remember—vividly."

Anna had no trouble imagining the scene, or herself in the place of the gullible Becky. Except for holding him. "Did you believe that, the suicide?"

"It was certainly possible."

"Was this before or after you'd been interviewed by the police?"

"Let's see." She looked up at the ceiling, time traveling. "Before. The day before. Oh! Hold on. You think he was guiding me? Manipulating?"

"Did you tell them you thought it was suicide?"

"I said—yes, in fact! I said she was unstable, maybe more than people knew. Used that exact phrase. And I told them what I knew about her father, her background … Oh my God, was I actually influenced by that man? Well, of course I was. Let's face it—seduced. The only time he ever paid the slightest attention to me. I was just a homely kid. I had a crush on him, too, and I'm sure he knew it. He just—exuded. He used me. But why, that's the question." She looked at the clock.

"Oh, my God, it's almost noon! I absolutely have to move on. But look, I want you to see for yourself. Be right back."

The sound of rummaging came from the front room. Rebecca hurried back with an 8x10 photograph, black and white, and put it on the table.

As she'd studied Robert over the years, Anna had sometimes wondered what he'd been like earlier in life. Had he ever been approachable, innocent? Had he ever really enjoyed anything? Here he was, a very young Robert, standing in the snow in overcoat and scarf, extravagantly handsome with dark hair to his shoulders, his arms around a striking young woman. The glittering girl on skis, the graduate in black dress and pearls. She pressed against him, her head thrown back, a long-stemmed rose in her teeth. One hand was flung into the air in a playful tango, the cascade of her hair like molten jet against the snow. Clinging to him, she teased the camera while he looked only at her, at the same time wanting and afraid. Laura, Maura, a strong resemblance. But close up like this Anna could see, between Laura and Michele, a near perfect match. Laura's double, come back from the dead.

"There's something in Freud, isn't there?" Anna asked. The fog was beginning to seep in through the cracks. "If we find ourselves over and over in the same forest, say in our dreams. Or meet the same person again and again, wearing another mask?"

"The repetition compulsion? *Todestrieb*, the drive toward aggression, let's say, or death as Freud put it, overriding the drive toward pleasure." Familiar lecture material to Dr.

Guthrie, it seemed, since she'd gone to the table and begun organizing the chaos. "Or maybe it's Jung you're thinking of. The return of the repressed. Strongly related, a bit of a different spin toward the noumenal. *Heimlich* and *unheimlich*, you know, homey and uncanny, come from the same root, as well as *traum*, dream, and trauma." Rebecca turned to Anna. "Oh, sorry! You've turned white as a sheet."

"He's my therapist." Unwanted, it just came out.

"Who?"

"Robert Buchanan."

Rebecca's hands flew up to hold her head, as if it might fly off. She sat down suddenly and stared at Anna across the table.

"You're kidding. So, are you investigating, or what?"

"Yes, I am. Both are true."

"And you think what? Give me a minute here." She took a long drink of tea. "Has he done something to you? You have to report that! I mean, you should."

"Not to me. It's just, I learned about these things by accident. I grew up here. You hear things. I ..."

Luckily, Rebecca broke in. "So you think that he supplied the drugs to Laura? I think the police looked into that. She stole them, I think he said. Yes, he told me, I remember, she stole them to implicate him. To take him with her. Uh! It gives me chills!"

"There's another—worse—possibility."

Rebecca strained to imagine. Then her eyes popped open in disbelief. "You think he killed her?"

"I'm trying to understand."

Rebecca took a deep breath. "I have a thousand questions, and I'm not asking any of them. Do not involve me in whatever this is."

"No, of course not."

"I'm sorry, but I can't deal with this. I have to ask you to leave." She got up and took the Burberry from the back of the chair. She helped Anna into it. "Appearances are truly deceiving. You'd make a great spy." She started toward the door, then turned back. "I'm sorry for whatever happened to you. Is happening. Please keep the picture. I don't want it. I don't know why I've hung onto it this long."

"Thanks so very much. And, sorry to impose, but do you have the number for a cab?" She fished out the cell phone. "I have another stop to make."

Ryan's Pub, whose name and address Pinky had supplied without divulging his source, occupied the lower floor of a squat two-story building faced with dirty yellow brick and defended with pull-down metal armature. It stood just off Broadway in Somerville's Winter Hill, a neighborhood still resisting the spread of gentrification from Cambridge and Tufts. There seemed to be offices upstairs, apartments maybe, where dingy shades were drawn. But some effort had been made to liven things up. Ryan's yellow and green neon sign sported both shamrock and lyre, and a full color rainbow arched over the doorway. Hand-painted signs in the barred windows congratulated Boston College on their recent win against Rutgers and announced the Celtics upcoming season, along with Guinness on tap.

The bleak cheer of the place was daunting. From where the cab had dropped her, right in front, Anna crossed the street and took refuge in the doorway of a travel agency.

"Look at it this way," Robert had said. "You can call it depression, repressed rage, fear. How about laziness?" When was that? Early on, when both of them had thought she wasn't listening. "Whatever you call it, we have a weapon against it. The will."

Was it *that* Robert she was pursuing, Anna wondered? Would he be a lifelong companion? There was only one way out. Sheltering beside a display of Mexican beach resorts, Anna dialed Pinky's cell. He didn't answer. She told him where she was and not to come. Another North Shore Patrician would only complicate things. She tried to keep it light. Would he call at 2:00, pick her up for lunch? They'd trade adventures. Then she crossed over and left the bitter cold of the street for the heat of Ryan's Pub.

The place was dimly lit and when she entered several pale faces turned from the blaring NASCAR race to check out the new arrival. She was the only woman there. The bartender hurried down to greet her. He was a fair-haired man in his forties, ruddy-faced and burly.

"Well now, Miss, what can I do for you on this fine, sunny day?" When he got a better look he added jovially, "I hope you know you've strayed out of Cambridge, and you're now in darkest Somerville." A real Irishman, or talented actor.

"Yes, thanks. I do know." Anna sat on a stool. "I'll have an Irish coffee."

"Excellent choice." The man bustled about and in no time produced a steaming glass mug with chipped handle and faded shamrock. He grabbed a half-drunk beer and touched his glass to hers. "Cheerio and your very good health!" He leaned on the bar and pretended to watch the race for a second or two, then turned back to her. "I'm Patrick, by the way."

"Anna."

"I don't mean to be nosy, Anna, but you're not exactly our regular sort of customer. How did you find our little corner of paradise?"

"I'm looking for Larry Neal," she said as casually as she could manage.

Patrick held up his hands as though someone had pointed a gun at him. "Ay, shite," he said. "You're the lady that called on Saturday, then?"

That must be Michele, Anna thought. She looked Patrick steadily in the eye, hoping he'd say more, and he quickly obliged.

"Look, this is something for Mike. I'm sure you didn't like the way he spoke to you before, but if there's something up with the Mustang, he'll make good on it."

A Mustang again? Two in one day. What had Michele said to make him think that? Anna tried to hold an expression of grave concern. "Is Mike available?"

"Well now, I'm sure I don't know. But let me give him a jingle."

Patrick went to the phone while the other men looked around at her with open distaste. Soon she heard distant footfalls on some inner stair and then a man came in through a doorway that led, said a glittering red arrow, to the Ladies and Gents. So Mike lived or worked upstairs. Perhaps he owned the place. Perhaps he was involved. He came toward her, a lean, strong man about sixty, with thick black hair, a black moustache and a half-smoked cigarette dangling from his narrow lips. Even his clothes were aggressive—tight black T-shirt and pants, with a Redwings jacket and work boots.

"All right, so is this about the title?" With unnecessary force Mike pulled out the stool next to hers and straddled it, punching his cigarette out in the nearest ashtray. Anna felt a stirring in her heart, down where the ants lived. But she said quietly, "I didn't come about a title. And I didn't call on Saturday."

Mike turned abruptly to Patrick. "The fuck?" he said, getting a baffled shrug in reply. So he turned back to Anna. "The fuck?"

Anna considered telling the truth, but Mike's hostile black eyes stopped her. Michele would coo to such a man. She tried to coo. "It's nothing, Mike, really. My name's Anna. I met Larry years ago when I lived in Cambridge. I'm visiting from California and thought I'd look him up."

Mike looked incredulous. "You and Larry?" He turned to Patrick with a snorting laugh. The bartender smiled indulgently.

"It wasn't like that," Anna said. "I had some Irish friends who liked to come in here, and we had ..." again she called on Michele for help, "... we had some good times. Laughs. He was fun, that's all."

With Mike's eyes boring into her, she tried to look open and trusting. It seemed to work. Mike sighed, turning again to Patrick. "Larry's fun? Can you believe this?" Patrick laughed, and Mike turned back to her. "Larry's had some trouble, that's why I was so uptight. I've had to step in."

Anna sipped her coffee, and noticed her hand was shaking a little. She put the glass down so Mike wouldn't see.

"So anyway," Mike went on, staring down at the bar. "I'm sorry to have to tell you. Larry had a stroke a few years back. Completely incapacitated." That word again. Robert, what seemed like years ago: "And could we intervene with drugs?"

"I'm terribly sorry. And you're, what, an old friend?"

"I'm Larry's cousin. Sorry, I thought you knew. I told the other lady." For a moment Mike seemed genuinely sad, and Anna dared to take another step.

"Does Larry still live in Somerville? Is there any chance I could see him?"

"I'm telling you, he's not much fun now, if he ever was. He doesn't talk very well, he's in a wheelchair."

"I don't care," Anna said sincerely. "I'd like to see him."

Mike stared at her hard, as if testing her. It seemed she passed. "Well, what the hell. It might do him good. He lives with his sister, Kathy Whelan. Not too far, over on Meachum. I know they're home. We talk every day, me and Kath. Look, I'll drop you. Make up for being such a prick. Sorry—jerk. Wanna?"

"Sure. Thank you." Anna took out a twenty to pay for her drink.

Patrick put up a hand and whisked away her glass. "On the house. All's well that ends well!" He winked and added, "Don't be a stranger!"

Mike led Anna into the grubby alley beside the pub, bounded on one side by a tall unpainted wood fence. Against that a two car garage sagged, its old fashioned double doors advertising the pub's wares: Guinness on one side and Harp on the other. Mike opened a large padlock and swung the doors open. A Ford Bronco was parked inside, along with a smaller car on blocks covered with a tarp. Part of a red fender was exposed, along with the grill and its famous galloping pony. Mike drove the Bronco out onto the drive, then closed the garage doors leaving the padlock hanging open. As he helped Anna in, he said, "Just so you know—Larry's stroke was an accident. What I mean, a drug accident. So don't ask him about it, or Kathy, okay? It's a sore subject. Just so you know."

19

"So this is where Larry washed up," Mike said. They'd gone only a few blocks and were parked in front of a two-story frame house, painted a painful brick red with pale green trim. "Better than a nursing home, I guess."

The house sat on a small rise with a short flight of stairs leading up from the sidewalk, then a strip of pavement across the sad lawn, then another short flight up to a concrete porch. A wheelchair ramp, leading down to the driveway, had been attached at the side. But for all its awkwardness the house seemed cared for. Roses in a bed had been pruned neatly back for the winter, the brown grass on the strip of lawn would be thick in summer, and two pots of plastic geraniums decorated the front stair.

On the way over Mike had called to tell Kathy they were coming. She was standing now at the door, a large woman with thick muscular forearms left bare by a short sleeved nurse's uniform. This was mostly covered by a much-washed pale green apron. *Durgan Park*, its faded letters said. Kathy seemed to be about fifty and looked worn out, with brown circles under her eyes and a slouch as she stood there. Her auburn hair, cut efficiently short, was going delicately gray. But as they came closer Anna saw a lively curiosity in the woman's green eyes and imagined that she might once have been quite pretty.

"So, come on, then!" Kathy called out. They were taking their time, mincing along the icy walk. "You're letting the heat out."

All starch and hurry, she ushered them into a cramped, dark foyer. As in Robert's building, a staircase went up to the second story and a hallway led back, here to a brightly lit kitchen where they heard the cheerful roaring of a football game. Anna could see the corner of a table, the back of a large electric wheelchair and the top of a man's head. His hair was a silvery blond, trimmed in a tight crew cut.

"Kathy, this is Anna, an old friend of Larry's from California."

"Right." Kathy hustled them into a small parlor as Larry twisted in his chair, calling out in a thick, strangled voice, "Gady! Gady! Oo id?"

"Y'see!" Kathy said to Mike, "Ears like a fox. I told you it might upset him."

"So what," said Mike, "he's always upset about something. Might as well be something interesting."

"Easy for you to say," said Kathy. Then she turned to Anna. "Sorry, I don't mean to make you feel unwelcome."

"Gady!," Larry called. "Oo id?! Gady!"

"Hold on a sec." Kathy bustled down the hall, her voice filtering back. "Larry, sit down, okay? This doesn't concern you."

"He can walk?" Anna asked Mike.

"He tries. Kathy walks him a couple times a day, but it's easier to keep him in the chair. Hey, listen, I gotta take off. You got a way back?"

"Yes, thanks. Thanks, Mike, for your help."

"Yeah, sure. I'll hear all about it from Kathy." He went into the hall. "Hey, Kath, I'm takin' off. Talk to you later."

"Yeah, Mike!" Kathy called and without a breath went back to her duties. "Please, Larry, sit down. You'll see Mike later. Watch your game. Oh, look! They're about to make a touchdown!" Larry's cheering faded as Kathy closed the kitchen door and came thumping back to Anna. "Same game over and over. Those DVRs are great. So." With a deep sigh she lowered herself into a well-worn recliner. "Sit down, take off your coat. You say you used to know Larry? Did we ever meet?"

"I don't think so." Anna took her time with the coat, trying to decide which way to go next. But Kathy rushed in again.

"Mike said it was back in the '90s. Weren't those the glory days? That stupid Gulf War was over, we'd got that bastard Saddam, we thought. I couldn't get enough of my brothers, lotta time at Ryan's. All three had signed up. Sean got killed, you might know. One of the few. The others were sick for a long time. Larry backed out, thank God. Faked a breakdown and now look." She looked sharply at Anna. "What year was it? You'd think I'd remember you. You're memorable." But before Anna could respond, Kathy seemed suddenly to run out of steam. She put her head back on the headrest and closed her eyes. "On the other hand, it's a long time ago. Plenty of time to forget you."

She sighed deeply and seemed about to nod off. In the silence, Anna made up her mind. "You don't remember me, Kathy, because I never met Larry. I'm here because of Robert Buchanan."

Kathy's eyes popped open, wary and alert. Anna imagined she had only seconds before Larry's powerful sister would take her by the scruff of the neck and throw her down the icy stairs. But one thing was clear: Robert Buchanan meant something to her. Anna rushed on.

"I'm a patient of his, in California. He lives out there now. I heard disturbing rumors about his time back in Boston and I was hoping you could give me some information."

Now was the time for Kathy to heave herself up, screaming and cursing. Instead she said softly, "Well, that's not a name you hear much anymore, thank God. I can tell you, though, it's not someone Larry wants to talk about, if that's what you were hoping. But I'm being rude. Want anything? Coke, some coffee? I'm having a Coke."

"Sure," Anna said. "Let me help you."

"Okay, you might as well meet Larry. But don't get into it with him, don't mention the B-word. He's at risk. He can't afford to get upset."

Anna followed Kathy down the dim hallway. As they approached, Larry twisted toward them, his muddy eyes peering over the top of his chair. With professional efficiency Kathy pulled him back so he could face their guest. "Larry, this is Anna," she said, as if she were speaking to a five-year-old. "She's visiting from California, isn't that fun? Want a soda?" And she bustled off to the fridge.

"Goat," Larry ordered, and gave Anna his full attention. His face was unusually long and pallid, spotted all over with gingery freckles. His pale eyebrows keep moving up and down, like someone with a thousand questions, and his mouth was drawn into an upside down U. The stroke had put him in permanent mourning. "Ha. Owie," he said to Anna and with effort extended his left hand. Anna took it. It was ice cold.

"Owie, that's what he calls himself," Kathy said over her shoulder. "That's a good one, huh?"

"Hi Larry." Anna looked down at the crippled man. A powerful sedative mixed with alcohol, Rebecca had said. Anna tried to pull away but Larry's grip was like a spasm.

"Gavorna," he said, crinkling his eyes almost shut. It seemed to be his way of grinning. Mercifully, Kathy came back with the Cokes dangling in the plastic rings of a six pack. She plunked them down on the table, seized Larry's arm, gave it a quick squeeze to force open his hand and popped a Coke into it.

"Yeah, nice and sunny," she said. "There you go." She pulled back the tab and put in a straw. "We're going to chat for a bit. Call if you need anything." And she marched off down the hall with Anna trailing behind. Back in the airless parlor she closed the door, handed Anna a Coke, and went back to her recliner. There were only a couple of other seats in the cramped little room. Anna picked the lumpy orange corduroy couch.

"A patient, huh?" Kathy took a swig of soda. "That's frightening. But I'm curious about you, Anna. Tell me a little about yourself. Anna what, for starters?"

"Sheffield. I'm an artist. I'm a sculptor and I teach at an art college in San Francisco. And I suppose you'd like to know why I'm seeing Dr. Buchanan."

"Oh no, we don't need to get into all that. I'm more curious how you found us."

"I grew up around here. There's a public record."

Kathy replied with a weary smile. "North Shore." In the musical lilt of Irish Boston, it was Nahth Shoah. "Nice up there. Well, it's all water under the bridge. You seem like a good person." She took a deep breath, let out a long sigh. "Alls I know is, Larry met Buchanan back at Mass General, when he was a technician just out of junior college and Buchanan was a psychiatric intern. I'm a nurse myself, as you can see. Following in Larry's footsteps. That's a good one, huh?" A hollow laugh and another sip of Coke. Then Kathy got up, went to the front window and pulled aside the lace curtain. "An artist," she said wistfully. "That must be fun. I love art."

There was a long silence. Finally Kathy turned back and came to sit beside Anna on the couch. "I haven't talked about this in ages, but I'll help you out if I can. What I know, Robert Buchanan is not someone you'd want to trust with the family jewels." She shifted around, trying to get comfortable on the creaking couch. "Darn it, I gotta replace this thing," she said. "Would you be a doll and grab my Coke?"

Anna did, and Kathy sat back cradling it in her lap. "Larry had a drug problem. Speed. To be honest, I don't know if he was supplying the doctor or what—you know, through his residency and all that, a lot of the docs take speed. But they got involved somehow around 1976. He told me about it when this thing happened with Buchanan's girlfriend." Kathy stopped, sipped, considered for a moment. "She committed suicide. It was in all the papers because her father was some big shot tycoon from South America who turned out to be a Nazi. I didn't know they had Nazis down there, but anyways, Larry kept saying the police were going to be looking for him—Larry, I mean—but they never did, and I just thought he was paranoid because he knew the doctor. Like I said, he had a drug ..."

Kathy broke off, listening. There was a dull shuffling sound and Larry's muffled voice asking something. He seemed to be just outside the room. Kathy called out, "This is not about you, hun, go back ..." But something thumped against the door. Kathy struggled up and opened it. Larry was standing there holding onto the handles of his chair, pushing it in front of him.

"No, no, you can't come in here, Larry. You're being a very bad boy." Kathy went into the hall and hustled him back into the chair. "You can take a bad fall. Now go back to your game. I'll be in in a minute and get you another soda."

The wheelchair whirred and bumped as Larry turned around in the narrow hall. "Curious as a cat," Kathy said. She closed the door and put her ear to it. Then she asked in a conspiratorial whisper, "So where was I? Oh! The cops." She came back to the couch and sat on the edge, rushing on with a new sense of urgency. "Okay, so anyways, a few years later Larry's cleaned up pretty much and stuff, and all of a sudden he starts acting weird, like before. You know, unreliable, not making eye contact when you talked to him, that sort of thing. My kids were getting into their teens and I did not want this shit, pardon my French, around them in any way, shape or form. He was living with us, see, dead broke. So I asked him what was going on, and he wouldn't say, just very jittery and peculiar, and lo and behold what should I read in the paper right about that time but another thing involving this Buchanan character. A paternity suit, with a patient no less. You probably know, yeah? From the public record?"

Anna nodded that she did. Kathy hurried on.

"I don't know if it was deeja view or what—." Kathy stopped, looking uncertain. Anna's face must have betrayed her. "Deeja view is a foreign expression," Kathy explained and rushed on. "You know, stuff that's happened before—imagining the police were after him. But anyways not long after all this Larry starts buying stuff, stereo equipment and all kinds of stuff. Said he'd landed some high-paying work. Oh, and he got that gorgeous red Mustang. But then, that very night he had his stroke, not that that was any big surprise to anyone. He'd abused his body horribly for many years. Of course I got to be the one to pick up the pieces. Had to turn around and sell the darn car for medical costs. The title wasn't exactly clear, so I was going to have to give it away, practically. But Mike gave me a really good price for it. Said it was going to be a Classic someday."

The Mustang again, still troubling Mike three decades later. Because the car was stolen? Or because the dead broke Larry suddenly had a Mustang and then a near fatal stroke? Robert, too, had had a Mustang. Red. A convertible. The room seemed stifling and Anna went to the front window hoping it would be cooler there.

"God knows," Kathy went on, twisting around to face her, "I used to tell him, 'The body is the temple of your soul, Larry, you really need to clean up.' But of course it all fell on deaf ears." She stopped suddenly and said, "Are you all right, Anna?"

"Yes, just hot. And wondering, did you have any thought that Robert—Dr. Buchanan—might have been somehow involved with Larry's, Larry's ..." She couldn't bring herself to say it.

"Larry's *stroke*?" Kathy was amazed, appalled. "Oh, Lord no! Maybe fraud or something, but not that. I was right here, a couple of rooms away. I heard him hit the floor."

A loud bump on the door startled them both. Kathy jumped up and flung it open. "Larry! Darn it all, have you been listening? I cannot believe this! Now I'm really angry."

But Larry, now sitting in the chair, came forward like a charging bull, forcing her back into the room. He seemed to be trying to get to Anna. Kathy stepped nimbly aside, flicked Larry's hand away from the controls and brought the chair to an abrupt stop. A Coke was on Larry's tray. He picked it up awkwardly and flung it into Kathy's recliner. It hit the back, splashing soda over the seat, the wall, the floor.

"Larry!! Now look what you did. I cannot believe this behavior!"

While his sister berated him, Larry sat straight up in his chair, looking past her to Anna. He was sweating and his eyes were bulging with effort and anger.

Kathy stormed past him, calling "Don't you move. I'll be right back." She was heading for the kitchen, for a mop or something. They had only seconds. Anna went to Larry and took his hand.

"Is there something you want to tell me?"

"Ye. Uduzay uduzay uduzay." He frantically pointed at her, then at his mouth. At her, at his mouth.

"What I said?"

"Ye." Larry bobbed his head furiously, unconsciously crushing her hand in his grip. "E dib. E dibby. Eye dowa. Owa. No nell Gady."

Owa. Eye dowa? What did that mean? I'd rather? I doubt her? But she'd understood "no nell Gady." And now Gady was coming back down the hall, muttering angrily to herself.

"Okay," Anna whispered. "Okay, Larry, I understand. Let's be quiet now."

This seemed only to make the man more frantic. "Be," he pointed to his chest, "buding, buding, buding." He pointed to his head: "Doobit!" he suddenly began to cry, hitting his forehead with the ball of his hand. "Doobit! Doobit!" He took hold of her sleeve, tried to pull himself up, but only succeeded in dragging her down almost on top of him. Kathy stormed back in with a wad of paper towels and stopped dead in the doorway.

"Now what the heck's all this?"

"I'm so sorry," said Anna. "He got very excited, I'm sorry ..."

Larry let Anna go and with his working hand pulled on Kathy's apron. "Gady, nahwy. Nahwy, Gady." He cringed like a beaten dog.

Kathy threw the towels in the chair and furiously attacked the spill. Then she tossed the sticky mass onto Larry's tray. "You should be sorry, you big lump," she said. Seeing his face wet with sweat and tears she wiped it with a corner of her apron. "It's okay." Her face softened as she ran a hand lightly over Larry's stubbly hair. "My baby brother. What can you do?"

Anna saw a chance to get away and quickly put on her coat.

"Yeah," Kathy said wearily, not looking at her, "you better go. I shouldn't have started this. Like I say, we don't use the B-word around here."

20

Anna stood on the corner of Meachum and Moreland trying to sort out what had just happened. Larry's frenzy, grabbing at her with his powerful hand, his babbling, had started the ants crawling. She needed to be somewhere safe, to think, to breathe. She tried Pinky's cell but got his service again. Pacing in frustrated circles she realized it wasn't really Putnam she wanted to talk to. She wanted Michele, she wanted those papers. But she hadn't even brought the girl's number. Maybe she'd erased Michele's message altogether. She couldn't remember.

She checked her watch. It was after 4:00, well past the time she'd asked Pinky to call. The weather had changed and the air had the metallic smell that comes before snow. She needed a warm place to wait. Broadway was a major thoroughfare. There must be stores and cafés there if she could find her way back. She walked briskly along Moreland, pushed by a cutting wind blowing up the Mystic River behind her. After three blocks she recognized a street she and Mike had taken earlier. Hoping it led back to Broadway, she turned. There was Ryan's golden lyre flashing from the next corner. She could go in to get warm, but then Kathy had probably gone straight to the phone to call Mike. He wouldn't like being lied to.

Anna stopped to consider. The walk had calmed her, and she could think about Larry without shaking. "Be, buding, buding, doobit." That was what he'd wanted to tell her. That thought had driven him wild. In his way, Larry was an artful speaker, so there must be some pattern there. She leaned against a fence, thinking it through. "Buding." Larry's d's are t's, so it should be "butting," but that didn't make sense. What about "be" as "me?" "Must think," maybe? "Doobit," hitting his head. That could be "must think I'm stupid." "Me," or maybe, "he," "must think I'm stupid?" Why would that thought make him weep?

The cold was creeping in, so she started off again. As she approached the pub she saw Mike's Bronco parked in the alley and, just visible behind it, the garage door and the open padlock hanging there. Inside was the Buding. Anna stopped, a piece of the puzzle unlocking. Me, the Mustang. And another thing he'd said, the first thing: e dibbe. Could that mean, he did me? *That* had brought the tears, the car personified as a man. Stupid! Stupid! But, no. Everyone agreed it was self-administered drugs, not an accident, that had ended Larry's criminal career, his youth, almost his life.

Anna looked along the street. There were more people now, doing afternoon chores—walking kids home from school, unloading groceries, bringing in mail. That would make it easier to slip unnoticed down the drive. Before she could decide what to do she heard raucous laughter coming up behind her. Three men in muddy work clothes, heads down against the wind, were heading for the pub. When they saw her they fell silent and passed her with veiled glances.

She caught their wake and walked casually along a few yards behind, turning into the alley as they opened Ryan's door. Van Morrison's voice drifted out, *Rave on John Donne* filling the evening air. Michele was suddenly there, with her uncanny likeness to Laura Blaufeld, her look daring, goading. You don't permit *me*!

Anna looked down the alley. Mike's Bronco would offer protection, just enough to get inside the garage. She'd stay only long enough to jot down the Mustang's license number. She took a small sketchbook and pen from her purse and put them in her pocket for easy access. But the driveway was slick with frost, and in the dim light she had to pick her way along. Even worse, when she pulled the padlock away both garage doors swung wide open, and she saw right away there was no plate on the Mustang's front bumper. To get to the back would take time. If she closed the doors she wouldn't be able to see. Crouching behind the Bronco, she looked at the pub. The wall facing her had only one small window toward the back, probably the bathroom. But upstairs were several windows, the shades up now. She could see the back of a computer against one of them. As she hesitated, Mike Neal appeared at the window, the computer's blue glow flickering on his face. Was he looking inside, or out?

She darted into the garage. The space in back was filled with tools, lawn furniture and old car parts, leaving only a narrow passage to the Mustang's rear bumper. Even that was blocked by a large trash can full of leaves. She dragged it aside and hunkered down in the shadows, feeling for the car's license plate. A door banged open, Van Morrison sang out, and Mike shouted, "The fuck's going on!" She fumbled for her pen, straining to see in the dim light. She wrote quickly on her palm and only realized Mike was there when the trash can was kicked aside.

"Patient, my ass," he said. "That fuck send you?"

Leaves fluttered around her. Thick hands grabbed her by the front of her coat and pushed her up against the car.

"If that fuck thinks he's getting this back, he's crazy. You tell him, I know what this is. This is a murder weapon and I know it."

Anna tried but couldn't stop the squealing gate. "I'm trying to understand …"

Mike shook her to shut her up. "Understand what?! You tell him, if Larry wasn't such a dumbshit we'd have got him. You're a PI, is that it? What!" He dragged her stumbling out into the open as the grave stones closed in around her.

"Please, you don't want to do this." She begged the man as he hauled her, slipping on the ice, toward the dark yard. She tried to focus on him. Was it, after all, Mike Neal? He seemed to have a short ponytail, tied back with a strip of leather, and a tattoo on his neck, a crown of thorns dripping two crimson drops.

"… find out who you're after if I have to beat it out of you …" he snarled, while Michele whispered, "I hope you got a piece of 'em," and time slowed as it does when something terrible is happening.

Anna looked down at the man's hand. His grip was unsteady, tightening and loosening as he stumbled across the frozen ground. As if moving underwater, she took hold of the front of her coat, waiting for the next misstep. It sent him sliding back toward her, and as his fingers opened she wrenched free and ran toward the pub's back door. Behind her there was a thud, the man falling on the ice.

"Fuckin' hell!"

The door opened, the man scrambled up. Anna ran down a dark hallway toward the music and babble of the pub. Under the glittering arrow the man caught her arm and spun her toward him. The talk and laughter stopped, an odd hush settled over them all. She looked into Mike's contorted face. He'd come back to himself. The ponytail was gone, and the tattoo. Not so bad, then, even though he was raising his hand to hit her. A cold ache drew her attention to her left hand. It had a grip on something. Her purse. She swung it blindly, hitting him hard on the side of the head. A cry went up from the barflies, Mike let go of her, and she bolted for the street. Chairs scraped, people leapt up. She threw open Ryan's door and was met by the round florid face of Putnam Graves. Behind him the Jaguar was parked in the alleyway.

"So there you are," he said. Seeing the crowd gathering at the door he added, "Oh! Well, then," and pushed her behind him toward the car. As Mike charged toward them he held out his hand. Mike stopped, staring at the plump, manicured offering. "How do you do? I'm Putnam Graves, Anna's attorney." He held the smaller man in place. "Do we need the police?"

"Sure, why not?" Mike said weakly. "She fuckin' assaulted me."

"I very much doubt that. But I am sorry you had to be inconvenienced." Hearing the car door close behind him, Pinky disengaged, climbed into the driver's seat and flipped the locks.

"Hey!" Mike came to the window, shouting. "She lies to me, upsets my crippled cousin, now she's crawling around in my garage. Who the fuck are you people?"

Pinky pulled smoothly out into the street. "We won't trouble you again," he called affably, picking up speed. He glanced toward Anna. "I sincerely hope that's true. What on earth have you been up to? What did he mean, assault? And crawling around some garage? That's not even plausible." A light snow was beginning to fall. Ryan's Pub faded away into the swirl.

"It was Mike, after all." To Anna's surprise, her voice was calm and steady.

"Mike?"

"The man I saw. Never mind. I *was* crawling around, looking for this." She opened her hand. The numbers were smeared but legible. "We need to make a call before things close."

"And 'assault'? What was that about?"

"Nothing. It's over now. I have to get to Logan. I have to get out tonight."

But that wasn't to be. Rush hour was well underway, and as they crept out of Somerville through stiffer winds and heavier snow, Pinky called the airport. There'd be whiteout conditions within hours and all flights were cancelled until morning.

"It's not wise to try for Manchester," Pinky said, as they made their way across the Charles toward Cambridge Street and Storrow Drive. Cars were honking and weaving, drivers raging. "How about this? My treat, a night in town."

Anna tried to pull herself out of the churn of her thoughts. A murder weapon. Michele, alone. Colin, alone. The fugue of dreams. Fate. And the dripping thorns, the face inside still hidden.

"I just need a place where I can draw."

"You're safe now, Anna." Pinky, from the warmth of a plush armchair, put a reassuring hand on her arm. They'd checked into the Ritz Carlton, Pinky's home away from home, and gone straight to the lounge. Then Pinky had gone to order their drinks, taking forever, Anna thought, and finally reappearing with a whiskey and something steaming.

"Come on, drink. We want to stop that shivering."

Until he said it she hadn't realized that a kind of quivering had set in, like water in an earthquake. It was an unfamiliar sensation, quite different from fear. More like the feeling when she'd opened her door and found Colin standing there. Maybe Robert was right, a dam was breaking. And then what? While Pinky was away she'd taken out the sketch book she always carried and drawn urgently without a plan, summoning from the dark the man with the ponytail. He'd been the one with the knife, she was sure of it. She looked down at what she'd made. A snake-like coil was forming, a kind of nest in which a smooth stone lay like an egg, and in the stone, an eye.

"Anna?" Pinky held up the toddy, hot buttered rum in a Russian tea glass nestled in silver trestles. The fragile comfort of wealth. She took it and drank. Pinky leaned across the table, watching her like a father at a sick bed. "I'm now officially worried about you," he said. When she didn't reply, he went on. "You and I come from the same stock, Anna. New England to the stony core and back to the Mayflower. We leave the room when a child cries, knowing he'd rather cry alone. Certain of it! Throw your arms around someone and sob like a baby? Unheard of!" He stopped, waiting for her to say something. She couldn't leave him stranded there.

"Yes, that's it, Uncle Pinky," she said. "I'm sorry I've involved you."

"Too late, I'm afraid. By the way, I called your mother. She's fine, of course. She agrees with our decision to stay over. But that wasn't my point. I know you want to be on your own. I've ordered dinner for you in your room in half an hour. But my day was quite productive and you should know what I found. So I'll be quick. All right?"

"Yes, of course. I want to hear."

"All right then." Pinky unwound the silk paisley scarf from his neck and threw it over the back of his chair. A whiff of expensive aftershave drifted across the table. "Last things first. While they were mixing our drinks I made a couple of calls about that number, the one on your palm. Two groups of three, that meant an old-style license plate, our man at Harvard in the '70s. And a honey of a car, by the way. Worth a lot of money now, if the title were clear. Your doctor was a forward thinker. A 1967 V8 convertible, absolute collector's item today, registered in the name of one Camilla Buchanan. Is there such a person, do you know?"

"Robert's daughter." Who, Anna remembered, was a baby in 1988. She kept that to herself. "The car belonged to Larry for a while. That's what made me wonder."

"Almost thirty years on, the title still held by the daughter." Pinky took a long drink of his whiskey. "Ah, that hits the spot." He settled back in his chair while Anna went back to her drawing. "The question is, how did our jolly Irishmen get hold of it, and did they know they'd be stuck with a car they didn't own and couldn't sell? That question takes us to Mass General, which took some doing and a fistful of business cards. But I managed to wrest the following from the Ministers of Health: that Mr. Neal had worked as a pharmacist's assistant, up to the fall of 1978, when he'd suddenly departed for parts unknown. Robert Buchanan was a first year resident that year and so wasn't licensed to, well, for instance, have his own patients or write unsupervised scrip. He, too, vanished for a spell that fall, but came back to complete his residency and go on to a specialization in psychiatry. No one remembered either of them personally, all too long ago. So."

Pinky leaned forward and waited for her to look up from her sketching. "What do we know about the fall of 1978?" He seemed determined to draw her out and she let him.

"That was the year of Laura Blaufeld's death," she said. "She died that summer."

"Exactly!" Pinky pointed an accusing finger at no one, as if he'd caught some dull lawyer in a carefully laid trap. "And did Professor Guthrie enlighten us further?"

Avoiding its dark center, she told him briefly about her visit with Rebecca Guthrie. An accidental overdose was likely, a strong sedative had been used, not easy to come by. She didn't say that the suicide ruling had come with Robert's help.

"All right then," Pinky went on. "That takes us to my next finding, the MedSource business. Now ten years have passed, and the good doctor finds himself once more up to his neck in boiling oil. And who should appear again in the frame but Larry Neal. In some sort of poetic justice, MedSource Labs have been absorbed by an outfit called Forensic Science Laboratories. FSL, for short. I learned that from a very helpful source, an attorney by the name of Patricia Stimson."

FSL. Your monkey. Same old. And now this. "Maura Quinlan's lawyer! Had I mentioned her?"

"No, no, but one thing leads to another. And we legal beagles have a way of finding each other. She had a name for me, the FSL technician who'd done the blood work in the Quinlan case. Not Larry Neal. One Gerald Whelan."

"Whelan?" There was Kathy Whelan, standing over her wreck of a brother, stroking his hair. And Michele shouting out Robert's letter, "Mr. Neal and his associates!" And she, with her hands over her ears.

"So off I go, to FSL. A helpful HR manager dug through the files and found that this fellow had lived in Somerville, at the same address that Larry Neal had given Mass ... Anna! You've gone pale. What am I thinking? You probably haven't eaten since breakfast."

Pinky called the waiter and ordered something quick, bread and olives. A baguette, warm and fragrant, arrived at a snap of the waiter's fingers. While they ate Pinky looked thoughtfully out of the picture window onto Arlington Street. Anna followed suit. Heavy snow had begun to fall. It swirled around the street lamps and made ghosts of the trees in the Public Garden and the Common beyond. Only five miles west, across the Charles River, Robert had posed in a snow bank with Laura Blaufeld. They'd driven these cobbled streets in the flashy red Mustang, the Duke and Duchess of Cambridge, a honey of a life. Snapshots flickered by: the glittering Laura on an Alpine slope, Maura and Gary Timms among the palms, Michele raging as Anna locked the door against her. "Obsession," Michele whispered.

"I'm sorry, what?" Pinky asked. Anna hadn't realized she'd spoken out loud. He was eyeing her with something darker than concern. Her father had been right, he was a sharp one and must guess she was holding something back.

"Warm bread," she said. "Such a simple pleasure. Thank you, Uncle Pinky." She reached across to squeeze his hand.

Pinky held her hand for a moment, then let it go. "Glad to help. But I'm not quite finished. I made a brief visit to the campus police at Harvard, the Blaufeld business. That summer they'd liaised with the Cambridge police, since the girl had just graduated and Buchanan was on the faculty. A toxicology test had been done, of course. The lethal combination was alcohol and a dose of—wait a minute." Pinky patted his jacket pockets and retrieved a little notebook. "'Ativan,'" he read. "A potent sedative used by psychiatrists for anxiety disorders. Now where did that come from? Naturally they looked at Buchanan, but he passed a polygraph so that was that."

Even a polygraph, Anna thought. Could you lie to yourself at such a depth? Anything, anything to protect the core. Anna imagined the scene in Laura's apartment. Give me one more chance, Robert says, let's have a drink, one last time together—like Marco the day Anna left. Just hold me one last time, he says, and then an eruption of primal energies. But whose?

"Anna?" Pinky had gone on, but Anna hadn't heard a word. "My conclusions. Want to hear them?"

"I do."

"Going back to the Mustang, let me hazard a guess. Based on what I know about hostile takeovers—that's one way you might look at blackmail—there's always the temptation of greed. There's Neal, in the shadows for the Blaufeld death and again in the Quinlan business. He must have been reaching for the heart. First the valuable car, then what would be next? The house? Anonymous letters to the wife, who might have money of her own? So I think it was Buchanan's idea of revenge, giving Neal the car but somehow not the title. A kind of joke. Merry Prankster sort of thing. I guess he was the brighter man."

He looked to Anna again with that penetrating gaze.

"Brighter? Yes, he's brighter." Was it Robert who'd said, people look at the world through distorted lenses? We see only what we're capable of seeing. The car was a weapon, Mike Neal had said. To end the blackmail? Or was it, as Mike thought, somehow to end the life of the only man who knew the truth about Laura Blaufeld? She hoped Pinky would keep looking through the lens of the Manchester Gentleman and not the courtroom commandant. Otherwise he'd never let her go.

"Still," Pinky was saying, "I was thinking, to get to the heart Mr. Neal must have gone through all the doctor's cash. Buchanan must have been pretty well-heeled by the mid '80s. That's a lot to pay to wriggle out of a paternity suit."

"His career," Anna said, steering him away. "Wouldn't he lose his license? And then there's his family, his marriage."

"Yes, I suppose. And you learned nothing more from Neal himself?"

"He's badly disabled. He was an addict and overdosed. He can hardly speak."

A question—a doubt?—crossed Pinky's face. Then he gave way to resignation. "That's too bad. There's more to it. There's more to it, I'm sure. Ah well. You're safe and sound, that's all that matters." He sipped his whiskey. "Now what's that you're drawing?"

Anna hadn't realized the sketchbook was lying open on her lap. She looked down at the snake-like nest and the stone, now seeming more like a head with a pair of quiet wolfish eyes. From above a crown of thorns dripped two drops of blood onto the stone. In a corner of the page, hidden by shadows, a man's face was forming. She held it up for him to see.

"Who is this?" Pinky spoke gently, carefully.

"One of my men, the one with the knife." But really, Anna thought, it looked more like Robert Buchanan. "I saw him tonight, for the first time. Parts of him. Now its gone blank again."

Pinky leaned across the table. “Since I’m standing in for Johnny I need a promise. You’ll get this Buchanan fellow out of your life. Whatever the truth of all this, finally it doesn’t matter. Complete break. That’s the only way.”

Anna took his hand. Behind the boyish blue eyes wheels within wheels were turning. “I got what I came for, thanks to you. Now I have to call the airline. I have to get on the first plane tomorrow.”

21

Michele reached for Joe's watch on the bedside table. 5:48. Finally. It was Wednesday. She'd slept maybe four hours, what with Joe coming in late and Robin waking up screaming. What the hell, sleep is overrated. She got up and flipped on the lamp but nothing happened. Right, Joe hadn't paid the bill and everything was shut off. And the fuck still hadn't replaced her cell. At least he'd scored some coke. That should perk things up.

Now Joe was sprawled across the bed, dead out. He'd slept over so she could take the car, then he'd wait for Aunt Ruthie to pick up Robin. The reason she needed the car, she'd told him, was an audition, a little girl/girl flick. He was happy for her getting work, decent money for a change, in something that didn't make him jealous. Good old clueless Joe. She tiptoed to his jacket hung over the back of a chair and transferred the coke to her purse. Lighting a couple of matches, she checked all her papers. Finally she put in Anna's little Buddha, for good luck. She lit a cigarette. Luckily the stove was gas so she could boil water for coffee.

So this is it. This is the day that everything turns around. Since Sunday when Anna had walked out on her she'd thought it over a million times. Every road she went down came back to the same place: Robert would be nuts not to pay her off and get her out of his life. Yes, he'd be angry, but so what. She knew how to work him. And what could he do, kill her? In the middle of the day in the middle of his office? Afterwards there might be more shit to wade through, but at least she knew where she was going. She could start looking for a place, somewhere up north, like Ukiah. She'd heard you could get a pretty nice house for a hundred thousand up there, and Robin could have a puppy or something. She'd have a new life, a car, some clothes. Maybe even Anna, who'd come around once the whole thing was settled. For sure she'd want to help Robin, like a grandma. And her, like a daughter. And some guy would come along. They always did. Or maybe Joe. Whatever.

While the coffee was dripping she stood over the crib and watched Robin sleep. In the lurid orange light spilling in from the street she looked like those dolls you get at Great America. "Fuck, girl," Michele said softly, "you really put me through the wringer. But it's gonna work out. It might even be a good thing you came along." Trailing smoke and ash, she danced. Nine Inch Nails, *Burn*. The baby slept on, dead to the world.

Across the Bay, Robert woke at 8:30 feeling groggy and disoriented. He lay for a few minutes staring at the ceiling, wondering why he was being dragged so painfully back from oblivion. He dimly remembered a fitful night, a sleeping pill taken around 2:00. Then it slowly came to him that it was the middle of the week, a day of patients and problems. He formed a mental picture of his calendar. Anna. He bolted up and raced for the shower.

As he bathed he went over the preparations he'd made for the day. The prescriptions had been delivered Monday by messenger and were now neatly arranged in his meds drawer. He'd persuaded Janice to take the day off, and Kara was on vacation, minimizing the witness factor and shock to any waiting patients. It was never a happy thing to see someone led away by uniformed orderlies. And it would be essential to have everything taken care of by the time Craig arrived at 10:30.

What exactly that meant he couldn't force himself to imagine. He had a vague notion of leading Michele to her car in an Ativan stupor and sending her down the freeway to her fate, goddamn the greedy little bitch. But that would be grossly irresponsible. Innocent lives and so on. A suicide would be better. Yes, a suicide on his doorstep, about which he was ignorant, waiting innocently in his office for Anna to arrive. The act of a lunatic, and the trigger for a psychotic break in the sensitive Ms. Sheffield. Well-framed by him, whatever she might say would seem the ravings of delusion. Then Craig would come, call the police, and testify to everything. But it shouldn't come to that. The papers Michele had shared were, after all, ambiguous, all the legal matters settled. And she didn't have the most damning bit, that scrap of a note from Larry Neal.

Wishing Michele a long season in hell he rushed through his morning rituals of grooming and dressing. As a last touch he made sure his half of Larry's note was in his pocket. He made a quick breakfast since he'd have to skip his croissants. As he stood at the kitchen counter sipping coffee and staring out at the leaden day the phone rang. It was Camilla, wanting to know what he had planned for later and could they grab lunch. She'd noticed that he was preoccupied, he seemed worried about something, and she wanted a heart-to-heart before everybody showed up for Thanksgiving. Fran too, she thought, was weirder than usual, sloshing around the house singing to herself. She wanted him to know she loved him and was there for him.

Hearing this he felt suddenly weak and afraid and had to sit down. He wanted to cry. He wanted to tell his daughter everything, have her hold him and stroke him and say she understood. He couldn't answer her question about lunch. The truth was, he had no idea what might happen today, whether Michele was someone he could control, whether even Anna was if it came to that. And he couldn't imagine what he might have to do between now and noon. If it should all get out of hand, and it was the last day of comfort for him, then it was for Camilla, too. And Ben. And Fran. Well, that might make it all worthwhile.

"Daddy? Daddy?"

"Yeah, honey, sorry. I *am* preoccupied. I've got to go. I have a 9:30. I'll call about 11:00, see how the day's shaping up. Let's have a drink later if we can't do lunch. At César or something. We'll have to see how the morning goes."

"Okay. Call my cell. I might go shopping."

"Get whatever you want, on me. As much as you want, sweetie. Anything."

They couldn't take the clothes off her back.

As it happened, the Mercedes turned onto Santa Cruz from Solano just before a little VW, trailing a thin line of black smoke, came in the opposite way from Marin. Robert was turning into his driveway when he heard an engine whine and looked up to see Michele pulling to the curb. He fought a rising panic. Whatever might happen, their meeting must not take place on the street. Throwing dignity to the wind he sprinted toward the door fumbling with his keys. When he glanced back, Michele was laughing and taking her time. The lock finally yielded. He ran upstairs and slammed his office door behind him, turning the deadbolt for good measure.

The office was dim and cold and he hurried to turn on lights—all the lights—and light the fire. He heard the door open downstairs, but no footsteps followed. That would be like her, he thought: to sneak up the stairs, knowing he was waiting, and time her entrance for maximum shock value. He took off his coat, went behind his desk and opened the top right drawer. Two phials of Ativan were readied, with two new syringes in their plastic wrappings. He closed the drawer again and strained to hear. Not a footfall or even a creaking board. Maybe she'd gone to the bathroom downstairs. Maybe she was cowering there. Maybe after all she was as frightened as he was. He stood behind the desk and waited.

Her knock, when it came, was dramatically loud. Even though he'd known it was coming it made him jump. Fine then, two can play. He sat down and worked on his breathing. Seconds later she knocked again, but he didn't move a hair. Perhaps he could simply wait her out. More time passed. He was beginning to relax a little when the deadbolt clicked and Michele stood in the doorway. She was wearing her favorite getup, the long black skirt, a crop top that let the serpent's eye stare out, and a ridiculous oversized leather jacket. Wagging a key at him, she nailed him with her ice-blue stare, even more glittering than he remembered. Her pupils were pinpoints. A tiny trail of white powder dusted her upper lip.

"Oh yes," she purred, "Mama's just full of surprises." She held up a stained envelope stuffed with papers.

Robert went to her, hoping to regain command. "Stop acting like a child. Come inside." She came in and he slammed the door behind her. They stood toe to toe. "This is the second time you've broken into my place of business." He looked down at her, relishing his superior height and strength. "Give me that key or I'll call the police."

"Bite me," said Michele and dropped the key in her purse. Then she took a piece of newsprint from the envelope and held it up for him to read.

Ivy League Boy Wonder Faces Licensing Board

"You think that surprises me? You stole that from me." He hoped he sounded as brutal as he felt. "That and a lot of other things. Do you imagine you're going to blackmail me? I was exonerated in a court of law. My record is clean. You think you know what those papers mean? You don't."

Michele smiled and batted her lashes. "Then why haven't you called the cops?" She slithered past him, went to his desk, pushed his things aside and perched there facing him. "Doctor Feelgood," she said, cocking her head at him like a bird. "Let's see what else we have here." She took from the envelope an older, yellowed paper. "Hm. 1978. 'Harvard Student's Death Ruled Suicide.' Wonder what that could be about?"

Robert felt his stomach tighten. "Old news, Michele. As I said, that was long ago, all settled. And I have a patient coming in a short time, so how about getting to the point. Which I assume is blackmail."

Michele considered for a moment. Did Robert know for sure that Anna was coming? Was that who he meant? Her brain was skipping and twitching, and she almost wished she hadn't snorted that coke.

"Yeah, that's Anna, a new friend of mine," she heard herself say. He didn't deny it so she kept the plan moving. Trying to look cool, she put the papers back in the envelope. "And I don't need to blackmail you. I'm not in this alone any more. You know Anna's rich, but you might not have noticed how smart she is. She makes things happen and she doesn't like what you've done to me and to your daughter. Robin, I mean, not Ca-mi-llaaa. Robin. The daughter you have with *me*. Anna's very unhappy about how you've treated us. And this stuff?" She held up the envelope. "This is just a tease. Anna's got the rest, all set to mail to the cops if anything happens to me."

That's better, she thought, watching him stand there glued to the floor. "And guess what?" She kept going, to see if she could make him crack. "We've talked to Maura. 'Member her? We know all about her and the blood samples. *Maura and Laura went up the hill,*" she sang, "*but when they met Robert they took a big spill.*' Or maybe a pill. I'm not interested in a fat payoff. I want support, that's all. Just what you owe me. Soooo ...," she threw her arms up, Vanna White, announcing the winner of the hot red SUV. "It's time for D-N-A! Anna's going to get tests and lawyers and everything." But Robert wasn't cracking. Instead he'd started to smile.

"You can cut the cheap theatrics, Michele." He took a small, wrinkled paper out of his pocket. "This look familiar?" He smoothed it out and held it up. It was Larry's note, half of it anyway. That was supposed to be with the stuff she'd left at Anna's. She tried not to show the panic.

"Without this thread you've got no clothes, baby." Robert walked over to the fire and dropped it in. It flared up and turned to ash. Michele's mind went into orbit. All the possibilities, what she knew and didn't know and might invent, came crashing together like wreckage in a tidal wave. She grabbed for the first thing that floated by, the other half of that note.

"I'm not sure, Doctor, but did that piece have the 'L.' on it? L for Larry Neal and his friends at F-S-L?" This might be a good time to take out Peabody, Hawkins, Schultz & Graves. She did. "Oh, and by the way you might notice this is a copy? Anna has the real thing, ready for the cops."

For a moment Robert froze. He looked like an ape, his face was so slack. She wondered if it was possible for someone to have a stroke and not fall down. When he spoke he sounded like a zombie. "It doesn't matter. Larry's as good as dead."

Michele laughed out loud. "Larry's dead? Wow, that's funny, then I wonder who I was talking to in Somerville? They still have the same number, after all this time. And what about the other half of that note? The half with the logo from MedSource Labs. Who do you think has that?"

Now Robert should explode and rage around the room or fall to his knees sobbing and beg for mercy. But he just stood there, gray as smoke, barely breathing. That could only mean Robert knew Anna was coming for sure.

As if he'd read her mind, Robert said, "All right, it seems all roads lead back to Anna. Let's wait for her, then."

So there was hope and a lot of new possibilities. For a second Michele felt a sort of love for the woman. And somehow out of that came a craving, a hunger for a special kind of revenge. She hoisted herself farther onto the desktop, letting her legs dangle carelessly, kicking her thick black heels lightly against Robert's walnut treasure. Bits of mud and wet grass dropped onto the precious Persian rug.

The silence grew longer as Robert struggled to master his thoughts. If Anna was involved, the police might already have been called. And he didn't know for sure where those papers were or the other half of that note. Anything could have happened since he'd seen it under Anna's couch. It rose again, the terror of being absolutely trapped. He wanted to get to that meds drawer, but Michele was too close. When she saw what was in there she'd react like a cornered cat.

"Come over here," he ventured. "Sit on the couch. Let's think this through."

Michele looked at him unmoving, so he went toward her, warily as you would toward a wild animal. Strangely, she began to smile, that beckoning smile he remembered well. He stopped, their eyes met and held. He willed her to yield to him and it seemed to be working. With that porn star pout, she languidly raised her long black skirt, inch by inch, up to her knees, up to her thighs. As she raised it she opened her legs bit by bit until she was fully exposed. The snake's red tongue curled around her thigh, and Robert noticed she still had the Brazilian cut. No thong, no scrap of cloth to hide the little pink tongue sticking tauntingly out, that told him she was really enjoying herself.

She let out a low, stagey moan. "One last time? With me in charge?"

The whole idea made Robert sick, but he saw a spark of hope and with it came a burst of vital energy. He walked slowly toward her like a bull toward a matador. "You in charge? What does that mean?"

"Oooo, the zombie's coming back to life. It means, you do what I say, whatever I want."

"That sounds good, Michele." Guardedly, he put a hand on her naked thigh. It was hot, as if she had a fever. How he'd loved that about her, the slippery strength and the heat. "You know, I've missed you." He came closer still. "I'm sorry it's been so hard for you. Maybe I've been unfair ..."

Michele laughed harshly. "Unfair?" she said. "That's a good one."

She recoiled a little from him as he went on, "... but you don't know. You don't really know the truth."

The hand was now between her legs, expertly stroking and probing. With this leverage, Robert turned her around on the desktop, knocking over pictures and sending papers fluttering to the floor, until he stood between the desk and his leather chair.

"Oh, yes I do, Robert," she was saying, imitating his deep growl. She dragged the hand away. "And that's not what I mean by being in charge."

She grabbed his belt and pulled him to her with surprising strength. It was all he could do not to take her by the hair and throw her to the floor. His stomach tightened, he started to sweat. While she was opening the buckle he slid open the drawer. Go for the neck, he thought, so the drug takes effect in seconds. When she was fully sedated he'd get the information out of her, where he could find his papers. The beauty of Ativan, the patient able to speak, conscious and defenseless. When he had what he wanted he'd give her a second dose. In combination with the cocaine a seizure would almost certainly shut her up for good. Her body would be lying in the hall when Anna arrived. He felt the long body of a syringe. Michele was tugging his belt out of the loops, making it hard to get a grip. Then she suddenly grabbed his sleeve and yanked his hand back.

"What are you doing, you bad boy?"

Christ, he thought, she's going to whip me. Or she's after my DNA. "Condom," he managed. "We don't want to make matters worse, do we?"

"What makes you think I want that?"

"We've always wound up there in the end." Some inspiration made him glance at the clock on the mantle. "And it's 9:45. Anna's coming soon."

Reflexively, Michele turned to look at the clock. Now! He slipped both hands into the drawer, seizing a syringe and the Ativan phial. He turned quickly away, tore off the paper and plunged the needle through the cap of the bottle, hiding the operation below his waist so she'd think he was dressing for the occasion. But Michele was quick as ever.

"What the fuck are you doing?"

She jumped off the desk as nimbly as a monkey. Filling the syringe, he kept his back to her shifting from foot to foot to hold her behind him. She took hold of his jacket and tried to pull him around, a ploy he knew very well how to frustrate. He wheeled toward her, sending her flying backward into the chair. He went for her with the needle, but she had his belt and hit out with it, catching him on the chest. It stung, but not badly.

"Pathetic," he said. He snatched a handful of her hair, yanked her up and pulled her out into the room, squealing and clawing at him. She dropped the belt, he kicked it away. With his other hand he pushed a bit of fluid out of the syringe. He needed her conscious and didn't want an embolism. But all this noise! If Craig came in early he couldn't explain a scene like this. He had to shut her up. He threw himself toward her. They fell backward together across the room and onto the desk, landing on their sides face to face. Michele's eyes, filled with animal rage and terror, reminded him of his years in the psych wards in Cambridge. She might be hurt, she must have been, but with all the cocaine in her system she didn't even know it.

Keeping his hold on her hair, he rolled on top of her and raised the syringe, aiming at a vein pulsing in her throat. But she writhed backward, grabbing his left arm with both hands and baring her teeth. Hampered as he was by holding the needle, he could only buck and squirm and before either could be effective she bit, right through his shirt, with all her strength. His hand flew open, letting go her hair.

Michele flailed wildly to free herself from his weight. The syringe was coming toward her face. She raised one arm to keep it away, pressing the other back onto the desk to save herself from being crushed. Her hand landed on something hard and she groped for it. A small, metallic thing—a pair of scissors. She knew the ones, they were always there on the desk. Thin blades carved with fancy scrolls like feathers. She let out a shriek, and for one second Robert paused, just long enough for her to slither free, leaving him sprawled across the desk. Before he could recover she jumped on his back and drove the scissors into the right side of his neck.

A strange creeping numbness spread across Robert's face. He felt Michele's weight fall away and whirled around, lashing out with the needle. It connected. The force of the blow sent her stumbling away, the needle dangling from her wrist. So the moment had come, never as bad as you'd imagined. Better than that. He actually wanted the thrill of watching her melt under the drug's power. He lunged at her to drive the plunger in. In one deft move she stepped away, pulled the needle out and buried it in his shoulder. The searing pain told him she'd delivered the whole package. He pulled the burning thing away and threw it across the room. But that was all he could manage. A strange weakness came over him and he sank to his knees.

"God," he said, looking up at her.

Both hands were over her mouth, her eyes huge and terrified. "Sorry," she whispered, like a child caught in some mischief. Before he could stop her she reached down and pulled the scissors out of his neck. With a delicate spasm a vessel opened somewhere inside. Its warm fluid ran down inside his clothes. He clamped both hands hard over the place and sat down on the floor. She held the bloody scissors against her chest, shaking like someone freezing. On her wrist was a tiny spot of blood where the needle had pricked her.

"Stupid bitch." His voice was hoarse, and only one side of his mouth was working. "You've killed the Golden Goose."

"What should I do?" Now she was a frightened child, wondering how such an awful accident could have happened. Blood was seeping out between his fingers and he felt his strength ebbing away.

"Call 911." He wanted to lie down but didn't dare. It was important not to stain his lovely rug. When she didn't move, he said gently, "Please, Michele." She got the phone, then stood there chewing her lip, quivering and sweating, her eyes darting around the room, over his face, up to the ceiling.

"Michele." He tried to be calm and forceful. "Please—dial 911."

She put the phone down beside him, found her purse in the debris and stuffed the scissors in. The envelope and papers lay on the rug. She took those, too, and started for the door.

"Michele!" She turned. "I can't let go. This is serious. Please."

She darted back, dialed 911 and pushed the speakerphone button. Then she took two steps toward the door, hesitated and came back with something hidden in her hand. He recoiled from her, but it was only a little Buddha sitting on a lotus. She put it on the rug beside him and ran. He heard the front door slam behind her as the phone beeped and a recorded voice said:

"All circuits are busy at this time. Please call back, or dial 611 ..."

"Christ!" he yelped. He looked at the clock. 9:49. How tricky time is, he thought. Only four minutes had passed since he last saw that clock. The most precious four minutes in all of eternity, the ones he most wanted back. Using his elbow he pressed zero.

A robotic voice said, "Operator, may I help you?" He had to laugh, a gurgling chortle.

"I hope so," he whispered. "I'm calling from Berkeley. I can't reach 911. I've been injured. Seriously. Maybe fatally."

The operator, if she was human, seemed unmoved by this news. "All right, sir, I'll connect you to 911. Please hold on."

Ringing, seconds going by. Robert tried to recall his anatomy books, the nerves and muscles of the neck, the veins and arteries and lymphatics. Oh well, he thought, the damage is done. What difference does it make?

"911," said another vacant voice. "What is your emergency?"

A kind of fuzziness was coming over him. He leaned against the desk, pulling the phone toward him with minimal success. He'd have to strain to be heard. "I'm injured. I've been stabbed."

"Stabbed, sir? Are you saying you've been stabbed?"

"Yes. Stabbed. Stabbed." He wanted to be clear but his jaw didn't seem to be working. Could be damaged nerves or just the Ativan. The little Buddha was sitting beside him and he picked it up and held it against his chest.

"Are you alone there, sir? Is the assailant still on the premises?"

"It's a neck … neck …" He thought he'd better lie down and tried to turn so that his head was near the phone, but it didn't work.

The operator was saying, "What is your location, sir?"

Downstairs he heard faintly the door open and close, then footsteps come slowly up. He looked again at the clock, which had taken on the ominous character of an executioner: 9:55. For once she was on time. He tried to call out, "Anna," but couldn't. There was only a wheezing sound like a leaky bellows.

High above, he could hear a little voice saying, "Sir? Sir? We have your location. Paramedics are on their way. If you can hear me, try to let me know."

The footsteps stopped at the top of the stairs. He gathered his strength and forced out a sound, a groan and scream together, which sent a spurt of blood onto the rug. Someone hesitated outside the door. Goddamn the woman and her fears, her manners, her patrician hauteur. Feeling deep sorrow for his darling Shiraz, he let go of the wound, curled up on the rug, and drifted away.

22

When the sirens started wailing Michele found herself on the corner of Solano and Santa Cruz, across the street from the Matrix Café. She had no idea how she'd gotten there or what to do next. She guessed she'd gone that way by reflex, and she'd forgotten all about Joe's car. She looked back toward Robert's where two cop cars and a white van were pulling up. Just past them, the rusty yellow Bug seemed to scream, *I don't belong here*. But now it was too late, there was nothing she could do about it. And what about Anna? Where the hell was Anna? She'd just have to hang, see how things developed. If only this pain didn't get worse.

She took a quick inventory. Her head hurt badly where Robert had grabbed her hair. Throwing her up against the desk had probably cracked her ribs. They felt hot and bruised. And there was a little black mark on her wrist where he'd stuck her with the needle, that evil son of a bitch. But the shakes were gone, replaced by a creeping numbness that threatened to shut her brain down all the way. She wondered if it might be that drug, whether it might make her pass out. She couldn't afford that, since she'd probably just killed someone.

A crowd started to gather, attracted by the commotion. Next to her a blue-haired lady was trying to keep her Scottie from sniffing Michele's shoes. The little black dog cocked a jet black eye at her, then jumped up going for her purse. It must smell the scissors, Robert's DNA. Secretly, she checked herself for blood. There was only a tiny smear on the front of her shirt, barely visible on the black cloth. Tugging on the leash, the lady looked at her with an anxious, curious smile. To direct her attention elsewhere Michele asked, "What's going on?" Whatever the lady said was drowned out by a siren burst right behind them. A fire truck and a plain black sedan screamed around the corner, bringing a new wave of gawkers. The beat-up looking black guy who usually sat outside the Matrix lugged his plastic milk crate up front and staked out a choice spot.

"Looks like a big one," he said. "Looks like a good one!" He grinned around at everyone, showing blackened teeth. "Prob-ly a heart attack. Fire trucks to a heart attack! Never did understand that." He flopped down on the milk crate and clapped his hands, a kid at the circus. Like a flock of birds the crowd fluttered away a few feet, leaving him alone with his glee. Michele was losing herself among them when the old guy jumped up shouting, "Whoa! There's guns!!"

Michele inched forward, trying to see. Cops were going sideways into the building with guns held out in front of them, while others snuck around the house and poked through the bushes and flowerbeds. They were looking for her. They thought she was still in there. They thought she was armed and dangerous.

"Yeah!" The old man hopped up and down on his teetery legs. "Oh yeah! This is a hot one! This is a good one!"

Michele pulled the leather jacket tight around her trying to hold herself together. A detective was climbing out of the sedan, a tall powerful guy in a long black trench coat, blond with a WWE SmackDown moustache. A real badass, Wyatt fucking Earp. It got very still down there, everyone standing around waiting. Then the cops came out of the building and the paramedics ran in. After a minute the detective went toward the house. That guy from Saturday, Robert's partner Craig, came out to meet him looking seriously fucked up.

They were talking when Anna's gray Volvo pulled around the corner of Marin. It must be ten o'clock and she was coming at her regular time just like Robert thought she would. Like nothing had happened, like Michele didn't even exist. Craig pointed, a couple of cops ran toward the Volvo, and then Anna got out. From here, she didn't look scared—not of them, anyway. More like those moms running to the school where the kids have just been shot. The cops led her to the detective, and after a minute they all went inside.

Michele felt weak, like she was going to be sick. A light rain had started. The crowd of watchers huddled under the eaves of the corner market and Michele joined them, backing around the corner and leaning against the wall. She sat down on the sidewalk, but no one seemed to notice. She rested her forehead on her purse, trying to get her breath. Okay, okay. Maybe Robert wasn't dead. But if he was or he wasn't, it was all over. If he was, Anna would tell. If he wasn't, he would. Or both. Murder or attempted murder, take your pick.

The crowd let out a small collective gasp, bringing Michele back to her feet. She peeked around the building.

Several people in matching windbreakers were carrying a stretcher toward an ambulance that had come while she wasn't looking. She saw Robert's tasseled loafers sticking out one end but couldn't tell whether his face was covered.

"Is he dead?" she said to no one.

"You better believe it!" shouted the man on the milk crate, though he couldn't have heard her. One cop started stringing yellow tape around the yard, another walked up the street toward the crowd, taking a little notebook out of his jacket. Michele melted away around the corner and down the avenue. She wanted to run but she'd attract too much attention. Besides, the pain in her ribs was intense, a deep throbbing ache. There was a Salvation Army a few blocks down, she remembered. She could dump this bloody shirt, the scissors, everything. Get new clothes, be someone else. And then what? The ground opened up beneath her, and in spite of the danger she took off running.

Anna sat on the couch in Craig Helsen's office waiting for someone to talk to her. Because of the shock she'd been given a blanket, tea and Dondrea Roper—a young black officer in a crisp black uniform who sat now just inside the door, writing diligently in a small red notebook. She seemed bright and disciplined and had obviously been told not to communicate with—what? The patient? The witness? The suspect?

Beyond that, Anna knew nothing. The officer who'd met her had said only, "You're Anna Sheffield?" And then a tall man like a cartoon gunslinger had introduced himself stiffly as Detective Richard Holzman. "Please come with us, ma'am." Any moment she'd expected to see Michele, handcuffed or wounded, or dead. As they were climbing the stairs another man had whispered to her, "Anna, I'm Craig Helsen, Robert's partner. Robert's been ..." Holzman had snapped at him, "Mr. Helsen? If you don't mind?" Which the partner seemed to take as a command to be quiet.

And then at the top of the stairs the door to Robert's office had opened. A group of blue-jacketed paramedics had emerged carrying Robert, or his body, on a stretcher. His eyes were closed, and he looked pale but strangely peaceful. It wasn't clear whether he was breathing. A bandage around his neck was leaking blood. Anna saw that the office was full of people in various uniforms, crawling over it like termites. A young woman with blonde spiky hair was on her knees holding up a man's belt. "The snake was about to leave the cage," she said. Everyone laughed. On Robert's beautiful Shiraz was a large stain of blackening blood. A police officer had held up an empty phial. "Ativan," he'd read from the label. Seeing Anna looking he'd rushed to close the door.

Now she waited, her mind churning with fear, exhaustion, and guilt. Late, on this of all days. Logan hadn't opened until Tuesday afternoon, and she'd had to take the red-eye. When she'd made it home at 9:00 a.m., things had gotten even worse. She'd found Michele's number and tried to call but the phone was out of service. There were five messages from Colin. When she'd reached him, they'd fought. She was going to Robert's, she'd told him, to meet Michele. She couldn't go into the Boston business, she couldn't be late. Colin had started to shout. Even knowing the cost, Anna had hung up.

She looked at Officer Roper, peacefully writing, and tried to form a plan. No one seemed willing to share information, so she must be under suspicion herself. Had Robert been conscious, even briefly able to talk? Had he implicated her somehow? Two psychotics in league against him? Robert's body lay innocently on the stretcher, but no time now for that. The important thing now was Michele. Had he told the police about her? Had the papers been found? From the detective's behavior, none of that seemed likely. Which left it up to her to tell what she knew. Now. Or later. Or never.

Rescue from her thoughts came in the form of the giant detective. He strolled in, trailed by Craig Helsen. Officer Roper jumped up and offered him her chair. He took it, turned its back to Anna and sat straddling it, while Roper stood ready to take notes. Oddly, Craig went behind his desk and sat there looking paternal, as if he were presiding over a group therapy session. But no therapy seemed forthcoming when Detective Holzman was the man in charge.

"How you doin'," he began coolly.

Since he obviously didn't care, Anna asked, "What's happened to Robert?"

Holzman narrowed his eyes, making his face hawkish. "You mean Doctor Buchanan?"

"Yes."

"You on a first name basis with the doctor?"

"Most clients are," Craig interjected, drawing an impatient sigh from Holzman.

"Could I ask you to just observe, Mr. Helsen?" He threw the question over his shoulder, then went back to his hard-eyed glaring. Craig sat back fiddling nervously with the buttons of his jacket.

"I've been seeing him for two years. He asked me to call him Robert on the first day. What's happened to him? Is he dead?"

"Not at the moment." Hearing this, Craig looked distressed, and Roper seemed to suppress a smile. Holzman flushed and hurried on. "What I mean, we don't have the current status. He has injuries that could be life-threatening. He's been taken to the hospital." Holzman squirmed in his chair and then asked harshly, "Where were you at 9:30 this morning?" He'd been shamed and now it seemed he was going to get tough.

Anna was surprised by a rising anger. So the police didn't know about Michele and in the absence of other possibilities were focusing on her. Craig must be there to give some sort of psychiatric evaluation. Or they were concerned that she might break down. Whatever had happened here, it had to be Robert's doing. Michele wanted money, not revenge, and he was the one with a reason to kill. But what were the chances that Holzman would understand? She'd spent two years in solitude, in armor of untouchable numbness. She'd retreat into that.

"Miss Sheffield? Trying to remember?"

"No," Anna said evenly. "I was at home on the phone with a friend."

"And what's your place of residence?"

She gave her address. Holzman then wanted to know how far that was and what route she took between here and there.

"And this friend's name?"

She should have known there'd be no way to keep him out of this. "Colin Mills."

"Who is …?"

"My … my partner."

"We'll need a number. An address"

Holzman snapped his fingers and Roper tore a page from her notebook. Anna gave Colin's home address and landline, knowing it would take hours to find him there. Holzman sat silently staring at it for a time. Then he reached into his pocket and took out a plastic bag. Inside was Sensei's Buddha, stained with blood. Anna gasped and reached for it, but of course the detective held it back. It was evidence.

"You recognize this," he said. He glared at her under his brows.

"Yes, it's mine." So Michele had taken it, the day they met, when she was left alone in the house. And then she'd brought it here. Had she known, then, what she was going to do? "Where did you find it?"

"Doctor Buchanan was holding it."

"It's been missing for a week. Please be careful. It's valuable. To me, at least."

"And how do you account for the fact that the victim had it in his possession?"

"I must have brought it with me last week, in my pocket. I sometimes do that when I feel …" She wanted to say, when I feel like murdering someone, but thought better of it. "When I feel shaky."

Holzman looked around the room with an unpleasant, knowing smile. Craig flushed and Roper's intelligent face went carefully blank. Apparently the detective's techniques wouldn't get a four-star review from this audience. Regardless, the big man jutted his face abruptly toward her and asked, "Can we have a look in your car?"

"My car?"

"Your automobile, your vehicle?"

"Why?"

"You don't want us to look in your car?"

Behind the desk Craig leaned forward. His look signaled that she should say yes. What were they hoping to find? Maybe they thought she'd attacked Robert, gone to her car to change her bloody clothes, then pretended to arrive after the assault. Or hidden a weapon or something. That's why they wanted the time and distance to her home. Craig was right, giving in was the best thing to do. She gave her keys to the detective. He went out, slamming the door behind him.

Roper looked at Anna with open sympathy. "Want some tea?"

Anna didn't, but for Craig this seemed to have broken the ice. He got up and stretched, then said to the ceiling, "I've read that the Berkeley Police have lots of officers with degrees in psychology, criminology, that kind of thing."

"Yes, sir," said Roper. "Detective Holzman's new to the department, transferred up here from Fresno." To herself she added, "The Wild, Wild West."

Craig sat again, put his elbows on the desk and his head in his hands. A few minutes later Holzman came in holding up a small bit of paper. "Okay! A parking stub from SFO, dated this a.m. You been somewhere?"

"I was visiting my mother in Boston."

Behind Holzman's back Craig looked up sharply.

"Boston." The big man came closer and stood over her. "That's Doctor Buchanan's hometown, am I right?"

"New Haven," Craig corrected, drawing an exasperated glare. But he went on undeterred. "He went to school in Boston, then lived there for some years."

Anna jumped in. "It was one of the reasons I chose him as my therapist. We had something in common."

Somewhat deflated, Holzman said, "So you were in a rush to get back?"

"Yes, to my appointment."

"That important, huh? Leaving your poor mother at Thanksgiving?"

It was obvious that Holzman didn't like her, any more than the men in Ryan's Pub had, or the townies from Gloucester she'd grown up with. She imagined him thinking *stuck-up bitch*. Well why not, she thought, and stood up almost eye to eye with him.

"My mother isn't poor. And yes, it was that important. If there isn't anything else, I'd like to go home now."

Holzman threw his hands up, surrendering. "Sure, just give all your information to Officer Roper."

Out in the hall Roper took her phone number and helped her into her coat. Behind her the door was slightly ajar and she heard Holzman say, "Well, Doctor?"

Craig answered, harried and unwilling. "Given what just happened here, she's holding up extremely well. Better than I am. I don't know what to make of it, except that Robert was wrong. And I'm not a doctor."

Wrong? About what? Anna didn't have time to think about it. She hurried to the car and as soon as she was out of sight called Colin at work. He was in court. At least she had a chance of getting to him first. She called his cell.

"Colin, I'm so sorry. Everything's changed. Meet me at home as soon as you can. And please, sweetheart, if the police find you don't say anything. Not until we've talked. I love you."

Robert woke up, sure that he'd missed his rounds. The familiar smell of the hospital was unusually powerful and distressing, disease masked by ten kinds of disinfectant, and he tried to shake off the dream he'd had. He was bound to his intern's cot by a web of clinging translucent cords. Someone was feeding him poison through an intravenous drip. But thrashing only brought on the pain, in his neck, his arm, his side. He tried to sit up but was restrained by strong hands. A young man's voice said, "Take it easy, Doctor Buchanan. Open your eyes. Open your eyes."

A welcome reminder. Eyes. They open. He tried it. The young man's face hovered near, too close for comfort. A sweet-faced Latino kid, an odd color of pink and smelling of mouthwash. Nurse, must be.

A voice floated through the room. "How do you feel? Any pain? Can you talk to me?"

"Am I?" Robert asked. It felt as if he'd swallowed sand.

The nurse chuckled. "You be, yes sir," he said. "You are one lucky son of a gun. Want a drink?"

"Martini," Robert croaked.

"Ha, ha!" The nurse held out a plastic water bottle with a straw attached, talking all the time. "Got the vein but not the artery. Delicate little instrument, whatever it was, just perfectly thread that needle. But you might be feeling a little disoriented. You got a load of Ativan, if you know what that is." He took the water away and began checking Robert's drip. "This is just saline, get that stuff out of you quick as we can."

A young woman's face flashed by, features twisted, teeth bared. "What happened?" he managed.

"You're going to have to tell us, when you remember." The nurse raised the bed, straightened the sheets and blankets. "Thing about Ativan, it can monkey around with short-term memory. And you got bit on your arm, not too bad, banged around some, nothing serious. Just the neck. You were stabbed. You lost a little blood, got a few stitches inside and out, and that's going to be uncomfortable for a while. But you'll be home for Thanksgiving." He bustled to the sink, filled the water bottle and put it within reach. "Now I gotta call in the cops. They're waiting to talk to you. Oh, and your family's coming." He put a small plastic object in Robert's hand, attached to a cord. "My name is Manuel. If you get tired, push this button. I'll make them leave you alone."

And he went out, leaving Robert with a storm of images battering his brain. Blood. It was oozing out between his fingers. He was holding a needle, he was searching through a drawer full of papers. There was a girl, looking up with eyes like deep lakes. *Blau*, they say in German. The girl gripped his hand, then slowly went limp, leaving him, enraging him. And another, much nearer, like a blue-eyed tiger wanting his blood. Like the other coming back in another skin to devour him. She, too, had talked about cops. Cops. Not at all helpful, not at all good. Cops mustn't find those papers, or the little girl with red hair, or the regal woman standing back watching from the shadows.

The door opened. A tall beefy man in a long black coat came in. His blond hair was cut like a soldier's and he sported a flamboyant reddish moustache. He looked a little like Robert's coach at Princeton, dressed up for Halloween. Robert started to laugh. It meant doubling painfully over, but he couldn't help himself.

Manuel stuck his head in. "It's okay. He'll be like this for a while. It's the drug."

"Gotcha." The man came and stood over the bed. "Hi, Doc. I'm Detective Richard Holzman. This is Officer Dondrea Roper."

He pulled a chair up and sat down. The young black woman, far more intimidating with her penetrating gaze and starched military stance, took out a notebook. Lying there between them, Robert felt hemmed in and suddenly frightened. Best to play dead until things were clearer. Seeing the detective about to speak, he murmured hoarsely, "I played for Princeton. You?"

"Fresno State. Tight end."

"Running back. Good team?"

"Nah, so-so. So how you feelin'?"

"No idea," Robert said and forced a laugh. Already it was easier to talk. The saline must be working. "Some pain here and there. Neck's the worst."

"And what can you tell us about who assaulted you? Anything at all."

There was a false neutrality in the man's voice that made Robert nervous. Feeling his way, hoping to sound pathetic, he asked, "Can you tell me what happened? That might help."

As if such things were beneath him, the detective nodded to Roper. She flipped back some pages of her notes. "Sometime between 9:30 and 10:00 a.m.—probably closer to 10:00, judging by blood loss—you were assaulted in your office. Your first appointment today was with a Ms. Anna Sheffield, who arrived on the scene shortly after 10:10 a.m. You remember Ms. Sheffield?"

Robert winced with pain. She was the one with the papers, someone had said. The woman in the shadows. Trying to sound daffier than he was, he asked, "Did she bring you anything? Was there anyone with her?"

Holzman stepped in. "What would she be bringing us? Who might be with her?"

That told Robert what he needed to know, and he muttered vaguely, "I don't know. Maybe that's something else."

Holzman and Roper exchanged a glance. "You think you can do this, Doc?" Holzman asked. "We wouldn't ask you, but the sooner you can tell us something, the sooner we'll track her down."

"Her?" Robert's hand slid along a woman's thigh, his fingers touched the hot darkness inside her, black hair lashed his face as he fought for the needle.

"The evidence points that way," the detective was saying. "And your partner, Mr. Helsen, was telling us you thought Ms. Sheffield was stalking you. You thought you might have to put her away for a while. The drug that got you, the Ativan—that was ordered for her, had her name on it. You recall any of that?"

Then it all came flooding back: Michele, the baby, the drawer with the papers, the path back to Larry Neal, and Boston where *blau* is for Blaufeld. And Anna Sheffield, ordering those drugs, the plan he'd made. And that stupid moment of weakness, telling Craig his fears. Anna might know a great deal but for some reason had told the police nothing. If they knew they wouldn't be speaking this way, concerned and sympathetic, regarding him as the victim of a violent crime. If he could just regain his strength he might beat them to her. For that he needed time.

"Doctor?" Holzman said. "You remember something?"

"Craig shouldn't have said that. Privilege."

"Not really. Ms. Sheffield isn't his patient."

"No, but I am, in a sense." Fearing he might sound too lucid Robert shifted and groaned. He went on weakly, "It was all speculation. Worried about her, exploring options. No, no. Not her. She'd never attack me, or anyone."

"And what if she thought you were attacking her?" asked Officer Roper. "I mean, whoever it was?"

Holzman turned to her sharply. "Excuse me," he said, and she bit her lip. "I can see you're tired out, Doc. Just a couple more things. Ms. Sheffield's appointment was at 10:00 this morning. She arrived late, said she was delayed flying back from Boston. You've lived in Boston, right? You know anything about that? She mention she was going to visit her mother?"

Blood freezing in the veins was the stuff of Gothic novels. Now Robert knew what it felt like. "She's always late," he whispered.

Holzman sighed. "Okay. One last thing. There was a struggle, pretty rough. A sharp instrument caused your neck injury. Possibly a letter opener, something like that? You have any idea what weapon we're looking for?"

"Scissors," said Robert, pretending to drift away. "Gramma's scissors. I have many patients, all women, some quite sick. She snuck up behind, I never saw her. Could be anyone. Ask Craig, a list." That should keep them occupied for a while. "So tired," he said, closing his eyes and pushing the call button.

Manuel appeared within seconds. "Okay, that's all for now." He came to the bed, lowered it, fussed again with the drip and the sheets. Robert heard a chair scrape, footsteps go to the door.

"How long 'til that stuff wears off?" Holzman asked.

"Couple, three hours. It's 1:15. Maybe 4:00?"

More shuffling, but the police still seemed to be in the room. Robert shifted, peeking out through slits. Holzman was gone and Manuel was standing with Roper in the doorway, leaning in to hear what the officer was saying. Robert himself could just make it out.

"Would a civilian know how to load a syringe?"

"Possible, I guess," said Manuel, "if they had some time and a lesson or two."

"How about in the middle of a brawl, flying furniture, that kinna thing?"

"Oh, no way. You got to be steady, not to break the needle or stick yourself. And then you got to flick, to get the air out. Even a nurse would have a hard time."

Robert closed his eyes as Manuel came back to the bed. In the hall Holzman's voice said, "Okay, let's go."

"Sir, just one thing," said Roper. Robert held his breath so he could hear. "I was talking to the nurse just now about that needle. 'Snuck up behind him?' That just doesn't make sense. And what about the marks on the desk, the dirt on the rug? Don't you think someone was sitting ...?"

Holzman's voice was rasping. "Listen, Roper, I know you're about to make Detective, and it's great the Lieutenant could spare you. You show a lot of initiative. But if I want your help I'll ask for it, okay? Let's go."

Robert sat up suddenly, startling Manuel. "What's up?!" the kid said. "I thought you drifted off."

"Where are my clothes?"

"Ooo, man of action! Police took them for evidence. Your daughter is bringing some for you. She came by a while ago, you gave her your house keys. Just take it easy if you can."

Yes, dear little Manuel. One mustn't run naked in the streets, no matter how urgent the need. Robert lay back, his thoughts swirling. Every act has its reason for being and cannot be otherwise. Who said that? Dostoyevsky? And what is crime after all? Simply breaking from the strictures of social norms, the so-called law, the coagulation of societal fear. Refuse to be afraid. That would be his mantra, he would cling to that. I refuse to be afraid. Exerting every ounce of will, Robert closed his eyes and managed to strangle the cry rising inside.

23

Michele stood in the middle of the floor listening to Joe's recorded voice drone on. It had taken her hours to get home. At the Salvation Army she'd gotten jeans and a sweater and stuffed her old clothes into a dumpster out back. Then she'd had to walk a mile to the El Cerrito BART. Then some anthrax scare had stopped the trains, some white powder that turned out to be donut sugar. They'd said that on the radio news, which she'd turned on the minute she came in. It was still playing in the background, but nothing about Robert, nothing about a murder in Berkeley. Now on the answering machine Joe was saying some shit about Robin, and that Ruthie wanted her to bring a ton of Coke to Thanksgiving—if she could manage it. Oh, and by the way he'd paid the electric bill. Obviously.

Right, that's why they hadn't called—the police. The power had been shut off. Thank God for small favors. She paced around, thinking about Anna standing there with Wyatt Earp. You could tell at a glance she was smarter. And she'd come to Robert's after the murder, so they couldn't think she'd done it. But what would she do, what would she tell them? Michele couldn't figure it out, couldn't make her mind stop spinning.

She looked at the clock. It was just after 1:00, so maybe it would make the TV news. She turned it on. They were in the middle of it, a slick-looking Mexican girl in a black trench coat standing next to a policeman. He was small and waspy with little round granny glasses. They were both getting wet.

"… a psychotherapist," the girl was saying, "an author and a lecturer at the University. Apparently he was stabbed this morning after coming to work here"—she gestured backwards—"in this quiet residential neighborhood in North Berkeley. With me now is Sergeant Tom Baldwin of the BPD. Sergeant, do you have anyone in custody? What can you tell us about this shocking attack?"

Attack? Did that mean Robert wasn't dead? The Sergeant didn't really answer her question. "Well, Candice, first we want to reassure people in Berkeley, there's every indication that Doctor Buchanan was attacked by someone he knew. This wasn't home invasion or anything like that, so people shouldn't be unduly alarmed. We have a number of promising leads and we're pursuing them vigorously."

"And were there any witnesses?" Candice wanted to know. "Have you found a weapon? Do you have any idea what might have happened here?"

"As I said, it's too soon to release those details to the public. But we do want to urge anyone who was in the neighborhood this morning and saw anything unusual to call the Berkeley Police." He gave a number.

With nothing more to say the Sergeant was cut out of the picture, leaving Candice looking soberly into the camera. In the background, just in the frame, was the yellow fender of Joe's Bug.

"So that's all we have for now, Ken. A mystery unfolding here in Berkeley on this dark rainy day before Thanksgiving. Now back to you."

Ken the Anchorman pulled a long face. "Candice Sanchez, in Berkeley. A terrible beginning of the holiday for the family of Doctor Robert Buchanan." Then he brightened up. "Okay, well, let's take a look at the Bay Area's weather, 'cause we just might have some good news there. A break in the storm is expected..."

"But is he dead?" Michele screamed at Ken. "You didn't say if he's dead!"

She flipped through some other channels, but at only 1:04 they had all moved on. She stood for a second watching some bombs exploding in a desert somewhere, then threw the remote across the room and grabbed her hair as if she'd tear it out by the roots. She fell on the floor writhing and sobbing. The picture of Robert when she pulled out the scissors kept flashing in her head, his face turning to smoke like some special effect, his blood pouring down like lava. Between flashes she thought she should go to the kitchen, get a knife and slash her wrists. Just get the whole thing over with. But the neighbors might be listening. They'd call the cops to see what was going on now with that crazy bitch in 201. As suddenly as she'd started, she stopped the thrashing and crawled to the door to listen. Nothing and no one. It was the day before Thanksgiving. They'd all gone home to their families.

She sat with her back against the door. She was dying of thirst, but when she pulled herself up the pain in her ribs took her breath away. She went to the long mirror leaning against the wall and lifted her shirt. A huge purple bruise was spreading across her right side. Even through the Garden's colors she could see it growing. She threw off the rest of her clothes. Seeing herself like this, all frail and battered, made her cry. She was so thirsty, and there was no one even to bring her a glass of water. With her arms around her waist, she stumbled to the sink and was drinking out of the faucet when the phone rang. She ran to it, turned on the monitor and waited, gasping with fear. It seemed forever until Joe's voice said, "You can leave a message for Joe, Michele, or Robin."

And then Joe came on for real. "Shelley, Shelley!" He was whispering. In the background the car shop was clanking and whirring. "Shelley, if you're there pick up. Pick up, goddamn it."

Her voice came out like a little girl's. "Joe, Joe … I'm hurt."

"What the fuck is going on? I heard this report on the news …"

Good, so he knew. That made it easier. She broke in sobbing, "It was Anna, that woman I met. I'm hurt. I had to leave the car. It's at Robert's, Buchanan's office. Please, don't freak, just go get the car. Then come home. Please. Please come home."

You had to hand it to him. Even if he was messed up behind it, he'd do it, she knew he would. She hung up and sat on the bed, tears pouring down. Maybe it was Joe after all, the one she was meant for. Maybe this would all blow over and they could go on like before. Curling around this comforting thought, she wrapped herself in a tattered robe and fell into an exhausted sleep.

Anna was wakened by the telephone ringing. She found herself on the couch, the fire she'd built earlier burnt down to embers. The clock on the mantel told her it was just after 4:30. Then it must be Colin. The ringing was stopped by the answering machine, then started up again. No, it was someone who didn't want to leave a message. Michele. She ran for it.

"Anna?" The man's voice was vaguely familiar. In the background there were muffled traffic sounds.

"Who is this?"

"Craig Helsen."

Anna hesitated, wary and alert. Holzman had been so careful to keep them apart. Was he hulking now beside Robert's partner, feeding him a script?

"Are you calling for the police? Are they with you?"

"No, no, of course not! I'm in my car. I just dropped Robert's car at his house. He's with his daughter, she's bringing him home." A softness in his voice made Anna think he'd been crying.

"Are you all right?"

"I should be asking you." He paused for a moment "I wanted to let you know that Robert's going to be okay. Amazing piece of luck. I was afraid the police might not tell you. And I'm upset about this morning, the way they treated you. Robert was your doctor after all, and I know you didn't do this."

"All right. Thank you for that." There seemed to be more. Anna waited.

"I wonder," Craig finally said, "if I could come by?" Of course, he'd overheard when she gave Officer Roper her address. "Robert doesn't live far from you. I'm right around the corner. I'm imposing, I know, but there are things I need to tell you."

Ten minutes later they were sitting at the dining table. While she'd slept the weather had changed. The storm had moved on and outside the French doors the sunset world was glowing with a deep golden light.

"I'll get right to the point," Craig said, taking the tea she offered. "I should be telling this to the police, but I don't understand well enough what's happening. There are implications for our practice, you see. Robert is our mainstay, our MD. Our building is in his name. If this goes badly we could all be out on the street in weeks." Craig looked at Anna with tired, red-rimmed eyes. "I knew he was wrong about you the minute I met you this morning. Robert made you out to be a wreck, on the brink of psychosis. But you're solid, that's clear. If it hadn't been for the rape you wouldn't have seen a shrink in your life, am I right? I'm relying on that."

"Nothing you say would surprise me," she offered. "If you're worried about damaging the relationship, there's nothing left to damage."

"So it's true," Craig said. "You did go to see Robert's wife. You found out about Maura Quinlan."

"You knew about Maura?"

"We knew in a general way—we partners, I mean. We knew there'd been a hearing, a trial. He told us, showed us some press. He was proud of it! Winning, you know." Craig shifted uncomfortably, ran his hands through his rumpled hair, then turned to her earnestly. "So, Anna. Was Robert ...? Did he try ...? Were you ...?"

Should she laugh or be sick? "God, no!"

"All right, don't worry. It's all right." Craig patted the table in front of him as if it were a hand, then got up and went to look out at the garden. A light wind had come up and drops of gold were falling from the trees. "Do you know who said, 'I am vast, I contain multitudes'?"

"Walt Whitman, I think. And isn't it 'large'?"

"Pardon?"

"'Do I contradict myself? Very well, then I contradict myself, I am large, I contain multitudes.' It's more generous that way, don't you think? More on a human scale."

Strangely, Craig laughed. "What a perfect Robert twist. Instinct! Energies! You artists never know what happens to your work once it leaves you, do you?" The laughter soured, became bitter as he went on, gazing out at the fading light. "God, the things we don't see right in front of us, the endless distortion. I loved Robert but he used me—I realize that now—to pump himself up. I admired him. I'm good at that, and it's what he wanted most. Admiration. Narcissism is a hard thing to live with, horribly isolating. Torture, really. I forgave him all the time." He turned to look at her. "The shadow, you see. We're all floored by it when we meet it. Whether it takes the form of attraction or repulsion doesn't seem to matter.

He was a shadow for me, and maybe you for him. And he for you? He talked about you as if he were breaking a horse, and he's no horse whisperer. I'm sorry to be so blunt."

"I'm grateful. I need this kind of clarity."

Craig came closer and stood looking down at her. "What happened was, he was stabbed and drugged. There was a violent struggle, obviously not with you. The drug that got him was ordered *for* you, though. A potent sedative called Ativan. You must have threatened him somehow—his professional image, his self-image. Nothing could be more enraging. He was going to put you in care. Maybe—Jesus, I can't say it—disable. Even kill. You, or someone." Craig dropped the soft manners. "Who is it? You know, don't you?"

Anna stood up. "You *are* here for the police!"

"No! No, I'm not." He came to her offering his hand. "I'm here to warn you. And her, whoever she is. Someone from his past? Never mind, I won't press you. But if you can you should tell her, Robert is not someone to toy with. He won't back down. The police may not know who she is, but obviously he does."

"What do you think he'll do?"

Craig gazed into space, conjuring terrible futures. "Try to regain control. What form that might take I don't know. Beyond my imagination, I'm afraid. So we all have to think carefully what to do now. We who know things." He looked at her, begging for help. "I hope I haven't made things worse."

But there was nothing she could do for him. After a long silence he admitted defeat. "I should go." He hurried into his coat, looking stricken and ashamed. At the door he said, "Don't worry, I won't go to the police. It's all conjecture, and after all Robert's still with us. I'm sorry. Truly, truly sorry."

When the door closed behind him Anna leaned against it, unable to move. What might happen next was beyond Craig's imagination, but not hers. Larry Neal's muddy eyes searched her face, his maimed hand pulled her down. There was something else he'd said, that she'd forgotten until now. E dibby. Eye dowa. She'd thought he meant "I" something. But what if it was "i", as in, "like." He called himself Owie, Owie for Larry. So Owa was Laura. It was perfectly clear. He did me. He did me like Laura. And now Michele.

As far as Anna knew there was only one place Michele could go, and that was home to Robin and Joe. She grabbed her coat and purse and was running out when Colin's car turned into the driveway.

"No, no," he said as he stopped beside her. "This time you're not leaving."

"Okay, we're home!" Camilla said merrily.

Robert followed his daughter into the living room. He let her help him with his coat and guide him to his favorite chair. The Ativan had been flushed out, and, if it weren't for the pain, he'd feel close to normal. Still, the house looked like a stage set, and the rooms seemed dressed for a photo shoot. Even Camilla looked fake in her L.A. gear, the silk-soft leather jacket, super-tight stretch pants, acid-green tank top, some filmy little lace shirt over it. All new, thanks to him. Perhaps his distress was the fault of Vicodin, or the trauma.

Or was it the knowledge that this was the whole package, all he had gained from his long struggle?

"Is that how you spend my money?" he heard himself say. "Don't you know it's winter?" Camilla just laughed.

He sat down and looked out of his huge picture window. A spectacular sunset was forming over the Golden Gate—the kind of night he'd always loved, nature unleashed and madly dramatic, Count Basie on the piano, a bottle of Veuve La Grande Dame on ice, some woman melting on the couch. Now it was like someone shrieking in pain.

"What can I get you, Daddy?" Camilla stood over him looking down with motherly concern. "Want your pj's?" She'd brought jeans and a layering of shirts to the hospital, and now she wanted him undressed again and helpless. Her manner was cloying. It made his skin crawl. Luckily he hadn't forgotten how to pretend.

"No, honey, I'm not sick. I got worse than this playing football. It's mainly the drugs. A strong cappuccino, three shots, that's what I need."

Camilla cocked her head to one side and laughed dismissively, for a moment horribly Fran-like. "I don't think so," she said.

Before he could check himself he stood up and snarled, "I am a doctor and I know what I need. Get me the goddamned coffee!"

"Fine! Kill yourself!" Camilla ripped off her jacket and threw it in a heap on the floor. "They said you'd be like this," she called on her way to the kitchen. The espresso machine ground and hissed and soon she plunked a mug down on the table beside him. "Knock yourself out. Now I'm making you some dinner."

"Just soup, please."

"Yes, my Lord and Master." And she stomped back into the kitchen.

He sat and drank. She'd made the coffee boiling hot, her little revenge, so he had to take it in tiny sips. But soon he felt it working and he turned his attention to the one thing in life that really mattered now: Anna Sheffield and his papers. They had to be found and destroyed. Once they were gone, the written history—mostly press accounts—would be old news, not evidence. With the benefit of caffeine it all seemed brighter now. Fran, for instance, was unlikely to reopen the Quinlan affair—she'd want to keep Robert up and earning. Larry, even if he could talk, would not be taken seriously, and the gang of felons that surrounded him had everything to lose by getting involved. As for Laura, a court had ruled. Unless new evidence had come to light, that was final. Besides, he was innocent, as anyone would understand when they knew what had really happened that night.

But Anna, there was the rub. What a cool one she'd turned out to be. When he'd gone to her home on Saturday she must have had the papers there. Of course she couldn't be bought and she'd be cold to any appeal to reason, at least from him. Worst of all, she'd gone to Boston after he'd left her. Had she gone on Michele's behalf? Is that what Michele meant when she said they had talked to Maura? If so, then why hadn't Anna given his papers to the police? They'd prove, or at least suggest, a strategy of self-defense in any case brought against Michele.

Robert gazed out toward the city where the girl was surely hiding. It was growing dark now, only a few streaks of brilliant rose highlighting the massive cumulus clouds rising out of the Pacific. Behind them another storm was gathering, jet black on the horizon. He imagined Michele surrounded by these wonders, running like a rat through the alleys.

And then it came to him all at once. What an idiot he'd been. She'd lied. Anna didn't have his papers, had never had them. Michele had them herself and Anna was protecting her out of a misguided noblesse oblige. How deep that went he couldn't be sure. But he could count on Michele always to put her own interests first. If he had Michele, Anna might be persuaded to stay out of it. Colin had come back. She now had something to lose. And, he thought with a rush of inspiration, there was one certain way to Michele's heart. As far as he knew she wanted only one thing—him. And as things stood now, he was willing to give himself, or seem to. He saw them standing together in a world of neon hearts, a place of pink plywood pews and white paper wedding bells—the Chapel of the Chimes he'd once seen on a biopic about Elvis. Only the sound of his daughter rattling in the kitchen kept him from howling with laughter. It could actually work! Michele's back is against the wall. God knows she's crazy enough. And for once she'll wear white. But he had to find her first.

He got up from his chair and began to pace, the pain in his neck throbbing with every step. He'd been rash not to get a number and address when Michele had come last week, one of many mistakes. He'd given in to panic, but that wouldn't happen again. Still there must be some trace, something she'd said. When they'd met she was working as a stripper. That meant North Beach, or the Tenderloin. A name flickered at the edge of consciousness, something to do with Joe. His father—cousin? uncle?—owned a place where she danced and tended bar. It had a silly name, making him think of candy.

He went to the telephone table and brought the Yellow Pages back to the couch. Sex clubs, that's what he needed. Under *Adult Entertainment* he scanned along the names: Crazy Horse, Kit Kat, The Garden of Earthly Delights. Then Sweetcakes. Michele stood, her back to him, the serpent's coil around her waist rippling in the firelight. With her hands she stroked her sleek white haunches, inviting him to her. Sweet indeed. She'd gripped the mantel as he took her from behind, sinking his teeth into the pale flesh of her neck. He should have gone right through to the bone. He looked up. Camilla was standing over him with a steaming bowl. He closed the book, too late.

"Whatcha doin'?" His daughter eyed him with amusement. "The drugs punching up your libido?"

He tried a laugh. It sounded hollow. "A guy can dream," he said.

"Seriously." She put the soup down and sat, pinning him with a hard look. "Are you remembering something?"

"My mind's a mess right now, honey. Sorry to put you through it. More than anything, I need to be alone for a while. Your mom will want you home. And we'll be together tomorrow. I just need to sleep."

"You just had three shots of espresso, Dad."

"Different strokes, sweetie. It calms me sometimes."

Camilla sighed but got up without questions. As she was getting her things another inspiration hit. "Take the Mercedes, honey. I know you love to drive it." Better to have her RAV4, a less conspicuous car. It was brand new, her birthday present, and the dealer plates would serve him better. "Just leave your keys. Makes me feel safer to have a car around."

"Okay, Daddy. Call if you need anything." She kissed him carefully on the cheek. "I hope they kill whoever did this to you."

"Easier said than done."

The moment he heard the Mercedes leave the driveway he went up to dress. His pearl gray Armani slacks were just the thing, with a black turtleneck to hide the bandages. His Eddie Bauer jacket completed the look, a wealthy bachelor on the hunt for kicks. He stood in front of the mirror, seeing himself for the first time since morning. A little the worse for wear, he judged, but good enough for a midnight ceremony in Reno. From there it would be easy, if it came to that, to slip through the moonscape of central Nevada, along the desolate Arizona border and on to an extended honeymoon in Mexico. He packed a small bag, laughing to himself. Then he gathered cell phone, credit cards, check books, birth certificate, passport and bundles of cash he had hidden here and there. Downstairs he added Vicodin and Ativan tablets, and with a rising thrill ran out into the gathering dark.

24

When the hand touched her shoulder Michele scuttled, half-conscious, to the corner of the bed and turned to fight the man with claws out and teeth bared. But when she opened her eyes it was only Joe. In her crazed state she thought she must be dreaming. He seemed to have a sleeping baby in his arms.

"Joe! What the fuck?"

He knew what she meant. "I had to get her, Shell," he said. "That's why it took me so long. Ruthie was freaking out. But I got the car. Relax, babe, it's me."

Michele looked at the clock. It was already past 5:00. Joe tiptoed away and put Robin in her crib, giving Michele just time enough to get out of bed and stand ready to show off her bruises. She wanted him to get how much pain she was in. It might keep him from asking so many questions. He came around the partition and stopped dead in his tracks.

"What'd he do to you?" He came to her smelling of car grease and sweat and for once she didn't care if he smeared her all over. When he pulled her to him she screamed for real. He let her go, ran to the wall and smashed it a couple times with his fist. "Fuck! Fuck! I'll kill the motherfucker!"

"He's already dead, Joe." Michele started to sob.

"Dead?" Joe wheeled around and gave her a weird look. "Where'd you get that? He's not dead. He's in stable condition at Alta Bates Hospital."

Michele had thought the one thing she wanted in the world was for Robert to be alive. But the feeling of his hands on her throat, the needle coming toward her, rushed back in behind a bolt of fear. That wouldn't be the end of it, he wouldn't leave it there. "How do you know?" she heard herself ask.

"I got it out of them when I picked up the car. Cop came right up, wanted to know what time I parked and if I noticed anything. Shit, girl, you get me in some situations. Plus, I got a ticket! Now what the fuck happened? What were you doing there?" Seeing her face all twisted up, Joe pulled her close again. "Come here, sit down." He led her to the bed and sat facing her, holding her hand. "So what happened? You said it was something to do with that woman?"

Like someone else was telling it, a story started to spin out. How Anna had some big thing going with Robert, how she'd found out he'd made it with some patient back in Boston and didn't trust him anymore. How Anna was rich and used to suing people and wanted to "get him," as she'd put it. Michele had felt sorry for her, she seemed so lonely—all alone, raped and all. But then things had gotten complicated. Anna had started giving Michele presents and money and sucking up to her, and Michele was just beginning to wonder what it was all about when Anna asked her to meet today at Robert's. She was going to have it out with him and wanted Michele's support.

"What's that mean?" Joe asked.

"She'd found these newspaper articles about the woman in Boston. She had proof. She knew he'd be pissed and I think she wanted a witness."

Michele paused for a minute. So far this sounded all right, just changing places with Anna, but soon she was going to run into trouble. Stuff would come out in the news later on. They'd already said they didn't have a suspect. What would Robert say when he talked? And Anna? The main thing now was to get an alibi from Joe, for when the police found her, then find a way to get those papers to the cops. She tried it out in her head, what she'd say. Look in her studio, you'll find something there. I saw the whole thing! She's crazy, a psychopath, not what she seems. She's jealous, angry, vicious. But she didn't mean it, she didn't mean to do it ....

The silence was getting deep, so she looked up at Joe to see how he was taking it. He had that mad dog look, his jaw jutting out, his eyes hard and scary. Carefully she put her hand on his face and stroked his cheek. She tried to sound small and sorry.

"Hey, Joe, you look like you don't believe me."

"I just don't get it, Shell. I mean, why? Why would that lady—I mean, she looked like a college professor—why would she try to kill a guy for something he did when she didn't even know him? And she wanted you there? Is that what you're telling me?"

Michele tried not to scream at him. "Haven't you heard what I've been saying? She has a thing for me, and Robin. She's messed up. Maybe he was fucking *her*, I don't know.

Anyway, she didn't try to kill him. Just—we got in there and one thing led to another. The two of them were arguing, and Robert just went to the desk and got out this needle, and he was trying to give Anna, like, this injection. Poison, I don't know. I couldn't let that happen, so I jumped him. He threw me across the room. And then Anna came up and stabbed him. She stabbed him in the neck with a pair of scissors."

"Holy shit!" said Joe. "What'd you do?"

"I ran. I ran away and left her there." She started to cry for real. "She must have gotten away somehow. I didn't know what to do. And now she's going to say it was me! She knows I have a criminal record, I told her. I know it was stupid. I should turn her in, but it'll be me against her, and who are they going to believe?"

"Well, she hasn't said anything yet or there'd be cops all over this place." Joe held her and stroked her hair but she could tell he was still thinking. After a minute he said, "Hang on a minute—Buchanan will tell them what happened."

"Not if he's worried about that woman. The thing in Boston. Maybe not."

"Maybe," Joe said. "We just don't know. We'll just have to wait and see."

"But I was with you, Joe, right? You'll say I was with you."

"I got to work at 10:00. I can say you dropped me off."

"And what if they see the car, find out it was there?"

"I'll take it to Frank's for a while, borrow a junker from the shop. Fuckin' hell." He sounded bone-weary.

And then Robin called out from behind the partition: "Dada!" In a way it was a relief, to get away from the questions and Joe's dark, searching looks. Michele went, gave her a bottle and stood absently stroking her hair until she drifted off again. It was maybe five minutes, but when she went back it had all gone to hell. Joe was standing in the middle of the room with his head down and his arms crossed over his chest. Behind him, her purse was turned upside down on the bed, her stuff scattered all over. Joe held some papers in his fist. He shoved them out toward her as she came across the room.

"I was looking for cigarettes. So what about this?"

It was the letter and the envelope with the clippings. She was sure she'd dumped all that behind the Salvation Army. Her mind was going crazy, trying to find something to say, someone to blame.

"You blackmailing him?" Joe took a step toward her.

"It was her," Michele said. "Anna must have put them in there."

"Bullshit." He'd seen through the whole thing and now his tone was deadly. "You didn't say there was a baby, with that chick in Boston. So? Is this baby mine?"

"You know she is, Joe."

"You fucking cheap lying little whore. I remember when you told me, I thought, wait a minute. We'd been broken up for two months. That's when it started with him, didn't it? Didn't it?!" He came to her, right in her face, and she was sure he was going to strangle her. Instead he took her hand and shoved the empty envelope into it. "This has blood on it. His, right? Good for you, you can get a paternity test." He started for the door, shoving the papers in his pocket.

"Joe! Jesus! You're going to the cops? What are you going to tell them? Don't do this! You're Robin's Dad, no matter what. You can't just walk out on her."

"I'll tell them whatever I feel like when it happens. And hey, watch this!" He went to the door, stood there with his head down and his hand on the knob. "No. No. No," he said to himself. He turned back, his face a mess of rage and tears. He brushed past her and disappeared behind the partition. *Man Kills Self and Family*, Michele imagined. It happens. It happens all the time. She ran toward him, but he came out carrying Robin, her blanket, her favorite rabbit. He threw open the door. "You're on your own."

The door slammed, feet clattered down the stairs, and they were gone. Everything got blurry. Michele's knees gave out and she sank to the floor. If she didn't do something quick this emptiness would swallow her whole. She crawled to the phone, dialed 411, and asked for the number of the Berkeley Police.

"Okay, Anna, why did you go to Boston?" Anna and Colin stood together in the hall. He'd persuaded her to come inside, but she wouldn't sit or take off her coat. When he'd heard she was going to find Michele all the sweetness had gone out of it. "You're putting me in a tight spot," Colin went on, his lawyer face sharp and pinched and ready for a fight. "We're withholding evidence in a felonious assault. Possibly attempted murder. We know about Michele and we should come forward. I should, anyway. At the very least I'm coming with you now."

"You can't." Anna moved into the living room, leading him away from the door. "She doesn't know you. And, just to be clear, it was an assault by him on her."

"That's what you believe. It could have been anything. We don't know what happened. She had motive—the baby, if Robert refused to take responsibility."

"Yes, and she's half his size. His belt was off, Colin. I saw it when I went past the office. Do you think he'd let her do that to him? He took it off himself, to beat her, to rape her ..." Anna felt tears coming and wiped them angrily away. "She's just a child. All she wanted was support. She didn't understand what she was caught up in. You don't understand."

"All right, then tell me." Colin came closer. His voice was edgy and demanding. "You went to Boston because of Robert, yes? What did you find out?"

"If I tell you you'll only have more to lie about. The police know we talked earlier, and they're going to want to talk to you. They're looking for you now. The more you know the worse it will be. All I'll say is, Michele has some of Robert's papers."

"You mean besides the press, the Quinlan business?"

"She got back into the office."

"Papers concerning what?"

He leaned into her, making her want to run. She went to the fireplace, trying to find the right distance from him. "I can't tell you! But she was fighting for her life today. Colin! She was fighting for her life."

"And aren't you? Haven't you been?"

"Oh, sure! I've been fighting—with three million dollars in the bank and more coming, two houses in the Berkeley Hills, a loving family, devoted friends I could afford to drive away. And you. Most of all you. I don't blame you for leaving. Who can stand by and watch someone, someone they love ...?"

"Disappear? Vanish into some unknowable hell? How about asking me to stand by now and watch you step on a land mine? Jesus, Anna!" Colin went back to the hall as if he might walk out, then came back to her. "Two people tried to kill each other today. From what you've said Michele is a little bit smart and a little bit crazy. Look! She's trying to blackmail this guy. If you know about those papers you're involved in a conspiracy. At least that's what a prosecutor would argue. And Buchanan's only injured. He's going to recover and then what?"

Anna couldn't say what she was thinking. "It's my fault. I stirred it all up." She started for the hall but Colin blocked her way. Michele would hit him, shove him aside. Anna tried not to shout. "Don't do that. I'm only going to the city for a couple of hours. I may not even find her."

"Okay, that's great. But the police are going to be there when I get home. You expect me to lie to them? I'm a lawyer, Anna. This is obstruction of justice."

"Don't go home, then. Go to, I don't know—a movie. Just for a couple of hours. Then we'll figure it out together."

"A movie. Right. Got any recommendations?" She'd never seen him so tired and grim. "You are the stubbornest person I have ever known. But you're not stupid, and this is stupid."

"You're trying to control the uncontrollable." Anna said. "This is the way back to you, can't you see that? I won't abandon this girl, and no one can help me but her."

Colin pulled her to him and she let him. She let herself rest there. "Okay, then, here's what I'm going to do," he said. "I'm going back to the office. I'm calling Jack Warren. He's the best defense attorney I know. We'll be here when you get back." He pulled away and looked her hard in the eye. "And here's something *you* can't control. I'm sticking with you no matter what."

And he was gone. As Anna stood at the door watching him turn onto Cypress, a large black car pulled into the driveway and parked close behind the Volvo, blocking it in. Richard Holzman got out. He came to the door, cold and mocking. "You going somewhere?"

"What are you doing here, Detective?"

Holzman went all sugary, a style even more repellant than his bullying. "I'd like to ask you a few more questions, since you seem to have recovered from the shock."

"I shouldn't talk to you without a lawyer," Anna said and started to close the door.

"You talked to us before. What's changed?"

"If I answer that question I'll be talking to you without a lawyer. Goodbye."

Holzman seemed to find that amusing. He put his foot against the door. "So why are you afraid to talk to me without a lawyer? Buchanan wasn't that important to you? Or was it something else? We found some pretty amazing stuff in his office today. You ever see his notebooks?" Anna's heart started to race. "He had these nicknames for his patients. You were The Mouse, did you know that? Used to be the Artistocrat. Clever, huh?" When Anna didn't respond he asked, "Mind if I have a look around inside?"

"You're kidding," Anna managed.

"Well—no." He tried to look simple and good-natured. "I just want to be sure you're safe. You're a material witness. The perpetrator might have seen you at the crime scene. She might be watching us right now, waiting for you to be alone."

"What is it I'm supposed to have witnessed?" Anna asked.

Holzman grinned. "By the way, was that the boyfriend — oh, sorry, *partner*—leaving just now? Funny, we haven't been able to reach him all day. Putting your heads together?"

"I'm going to say goodbye," Anna said. But Holzman didn't budge. His thick body blocked the door. He smelled of Old Spice and sweat, and his breath was cloying—stale coffee and chewing gum.

"Please move away," she said.

Instead, Holzman leaned against the doorframe. "I'm just curious, though. If I found out my shrink was calling me The Mouse—man! I'd be furious. Makes you wonder how good he really is. At the very least." He was trying to sound cool but under the glare of the porch light his face was turning a dark unhappy red. Unbidden and unwanted, the old trembling began.

"Get away from the door," Anna said. Her car keys were heavy in her pocket, and she wrapped her hand around them to use as a weapon. Whatever might have happened next was interrupted by the ringing of Holzman's cell.

"Shit," he muttered. "Yeah?" He listened, then looked at Anna with a broad, delighted smile. "Okay, thanks a lot, Roper. That's great news." He walked over to the side of the house and looked down the path toward the studio. When he came back he was smirking. "Looks like the old worm has turned. Your story's sprung a leak, and we just might be able to get a search warrant. Later tonight, wanna bet?"

Saying nothing, Anna went into the house and locked the door behind her. Then she tiptoed into the living room and looked out between the blinds. Holzman sprinted down the driveway to his car. His screeching tires left a puff of smoke hanging under the streetlight. The Mouse—small, twitchy and frightened. So that's how Robert thought of her. And perhaps, after finding Larry's note, he thought The Mouse had scurried off with his papers. Could he be that brazen, using the police to find them for him?

Holzman had been looking for something at the back of the house. Something searchable. Anna ran out and felt for the key above the studio door. She found it far down along the lintel, in a place she'd never put it herself. Everything inside was as she'd left it on Saturday except there were odd marks on the floor, as if someone had tried to mop it without water. Looking more closely, she found a tiny handprint in the dust. The granite pillar towered over her, and as she looked up a serpent squirmed out of its bloody gash and danced for her. Stepping carefully, she took a flashlight from a shelf and shone the beam around the floor. A trail of boat-like shoe prints led to a far corner, to the closet where she stored her heavy tools. Keeping to the edge of the room, Anna went to it and looked in. The corner of a manila envelope stuck out from behind her polisher. Michele. A little bit smart and a little bit crazy. The police would be there soon with a warrant, but so would Colin and his lawyer. And so would she and Michele. She could still feel the big detective leaning in, blocking her way. It was all a game to him and this was the only piece she had to play. Holding the envelope in her teeth, she took the push broom and backed toward the door, sweeping away the little hand, the shoe prints. She locked the studio, ran out to the car, pulled up the back seat and dropped the envelope into the well underneath. Then she drove like a madwoman toward San Francisco.

When Robert finally fought his way through heavy traffic onto Broadway he found North Beach alive with the holiday spirit. This was the first real break in the storm and the town had turned out to celebrate. Because of the cars clogging every artery Robert left the Toyota on Sansome and walked the three steep blocks up to Sweetcakes. The Twitter and Facebook nouveau riche were out in force, bulling their way along through the spike and skull crowd, the City Lights artistes, and of course those like himself, the slumming gentlemen of the middle class. He walked with elbows out, protecting his injuries as he jostled through the throng.

His kind were the strongest presence in Sweetcakes, though the night was still young. He might have felt right at home except for the tastelessness of the place. The lights were low, the color red, the music thumping out fake orgasmic beats. Lap dance couches were hidden by plastic palms and a hall in the back led away, said a tacky sign, to a half-dozen Private Pleasure Booths. The whole thing was borrowed from some B gangster flick, a reflection of a reflection. The bar was an oval horseshoeing a smallish stage with the obligatory slick brass poles. Inside, a stocky middle-aged guy was chomping on an unlit cigar, not even trying to look busy. Robert guessed he was the owner, Joe's relative.

Robert sized him up, wondering if after all this was the best approach. The man was paunchy and balding, with the lined face and battered eyes of a veteran nightcrawler. His Hawaiian shirt was splashed all over with pink hibiscus and stained in the armpits with sweat. Maybe it was the club's 85-degree heat. They had to keep the girls warm, Robert joked to himself, as he watched a pair in standard issue spike heels and thongs slither up and down, pretending to get off on each other. So far the ad outside was blatantly false: Red Hot Exotic Dancers, Girl on Girl, A Cut Above. Michele was the one who could fulfill that promise, though she'd have nothing but contempt for the men taking their secret pleasures in the booths out back.

Robert went to the bar and sat down near a group of Japanese business men. They bowed slightly and turned away. After a minute or two Joe's relative sauntered over.

"Evening. What can I get you?"

Robert was dying for a Martini but knew he didn't dare. "Club soda with lime."

The guy played for a moment with the wattles hanging from his chin. "That's no way to start the holidays," he said. A salesman, too, Robert thought.

"So true. But I'm recovering from an accident. On painkillers."

"Well, there's better things for you than alcohol," the man said with a wink.

Robert joined him in a sly chuckle, then looked toward the girls still drifting like sleepwalkers around the stage. So the guy wouldn't be a stickler for the rules, hands off the merchandise. "True again," he said. "Speaking of which, I was hoping to find a girl I saw in here a while back. Can't remember her name, but she had a tattoo, a snake in a garden …"

"Michele," the man interrupted. "Jolie, she used to call herself. Like that actress, Laura Croft. She tends bar some weekends. Funny you'd mention her. She's my, well, sort of daughter-in-law, more or less married to my nephew Joe. They got a kid together. That's why she gave up the dancing. And by the way, the name's Frank. Frank Pierello. I own the place."

"Oh. Well, I'm sorry. Hope I didn't offend you." Robert offered his hand, trying to look chagrined and carefully withholding his name. But he'd learned something important. Wherever Michele was, Frank was unaware of any trouble.

"Nah, don't worry about it," Frank said, sucking up to his well-heeled customer. "All business. What a honey, huh? Can't hardly keep my hands to myself when she's around. But of course, there's Joe. Loyalty. He's like a son. And then she can be a mean-tempered little something-or-other. But lemme get your soda."

"Thanks." Robert was glad to have a moment to think. Loyalty. That made it too risky to get Frank involved. When he came back with the drink, Robert changed his tack. "So, did Michele have any special friends here, anyone you might recommend?"

Frank laughed. "Not that bad an accident, I guess."

"All the important stuff's still functioning. The best R&R."

"Well, let's see." Frank looked around, surveying his domain. "What time is it?" Both men looked at their watches. It was a little after 6:30. "Yeah, there's Sharee. She should be in by now. Lemme go find her. Take a seat on the banquette. Make yourself comfortable."

A few minutes later the lithe, sweet-faced Sharee was sitting next to him under a plastic palm, a muscular leg thrown over his knee. "So you used to know Michele? How come I don't remember you? You so handsome. And Michele, she's my BFF, my special girlfriend. How come she didn't tell me about you?"

"Girls are funny things." Robert tried to stay patient. "Do you watch the news, Sharee? Radio? Read a paper?"

She twirled one of her auburn dreads. "That's a funny question. You scared we won't have nothing to talk about?" She laughed, a rich musical trill. "No, I never do. I used to, but now it's way too scary. I did watch those bombs in Boston about a hundred times and that's when I stopped watching for good. But let's not talk about sad things."

She straddled his lap, rested her arms lightly on his shoulders, and began to undulate, crotch to crotch, rolling her little honeyed breasts along his chest. When he didn't respond, she took his hands and cupped them on her naked bottom. He yanked them away.

"That's not what I'm after." He lifted her off, light as a feather, and set her back down beside him. "Don't be offended." He took out a hundred dollar bill. "I just want to find Michele. Where does she live?"

Sharee looked at the money, then at him. "Now that is really against the rules, giving out personal information." She tipped her head like a kewpie doll. "Really, really." She batted her false lashes with a pucker-lip smile. He added a second hundred. She knelt on the couch and peeked through the palms toward the bar. Then she took the money. "56 Dore, just this side of Division. Number 201. I hope she'll be happy to see you, or I'm really gonna hear about it."

Robert got up. He was straightening his clothes when Sharee tugged on his hand. She pointed toward the front door where Frank was talking heatedly with a young man in greasy work clothes. The kid was waving some paper in Frank's face and Frank seemed to be trying to calm him down.

"Don't go out that way," Sharee whispered. "That's Joe, Michele's boyfriend." Seeing Robert tense, Sharee guided him into the hallway leading to the Pleasure Booths. "All the way down, then turn left. There's some stairs, then a bright red door. You'll be in the parking lot out back." Again that rich little trill. She was high as a kite. "Say hi to Michele from Sharee," she called after him. "Tell her wussup."

25

Michele was standing by the sink, rummaging through the cupboard for something to eat. She'd managed to get herself bathed and dressed, back in the Salvation Army clothes. She'd taken a shitload of aspirin and was feeling totally weird, like she'd come unstuck from reality. Like when she was candy flipping, taking E and acid at the same time. Stuff from the past—blood and wounds, even Andy holding his gut—just kept coming like a drain backing up. So when a raw sound blasted toward her out of the wall she screamed and wheeled around to face the door, holding out a box of Cheez-Its to ward off the guns. But it was just the front door buzzer. Would the cops ring the bell? Would Joe, if he was coming to kill her? She wished the place had a window that looked onto the street. If she saw it was them, maybe she'd jump. The buzzer rang again, longer this time, and she stood frozen, trying to decide what to do.

Down below, Anna leaned against the building's gritty wall, imagining the scene when she came back empty-handed. She didn't know how long it took to get a search warrant—you called a judge, Michele's tip would have to be credible. Could the police be in her studio already, searching for Robert's papers? Without Michele the thing was bound to turn nasty. And Colin would be there, facing them alone.

She'd started to dial his cell when the intercom crackled. A frightened little voice floated away down the alley.

"Who is it?"

"Michele!" Anna shouted into the wall.

All that came back was a wracked sob. Then finally, "Are the cops with you?"

"Of course not."

"You sure?"

"Michele, don't be stupid! They don't know anything about you. If they did, you wouldn't be here now. Let me in!"

The door buzzed and clicked open. Her skirt pulled up around her thighs, Anna sprinted up the two flights of dark stairs. The corridor above was lit with bare bulbs, making Michele ghoulish as she looked down. Her face was deformed by anger and pain and it looked as if she might start screaming. Anna ran to her and took her in her arms.

"I'm so sorry." She held the girl against her. "I should have listened to you. Come inside, we have to decide what to do."

Michele let herself be led. They sat close together on the bed and she let Anna keep her arm around her shoulders. "Did he hurt you?" Anna asked.

Like a little girl, Michele pulled up her sweater and showed the bruises. "But I got him back," she said. "I stabbed him with those scissors."

"I know. Where are they now?"

"In a dumpster behind the Salvation Army."

"Okay, then. We have to tell the police." Anna held Michele's hands, didn't seem to care that they were cold and clammy. "Anyone can see you were acting in self-defense.

We're getting a lawyer. I'll pay for everything, you don't have to worry about that. But you'll have to explain the papers."

"They're gone," Michele said, turning so Anna couldn't see her eyes. "Robert burned them."

"No. He didn't," Anna said.

Before Michele could think what to say the buzzer sounded again. She squeezed Anna's hand so hard she felt the bones move, but the woman didn't flinch.

"It might be Joe," Michele whispered. She went to the intercom and pushed the button. But it wasn't Joe and the voice that answered brought Anna running.

"Michele." Deep and seductive. "Michele, it's Robert."

Michele turned to Anna, shaking so hard her teeth were rattling. "You told him. You told him where I live!"

"I'd never do that. Whatever he says, he's come for the papers."

Michele shook Anna off and started to pace in tight little circles. "Okay, he didn't burn them, only half of Larry's note. I don't know why I said he did, you're making me all confused." She had to think of something the woman might believe. "Joe has the papers. He found them in my purse and then he walked out on me. He took Robin. Maybe it was Joe told him to come here."

She stopped in front of Anna, who just kept staring into her eyes like she was trying to read her mind. She wasn't demanding anything, she looked soft and understanding, and it made Michele want to crawl back into her arms and tell her everything. But she couldn't do that. The cops were already in Anna's studio and when she found out about it she'd feed

Michele to the dogs. Who wouldn't? The buzzer sounded again, longer this time, making them both jump.

"It doesn't matter," said Anna. "We have to go. How can we get out?"

"There's a fire exit across the hall but it goes into the alley. That's a dead end. The only way out is back onto Dore."

Anna thought for a second. "Then let him in. My car's across the street. We'll go down while he's coming up. Get a coat, some clothes."

Michele did as she was told, stuffing things into an old duffel bag of Joe's. She was putting on his leather jacket when the intercom went off again. She ran to it.

"What do you want, Robert?"

"Michele, I'm sorry about this morning. It all got away from us, didn't it?"

Michele couldn't help herself. "You fucking tried to kill me, you asshole."

Anna came to her. "Don't let him do that to you," she said as Robert's sultry murmur came back. "I know you must be hurting. Let me in. Come on, Michele. I got it all wrong. I want to help you."

"Close the door, but don't lock it," Anna whispered. "He'll try to come in, don't you think? That will give us a little more time. You lead the way."

After putting the door on the latch, Michele went into the hall. Anna waited by the intercom. The fire door led onto a metal stair running down the side of the building. Michele opened it and looked back, locking onto Anna's eyes. Anna pushed the button. They heard the door slam open in the hall below, then feet thumping up the stairs—not the old, nimble Robert, Michele thought, I must have got him good. When Anna had passed her, she silently closed the fire door and followed Anna's fluttering skirts down the wind-beaten stairs.

At the door of 201 Robert stopped and listened. He'd half expected Michele to be waiting there, the picture of Pathos with the baby in her arms. But the little bitch never stopped gaming. He knocked. When no one came he tried the door. Surprisingly, it opened, and he stepped into the awful mess of Michele's life—clothes and junk and dirty dishes, the place turned upside down. For a moment he wondered where she might be hiding. He held his breath, listening for any sign of life. Far below he heard the clatter of running feet. However she'd done it, she was gone. He threw himself down the stairs, the stitches in his neck tugging painfully at his wound, and hit the street door like a linebacker. But too late. The street was deserted. There was only one place he knew that Michele might find shelter. He sprinted to his car and careened through the city, back the way he'd come.

The Thanksgiving rush had almost cleared and it took only minutes for Anna to get onto the bridge. It was jammed in both directions but at least they were moving. Michele stared ahead, jiggling her legs up and down. She looked old and ill. Her cheeks were hollow and there were deep brown circles under her eyes. Since they'd left the apartment, she'd only glanced in Anna's direction, never quite making eye contact.

Finally she asked, "Where we goin'?" Her voice was tight and suspicious, all the softness gone.

"We're going to my house. You remember Colin? He's getting a lawyer." When Michele didn't respond, Anna went on, picking her way carefully. "We'll get you taken care of and then go to the police. Unless they're already there. There's a Detective Holzman investigating." Anna glanced over. Michele looked quickly away. "He said he was getting a warrant to search my studio. Do you know anything about that?"

"You crazy?" Michele said dismissively.

Anna didn't press it. There'd be time enough to sort that out. There was a long silence while they crossed Treasure Island and started their descent into the East Bay. Behind them, Anna noticed, the brilliant sunset had been swallowed by a black mass of clouds, another round of storms only hours away. Finally Michele spoke.

"Attempted murder starts at fifteen."

"Fifteen?"

"Years. I think. I don't really remember. It only happened once before and I was a juvenile. Maybe that's different."

"This wasn't attempted murder."

"It's me against him and look how that went before."

There was no answer for that. Anna could only hope that it would be Colin and the lawyer, not Holzman and the police, who were waiting when they arrived. They were curving around onto I-80 East, passing Emeryville, only a couple of miles to their exit and another ten minutes home. But Michele wasn't going quietly. She shifted in her seat, more and more agitated as they passed the first Berkeley exit, then the second. Suddenly she screamed, "Stop! Stop! I won't do it!"

Anna took hold of her arm. "Stop it, Michele!"

But the girl wrenched free. She screamed. "You don't know what they'll do to me. You've never had a judge look down at you like something he stepped in." She fumbled with her seat belt, trying to unlatch it. "You don't get it! You can't, you never will!" Before Anna could react, she was out of the belt and fumbling for the door latch.

"Michele!" Anna started toward the shoulder. "Don't do something stupid. I'm pulling over." The Albany exit, the way home, was only yards ahead.

"No! No, keep going!" Michele found the door handle. "Keep going or I'll open this door. I'll kill myself, I swear to God."

Anna swerved back into the lane, horns blaring, angry drivers mouthing curses as they shot past. "What do you want, then? Where do you want me to go?"

"East," said Michele. "Toward Sacramento. I know a safe place. Go east."

In the lot behind Sweetcakes, Robert paid a small fortune to park in the handicapped spot, the one closest to the door that led into the club's back hall and the Pleasure Booths. On the drive over he'd called Sharee. Michele wasn't home after all. Was she there? No, but it was funny he was asking, because Joe and Frank were pissed. It was something to do with Michele. Unsure of the next step he'd told the girl to meet him out back in fifteen minutes, but there was no one. If she'd told Frank about him the fat man or his bouncer would be waiting out there with a baseball bat. He just needed to stay cool.

He took another Vicodin and was doing his yoga breathing when the door finally opened and Sharee's baby face peeked out. She beckoned him inside. She must be on a break, judging by the leopard-spotted body suit and feathery pink mules. Together they slipped up the stairs and into one of the Pleasure Booths, a claustrophobic place with low light, red plush banquettes and air heavy with potpourri. A large drape hanging on one wall hid the business end of the room, the picture window looking in on the girl or girls working it inside.

"You gonna get me in so much trouble!" Sharee giggled. She threw herself down on the banquette. "Now how much you gonna give me?" But when she turned to face him the laughter stopped. "Is that blood on you?"

He felt his neck. With all the exertion the bandage had slipped and must be visible over the top of his turtleneck. The edge was damp. His fingers came away tinged with red.

"An accident," he said. "I need to find Michele."

Sharee sat up, looking sober and serious. "I don't know where she is if she's not home. She better not come here, that's all I know."

"Why not?"

"Frank and Joe, I told you."

"Yes, but you didn't say why." Robert sat beside her, summoning his best bedside manner. "Can you tell me why?" he purred, and was surprised when she backed away.

"I don't know, just what I heard passing by. Some shit Michele's mixed up in, some doctor she was seeing got attacked." Little knots of worry gathered around the girl's eyes as she took in the meaning of the bandage and the blood. "That isn't you, is it?"

When Robert didn't say anything Sharee eased away, then suddenly bolted for the door. He couldn't let that happen. He grabbed her arm and pulled her back down beside him. She tried to pry his fingers from her wrist but of course he was the stronger.

"All I want to know is where she'd go," Robert said, trying to stay calm. Easy as it would be, there was no point in breaking her arm. "I'm happy to pay for the information. And I don't want to hurt her, or you. I want to help her. The police are looking for her."

Trapped there beside him, Sharee tried to act nonchalant. She shifted around and crossed her legs. "Who goes out messed up like you are? You should be in the hospital." She lifted her free hand and began examining her nails, sending Robert over the edge. He yanked the hand out of the air and jerked her to her feet.

"Where the hell is she?"

"Shit! I don't know!" Sharee squealed.

"You're her best goddamn friend, you must know! Would she go to your place?"

"No! She doesn't have a key."

Robert took her by the throat. "Does this help you think, you little slut?" His hand almost encircling it, her neck felt fragile as a bird's.

Now Sharee looked really terrified. Her voice came out high and wheezing. "Only place I know, there's a cabin up in the woods …" Robert relaxed his grip so she could speak, but kept her pinned against the wall. "Frank's place, him and Joe go hunt and stuff. She was just talking about it, how she loved it up there. Outside Placerville."

"Where exactly?"

Sharee wriggled and rolled her eyes. "I never been! Why you doin' me like this?!" He squeezed a little harder. "All's I know is Wildcat Ridge. That's where the place is. You can prob'ly ask anybody up there. That's how it is in the country."

With one hand still holding her throat Robert took the last hundred from his pocket and shoved it into her cleavage. He felt blessedly relieved, almost serene. "If you say anything about this I will know about it," he said pleasantly. "Enough said?"

Sharee nodded, her dollbaby dreads bouncing up and down. Robert let her go, stepped away and opened the door for her. "You one crazy fucked up motherfucker," she shot at him as she went by.

Robert brushed her aside. "That kind of talk doesn't become you," he said on his way down the hall. "But I can see why you and Michele get along so well." Then the door to the parking lot crashed shut behind him.

26

Anna pulled to the side of the road and looked out. A sign, twisted and bent from some drunken collision, said *King of the Mountain Road*. Beyond it the night was a void. She sat for a moment listening to Michele's labored breathing. She'd been curled up like a cat in the back seat, asleep for over an hour. She was wrapped in a thin blanket they'd bought somewhere around Davis, at a truck stop where Anna had gotten gas, groceries, painkillers, and a map. Michele had drawn a winding path from the Highway 50 turnoff, out into the hills east of Placerville, north of a tiny town called Pollock Pines. Then she'd crawled into the back seat and fallen dead asleep.

That's when I could have turned back, Anna thought. But what if Michele had woken up? What mayhem then? Instead she'd gone to the restroom and called Colin. She'd left the message at the apartment, in case the police were with him. She wanted him to know that she was safe, alive anyway, but not where she was going. If he knew, the Highway Patrol would soon be behind them. The girl needed rest, a moment of peace. As *she* did. She'd only said she'd call soon.

Now she found herself in a frozen oasis. Outside, the cold blue glow of the headlights lit the trunks of overhanging pines and a few flakes of snow drifting down. Inside, the old protective fog held her close. All that mattered was to stop, she thought dully, to rest and heal for a day. She'd persuade Michele to come back with her, make her see it was the only path to take. If only they could find this cabin.

Michele's panicky voice startled her. "What's happening?" Her hands were up as if warding off a blow. "Why'd you stop?"

"It's all right. I'm just wondering which way to go."

Michele scrambled up and to the window. "King of the Mountain. Turn. Turn here." They went on silently, Michele leaning into the front seat. After a mile or two she pointed ahead, to the mouth of a dirt road leading off into the forest to their left. It was marked by several mailboxes, among them a bright red one with the name Pierello nestled in ivy and violets, a hummingbird hovering over the P.

"Ruthie's freakin' birds," said Michele. "It's not far now."

Anna left the paved road and slowly climbed, bouncing over ruts, winding back and forth for what seemed like miles. Finally Michele pointed to a narrow track that snaked away into the ghostly trees. After a few yards the headlights swung across the front of a cabin—logs with white plaster in-between, standing on pilings above a lawn of old snow. A stairway led down one side, from a bright red door into a small drift. Between the pilings a mountain of wood was partly covered by a tarp. Anna stopped in a turnout some yards from the house.

"This is weird," Michele said. "Frank said it doesn't snow up here."

She got out and worked her way up the stairs, kicking off crusty snow with furious energy. At the top she lifted a sodden doormat to retrieve a key. Anna followed her up, carrying the groceries. Inside the cabin was cold and damp. Michele groped around for a flashlight hanging on a nail by the door.

"They stop the electric in the winter," she said, sounding aggrieved. She shone the light around the room until she found a kerosene lamp. "There's propane in the kitchen but it takes forever. They heat water on the wood stove."

She lit the lamp, illuminating a pine-paneled room with a high chalet ceiling. There were two living areas: a threadbare sofa and arm chairs around a large wood stove at the far end, and a simple dining set near the entrance. A couple of chests of drawers, a hutch and a card table with four folding chairs made up the rest of the furnishings. A row of windows along the front wall, without blinds or curtains, gave back their reflection as they moved into the room. Beside the front door was the entrance to a small kitchen. At the end of the living room a ladder-like stairway led up to a loft. Below it was a dark room, perhaps a pantry or storage area. On the wall between kitchen and loft a moth-eaten deer's head, modestly antlered, stared out. A gun rack held two guns.

Michele must have seen her looking. "They're not loaded," she said.

She stood on a chair and took one down, pushed a lever to open the breech and held the shotgun out so Anna could see that its two barrels were empty. Then she climbed down with it. She used it to point toward the darkness under the loft.

"Bathroom's back there. There's a bed upstairs." She sank down on the sofa, the gun across her knees.

"I'll make a fire," Anna said. "Can you put a kettle on the stove?"

"No." Michele yanked up her blouse. Both serpent and garden were lost now in a welter of contusions and bruises.

"I know, Michele. You need a doctor."

"But I'm not going to get one, am I?" She tucked the gun into the sofa cushions and lay down beside it, glaring up at Anna. "You left me. You went away and left me."

"I went to Boston. To find out what happened."

"I told you what happened."

"You were guessing. Now I know. Some of it, anyway. I'll tell you if you'll listen."

"What good is that? You left me." She rolled over, shutting Anna out.

"I'm here now. And you will have a doctor, tomorrow."

"Yeah, while you turn me in to the fucking police. Just make a fire, make the bed. Sheets are in the bathroom. Fuck! I'm freezing."

For once Anna was grateful for the sheltering fog. The girl's anger rolled over her in a harmless wave. Michele was a willful child, after all, trying to regain control. It was only twelve hours since her world had flown to pieces. Making a fire, making the bed—the sweet familiar tasks, she'd pretend, of a night in the country.

She set about it. Once the fire was blazing she took the flashlight and made her way through the small room under the loft. It was stacked with boxes and baskets and lined with shelves holding dozens of large tins labeled Emergency Rations. Maybe this was where the Pierellos planned to sit out Armageddon. At the back she found the bathroom, a small space done up in blazing yellow with red trim and bird decals everywhere. A dainty porcelain tub on lion's feet, too small to lie in, had somehow been fitted in. Anna imagined the hunters, smeared with dirt and gore, crushed in together knee to knee waiting for the Rapture. In her old life she would have laughed. She found the sheets and made her way up the narrow ladder to the loft.

A Coleman lamp hanging from a hook splashed the cramped space with a cold white light. The bed—a mattress and box spring on a plywood platform—was shoved into one corner, just making room for a pair of low bureaus against the opposite wall. But there were plenty of blankets and pillows piled in a corner. As she worked, the heat from the fire quickly warmed the place, releasing scents of pine and wood smoke and bringing memories of New Hampshire—her father with his long sure cross-country stride, Claire in pink and white, always the perfect little bunny, the evenings playing Scrabble and bridge, reading and drawing—how little that had prepared her for the knives and screams and drowning forests of the Real Thing. Michele's voice, full of sullen self-pity, snapped her back into it.

"What's the matter?" She was standing at the top of the ladder, wrapped in her blanket and holding the shotgun. In the harsh light, her eyes were reptilian. "What have you got to cry about?"

Anna hadn't realized she was crying. "I'm almost done," she said coldly. "You can sleep. Are you in pain?"

"He broke my ribs. They hurt like hell."

If the girl expected sympathy, Anna thought, she'd get as little as she gave. "I hope you'll sleep. Tomorrow we'll get you back to a doctor."

She went on piling pillows against the wall, protection for Michele's injuries. The girl moved behind her and she felt the hair rise on the back of her neck. She looked around, half expecting to see the gun in her face. But there were only those glassy blue eyes.

"You're so stupid," Michele said. "If I go back I'm going to jail. No, prison. *Prison*!" It came out in a strangled hiss. "And it's gonna be because of you."

It was like an electric shock, the blistering heat that shot through Anna's heart. Before all the reasons not to caught up with her, she was standing over the girl. "Not me, Michele—you! It's you! All of it! *You*!!"

"Don't yell at me, I'm hurt!" Michele whimpered. She dropped to the floor, the gun beside her.

Anna stood over her. "You used me from the first minute you saw me! You were waiting for me, weren't you, sitting there on Robert's stairs? What was it you saw in me, that said 'rich bitch?' That said 'pushover?' My clothes, my car? Or was it only after you'd gotten a free lunch and you saw me with your baby? You used Robin to get to me. Your own child!"

Michele shrank away from her. "You wanted it, you wanted to know about Robert. You went through my stuff and found those papers! You told me to call you. You said that you'd pay. It wasn't me that went to Boston!"

"You've implicated me in a crime!"

"You said it wasn't, it was self-defense!"

Fighting an impulse to grab the girl and shake her, Anna stood back, wrapping her arms tightly around herself, holding herself together. "I'm talking about the theft of Robert's papers. The ones you left in my studio."

"You weren't supposed to go in there!" Michele slunk farther away until her back was against the wall.

"And then there's the souvenir you stole while I was taking care of your baby. Robert was holding it."

"That was for luck," Michele broke in. "Robert was hurt, he needed it."

"Hurt? You tried to kill him! For whatever reason. You! You, Michele! And you wanted the police to think I was there. Now the police have it. Because *you* left it there! And because *you* called the police and told them where to look they've gotten a warrant to search my home. If they found those papers they'd suggest conspiracy, blackmail. That's implicating me in a crime, as I'm sure you know."

"Okay. Okay, okay, okay," Michele whispered trying, it seemed, to calm herself. She sat there for a moment, the blue eyes chasing her thoughts around the room. "What did you do with them?"

"They're safe. The police have no idea."

"Where?"

"I'm not going to tell you! I can't trust you."

Michele scrambled up, pleading. "No, no, no! Come on, Anna, think about it! We can send them back to Robert. If he's got the papers he won't press charges. He doesn't want anyone to know about me. We'll just go back to the way it was, me and Joe, you and the boyfriend. Robert and his fucking secrets. Just forget about it."

"That's insane! It's gone beyond the papers. I've followed the trail back. The drug in that needle had my name on it. He wanted to destroy us both." Michele's eyes darted down to the gun on the floor at the foot of the bed. There'd been plenty of time, Anna thought, to load it while they were apart. She snatched the thing up and held it against her chest. "I've seen Larry. I think I know what Robert did to him. And Laura. Those papers are my best protection, and yours. They explain everything."

Michele backed away again. It was the first time Anna had seen her frightened. "What's going on with you? It isn't loaded. I told you."

"And I told you I don't trust you." Anna found the lever. The gun fell open, empty. She looked at Michele, wounded and trapped in her own dark places. I'm becoming someone to fear, she thought. The stark room, the girl, the confusion of roads and reasons that had brought her here, all tangled together and fell away.

"I'm sorry. I'm sorry." She sat on the bed, put the gun on the floor, and covered her face with her hands. The only sound was the wind and wet snow slapping against the narrow windows above the bed. Snow would make it harder to get out in the morning, Anna thought vaguely, if it kept up all night. But Frank says it doesn't snow. She was startled back by a rustling sound. It was Michele crawling toward her. Head down, she curled shivering against Anna's knees like an injured animal.

"You're mad at me. You hate me now," she whimpered.

"I don't hate you," Anna said, wishing she could sound more gentle. "We've got a lot to go through still. We should try to be friends, stop lying anyway."

"Okay. Okay, I promise."

They sat there exhausted, listening to the wind moaning in the trees. Anna finally asked, "Is there another place to sleep?"

"The sofa folds out." Michele got slowly up, holding her side. "But stay with me," she said simply. "I don't mean anything by it, I'm just really scared. Please stay with me."

They took off their shoes and lay down together in their clothes. Anna settled a blanket over them and switched off the lamp. Michele turned her back and curled herself around a pillow for comfort. Out of the dark a small voice said, "Please hold me." The simple, innocent plea of a lost child, calling to the mother she'd never had, and never been, and probably never would be. Anna drew Michele to her. There was a tremor coming from her, and a sickly heat. On the pitch black canvas of the night another Michele drew a naked figure, mocking, *how about those drives*? Only a week ago, the map of the world redrawn. As it had been when she passed the churchyard, the wall, the iron gate. Three men were strolling along the street, heads down, whispering in Spanish. So. She had seen them without realizing it. One was very short and wore a hooded sweatshirt. One had a headband and long black hair, something sleek and handsome about him. And the third—blockish and concealing a knife. The sweatshirt black, the headband red, hair tied with a leather thong. And the strong one, jaundiced and pockmarked, with a tattoo of thorns dripping blood. She came nearer, they looked up. But someone had erased their faces. She needed paper and pen, but had no hope of finding them here.

"I won't let them hurt you," she said. The girl didn't answer. With snow lashing against the windows, Anna lay for a long time, conjuring.

It wasn't the first time Robert had considered the Mexico option. As he drove east, swept along I-80 in high speed bumper-to-bumper traffic, he let himself drift back to the time it had first occurred to him. Christmas, the first holiday with Fran. She was open to adventure in those days and they'd avoided the usual tourist spots. It was some years after the Laura nightmare, but he was haunted still by terrors in the night. And there, in the little jungle town of Papantla in the state of Vera Cruz, for the first time he'd felt free of it. He'd wanted to stay there forever, start a clinic, live a Hemingway existence. But Fran had been trotting along beside him and a longer nightmare was just beginning.

Now as the miles slipped by he began to consider what it would be like—*for real* as Michele liked to say—submitting to the fate that had been stalking him for years. Years in which he'd endured profound misunderstanding, been held to account by small minds who saw only victims and perpetrators. There'd be capture, entrapment. And the irony was, he'd done nothing to deserve it, had been groping in the dark like the rest of them, for all his sincere belief in Will and Action. Nietzsche was right, he'd been sleepwalking all this time, and here, now, was the moment of choice. Not the sweaty confusion of that last night with Laura, not Larry's dark comedy or yesterday's bungling. Or Fran and Maura, not even worth mentioning. Choice with a capitol C, that comes once and not again.

Yes. Mexico. The real Mexico, where death stands on an equal footing with life, and the laws favor the strong—that was the place of absolute sanctuary. Even more so now, with everyone looking toward the Middle East, ISIS, the great terrors of the day. All he had to worry about was getting across the border. The money he'd stashed around the house came to almost five thousand dollars. That should do it until he found a way to access more of his funds. Who would notice, he thought as he blazed along eastward, one American doctor moving quietly from town to town? Who would ask questions when he found the refuge with bribable officials, just enough gringos and a clinic up for sale? And who would care that another dissolute American girl had passed quietly away without ID or connections? Who would even know, if the girl had wandered off a jungle trail? He was confident he could woo Michele away, a trivial matter. But the papers—that was the most pressing issue that had still to be resolved. If he had those, perhaps his time in Mexico need only be another long, distasteful honeymoon. Sleepwalking or not, he did love his house, his position at the University …

He was just moving on to consider other problems—Fran, Craig, his practice and most of all Anna Sheffield—when the insistent ringing of his cell phone dragged him back to the present. He looked out and found Sacramento's glare all around him. In his confusion he answered without thinking.

"Doctor Buchanan?" said the phone, "This is Detective Holzman."

Someone had spoken to the police, given his cell number. Craig? Camilla? If they were all turning against him he'd better have his wits about him. He slowed from 80 to 65 and drifted over toward a slower lane.

"Doctor, are you there?"

"Yes, Detective," he said brightly. "How are you?"

"Sounds like you're on the road. Where are you, sir?"

"I'm not quite sure," he said and threw in a hearty laugh for good measure. "And you? How are things? Any progress?"

"I'm here with your partner, Mr. Helsen. He came by your house to see how you were doing and found you gone. Where are you, sir?"

Robert didn't answer for a moment, distracted by a welter of signs for highways going off to all corners of the Golden State. Highway 50 was the smallest of them and he had to swerve to make the connection. Horns blared.

"Sounds like you're in heavy traffic." Holzman was nonchalant, might be sitting in some office with his feet on a desk. "You in the city? Why don't you pull over, Doc, so we can talk?"

"No, no, I'm fine, hands-free. Now what were you asking?"

"We've talked to your daughter. Seems you've taken her car."

This made Robert petulant. “Well, I gave her mine. I needed some way of getting around. I’m just gathering my thoughts.”

“Sure, that makes sense.” The insufferable man clearly didn’t believe him. “But I wanted you to know we’ve got a lead on a young woman. Former patient of yours.”

Robert knew silence was the wrong thing but his mind went blank. After an interminable pause Holzman went on. “We’ve learned about her from Colin Mills, Anna Sheffield’s boyfriend. Name’s Michele, that’s all we know. Except that she’s a stripper.”

All the parts of Robert’s brain fired off alarms at once. A shot of adrenaline, a wrenching of the heart that Anna had been so weak, a paradigm meltdown. “Michele?” He wasn’t pleased by the geriatric quaver in his voice.

“Yessir. Apparently Ms. Sheffield went off looking for this person and never came back. We could use a last name.” Holzman stopped, letting the bait dangle.

If the news of Anna’s involvement was meant to make him panic, the big cowboy had miscalculated. It brought the first real promise in hours. Anna must have been with Michele at the apartment. And if they‘d gone together to this cabin life would be infinitely simpler. Everything he needed, there in one package. One of them must know where his papers were. His thoughts were interrupted by the gruff detective.

“I’m putting Mr. Helsen on.”

God, of all things. Craig's voice, full of strain and pleading, said, "Robert. Robert, what are you doing? Think how this seems. Please, where are you? Let us help you."

Et tu, Robert wanted to say, but kept still, pursuing more pressing matters. Of course Anna's money could take the women anywhere, but that wasn't her style. She was The Mouse, after all. Home, hearth, nice tidy resolutions. She'd want him punished, but would she be willing to live with the consequences? Destroying his children, Michele, his patients, all for something she didn't understand? To make her see, that was the thing. He summoned her, held her calm knowing gaze. She had the capacity, if she'd listen. And if she wouldn't? Michele was a harmful thing, like Larry, a thing to be excised. But Anna .... His mind froze, held by the image of blue eyes looking up, going cloudy, lips like ripe plums in a chalk-white bowl.

Craig's voice cut in. "He's not responding." Only seconds had past, and Robert had forgotten all about him.

"I'm useless, Craig, honestly," he said. "I still have no memory of the attack, or really much before it. Things should improve, though, in a day or two," he added helpfully. "Meantime you keep up the good work."

But instead of his malleable partner, Holzman answered. If Robert wouldn't come home, he had no choice but to put out an APB for the Rav4, and Robert should consider the negative publicity that was bound to follow. Robert decided quickly.

"Oh, no, no. There's really no need for that. Such an expense for the taxpayers." He looked intently ahead, hoping for signage. He was in luck. A sign announcing that Placerville was 35 miles ahead flashed by. "Look, I'm down around Santa Cruz." That should buy some time. "I'll come to you. I'll come straight home."

They agreed to meet at midnight, Holzman insisting on the BPD in downtown Berkeley—the benign round building standing sweetly beside the City Hall, the courts, the jail. Not trusting the former tight end to keep his word, Robert hung up and moved back into the fast lane. Soon he disappeared into the thick stream of ski-racked SUVs gunning it toward a holiday in the fabulous Sierra snows.

Sometime in the night Michele startled awake, adrenaline pumping. She'd been standing at the end of a long corridor, shiny clean under hard glaring lights, doors and doors along both sides all closed and locked. Juvie, it must be. Joe was in there somewhere. She'd seen him, leaving one room and going into another, dragging something behind him. It was a metal door clanging shut that had waked her. Or was it the thick throbbing in her side? Or something moving around downstairs? She sat up, but there was nothing to see in the absolute dark, and the only sound was the wind moaning through the trees.

She put her hand out and felt a soft body lying beside her. Anna, the person she was supposed to trust to get her through. Who'd stood over her with a gun and screamed in her face. Who'd made her beg. Who'd somehow gotten control of her whole life. The adrenaline rush was turning to rage when a little squeal and click, metal on metal, broke in—the door of the stove closing down below. The loft was warm, she realized, like someone had been feeding the fire. It was just possible that Joe had figured where she'd go and had come to find her. He was waiting for morning, letting her sleep. Or had he brought the cops? No, the cops don't let you sleep.

She slipped out from under the covers, down to the end of the bed and off onto the floor, then crawled to the edge of the loft and looked over. A pool of weak orange light lay around the stove, but outside it you couldn't see a thing. Taking the gun in case, she lowered herself silently down the ladder.

27

Anna startled up, awakened by the silence and the heat. The wind had stopped, there was no sound of breathing beside her, and the loft was stifling. Someone had been feeding the fire, but nothing was stirring down below. Where was Michele? Had she gone down to sleep on the sofa after all? Or had the pain kept her awake?

The little windows above the bed let in a soft, white light. Anna checked her watch: 6:20. She got up and looked out. The cabin backed onto a steep hillside whose manzanita and pine drooped under the weight of new snow. The car would have to be dug out, maybe even the road, and the trek back would be difficult. But the work would give her a reason to be outside and alone. The phone was downstairs in her coat pocket, where she'd left it yesterday—the unwanted gift from her mother, now the most precious thing she owned. She'd manage to call Colin, and Sarah, who must know by now that she was "missing."

She threw off the covers and made her way carefully down the ladder. When she turned at the bottom, there was Robert Buchanan, lounging on the sofa like a pasha. Michele rested against him, eyes half open, pale but breathing. Nearby, the gun lay across the arms of a chair.

This is the sort of moment, Anna thought, when people scream. Instead, there was only a sharp intake of breath, then emptiness. It was almost as if she'd expected him. The man looked sallow and drawn, his eyes sunken and circled with brown. A thick bandage, hidden by the collar of a black turtleneck, covered what must be the stab wound, and above it his neck and jaw were purplish and swollen. The violent scene in his office, less than twenty-four hours ago, played out between them as they looked into each other's eyes. Finally Robert disentangled himself and got up. There was an edgy, ragged energy about him.

"Well?" he said. "'What are you doing here?' 'How did you find us?' 'Happy Thanksgiving?' Something?" Behind him Michele watched with hooded eyes.

"Are you all right?" Anna asked her, but got no reply. "What did you do to her?"

"Vicodin, quite a bit. She won't be very helpful for a while, I'm afraid. If you're thinking it's poison, you're wrong. We all need our wits about us."

Of course he'd come for the papers. Of course Michele would have told him that Anna had them. Would he use Michele as bait? Threaten to kill her if Anna didn't give him what he wanted? Whatever his plan, he seemed to think they had all the time in the world, that no one was looking for them. In that case there was one thing she couldn't let him have. Her coat, the phone in its pocket, was only a few yards away, thrown over the back of a chair near the kitchen door. A journey of a thousand miles. But the Artistocrat had one weapon that never failed to disarm him. As much as she hated the snobs she'd grown up with, she'd learned something from them. Don't hesitate to put him in his place—a Townie, a Scholarship Boy, not in her league. Brushing past him, she went to the coat and put it on.

Robert followed. "Going somewhere?" He chuckled, Holzman with a Harvard veneer.

"I'm cold. You might remember, that happens when I'm frightened."

A little shadow crossed his face. Guilt, Anna hoped, or shame. "Sure, sure. I remember."

"And I've just gotten up. I need the bathroom. I assume you'll give me some privacy."

"Of course." Robert stepped aside so she could pass. "But I do want you to know," he went on politely, "that just in case you have some notion of using the window in there, jumping out or something, I have this." He held up a knobby black object. "Don't know what this is? It's a distributor cap. Your car won't run without it." Anna was about to speak when he rushed on. "Don't look so affronted. Don't scold. Please. The partners, the daughters, all full of self-righteous bullshit. Not you, too. Please!" Out of nowhere he hit the wall explosively with his fist. "Sorry," he said. "I've had a stressful week."

Anna didn't flinch. "We all have. I'll let you rest. I'm going to bathe."

"Don't be long," Robert whispered after her. "We have a lot to talk about."

Anna shut the bathroom door and latched its flimsy hook and eye against him. She turned the bathtub taps on full, considering what might happen if she called Colin, the police, her mother. The questions, pleadings, delays while the proper authorities were found, were all too risky with Robert only steps away. There seemed to be only one real possibility. She undressed, piling her clothes on a wicker hamper. When she pushed it against the door it seemed remarkably heavy. She dialed Putnam Graves. He'd always hosted a large family Thanksgiving and would surely be there now, in the rambling old house on the shore, sharpening the carving knife. But the phone rang once, then said, "You've … eached the … 'raves … Do … sage." There must be something wrong with the signal—or the battery?—she wasn't sure. But one ring, she remembered, meant that he was using the phone.

She raised her voice a little. "Uncle Pinky, listen carefully."

"Did you say something?" Robert's voice intruded. He was right outside the door.

"Talking to myself," Anna called back.

Having no idea how much of this might get through, she went on loudly, "But I am curious, Robert. As long as you're there, tell me how you found the Pierellos. I mean, who would think to look for Michele in Pollock Pines?"

"Country places, everyone knows everyone." That was evasive but it didn't matter, the message had been sent. "Why don't you open the door? It'll be easier to talk." The handle turned and the latch strained against the frame.

"Because I'm not dressed." Reflexively she put out a hand to ward him off—the one holding the phone—just as her message was cut off with a single clear beep. She pressed the red button but it was too late.

"What was that?" The door was like paper, he'd heard perfectly.

Anna sat on the hamper for extra weight.

"That sounded like a phone," Robert pushed against the door, felt the resistance. "Damn you, you've got a phone!"

Anna looked frantically around for somewhere to hide the thing. She jumped up and threw the hamper open. A mound of sheets caked in dried blood was stuffed inside. How angry Ruthie would be that the hunters hadn't done their washing up.

"I didn't hear anything," she called out and shoved the phone deep inside the crusted mass.

Robert responded with a harder shove. Fran and Maura had warned her, he has no conscience, he has no shame. But after all the hours she'd spent sparring across the three-foot battleground of Robert's office she was sure she knew his Achilles' heel at least as well as he knew hers. She stepped away from the door and turned to face him. The latch flew apart. She took an imperious stance, only covering herself with her arms as Robert stumbled into the room.

He stared for a moment, then turned away, pink blotches breaking out on his cheeks. "I'm terribly sorry," he said.

"At least you have *some* decency left," Anna said, driving her advantage home. How long would it take for the police to find them? If Putnam had gotten the message. If he understood what it meant. Hours, she imagined. She wrapped herself in a towel.

"I thought ..." Robert was saying.

"You thought I had a phone. I told you I didn't."

"I heard something," Robert said, trying to rally. "I haven't slept, I haven't eaten ..."

"I'll finish here, then we can talk." Anna said sternly. Seeing a chance to gain some time, she added more gently, "I'll make breakfast." Pushing it to the limit, she softened into motherly sweetness. "It's all right, you're exhausted. Why don't you rest?"

Robert sighed, his eyes still averted, then turned sheepishly to go. He paused in the doorway, trying briefly to repair the broken lock. "Sorry," he said again and went out, closing the door carefully behind him. Anna sat on the side of the tub feeling she might be sick. Then she pushed the hamper back against the door and took her time with the bath.

When she came out again it was close to 8:00, but the light in the cabin had a snowy evening glow. Someone had lit a couple of lamps—Robert, it must be. Outside the day had turned gray and forbidding. Michele had moved to an arm chair and was languidly thumbing through a dog-eared *Glamour*. There was no sign of Robert. Anna went to the front windows and looked down. A wide meadow, downy with new snow, ran all the way from the house eastward to the edge of a dense pine forest. Faintly, a radio news program drifted up from an SUV which Robert was furiously digging out of a small drift. He threw the snow toward Anna's Volvo, burying it deeper and deeper.

Behind her Michele spoke. "We're taking off." The slur had gone out of her voice and when Anna turned to look her eyes were clear and shrewd. "Didn't think of that, huh? You are so far behind the curve, girlfriend."

"What's going on?" Anna asked. "A minute ago you couldn't hold your head up."

Michele laughed harshly. "You really do think I'm stupid." She dug in the pocket of her jeans and held something out. Three tablets, one of them bitten in half. "You think I'm getting fucked up on Vicodin? It's an old trick from juvie. Put it under your tongue. He might be straight up or he might not. I took just enough to deal with the pain." She looked at Anna with a self-satisfied smile. "Who gives a shit, right? We're going to Mexico. He's gonna marry me in Reno. Now all we need are those papers."

So this was the curve Anna was behind. But she knew the papers were the least of what Robert needed. What if she'd miscalculated, shaming him as she had? With Michele contained, what might he be willing to do?

"It's not just the papers, Michele. It's us and what we know. A marriage in Reno isn't worth the paper you sign. And you really think he'll take you to Mexico? The police will be looking for you. They're looking for him now."

Michele gave her a searching look. "Where's your phone?" she asked.

"The battery's dead. I just meant, they must be, don't you think? And what about Robin? Wasn't all this for ...?"

"Shut up!" Michele broke in. "He wants me! We're going to start over. When we get settled we'll come back for her. He'll take the test. He's her father and Joe can eat shit for all I care. I've dreamed about this since she was born, nothing else but this. Robert just needs the papers. And I've been thinking. You've got them with you, don't you? You said the cops don't have a clue where they are, and what else did you have time for?"

"Did you tell him that?"

"Are you kidding? I'm talking to you first. Why give him a reason to hurt you? You're in this shit because of me and this is how I want it. Just let him have the papers and we're gone."

"Michele, you can't believe that. Look, he's already drugging you, yesterday he tried to kill you. Mexico is a dangerous place. You'd always be wondering, you'd never sleep."

"That cuts both ways." Michele laughed, a little girlish ripple. "I didn't quite tell you the whole thing, how it went down in the office. I was fucking with him, getting to him like I do. Really, it *was* me tried to kill him, kind of. So we're both in deep."

"Sure. And you hatched your great escape when?"

"Last night. We went out to the car so we wouldn't wake you up. I heard a noise and went to see. He was standing behind the ladder. He grabbed me, because of the gun. I can't believe you didn't hear it. I was kicking like a cat in a sack." She laughed again. Was the whole thing a big lark? "So, I don't know exactly what he's thinking, and he definitely doesn't know what I am." She paused, taking Anna in with mocking appraisal. "Poor Nana," she said, "you just don't get it. I've got something on him, and him on me. Not knowing how we'll use it is part of the thing between us."

"And what do you think his plans are for me?" Anna asked.

"Nothing much," Michele began, but a thumping sound under the house interrupted. They froze, listening. It was Robert starting slowly up the stairs, stamping on each one to get a footing on the ice. Michele lowered her voice. "Just leave you here, give us time to get out. There's plenty of food, somebody will find you sometime. Or you can walk out when the snow stops." As the door opened, she hissed, "That's if you give us the fucking papers!"

Anna jumped up. "You should eat some breakfast," she said loudly, as if talking to a child. "Can you do that for me?"

"Okay, why not," said Michele, all soft and drugged again.

"So!" Robert said. "Venus has risen from her bath." He was taking off his coat, his clothes steaming in the sudden heat. It was the tone he used when Anna came in late to a session—ironic and insinuating. He looked at his watch, then toward Michele. "A storm's coming in. Two hours, they're saying." He draped his coat carefully over the back of a dining chair, then sat down as if waiting to be served. "That gives us an hour or so."

"Until?"

"We'll be on our way. But you and I will sit and chat." As Anna passed him to get to the kitchen he winked and added, "Like old times."

28

Robert and Anna sat facing one another across the table. During their short silent breakfast Michele had joined them, sitting vacantly at the far end. Even though she must be starving, she'd kept up her charade, lazily sipping coffee and toying with her food. Now she wandered back to the sofa where she lay dozing, or pretending to. Robert leaned back in his chair, lacing his fingers together over his heart.

"Well, Anna," he said as if starting a session. "I'm sorry about this morning. I'm not myself." He picked up something from the table and turned it in his hands—a thrift store spoon, a stand-in for the scissors. It seemed he was a little lost without his leather chair, his desk, his notebook. "I hope you haven't felt neglected in all of this."

Neglected? Anna explored the craggy, ashen face, wondering how much Vicodin he'd taken. "Not at all, Robert," she said graciously, "but thank you for asking. And I'm sorry, too."

"Good. But still, I'd like to include you. So tell me about Boston."

She sat silent for a long time, trying his patience. "I saw my mother," she said finally, turning away to look out at the snowy stillness. "She's doing very well. The house could use some attention."

Robert threw the spoon clattering down onto the table. "Don't test me! That game's over. Your mother is not why you went, is she?" He sat back, recomposing. "You shouldn't take all this so personally. It has nothing to do with you—none of it."

Anna turned back to him. "I'd hoped to find that none of it was true. I'd hoped to come to trust you. I understand now why I never did. I also understand that I'll never recover."

"Recover?" He sounded genuinely surprised. "Why should you recover? The best you can hope for is to surrender, let life live you."

"As you have."

Robert waved the remark off with a fluttering hand. "So the trip was worthwhile? Your great 'Quest for Truth'?" He made large, mocking quotation marks in the air.

Anna took a moment to calculate. Stopping time was all that mattered now. "I came away with more questions than answers."

"Michele said you found Larry. Talk to him?"

"Yes, very sad."

"He can talk, then?"

"Not well. It's all a matter of interpretation."

"Really?" Robert sat eagerly forward, reckoning, Anna guessed, how this might play in his favor. "How did you find him?"

"Through Ryan's. His cousin Mike, but that was mostly about the car."

Suddenly Robert threw his head back and laughed. "Mike Neal! What a character! Comic book villain, don't you think?"

Before Anna could answer, he hurried on. "And where is it now, if you know? The Magnificent Mustang?"

"On blocks in Mike's garage."

"Ha, ha! That was a good one, wasn't it?" Robert thrust his fists in the air: touchdown!

"I'm not sure," Anna said, drawing it out. "A car? I didn't really understand what that meant. Why did it matter?"

"Your blessed naiveté," Robert said. "It's incredibly easy when you understand Larry's mind. So obvious and shallow. He had his hand in my pocket and intended to keep it there. But there were two things that made him lose whatever small judgment he'd been born with. Cars and drugs. Especially *that* car. His idea of glory. So when he'd exhausted my liquid assets, and I saw he was going for the jugular, I put the Mustang in trust for Camilla. I gave it to him the minute he made his demand."

He looked at Anna, wanting praise it seemed. When she didn't give it he started to scold. "Of course you don't see it, because you don't know—I bought it for *her*, for Laura. You know who I mean, you've got her picture. In 1977 it was already a Classic, a cherry red '67 2-door convertible, 360 hp, concourse ready, the last of the breed. But you missed the '60s, you weren't even born."

He stopped for a second, withdrawing again into his memories. "You should have seen us in it. Fantastic! Jaw dropping. But now it's 1987. I need to get rid of it, but I can't. I can't let it go." A spasm of pain distorted his features. He wiped it away with his hands and rushed on. "Maura is coming after me, and Larry is coming after me, and finally there's a worthy cause. Laura called Larry 'The Worm,' loathed the man. She'd love this.

"So I drove the Mustang over to Ryan's, top down, beautiful summer night. Got Larry, tight as he was, to come out with me and drive it down the Mystic. When I showed him the pink slip he barely looked at it. But of course I knew eventually somebody would, probably Mike. All business, that guy, not an imaginative bone in his body. If something happened to Larry he'd pick up the pieces, and since they couldn't sell the car he'd probably wind up with it. He might drive it, but if anything happened to it he'd be sued by the trust. If anything happened to me, it was Camilla's.

"So I told Larry it was all his. Just drive it home and I'll take a cab from there. We went to his sister's place, and then I told him there was another gift for him in the glove compartment. He'd been clean—clean but not sober—oh, maybe two months at that point, the perfect moment for a small intervention. Just try this, it's incredibly good, a real stress reliever, a one-time deal. The joke was, it was Ativan, tiny white pill, something Larry had been supplying me for years. I made up a name, Blisserion or some such nonsense."

Robert laughed. Restraint gave way to hilarity. Anna fled to the middle of the room, pursued by the memory of Larry, trapped in his chair slack-faced and drooling. From there she could see Michele propped up on the sofa cushions, alert and listening. Their eyes met, sending complicated warnings and commands. Then the laughter stopped and Michele dropped instantly back to sleep. But it was only Anna Robert wanted, a child demanding his mother's attention.

"Come back. Come back. Sit down."

She did, trying to look open and forgiving.

"Sorry," Robert said, still chuckling. "But really, the man's gullibility! It just went on and on. That wasn't all, you see. There had to be something with a little more kick. So I wrapped the pink slip around a nice little bag of crystal meth, and told him, 'Be sure to look this over when you get inside.' I put it in his hand so he could feel the bag. I knew he couldn't resist. And apparently he went inside and did what he had to do. A few minutes later I guess he seized."

He paused, sober at last, still hoping for approval. When he didn't get it, he rushed on. "The car was just the vehicle for the drugs, you see. He never would have taken them without it. A package deal! He could have died, the idiot. Luck of the Irish. Still, the outcome was workable, from what you've said."

He looked at Anna, now with fatherly concern. "You don't look well," he said. "Want some tea?"

"Robert, I met the man. His life is wretched. This is very hard to hear. Sickening, really."

"Oh, now you see, this is astonishing." Robert leaned across the table. "This is why your work is merely pretty, why you've never unlocked the guts of your talent. I've wanted to say this to you for years. You want to dive into the deep and you don't."

He got up, started toward the kitchen, then came back and stood over her. "Why did you go to Boston? Why did you interfere? It's a matter of interpretation, as you said. I never set out to hurt him, I thought you'd understand that.

Just put a little pressure on the fault lines, let him know I could. He could have resisted, he could have chosen otherwise. Can't you see he did it to himself?"

He was standing too close. Anna could smell the sickly sweet of his wounds but she didn't back away. "And Laura? Did she do it to herself?"

As if catching her thought, Robert's hand went to his throat and pressed the bandage, stifling a sudden pain. "Why do you ask that? You've seen the Globe piece. You have it, Michele tells me. That was ruled on. Suicide. It's a non-issue."

"Not to you. Not to me." She waited while Robert struggled. He looked at his watch, went into the kitchen and poured two cups of tea. He put one down for Anna, then went back to his place and drank, staring at her over the cup's rim.

"All right," he said. "Tell me. Why in hell does it matter to you?"

Because I want Michele to run from you. Because I want something to give the police when they come. Because I want to see the men behind the masks, the rubbed-out faces. But she knew what he wanted and she gave it. "Because I want to understand."

Robert's head dropped forward as if he might cry. "I need my papers," he whispered. "You have her pictures, her letters. I can't lose those."

Behind him Michele sat up, looking at her with wolfish concentration. Put pressure on the fault line, now, she silently ordered. Anna came around the table to sit beside Robert.

"I'm ready to give you your papers if you'll tell me what happened with Laura." She laid a hand gently on his arm. "You've never told anyone, have you?"

To her surprise, he covered her hand with his. "Clever girl," he said, not looking at her. "Change places—why not?" She wanted to pull away but didn't dare break the flow. "I like it," he purred. "I like it." He began to stroke her long fingers as you might stroke a pet, and to murmur almost to himself. "I was deeply, deeply in love with her, more than you can possibly imagine."

His touch was damp and oppressive. Anna slipped her hand away but he seemed not to notice. He got up, went to the front windows, and looked out into the featureless gray.

"When we first got together it was fire and dry timber. Untamed, unattainable, and it was me she chose. Me!" He turned back, giddy with pride, but the mood soon darkened. "Then she went off to Switzerland our first spring together and met some Count, some Fascist Spaniard. The truth about that might never have come out except for that dreadful father of hers."

Robert sat again beside Anna, sipped his tea, and let himself drift back. Anna waited, perfectly still.

"It was her graduation. Call it fateful. No, fatal. Fatal!" He laughed in spite of the pain. "She'd prepped me for it by finally talking about her parents, something she'd avoided all those months. 'Absurd as it might seem'—that's how she put it—'my father was a member of the SS. Really!' Frankly, I'd suspected as much. 'Well, someone had to be!' Sure, why not, what's the big deal? Daddy hadn't done anything awful, she was sure of it. Not a camp Komandant with whip and snarling shepherd, nothing like that. He was educated and sophisticated, the son of an industrialist, had a talent for the violin. He'd held an important desk job in Berlin, ambivalent about Hitler as things developed. Laura had a lot of reasons why everything about her father was above reproach."

Anna played for time. "Was he prosecuted, then? Or did he escape?"

"Herr Blaufeld was helped by some nice OSS men to safe harbor in Argentina where he met the mother, the daughter of a mining magnate. He knew things, you see, he was helpful. They lived high, although Daddy was often depressed and drank a lot, maybe drugs, too—opiates, Laura wasn't sure. But the three kids had the best and he was just 'Papito.' 'Really, Robert, you shouldn't worry about such silly things.' Now what do you think, Dr. Sheffield? Was that reassuring?"

"Or possibly thrilling? With a childhood like that, maybe she aroused ..."

Robert broke in, "We'll have to send you to graduate school, my dear. Nice try, but no. I was terrified. Not because Papito was a Nazi. No! He was going to ask about *my* background. We'd be rivals for the daughter's love—Freud 201—and how could I compete with a sojourn in Hitler's bunker? But once we were there, at the Plaza—after the ceremony we all took a limo down to New York—I confess I felt a great superiority. The parents were like two bodies dug out of a peat bog. Papito! His leathery, dissolute face, his dark eyes bruised and swollen, in a perpetual prizefight with sleep, or maybe memory. And the mother! Coppery snake's skin, multiple facelifts stretching her features past any possibility of expression, meticulously dyed blonde mane. No no no no. Pity and contempt. Or that's what I thought."

Robert drained his cup of cold tea. There was a new vitality, the story bringing him back to life. "But then, toward the end of the evening, Papito deigns to approach. He has a surprisingly thin, nasal voice. A cartoon Nazi. 'Zo, Ropert, dell me zomzing about yourself.' I couldn't resist. I said, 'My father is a garbage collector in New Haven, Connecticut. That's where Yale University is, but he didn't go there. And my mother is a fat housewife with five children and heart disease from too much smoking.' Laura gave me that killer stare. 'Sorry, just kidding.' I was flippant. 'Dad's in sales. You know I'm a Doctor, don't you? With two degrees from Harvard University? Isn't that enough?'"

"Beating him at his game," Anna said, but Robert rushed on.

"And Herr Blaufeld says, 'Apparently your degrees did not bring with them manners. I was merely asking to be polite. In fact your history does not interest me in the least.' He takes a leisurely drink of Dom Pérignon. 'And you know, Dr. Buchanan, if you have any intentions of becoming a member of our family, I can promise you that that will not happen. Not because I am opposed—Laura has a will of her own—but because she has other prospects. So you should ask yourself whether your degrees and so forth are enough to satisfy *you*.' But that doesn't hurt enough, oh, no. 'Humility,' he says, very softly. He raises a mummified finger." Robert demonstrated, pointing delicately toward Anna's nose, as you might in speaking to a child. "'Believe me, you have no idea what things can happen in this life. Cultivate humility, that's the best idea.'

"Humiliation, he should have said, the consummate bastard. But he was right about the other. Anything can happen. We went back to Cambridge. We were supposed to spend that summer together but all hell broke loose. What had Papi meant by 'other prospects?' Laura stood by a window, dazzlingly Latin. Flashing eyes, white teeth, sleek black hair down to her waist. 'Do you think when I go on vacations I just sit around mooning over you?' she says. 'I met someone, that's all. A Spanish businessman, son of a Franco general.' She has a picture of this guy in her purse. She holds it up. He's thin, dark, smooth, with pomaded hair. All he needed was a pencil mustache to be the laughingstock of a screwball comedy. 'Super on skis, so everybody's happy.' She had this way of tossing that mane of hair. Michele does that, too. And she laughed. And I said, 'Then you came back and hopped right into bed with me?' She turns on me. 'So? Why not?! You do not own me!! Besides, I had a primal urge.' She purses her lips at me. 'Both times.'"

Robert got up and drifted away again to the windows and the snow. "Nazi Peronistas, the past they shared, military elites awash in booze and drugs, every kind of perversion. It made her ruthless. And magnetic, everybody felt it. And her beauty, of course, that too. She wanted to break it off, just like that. But ..." He paused for a long moment, staring out. When he spoke again his voice had gone dark and stony. "What she hadn't told me was that she'd been pregnant.

She'd been carrying my child. Mine. She'd had an abortion. That's what the trip was really for. To kill my child."

As he spoke he'd come back into the center of the room, ignoring the other child lying on the couch. At the same time a muffled chuffing sound came from outside but Robert was too absorbed in himself to notice.

"I found out the hard way," he was saying, absently following Anna with his eyes as she retreated to the fire and Michele. "Our last night together she said she was in pain, female stuff, and could I bring her something. We'd often experiment with things I'd get from the lab, from The Worm."

As he spoke Anna glanced past him to the window that overlooked the meadow. Michele was pretending to sleep, so only she saw the twirling blades of a helicopter disappear over the far eastward trees, throwing billows of snow into the air.

Robert raised his voice. "So I brought the Ativan. When I got there we had a couple of martinis and then she told me it was over. 'Aborted.' She made an awful gesture."

Anna forced herself back to him, went to the table and sat facing the windows. She pretended to sip her tea. As she'd hoped, he followed, the story driving him toward its revelations.

"But still I wanted to be with her, one last time. *With* her, you know what I mean. That was essential, to replace what had been lost. I insisted, whatever excuses she might make. Even under the drug she fought me off, and then she spit at me, 'You think I want more of you? Besides, Antonio would never have me with a little garbage man growing inside me.' She was like that, said the most god-awful things. I couldn't take it. She was tearing me to pieces! I gave her another shot to shut her up and finally she was willing to give in. It was the only way to make her stop. And she was warm like that—fell into my arms, yielding for once. But I hadn't thought about the alcohol. The drug was new to me. I didn't mean to hurt her, she just made me so angry. And then she left me." Robert reached out to Anna. When she didn't respond, he slammed both fists down on the table. "Open your eyes, can't you? She left *me*! Over and over, again and again. She's killing me with the slowest poison—insatiable hunger."

The silence gathered around them. The helicopter had gone, maybe had missed Anna's car buried under the snow. Still, they must have seen his. She had to draw it out, whatever the risk. "But Robert, you've had that child over and over, without her. With Maura, with Michele, even with Francis. And you've left them all. Again and again."

"Because they promised something they couldn't deliver!"

"They were in your care. They trusted you. In some crazy way they loved you. Promised what?"

"They weren't enough!! Can't you see that?! With those big deep artist's eyes? They weren't *her*. Depths as great as mine—to meet myself in another form, a child from that, from us, to go on and on …."

"This child, then." Anna went to Michele, now gazing emptily at the ceiling. This might be the last chance to make her see. "She's yours, isn't she? The whole feast. Everything you've abandoned, everything you've denied? Look! She's come back to you! Here she is. You chose her. Take her, then. Just as she is."

"No!!" Robert cried out.

Then the room went silent, bringing him up short. The story lay mangled around him, wrecked and ruined. The depth of it, the real meaning had slipped out of his hands. He'd thought that telling it would bring release but there seemed to be only quicksand. To Anna these were just the blunders and compulsions of an ordinary man, a confused and stumbling man. He could see the judgment in her eyes. Maybe he'd miscalculated. She was concerned only for Michele, was looking through him now as if he didn't exist, toward the creature coiled on the couch, tense and nervy, as if the drug had suddenly worn off.

He stood, throwing his chair aside. "What's going on? What's going on here?"

They froze like rabbits. Cutting the silence was the sound of an engine, a car far off but coming nearer. He charged across the room and dragged Michele to her feet. "You bitch, you told someone!" Anna dodged past him and threw on her coat.

"Who would I tell? It's just the road, there's people all along this road!"

"We have to go now." He struggled with Michele toward the door.

"I'm not going!" She kicked and squirmed free. "It's me, or nothing. I won't be *her* for you!"

He lunged and snatched her back again. They were back in his office, fighting for their lives. He'd been too careful then. He raised a fist but Anna was suddenly there pulling Michele out of his hands. He had to choose. He let Michele go and wheeled toward Anna, catching hold of the front of her coat.

"Give me my papers. I've kept my end of the bargain." When she didn't move, he hit her hard with the back of his hand. "Scheming bitches, both of you!"

"I will, I'll get the papers." She was holding her face and trembling. Good. Finally she was afraid. "They're in my car. I'll give them to you. Then go. Leave us here."

"I'll leave *that*," he jerked his head toward Michele. "But you'll be left by the side of the road and then we'll see how clever you are."

Could he do what he was thinking? Throw her out on some remote mountain pass? She'd exposed him, stripped him bare. She was the only one they'd believe. But strangle the life out of her? The meaning was draining out of everything. He pushed Anna hard, sending her stumbling into the table, then grabbed her again by the back of the neck. Michele's voice cut through.

"Get your hands off her." It was the gun she'd brought down the ladder hours ago, that she'd said was empty. Its gaping double barrels were pointed at his chest.

"Not loaded, you said."

"That was then." He held up his hands. She shouted past him, "Go, Anna! Go!"

Behind him the door crashed open, and Anna disappeared down the stairs. The car he'd heard was coming closer.

"You want to go to prison? Do you!?"

Michele's crazy eyes were giving off blue sparks. "There's no getting out of it now." She'd certainly had time to load the gun, and with her you never knew.

"Just let me see. Let me see who's coming." He inched toward the windows. "Could be Frank, or Joe. Maybe Sharee told them."

As he turned to look, he heard the gun cock. He stopped, craning to see from where he was. There was a white SUV with a logo on the side, El Dorado something, and a blue one closely following. They were churning along the icy road. Both were full of people in uniform. Behind them an ambulance had stopped beyond the trees. Anna was clawing at the snow he'd piled on her car. She got the door open, lifted the back seat, and took something out. A thick manila envelope. His. She seemed not to see the cars. Maybe they were hidden by the Volvo under its mountain of snow. She put the envelope inside her coat and started clumsily across the meadow, maybe trying to reach the woods.

Robert looked back. Michele was coming at him across the room. Down below the cars had stopped and the men were climbing out. From the white one County Sheriffs with cowboy hats and rifles. From the blue one Holzman, Roper, and a man in a tuxedo. Anna stumbling away with his life, the guns below, the gun behind, but a good running back could thread that needle. "Gun, gun, gun!!" he screamed. He picked up a chair, charged the window, and smashed it open. The flying glass didn't faze him. He leaned out. "Gun! Gun!" He pointed toward the meadow. "She's got a gun!"

They all looked up, then followed where he pointed. The cowboys ran toward the meadow, at the same time readying their rifles like hunters chasing deer. Behind him, Michele shrieked like someone under torture. She careened to the door and out onto the porch, the gun pointing down toward the cops.

"No! No!" she screamed at them.

The cowboys stopped and turned, looking confused. Anna, too, had stopped, turned, then slipped and fallen to her knees. She was looking up toward Michele, calling something that was carried off by the wind. Down below, Holzman was drawing a large black hand gun. Sliding clownishly in his city shoes, he stumbled toward the house shouting, "Drop the weapon!" Robert ran to the door just in time to see the man throw himself down commando style and fire.

Michele heard the first bullet smack into the wall beside her. The second broke a window, sending splinters of glass into the side of her face. She'd only wanted to help her friend but they wouldn't even give her that. See, this is how it is. You try to make it right and this is what they do. She looked toward Anna kneeling in the snow, holding something close inside her coat, and imagined she saw her baby's shock of red hair. Like the day they first met—Anna holding, protecting. She could see the little face, mouth open and crying like a baby bird. I'll make it up to you, she thought, as something hit her shoulder, throwing her against the rail. She heard Robin screaming—oh, that poor baby, please someone stop her screaming. Something hit her chest and she tried to hold onto the rail so she wouldn't be thrown off into the snow. Her mother was standing at the door with enormous horrified eyes, her hands over her mouth, and Andy was saying, this is one weird kid you've got here, now look what she's done to herself. Then somehow she and Robin were sitting on a park bench. An orange balloon, tied to the baby's wrist with a long white ribbon, had come loose and was floating away above their heads. They both reached up, but it was already gone, an orange dot in a deep blue sky. She cradled the little body close and they looked into each other's eyes. Then someone called her name.

She twisted back toward the cabin door. And there he was. All she'd ever wanted, dark eyes glowing with hunger and fear, like all those times she'd pulled him down and in. 'You need a part of yourself to come back to you,' he'd once said. She raised the gun. A blast of noise, then a cloud of red filled the air, falling like rain as she felt herself sliding down the snowy stairs, a Fun Park ride, tumbling over and coming finally to rest in a cold soft bed at the bottom of nowhere.

Anna knelt in the meadow watching first Michele, then Robert fall. The men who'd been chasing her turned and ran toward the cabin. One held a gun over Michele, the other knelt down, checked her pulse, shook his head. He climbed toward Robert who seemed to be trying to get up. Since everyone had forgotten her, Anna rose and walked slowly toward them. A flurry, more police, an ambulance appearing from nowhere. Robert, his clothes ripped and bloodied, was placed on a stretcher. As he passed, he reached out to her.

"No one leads the life he intended." He took a rasping breath. Then he looked up at the deputy walking beside him and whispered, "Seduced." He tried to sit up, then fell back and grew still.

Dreamlike, they faded away. Anna walked on. Holzman still knelt in the snow, looking dazed. But now a handsome

Asian man was helping him up, patting his back, taking his gun away. He was wearing tuxedo trousers and a short samurai kimono, apparently dressed for a party. It was Thanksgiving, it must be that. Under the kimono, a holster with a gun was strapped across his chest, some senior official. Holzman kept gesturing toward the cabin and the girl who was not getting up and would never get up.

Finally Anna stood over Michele, watching a river of steaming red spread across the snow around her. Her face was pale, eyes glinting dully like shards of beach glass. In the fall her clothes had been torn away, exposing her injured side, the serpent's head and its tail curling around her breast. The eyes used to wink, the fanged mouth breathe with the girl's breath. Anna waited, but there was nothing. Except the three men coming toward her along the churchyard wall, heads down, whispering. As she stared at the serpent's coils the men looked up. The short one was just a kid, with fat brown cheeks and bad teeth; the sleek one delicate and vain, with wide-set eyes. And the one with the knife—a flat face, square and pockmarked, a thick jaw made for crushing, and narrow predatory eyes. The others called him Coco. Anna knelt down and stroked the girl's black hair.

"Poor unloved." She lifted the girl's light body and held her. Then someone put a hand under her elbow and coaxed her away.

"I'm Lieutenant Ohira." It was the man in the kimono. "You're Anna Sheffield?"

"I have something." Anna took the papers from inside her coat. "Please, take these."

Ohira beckoned. An officer took the blood-stained envelope and dropped it into a paper bag.

"Where will you take him?" Anna asked.

"The gentleman has just passed away. I'm sorry."

"Did he say anything?"

"'This thing of darkness.' He asked who said it. Does that mean anything to you?"

She sat down in the snow. "Prospero. Caliban. *The Tempest.*"

"Let's get you to the paramedics," Ohira said, offering a hand.

"Not now." Anna took his hand and held it. "I've seen them, Sensei. I've seen them. He'd want to know."

Epilogue

Outside the studio a light April rain, the last of the season, was falling on the misty Bay, the town, the plum and cherry trees flowering along Anna's garden wall. Locked away behind the blue door, with the music of sitar and tabla dipping and dancing, she leaned in to the rough body of stone, weaving metal ribbons through and around. The ragged edges pricked and scored her but she wouldn't spare the time to protect herself. This was the day to end it. Finally, after months, following wherever it led.

At first that had been nowhere. In the days after Michele's death there'd been only police and lawyers, reporters and judges, hearings and procedures. And a deluge of family. And Joe. When he went through Michele's things he'd found Anna's number, and in the first weeks he'd called often to berate her or rip himself to pieces. She could have asked the police to end it, but she wanted something from him, too. And it helped them both to console and cry together. Finally they'd come to an agreement and he'd stopped calling. Except once to say the Pierellos were scattering Michele's ashes on Christmas Eve, and did she want to come? She and Colin thought they shouldn't, but when the morning came, they went.

It was a spot on the Marin Headlands, on a bright cold day between December storms. From there the little group could look out over the city and the Bay, down on the Golden Gate, and out to sea all the way past the Farallons. Joe was scrubbed up in denim and leather. Frank was bilious, weepy and leaning on Ruthie, who held firm in stilettos, flowered sun visor, and enormous hair. Sharee and three others from the club, in feathers and spandex and fur, huddled together like exotic birds, calling after the ashes, "Jolie, we love you! We'll miss you, girl!" The wind was in their favor. The gray dust went where they'd hoped, curling away toward the sea. "Like dragon's breath," said Sharee, making all the girls cry.

Then came the dream. She was sleeping beside Colin in a rented house up the coast. For days they'd lain together through winter storms and fog, finding their way back. On the third day Anna woke in the night to find they were lying in a small clearing, in a grove of massive oaks. Above them, graveyard angels were hanging upside down from the branches, in clusters like bats, scrolls like long tongues unfurling from their mouths. Their eyes were all vibrant blue. The scrolls were inscribed with some incomprehensible text, in tiny script impossible to read. "Binding, protection, emanation," she was saying to Colin when she woke up.

She'd begun to reimagine the work she'd abandoned. She saw it overgrown with vines and herself inscribing and engraving them, and then the vines became steel and copper ribbons. The names of long-abandoned friends came back to her, especially those at The Crucible in Oakland. Oak. Land. A forge, a fire. At the time, she'd found all that prophetic. By

February she had all the ribbons cut and flame-tinted, and was getting up in the middle of the night to engrave her dreams.

Then at last, only days ago, she'd taken the long journey two miles down to Berkeley Police Headquarters and the lineup they'd arranged. Even with her drawings and quick identifications the case had taken months to work its way through the system. But finally the men had been brought in from Pleasanton, the federal prison where they were serving time for armed robbery and assault. She and Lieutenant Ohira stood together, looking into their cage: Jesus Salcedo, smooth and hard as volcanic glass, and the child, Hector Morita, whatever qualities he'd once had erased by prison life. They pleaded guilty and had eight years added to their time. It could have been more, but Anna wouldn't lie. Neither of them had had the knife. That was Coco Nava, but he'd eluded them. The police showed her a photograph, and in spite of his vacant face she knew him, by the gold teeth and the tattoo. He'd been killed—executed, they said—in a gang shooting only a month after he'd raped her.

"Street justice," Officer Roper said, and seemed baffled when Anna couldn't stop crying.

But now the last long strands of steel and copper, torch blasted into shades of ochre, purple and acid blue, twisted in her hands. Just as she'd dreamed them, they wound in and out of the rock, appearing and disappearing as the light changed—a word, an image, here and then gone. She came off the ladder and stepped back to look. Two dancers, cut apart by jagged lines of pigment poured into the stone—some thick like blood, others flowing like streams of water. Apart but entwined together in the coils of their history. Or memory. Or fate. It was no longer up to her. Let others decide.

She was picking up the engraver to start again when there was a knock, small and light. When she opened the door Suki zipped in and jumped onto a counter. Colin followed with Robin, holding her hand. It was their weekly day together, Robin and her godparents. The child held out a sticky ice cream cone. Anna picked her up and held her.

"The tongues of men and of angels," Colin said. Exploring the tangled forest he found, "... *In gardens, doves were broken jars the wind blew through ...*"

Anna joined him, protecting Robin's curious fingers from the cutting shards. On a small gravestone she read, "*This thing of darkness I acknowledge mine.*"

Colin tucked a strand of Anna's hair behind her ear. "Want to add something?" he asked Robin.

"Cream," she said and licked her sugary palm.

Colin wound his arms around them. "*Love opens my chest, and thought returns to its confines.*"

They stood together, looking.

Author Biography

Abigail Van Alyn has led a colorful life as both actor and writer.

Born in New York City and raised in South Carolina, Van Alyn attended Wellesley College and UC Berkeley and earned two bachelor's degrees in philosophy and English literature. She later received a master's in theater arts.

After an early career in New York journalism, Van Alyn switched tracks and became an actor. She spent ten years as a company member of San Francisco's much-awarded Eureka Theater. Two of her plays have been produced: *In the Wilderness/In the Zoo* and *Lying to the Holy Spirit.* As pseudonymous George Fletcher, Van Alyn has also published two books for young readers, modernizing Roman myths.

Van Alyn now lives in Northern California near Mount Shasta and coaches business leaders in communication skills. When she isn't teaching or writing, she enjoys mountain walks and working in her garden.